linger

linger

maggie stiefvater

SCHOLASTIC INC.

This book was originally published in hardcover by Scholastic Press in 2010.

ISBN 978-0-545-68279-4

12 11 10 9 8 7 6 5 4 18 19/0
Printed in the U.S.A. 40

This edition first printing, May 2014

The text was set in Adobe Garamond Pro.
Book design by Christopher Stengel

To Tess,
partially for the clever stuff,
but mostly for the bits
in between the clever stuff

Prologue

· GRACE ·

This is the story of a boy who used to be a wolf and a girl who was becoming one.

Just a few months ago, it was Sam who was the mythical creature. His was the disease we couldn't cure. His was the good-bye that meant the most. He had the body that was a mystery, too strange and wonderful and terrifying to comprehend.

But now it is spring. With the heat, the remaining wolves will soon be falling out of their wolf pelts and back into their human bodies. Sam stays Sam, and Cole stays Cole, and it's only me who's not firmly in my own skin.

Last year, this was what I wanted. I had a lot of reasons to long to be part of the wolf pack that lives in the woods behind my house. But now, instead of me watching the wolves, waiting for one of them to come to me, they are the ones watching me, waiting for me to come to them.

Their eyes, human eyes in wolf skulls, remind me of water: the clear blue of water reflecting the spring sky, the brown of a brook churning with rainfall, the green of the lake in summer as the algae begins to bloom, the gray of a snow-choked river. It used to be only Sam's yellow eyes that watched me from between the rain-soaked birches, but now, I feel the weight of the entire pack's gaze. The weight of things known, things unsaid.

The wolves in the woods are strangers now that I know the secret of the pack. Beautiful, alluring — but strangers nonetheless. An unknown human past hides behind each pair of eyes; Sam is the only one I ever truly knew, and I have him beside me now. I want this, my hand in Sam's hand and his cheek resting against my neck.

But my body betrays me. Now I am the unknown, the unknowable.

This is a love story. I never knew there were so many kinds of love or that love could make people do so many different things.

I never knew there were so many different ways to say good-bye.

Chapter One

· SAM ·

Mercy Falls, Minnesota, looked different when you knew you'd be human for the rest of your life. Before, it had been a place that existed only in the heat of summer, concrete sidewalks and leaves curved up toward the sun, everything smelling of warm asphalt and dissipating truck exhaust.

Now, as the spring branches shared seldom-seen frills of tender pink — it was where I belonged.

In the months since I'd lost my lupine skin, I'd tried to learn how to be a boy again. I'd gotten my old job back at The Crooked Shelf, surrounded by new words and the sound of pages turning. I'd traded my inherited SUV, full of the scent of Beck and my life with the wolves, for a Volkswagen Golf just big enough for me and Grace and my guitar. I tried not to flinch when I felt the cold rush in through a suddenly open door. I tried to remember I was no longer alone. At night, Grace and I crept into her room, and I folded myself against her body, breathing in the smell of my new life and matching my heartbeat to hers.

If my chest caught when I heard the wolves' slow howls in the wind, at least I had the balm of this simple, ordinary life to console me. I could look forward to years of Christmases with this girl in my arms, the privilege of growing old in this unfamiliar skin of mine. I knew that. I had everything.

Gift of time in me enclosed
the future suddenly exposed

I had started to bring my guitar with me to the bookstore. Business was slow, so hours would go by with no one to hear me singing my lyrics to the book-lined walls. The little notebook Grace had bought me was slowly filling with words. Every new date jotted at the top of a page was a victory over the disappearing winter.

Today was a day much like the ones before: wet morning streets still devoid of consumer life. Not long after I opened up the store, I was surprised to hear someone come in. Leaning the guitar against the wall behind my stool, I looked up.

"Hi, Sam," Isabel said. It was strange to see her on her own, without the context of Grace, and stranger still to see her here in the bookstore, surrounded by the soft reality of my cave of paperbacks. The loss of her brother the winter before had made her voice harder, her eyes sharper, than they'd been the first time I'd met her. She looked at me — a canny, blasé look that made me feel naive.

"What's up?" she asked, sitting on the empty stool next to me, crossing her long legs in front of her. Grace would've tucked hers underneath the stool. Isabel saw my tea and took a sip before breathing out a long sigh.

I looked at the violated tea. "Not much. New haircut?"

Her perfect blond ringlets were gone, replaced with a brutal, short style that made her look beautiful and damaged.

Isabel raised one eyebrow. "I never pegged you for a fan of the obvious, Sam," she said.

"I'm not," I said, and pushed the untouched paper cup of tea toward her to finish. It seemed filled with meaning to drink from it after she did. I added, "Otherwise, I would've said, 'Hey, shouldn't you be in school?' "

"Touché," Isabel said, taking my drink as if it had always been hers. She slouched elegantly on her stool. I hunched like a vulture on mine. The wall clock counted off the seconds. Outside, heavy white clouds that still looked like winter hung low over the street. I watched a drop of rain streak past the window, only to bounce, frozen, on the sidewalk. My mind drifted from my battered guitar to my copy of Mandelstam sitting on the counter ("*What shall I do with this body they gave me, so much my own, so intimate with me?*"). Finally, I leaned over and pressed the PLAY button on the sound system tucked beneath the counter, restarting the music overhead.

"I've been seeing wolves near my house," Isabel said. She shook the liquid in the cup. "This tastes like lawn clippings."

"It's good for you," I said. I fervently wished she hadn't taken it; the hot liquid felt like a safety net in this cold weather. Even though I knew I didn't need it anymore, I still felt more firmly human with it in my hand. "How close to your house?"

She shrugged. "From the third floor, I can see them in the woods. Clearly, they have no sense of self-preservation, or they'd avoid my father. Who is not a fan." Her eyes found the irregular scar on my neck.

"I remember," I said. Isabel had no reason to be a fan, either. "If any of them happen to wander your way as humans, you'll let me know, right? Before you let your dad stuff them and put them in his foyer?" To lighten the impact, I said *foyer* like the French: *foi-yay.*

Isabel's withering look could've turned lesser men into stone.

"Speaking of *foi-yays,*" she said, "are you living in that big house by yourself now?"

I wasn't. Part of me knew I ought to be in Beck's place, welcoming back the other pack members as they fell out of winter into their human forms, looking out for the four new wolves that had to be getting ready to shift, but the other part of me hated the idea of rattling around there with no hope of ever seeing Beck again.

It wasn't home, anyway. Grace was home.

"Yes," I told Isabel.

"Liar," she said, adding a pointy smile. "Grace is such a better liar than you. Tell me where the medical books are. Don't look so surprised — I'm actually here for a reason."

"I didn't doubt that you were here for a reason," I said, and pointed to the corner. "I just had yet to ascertain what that reason was."

Isabel slid off the stool and followed my directions to the corner. "I'm here because sometimes Wikipedia just won't cut it."

"You could write a book about the things that you can't find online," I said, able to breathe again now that she had gotten up. I started to fold a duplicate invoice into a bird.

"You should know," Isabel said. "As you were the one who was once an imaginary creature."

I made a face and kept folding my bird. The bar code of the invoice patterned one of its wings with monochromatic stripes, making the unmarked wing look larger. I picked up a pen, about to line the other wing and make it perfect, but changed my mind at the last moment. "What are you looking for, anyway? We don't have much in the way of real medical books. Just self-help and holistic stuff, mostly."

Isabel, crouched beside the shelf, said, "I don't know. I'll know it when I see it. What's that thing called — that doorstop of a book? The one that covers everything that can go wrong with a person?"

"Candide," I said. But there wasn't anyone in the shop to get the joke, so after a pause, I suggested, *"The Merck Manual?"*

"That's it."

"We don't have it in stock. I can order it," I said, not needing to check the inventory to know that I was right. "It's not cheap new, but I can probably find you a used copy. Conveniently, diseases tend to stay the same." I threaded a string through my paper crane's back and got up onto the counter to hang it above me. "It's a little bit of overkill, isn't it, unless you're planning to become a doctor?"

"I was considering it," Isabel said, in such a stark way that I didn't realize she was confiding in me until the door went *ding* again, admitting another customer.

"Be with you in a second," I said, standing on my toes on the counter to toss the loop of string over the light fixture above me. "Let me know if you need anything."

Though there was only a heartbeat's pause, I was aware that Isabel had gone silent in a way that shouted the silence to me. I lowered my arms to my side, hesitating.

"Don't let me stop you," the newcomer said, voice even and overwhelmingly professional. "I'll wait."

Something in the tone of his voice made me lose my taste for whimsy, so I turned around and saw a police officer standing by the counter, looking up at me. From my vantage point, I could see everything he had hanging on his gun belt: gun, radio, pepper spray, handcuffs, cell phone.

When you have secrets, even if they're not secrets of the illegal sort, seeing a police officer in your workplace has a terrible effect on you.

I slowly climbed down behind the counter and said, with a halfhearted gesture to my crane, "It wasn't working very well, anyway. Can I . . . help you find something?" I hesitated on the question, since I knew he wasn't here to talk about books. I felt my pulse, hard and fast, pounding in my neck. Isabel had disappeared, and for all intents and purposes, the store looked empty.

"Actually, if you're not busy, I'd like to talk with you for a moment," the officer said politely. "You *are* Samuel Roth, right?"

I nodded.

"I'm Officer Koenig," he said. "I'm working on Olivia Marx's case."

Olivia. My stomach felt tight. Olivia, one of Grace's closest friends, had been unwillingly bitten last year and had spent the last few months as a wolf in Boundary Wood. Her family thought she'd run away.

Grace should've been here. If lying were an Olympic sport, Grace would've been champion of the world. For someone who hated creative writing, she certainly was an awesome storyteller.

"Oh," I said. "Olivia."

I was nervous about the cop being here, asking questions, but weirdly, I was more nervous because Isabel, who already knew the truth, was listening. I could imagine her crouching behind one of the shelves, arching an eyebrow scornfully when a lie fell flat on my unpracticed lips.

"You knew her, correct?" The officer had a friendly look on his face, but how friendly could someone be when he ended a question with *correct?*

"A little," I said. "I met her in town a few times. But I don't go to her school."

"Where do you go to school?" Again, Koenig's voice was completely pleasant and conversational. I tried to tell myself that his questions felt suspicious only because I had something to hide.

"I was homeschooled."

"My sister was, too," Koenig said. "Drove my mother crazy. So, you do know Grace Brisbane, though, correct?"

Again with the *correct?* stuff. I wondered if he was starting with the questions he already knew the answers to. I was again acutely aware of Isabel, silently listening.

"Yes," I said. "She's my girlfriend."

It was a bit of information they probably didn't have and probably didn't need to have, but it was something that I wanted Isabel to hear for some reason.

I was surprised to see Koenig smile. "I can tell," he said.

Though his smile seemed genuine, it made me stiffen, wondering if I was being played.

"Grace and Olivia were good friends," Koenig continued. "Can you tell me the last time you saw Olivia? I don't need an exact date, but as close as possible would be really helpful."

Now he had a little blue notebook flipped open and a pen hovering over it.

"Um." I considered. I'd seen Olivia, snow dusting her white fur, just a few weeks earlier, but I didn't think that would be the most helpful thing to tell Koenig. "I saw her downtown. Here, actually. In front of the store. Grace and I were killing some time, and Olivia was here with her brother. But that must have been months ago. November? October? Right before she disappeared."

"Do you think Grace has seen her more recently?"

I tried to hold his gaze. "I'm pretty sure that's the last time she saw Olivia as well."

"It's really difficult for a teen to manage on his or her own," Koenig said, and this time I felt sure that he knew all about me and that his words were loaded with meaning just for me, drifting without Beck. "Really difficult for a runaway. There are lots of reasons that kids run away, and judging from what I heard from Olivia's teachers and family, depression might have had something to do with it. A lot of times these teens just run away because they need to get out of the house, but they don't know how to survive out in the world. So sometimes, they only run as far away as the next house over. Sometimes —"

I interrupted him before he could get any further. "Officer . . . Koenig? I know what you're trying to say, but Olivia isn't at Grace's house. Grace hasn't been slipping her food or helping her out. I wish, for Olivia's sake, that the answer was that easy. I'd love it for Grace's sake, too. I'd love to tell you that I knew exactly where Olivia was. But we're wondering when she's going to come back just as much as you are."

I wondered if this was how Grace spilled out her most useful lies — by manipulating them into something she could believe.

"You understand I had to ask," he said.

"I know."

"Well, thanks for your time, and please let me know if you hear anything." Koenig started to turn, then paused. "What do you know about the woods?"

I was frozen. I was a motionless wolf hidden in the trees, praying not to be seen.

"Excuse me?" I said faintly.

"Olivia's family said she took a lot of photos of the wolves in the woods, and that Grace is also interested in them. Do you share that interest?"

I could only nod wordlessly.

"Do you think there's any chance she would try to make a go of it out there by herself, instead of running to another city?"

Panic clawed inside my head, as I imagined the police and Olivia's family crawling over the acres and acres of woods, searching the trees and the pack's shed for evidence of human life. And possibly finding it. I tried to keep my voice light.

"Olivia never really struck me as the outdoorsy sort. I really doubt it."

Koenig nodded, as if to himself. "Well, thanks again," he said.

"No problem," I said. "Good luck."

The door *dinged* behind him; as soon as I saw his squad car pull away from the curb, I let my elbows fall onto the counter and pushed my face into my hands. *God.*

"Nicely done, boy wonder," Isabel said, rising from amongst the nonfiction books with a scuffling sound on the carpet. "You hardly sounded psychotic at all."

I didn't reply. All of the things the cop could've asked about were running through my head, leaving me feeling more nervous now than when he'd been here. He could've asked about where Beck was. Or if I'd heard about three missing kids from Canada. Or if I knew anything about the death of Isabel Culpeper's brother.

"What is your problem?" Isabel asked, a lot closer this time. She slid a stack of books onto the counter with her credit card on top. "You completely handled it. They're just doing routine stuff. He's not really suspicious. God, your hands are shaking."

"I'd make a terrible criminal," I replied — but that wasn't why my hands were trembling. If Grace had been here, I would have told her the truth: that I hadn't spoken to a cop since my parents had been sent to jail for slashing my wrists. Just seeing Officer Koenig had dredged up a thousand things I hadn't thought about in years.

Isabel's voice dripped scorn. "Good thing, too, because you aren't doing anything criminal. Stop freaking out, and do your book-boy thing. I need the receipt."

I rang up her books and bagged them, glancing at the empty street every so often. My head was a jumbled-up mess of police uniforms, wolves in the woods, and voices I hadn't heard for a decade.

As I handed her the bag, the old scars on my wrists throbbed with buried memories.

For a moment, Isabel looked like she was going to say something more, and then she just shook her head and said, "Some people are really not cut out for deception. See you later, Sam."

Chapter Two

· COLE ·

I have had no thought other than this: Stay alive.

And to have had only that thought, each day, was heaven.

We wolves ran through the sparse pine trees, our paws light on ground damp with the memory of snow. We were so close together, shoulders bumping against one another, jaws snapping playfully, bodies ducking beneath and leaping over one another like fish in a river, that it was impossible to tell where one wolf began and another ended.

Moss rubbed to bare dirt and markings on trees guided us through the woods; I could smell the rotting, growing smell of the lake before I could hear water splashing. One of the other wolves sent out a quick image: ducks gliding smoothly onto the cold blue surface of the lake. From a second wolf: a deer and her fawn walking on trembling legs to get a drink.

For me, there was nothing beyond this moment, these traded images and this silent, powerful bond.

And then, for the first time in months, I suddenly remembered that, once, I'd had fingers.

I stumbled, falling out of the pack, my shoulders bunching and twitching. The wolves wheeled, some of them doubling back to encourage me to rejoin them, but I could not follow. I twisted on the ground, slimy spring leaves pasted to my skin, the heat of the day clogged in my nostrils.

My fingers turned over the fresh black earth, jamming it beneath nails suddenly too short to defend me, smearing it in eyes that now saw in brilliant color.

I was Cole again, and spring had come too soon.

Chapter Three

· ISABEL ·

The day the cop came into the bookstore was the first day I had ever heard Grace complain of a headache. It probably doesn't sound that remarkable, but since I met Grace, she had never mentioned so much as a runny nose. Also, I was something of an expert on headaches. They were a hobby of mine.

After watching Sam dance clumsily with the cop, I headed back to school, which by this stage in my life had become sort of redundant. The teachers didn't really know what to do with me, caught as they were between my good grades and my terrible attendance record, so I got away with a lot. Our uneasy agreement basically came down to this: I'd come to class and they'd let me do what I wanted to do, as long as I didn't corrupt the other students.

So the first thing I did when I got to Computer Arts was dutifully log in to my computer station and undutifully pull out the books I'd bought that morning. One of them was an illustrated encyclopedia of diseases — fat, dusty-smelling, and bearing a copyright of 1986. The thing was probably one of the first books The Crooked Shelf had stocked. While Mr. Grant outlined what we were supposed to be doing, I flipped through the pages, looking for the most gruesome images. There was a photograph of someone with porphyria, someone else with seborrheic dermatitis, and an image of roundworms in action that made my stomach turn over, surprising me.

Then I flipped to the *M* section. My fingers ran down the page to *meningitis, bacterial.* The back of my nose stung as I read the entire section. Causes. Symptoms. Diagnosis. Treatment. Prognosis. Mortality rate of untreated bacterial meningitis: 100 percent. Mortality rate of treated bacterial meningitis: 10 to 30 percent.

I didn't need to look it up; I already knew the stats. I could've recited the whole entry. I knew more than this 1986 encyclopedia of diseases did, too, because I had read all the online journals about the newest treatments and unusual cases.

The seat next to me creaked as someone sat down; I didn't bother to close the book as she rolled over in her chair. Grace always wore the same perfume. Or, knowing Grace, used the same shampoo.

"Isabel," Grace said, in a relatively low voice — other students were chattering now as the project was under way. "That's positively morbid — even for you."

"Bite me," I replied.

"You need therapy." But she said it lightly.

"I'm getting it." I looked up at her. "I'm just trying to find out how meningitis worked. I don't think it's morbid. Don't you want to know how Sam's little problem worked?"

Grace shrugged and turned back and forth in the swivel-back chair, her dark blond hair falling across her flushed cheeks as she dropped her gaze to the floor. She looked uncomfortable. "It's over now."

"Sure," I said.

"If you're going to be cranky, I'm not going to sit next to you," Grace warned. "I don't feel good, anyway. I'd rather be home."

"I just said 'sure,'" I said. "That's not cranky, Grace. Believe me, if you want me to bring out the inner —"

"Ladies?" Mr. Grant appeared at my shoulder and looked at my blank screen and Grace's black one. "Last time I checked, this was a Computer Arts class, not a social hour."

Grace looked up earnestly at him. "Do you think I could go to the nurse? My head — I think I have a sinus thing coming on or something."

Mr. Grant looked down at her pink cheeks and pensive expression, and nodded his permission. "I want a note back from the office," he told her, after Grace thanked him and stood up. She didn't say anything to me as she left, just knocked on the back of my chair with her knuckles.

"And you —" Mr. Grant said. Then he dropped his gaze down to the encyclopedia and its still-open page, and he never finished his sentence. He just nodded, as if to himself, and walked away.

I turned back to my extracurricular study of death and disease. Because no matter what Grace thought, I knew that in Mercy Falls, it's never over.

Chapter Four

· GRACE ·

By the time Sam got home from the bookstore that evening, I was making New Year's resolutions at the kitchen table.

I'd been making New Year's resolutions ever since I was nine. Every year on Christmas, I'd sit down at the kitchen table under the dim yellow light, hunched over in a turtleneck sweater because of the draft from the glass door to the deck, and I'd write my goals for the year in a plain black journal I'd bought for myself. And every year on Christmas Eve, I'd sit down in the exact same place and open the exact same book to a new page and write down what I'd accomplished in the previous twelve months. Every year, the two lists looked identical.

Last Christmas, though, I hadn't made any resolutions. I'd spent the month trying not to look through the glass door at the woods, trying not to think about the wolves and Sam. Sitting at the kitchen table and planning for the future had seemed like a cruel pretense more than anything else.

But now that I had Sam and a new year, that black journal, shelved neatly next to my career books and memoirs, haunted me. I had dreams about sitting at the kitchen table in a turtleneck sweater, dreams where I kept on writing and writing my resolutions without ever filling the page.

Today, waiting for Sam to get home, I couldn't stand it anymore. I got the journal from my shelf and headed for the kitchen. Before I sat down, I took two more ibuprofen; the two the school nurse had given me had pretty much killed the headache I'd had earlier, but I wanted to make sure it didn't make a reappearance. I had just clicked on the flower-shaped light over the table and sharpened my pencil when the phone rang. I stood and leaned over the counter to reach it.

"Hello?"

"Grace, hi." It took me a moment to realize that it was my father's voice. I was unused to hearing it, pressed and fuzzy, over the phone lines.

"Is something wrong?" I asked.

"What? No. Nothing's wrong. I was just calling to let you know that your mother and I will be home around nine from Pat and Tina's."

"Okaay," I said. I already knew this; Mom had told me this morning when we parted ways, me to school, her to the studio.

A pause. "Are you alone?"

So *that's* what this call was about. For some reason, the question made my throat tighten. "No," I said. "Elvis is here. Would you like to talk to him?"

Dad acted as if I hadn't answered. "Is Sam there?"

I felt like answering yes, just to see what he would say, but instead, I told him the truth, my voice coming out strange and defensive. "No. I'm just doing homework."

While Mom and Dad knew Sam was my boyfriend — Sam and I had made no secret of our relationship — they still didn't know what was really going on. All the nights Sam stayed over, they thought I was sleeping alone. They had no idea about my hopes for our future. They thought it was a simple, innocent, bound-to-end teenage relationship. It wasn't that I didn't want them to know. Just that their obliviousness had its advantages, too, for now.

"Okay," Dad said. There was an unspoken commendation in his answer, an approval of me being alone with my homework. This is what Graces did in the evening, and heaven forbid I should break the mold. "Planning a quiet night?"

I heard the front door open and Sam's step in the hall. "Yes," I replied as he walked into the living room, guitar case in hand.

"Good. Well, see you later on," Dad said. "Happy studying."

We hung up at the same time. I watched Sam silently shed his coat and go straight for the study.

"Hi, bucko," I said when he returned holding his guitar minus the case. He smiled at me, but the skin around his eyes was tight. "You seem tense."

He crashed down onto the sofa, only half sitting, and threw his fingers across the strings of the guitar. A discordant chord rang out. "Isabel came into the store today," he said.

"Really? What did she want?"

"Just some books. And to tell me that she'd seen wolves by her house."

My mind instantly slid to her father and to the wolf hunt he'd led in the woods behind my house. From Sam's troubled expression, I knew his thoughts mirrored mine. "That's not good."

"No," he said. His fingers moved restlessly over the guitar strings, effortlessly and instinctively picking out some beautiful minor chord. "Neither was the cop that came in."

I set my pencil down and leaned across the table toward him. "*What?* What did a cop want?"

He hesitated. "Olivia. He wanted to know if I thought she might be living in the woods."

"What?" I asked again, my skin prickling. There was no way that someone could guess that. No way. "How could he know?"

"He didn't think she was a wolf, obviously, but I think he was hoping we were hiding her or that she was living nearby and we were helping her or something. I said she didn't strike me as the outdoorsy type, and he thanked me and left."

"Wow." I leaned back in my chair and considered. It was really only surprising that they hadn't questioned Sam sooner. They'd already talked to me soon after Olivia "ran away," and had probably only just recently made the connection between Sam and me. I shrugged. "They're just being thorough. I don't think there's anything for us to worry about. I mean, she reappears when she reappears, right? How long do you think it will be until the new wolves start to change back into humans?"

Sam didn't reply right away. "They won't stay human at first. They'll be really unstable. It depends how warm the day is. It varies from person to person, too, sometimes a lot. It's like how on certain days some people wear sweaters when other people can wear T-shirts and still feel comfortable — different reactions to the same temperature. But I guess it's possible some might have already shifted into humans once this year."

I imagined Olivia darting through the woods in her new wolf body, before pulling my mind back to what Sam was saying. "Really? Already? So someone might have seen her?"

Sam shook his head. "She'll only have a few minutes as a human in this weather; I really doubt anyone could've seen her. It's just . . . it's just a practice run for later." He was lost to me then, his eyes someplace far away. Maybe remembering what it was like for him back when he was a new wolf. I inadvertently shuddered; thinking about Sam and his parents always got to me. A nasty chill clenched in my stomach until Sam went back to playing his guitar. For several long minutes, he walked his fingers up and down chords, and when it became obvious that he was done speaking for the moment, I dropped my gaze back to my resolutions. My mind wasn't really on them, though; it was circling the idea of young Sam shifting back and forth while his parents looked on in horror. I doodled a 3-D rectangle on the corner of the page.

Finally, Sam said, "What are you doing? It looks suspiciously creative."

"Slightly creative," I said. I looked at him, eyebrow raised, until he smiled. Strumming a chord, he sang, *"Has Grace quitted herself of numbers / and given herself to words?"*

"That doesn't even rhyme."

"Abandoned all her algebra / and taken to penning verbs?" Sam finished.

I made a face at him. "*Words* and *verbs* don't really rhyme. I'm writing my New Year's resolutions."

"They *do* rhyme," he insisted. Bringing his guitar over to

the table and sitting across from me — the guitar made a low, musical *thump* as it lightly struck the edge of the table — he added, "I'm going to watch. I've never written any resolutions before. I'd like to see what organization in progress looks like."

He drew the open journal across the table toward him, his eyebrows tipping low over his eyes. "What's this?" he asked. "Resolution number three: *Choose a college.* You've already picked a *college*?"

I slid the journal back to my side of the table and turned quickly to a blank page. "I did not. I got distracted by this cute boy who turned into a wolf. This is the first year I haven't made all of my resolutions, and it's all your fault. I need to get back on track."

Smile slightly faded, Sam scraped his chair back and rested his guitar against the wall. From the countertop next to the phone he got a pen and an index card. "Okay, then. Let's make new ones."

I wrote *Get a job.* He wrote *Keep loving my job.* I wrote *Stay madly in love.* He wrote *Stay human.*

"Because I'll always be madly in love," he said, looking at his index card instead of my face.

I kept looking at him, his eyes hidden behind his lashes, until he lifted them back up to me.

"So are you going to put *Pick a college* on there again?" he asked.

"Are you?" I asked back, keeping my voice light. The question felt loaded — we were edging into the first conversation that really addressed what life would look like this side of winter, now that Sam could live a real life. The closest college to

Mercy Falls was in Duluth, an hour away, and all of my other, pre-Sam choices were even farther.

"I asked first."

"Sure," I said, sounding glib rather than carefree. I scribbled down *Pick a college* in a hand that looked completely different from the rest of my list. "Now, are you?" My heart was unexpectedly thrumming with something like panic.

But instead of answering, Sam stood and went to the kitchen. I swiveled to watch him put on the teakettle. He brought down two mugs from the cabinet over the stove; for some reason, the familiarity of this easy movement filled me with affection. I fought the urge to go stand behind him and wrap my arms around his chest.

"Beck wanted me to go to law school," Sam said, fingering the edge of my favorite robin's-egg-blue mug. "He never told me, but I heard him tell Ulrik."

"It's hard to imagine you as a lawyer," I said.

Sam smiled a self-deprecating smile and shook his head. "I can't imagine myself as a lawyer, either. I can't imagine myself as anything yet, to tell you the truth. I know that sounds . . . terrible. Like I have no ambition." Again, his eyebrows drew together, pensive. "But this idea of a future is really new to me. Until this month, I never thought I could go to college. I don't want to rush into it."

I must have been just staring at him, because he added, hurriedly, "But I don't want you to have to wait, Grace. I don't want to keep you from going ahead because I can't make up my mind."

Feeling childish, I said, "We could go someplace together."

The kettle whistled. Sam pulled it from the heat as he said, "I somehow doubt that the same college will be ideal for a budding math genius and a boy in love with moody poetry. I suppose it's possible." He stared out the kitchen window at the frozen gray woods. "I don't know if I can really leave, though. At all. Who will take care of the pack?"

"I thought that was why the new wolves were made," I said. The words sounded strange in my mouth. Callous. As if the pack dynamic were an artificial, engineered thing, which of course it wasn't. Nobody knew what the newcomers were like. Nobody but Beck, of course, but he wasn't talking.

Sam rubbed his forehead, pressing his palm over his eyes; he did it a lot since he'd come back. "Yeah, I know," he said. "I know that's what they're for."

"He would've wanted you to go," I said. "And I still think we could find a school together."

Sam looked at me, his fingers still pressed into his temple as if he'd forgotten they were there. "I'd like that." He paused. "I'd really like — I'd like to meet the new wolves and see what kind of people they are, though. It'll make me feel better. Maybe I'll go after that. After I'm sure everything's taken care of here."

I put a jagged line through *Pick a college*. "I'll wait for you," I said.

"Not forever," Sam said.

"No, if you turn out to be useless, I'll go without you." I tapped my pencil on my teeth. "I think we should look around for the new wolves tomorrow. And Olivia. I'll call Isabel and ask her about the wolves she saw in her woods."

"Sounds like a plan," Sam said. He returned to his list at the table and added something to it. Then he smiled at me and spun the index card so that I could read it right side up.

Listen to Grace.

· SAM ·

Later, I thought of the things I could have added to the list of resolutions, things I'd wanted back before I realized what being a wolf meant for my future. Things like *Write a novel* and *Find a band* and *Get a degree in obscure poetry in translation* and *Travel the world.* It felt indulgent and fanciful to be considering those things now after reminding myself for so long that they were impossible.

I tried to imagine myself filling out a college application. Writing a synopsis. Tacking a sign saying DRUMMERS WANTED on the corkboard opposite Beck's post office box. The words danced in my head, dazzling in their sudden nearness. I wanted to add them to my index card of resolutions, but I just . . . couldn't.

That night, while Grace showered, I got out the card and looked at it again. And I wrote:

Believe in my cure.

Chapter Five

· COLE ·

I was human.

I was bleary, exhausted, confused. I didn't know where I was. I knew I'd lost more time since I'd last been awake; I must've shifted back to a wolf again. Groaning, I rolled onto my back and clenched and unclenched my fists, trying out my strength.

The early morning forest was absolutely freezing, mist hanging in the air, turning everything light gold. Close to me, the damp trunks of pine trees jutted from the haze, black and severe. Within a few feet, they turned to pastel blue and then disappeared entirely in the white fog.

I was lying in the damn mud; I could feel my shoulders coated and crackling with it. When I lifted my hand to brush off my skin, my fingers were coated as well — a thin, anemic clay that looked like baby poop. My hands stank like the lake, and sure enough, I could hear water slowly lapping very close to my left side. I reached out a hand and felt more mud, then water on my fingertips.

How did I get here? I remembered running with the pack, then shifting, but I couldn't remember making it to the shore. I must've shifted back again. To wolf, and then to human. The logic of it — or rather, the lack of logic — was maddening. Beck had told me the shifts would get more controlled, eventually. So where was the control?

I lay there, my muscles starting to tremble, the cold pinching my skin, and knew that I was going to shift back to a wolf soon. God, I was tired. Stretching my shaking hands above my head, I marveled at the smooth, unmarked skin of my arms, most of the scarring of my former life gone. I was being reborn in five-minute intervals.

I heard movement in the woods near me, and I turned my face, my cheek against the ground, to see if it belonged to a threat. Close by, a white wolf watched me, halfway behind a tree, her coat tinted gold and pink in the rising morning sun. Her green eyes, strangely pensive, met mine for a long moment. There was something about the way she was looking at me that felt unfamiliar. Human eyes without judgment or jealousy or pity or anger; just silent consideration.

I didn't know how it made me feel.

"What are you looking at?" I snarled.

Without a sound, she slid into the mist.

My body jerked on its own accord, and my skin twisted into another form.

I didn't know how much time I'd spent as a wolf this go-round. Was it minutes? Hours? Days? It was late morning. I didn't feel human, but I wasn't wolf, either. I hovered somewhere in between, my mind skating from memory to present and back to memory again, past and present equally lucid.

Somehow my brain darted from my seventeenth birthday to the night my heart stopped beating at Club Josephine. And that's where it stayed. Not a night I would've chosen to relive.

This was who I was, before I was a wolf: I was Cole St. Clair, and I was NARKOTIKA.

Outside, the Toronto night was cold enough to ice over puddles and choke you with your own frigid breath, but inside the warehouse that was Club Josephine, it was hot as Hades, and it would be even hotter upstairs with the crowd.

And there was a hell of a crowd.

It was a huge deal, but it was a gig I didn't even want to do. There wasn't really any other kind these days. They all ran together until all I could remember were gigs where I was high and gigs where I wasn't and gigs where I had to pee the whole time. Even when I was playing the music on the stage, I was still chasing something — some idea of life and fame that I'd imagined for myself when I was sixteen — but I was losing interest in actually finding it.

While I was carrying in my keyboard, some girl who called herself Jackie gave us some pills I'd never seen before.

"Cole," she whispered in my ear, as if she knew me instead of just my name. "Cole, this will take you places you haven't been."

"Baby," I said, shifting my duffle so that I wouldn't hit it on the rat's maze of walls beneath the dance floor, "it takes a lot to do that these days."

She smiled wide, teeth tinted yellow in the dull light, like she knew a secret. She smelled like lemons. "Don't worry — I know what you need."

I almost laughed, but instead I turned away, shouldering my way through a half-closed door. I looked over Jackie's highlighted hair to shout, "Vic, c'mon!" I dropped my gaze back to her. "Are *you* on it?"

Jackie ran a finger up my arm, tracing around the tight sleeve of my T-shirt. "I'd be doing more than just smiling at you if I was."

I reached down and touched her hand, tapping it until she understood what I meant and opened her palm. It was empty, but she reached into the pocket of her jeans to pull out a wad of plastic wrap. Inside, I saw a collection of electric-green pills, each stamped with two *T*s. They got an A-plus for pretty factor, but who knew what they were.

In my pocket, my phone buzzed. Normally I would've let it go to voicemail, but Jackie, standing two inches away from me, breathing my air, gave me an incentive to interrupt the conversation. I fished the phone out and put it against my ear. "Da."

"Cole, I'm glad I got you." It was Berlin, my agent. His voice was gritty and fast as always. "Listen to this: 'NARKOTIKA takes the scene by force with their latest album, *13all*. Brilliant but frenetic front man Cole St. Clair, thought by many to be losing his edge' — sorry, man, that's just what they said — 'comes back stronger than ever with this release, proving that his first release, at sixteen, was no fluke. The three —' are you listening, Cole?"

"No," I said.

"Well, you should. This is Elliot Fry saying this," Berlin said. When I didn't reply, he said, "Remember, Elliot Fry, who called you a surly, overactive toddler with a keyboard? That Elliot Fry. Now you guys are golden. Total turnaround. You've arrived, man."

"Brilliant," I said, and hung up on him. I turned to Jackie. "I'll take the whole bag. Tell Victor. He's my purse."

So Victor paid for them. But I'd asked for them, so I guess it was still my fault.

Or maybe it was Jackie's, for not telling us what they were, but that was Club Josephine for you. The place to find the new high before anyone knew how high it took you. Unnamed pills, brand-new powders, shining mysterious nectar in vials. It wasn't the worst thing I'd made Victor do.

Back in the dim lounge, waiting to go on, Victor swallowed one of the green pills with a beer while Jeremy-my-body-is-a-temple watched him and drank green tea. I took a few of them with a Pepsi. I don't know how many. I was feeling pretty bitter about the transaction by the time we got onto the stage. Jackie's stuff was letting me down — I was feeling absolutely nothing. We started our set, and the crowd was wild, pressed up against the stage, arms outstretched, screaming our name.

Behind his drums, Victor screamed back at them. He was high as a kite, so whatever Jackie had sold us had done it for him. But then it never took as much to get Victor high. The strobes lit up bits and pieces of the audience — a neck here, a flash of lips, a thigh wrapped around another dancer. My head pounded in time with the beat that Victor laid down, my heart scudding double time. I reached up to slide my headset from my neck to my ears, my fingers brushing the hot skin of my neck, and girls began to scream my name.

There was this one girl my eyes kept finding for some reason, skin stark white against her black tank top. She howled my name as if it was physically painful for her, her pupils dilated so wide that her eyes looked black and depthless. She reminded me of Victor's sister inexplicably, something about the curve of her nose or the way her jeans were slung so low, held up by nothing but the suggestion of hips, though there was no way Angie would be anywhere near a club like this.

Suddenly I didn't feel like being there. There was no longer a rush at hearing my name screamed, and the music wasn't as loud as my heart, so it hardly seemed important.

This was where I was supposed to come in, singing to break the nonstop take-you-to-the-moon pattern of Victor's beat, but I didn't feel like it, and Victor was too gone to notice. He was dancing in place, fixed to the ground only by the drumsticks in his hands.

Right in front of me, among a throng of bare midriffs and sweaty arms thrust into the air, there was a guy who didn't move. Illuminated sporadically by the strobes and lasers, I was fascinated by how he stayed still, despite the press of bodies all around him. He held his ground and watched me, his eyebrows drawn down low over his eyes.

When I looked back at him, I remembered again that scent of home, far away from Toronto.

I wondered if he was real. I wondered if anything in this whole damned place was real.

He crossed his arms over his chest, watching me while my heart scrabbled to escape.

I should have been paying more attention to keeping it in my chest. My pulse sped, and then my heart burst free in an explosion of heat; my face smacked against the keyboard, which wailed out a pulse of sound. I grabbed for the keys with a hand that no longer belonged to me.

Lying on the stage, my cheek setting fire to the ground, I saw Victor giving me this withering look, like he'd finally noticed that I'd missed my cue.

And then I closed my eyes on the stage of Club Josephine.

I was done being NARKOTIKA. I was done being Cole St. Clair.

Chapter Six

· GRACE ·

"You know," Isabel said, "when I told you to call me on the weekend, I didn't mean for you to call me so we could go tramping through the trees in subfreezing temperatures."

She frowned at me, looking pale and oddly at home in these cold spring woods, wearing a white parka with a fur-lined hood that framed her slender face and icy eyes, a sort of lost Nordic princess.

"It's not subfreezing," I said, knocking a clod of soft snow off the sole of my boot. "All things considered, it's not bad. And you wanted to get out of the house, didn't you?"

It really wasn't bad. It was warm enough that the snow had mostly melted in the areas where the sun could reach, and it was only under the trees that patches remained. The few degrees of extra warmth lent a gentler look to the landscape, infusing the grays of winter with color. Though the cold still numbed the end of my nose, my fingers were snug inside their gloves.

"You should be leading the way, actually," I said. "You're the one who's seen them here." These woods that stretched behind Isabel's parents' house were unfamiliar to me. A lot of pines and some kind of straight-up-and-down, gray-barked trees that I didn't know. I was sure Sam would've been able to identify them.

"Well, it's not like I've gone jaunting in the woods after them before," Isabel replied, but she walked a little faster until she was caught up with me and we were walking side by side, separated by a yard or two, stepping over fallen logs and underbrush. "I just know they always appeared on that side of the yard, and I've heard them howl in the direction of the lake."

"Two Island Lake?" I asked. "Is that far from here?"

"Feels far," Isabel complained. "So what is it we're doing here? Scaring wolves away? Looking for Olivia? If I had known Sam was going to squeal to you like a little girl about this, I wouldn't have said anything."

"All of the above," I said. "Except the squealing bit. Sam's just worried. I don't think that's unreasonable."

"Right. Whatever. Do you think there's a real chance Olivia could've changed already? Because if there's not, maybe we could take a morning stroll back to my car to get a coffee somewhere instead."

I pushed a branch out of my way and squinted; I thought I could see the shimmer of water through the trees. "Sam said it's not too early for a new wolf to change, at least for a little bit. When it gets to be a warm snap. Like today. Maybe."

"Okay, but we're getting coffee after we don't find her." Isabel pointed. "Look, the lake's up there. Happy?"

"Mmm hmm." I frowned, noticing suddenly that the trees were different than before. Evenly spaced and farther apart, with tangled, soft, relatively new growth for underbrush. I stopped short when I saw color peeking out of the dull brown thatch at our feet. A crocus — a little finger of purple with an almost-hidden throat of yellow. A few inches away, I spied more bright green shoots coming up through the old leaves, and two more blossoms. Signs of spring — and, more than that, signs of human occupation — in the middle of the forest. I felt like kneeling to touch the petals of the crocus, to confirm that they were real. But Isabel's watchful eyes kept me standing. "What is this place?"

Isabel stepped over a branch to stand beside me and looked down at the patch of brave little flowers. "Oh, that. Back in the glory days of our house, before we lived here, I guess the owners had a walkway down to the lake and a little garden thing here. There are benches closer to the water, and a statue."

"Can we see it?" I asked, fascinated by the idea of a hidden, overgrown world.

"We're here. There's one of the benches." Isabel led me a few feet closer to the pond and kicked a concrete bench with her boot. It was streaked with thin green moss and the occasional flattened bloom of orange lichen, and I might not have noticed it without Isabel's direction. Once I knew where to look, however, it was easy to see what the shape of the sitting area had been — there was another bench a few feet away, and a small statue of a woman with her hands brought up to her mouth as if with wonder, her face pointed toward the lake. More flower bulbs, their shoots bright green and rubbery-looking, poked up around the statue's base and the benches, and I saw a few more crocuses in the patchy snow beyond. Beside me, Isabel scuffed her foot through the leaves. "And look, down here. This is stone under here. Like a patio or something, I guess. I found it last year."

I kicked at the leaves like she did, and sure enough, my toe scuffed stone. Our true purpose momentarily forgotten, I scraped at the leaves, uncovering a wet, dirty patch of ground. "Isabel, this isn't just stone. Look. It's a . . . a . . ." I couldn't think of what to call the swirling pattern of stones.

"Mosaic," Isabel finished, looking down at the complicated circles at her feet.

I knelt and scraped a few of the stones bare with a stick. They were mostly natural colored, but there were a few chips of brilliant blue or red tiles in there as well. I uncovered more of the mosaic, revealing a swirling pattern with a smiling, archaic-looking sun in the middle. It made me feel odd, this shining face hidden under matted rotting leaves. "Sam would love this," I said.

"Where is he?" Isabel asked.

"Checking out the woods behind Beck's house. He should've come with us." I could already picture the curve of his eyebrows, close over his eyes, as he saw the mosaic and the statue for the first time. This was the sort of thing Sam lived for.

An object beneath the bench before me caught my attention, however, pulling me back to the real world. A slender, dull white . . . bone. I reached out and picked it up, looking at the gnaw marks on it. As I did, I realized there were more scattered around the bench, half buried in the leaves. Pushed partway underneath the bench was a glass bowl, stained and chipped, but obviously no antique. It took me only half a moment to realize what it was.

I stood up and faced Isabel. "You've been feeding them, haven't you?"

Isabel glowered at me, looking petulant, and didn't answer.

I retrieved the bowl and shook out the two leaves that lay curled in the bottom of it. "What have you been feeding them?"

"Babies," Isabel said.

I gave her a look.

"Meat. I'm not an idiot. And only when it was really cold. For all I know, the stupid raccoons have been eating it." She sounded defiant — angry, almost. I had been planning to goad her about her hidden compassion, but the raw edge to her voice made me stop.

Instead I said, "Or carnivorous deer. Looking to add some protein to their diet."

Isabel smiled a small smile; it always looked a bit more like a smirk. "I thought Bigfoot, perhaps."

We both jumped as a high-pitched cry, like an eerie laugh, came from the lake, followed by a splash.

"Christ," Isabel said, her hand on her stomach.

I took a deep breath. "A loon. We scared it."

"Wildlife is overrated. Anyway, I don't think Olivia's near here if *we* scared the loon. I think a wolf changing into a girl would be a little louder than we're being."

I had to admit her theory made sense. And the fact was that I still wasn't sure how we were going to handle Olivia's sudden return to Mercy Falls, so a tiny part of me was relieved.

"So we can go get coffee now?"

"Yeah," I replied, but I moved across the hidden patio toward the lake. Once you knew the mosaic was underneath your feet, it was easy to feel how unforgiving the surface was; how unlike the natural forest floor. I walked over to stand by the statue of the woman and pressed my fingers to my lips when I saw the view. It wasn't until after I'd taken in the still lake framed by naked trees and the black-headed loon floating on its surface that I realized I was unconsciously mimicking the statue's look of eternal wonder. "Have you seen this?"

Isabel joined me. "Nature," she said dismissively. "Buy the postcard. Let's go."

But my gaze had drifted downward to the forest floor. My heart sped. "Isabel," I whispered, frozen.

On the other side of the statue, a wolf was lying in the leaves, its gray pelt nearly the same color as the dead foliage. I could just see the edge of its black nose and the curve of one of its ears rising out of the leaves.

"It's dead," Isabel said, not bothering to whisper. "Look, there's a leaf sitting on it. It's been there awhile."

My heart was still thumping; I had to remind myself that Olivia had become a white wolf, not gray. And that Sam was a boy, safely trapped in his human body. This wolf couldn't be either of them.

But it could be Beck. Olivia and Sam were the only ones that mattered to me, but Beck would matter to Sam. He was a gray wolf.

Please don't be Beck.

Swallowing, I knelt next to it while Isabel stood beside me and shuffled in the leaves. Carefully plucking the leaf that covered part of the wolf's face, I felt the coarse fur brush the side of my hand, even through my gloves. I watched the banded gray, black, and white hairs keep moving for a second after I lifted my palm. Then I gently opened the half-lidded eye on the side closest to me. A dull gray eye, very unwolflike, stared at some place far beyond me. Not Beck's eye. Relieved, I rocked back on my heels and looked at Isabel.

At the same time that I said, "I wonder who it was," Isabel said, "I wonder what killed it."

I ran my hands over the length of its body — the wolf lay on its side, front legs crossed, back legs crossed, tail spread out behind it like a flag at half-mast. I bit my lip, then said, "I don't see any blood."

"Turn it over," Isabel suggested.

Gently, I took the wolf's legs and flipped it onto its other side; the body was only a little stiff — despite the leaf that had dropped onto its face, the wolf hadn't been dead long. I winced in anticipation of a gruesome discovery. But there was no visible injury on the other side, either.

"Maybe it was old age," I said. My friend Rachel had had a dog when we first met: a grizzled old golden retriever with a muzzle painted snowy white by age.

"The wolf doesn't look old," Isabel said.

"Sam said that the wolves die after about fifteen years of not shifting back and forth," I said. "Maybe that's what happened."

I lifted the wolf's muzzle to see if I could spot any telltale gray or white hairs on it. I heard Isabel's disgusted noise before I saw the reason for it. Dried red blood stained the wolf's muzzle — I thought it might be from a previous kill, until I realized that the side of the wolf's jaw that had been resting on the ground was caked with blood, too. It was the wolf's blood.

I swallowed again, feeling a little sick. I didn't really want Isabel thinking I was queasy, though, so I said, "Hit by a car and came here?"

Isabel made a noise in the back of her throat, either disgust or contempt. "No. Look at the nose."

She was right; there were twin trails of blood coming from the wolf's nostrils, running down to join the old smear across the lips.

I couldn't seem to stop looking at it. If Isabel hadn't been there, I don't know how long I would've crouched there, its muzzle in my hands, looking at this wolf — this person — who had died with his own blood crusted on his face.

But Isabel was there. So I laid the wolf's face carefully back onto the ground. With one gloved finger, I stroked the smooth hair on the side of the wolf's face. Morbidly, I wanted to look at the other side again, the bloody one.

"Do you think there was something wrong with it?" I asked.

"Ya think?" Isabel replied. Then she shrugged. "Could just be a nosebleed. Do wolves get nosebleeds? They can make you yak if you look up when you have one."

My stomach was tight with misgiving.

"Grace. Come on. Head trauma could do that, too. Or animals picking at it after it died. Or any number of disgusting things to think about before lunch. Point is, it's dead. The end."

I looked at the lifeless gray eye. "Maybe we should bury it."

"*Maybe* we can have coffee first," Isabel said.

I stood up, brushing the dirt off my knees. I had the nagging feeling you get when you leave something undone, a prickling anxiety. Maybe Sam would know more. I kept my voice light and said, "*Okay.* Let's go get warmed up and I'll call Sam. He can come look at it afterward."

"Wait," Isabel said. She got out her cell phone, aimed it at the wolf, and clicked a photo. "Let's try using our brains. Welcome to technology, Grace."

I looked at the screen on her phone. The wolf's face, glazed with blood in real life, looked ordinary and unharmed through the cell phone's view. If I hadn't seen the wolf in the flesh, I would've never known there was anything wrong.

Chapter Seven

• SAM •

I had been sitting at Kenny's for about fifteen minutes, watching the waitress attending to the customers in the other booths like a bee visiting and revisiting flowers, when Grace tapped on the other side of the streaked glass. She was a backlit silhouette against the bright blue sky, and I could just glimpse the slender white of her smile, and saw her kiss the air at me before she and Isabel headed around to the front of the diner.

A moment later, Grace, her nose and cheeks pink from the cold, slid into the cracked red booth beside me, her jeans squelching on the perpetually greasy surface. She was about to touch my face before she kissed me, and I recoiled.

"What? Do I stink?" she asked, not sounding particularly bothered. She laid her cell phone and car keys on the table in front of her and reached across me for the menus by the wall.

Leaning away, I pointed to her gloves. "You do, actually. Your gloves smell like that wolf. Not in a good way."

"Thanks for the backup, wolf-man," Isabel said. When Grace offered her a menu, she shook her head emphatically and added, "The whole car smelled like wet dog."

I wasn't sure about the wet-dog label; yes, I smelled the normal, musky wolf odor on Grace's gloves, but there was something else to it — an unpleasant undercurrent that rankled my still-heightened sense of smell.

Grace said, "Sheesh. I'll put them in the car. You don't have to give me that about-to-hurl look. If the waitress comes, order me a coffee and something that involves bacon, okay?"

While she was gone, Isabel and I sat in a kind of uneasy silence filled by a Motown song playing overhead and the clattering of plates in the kitchen. I studied the shape of the saltshaker's warped shadow across the container of sugar packets. Isabel examined the chunky cuff of her sweater and the way it rested on the table. Finally, she said, "You made another bird thing."

I picked up the crane that I'd folded out of my napkin while I was waiting. It was lumpy and imperfect because the napkin hadn't been quite square. "Yeah."

"Why?"

I rubbed my nose, trying to rid it of the scent of the wolf. "I don't know. There's a Japanese legend that if you fold one thousand paper cranes, you get a wish."

Isabel's permanently arched right eyebrow made her smile look inadvertently cruel. "You have a wish?"

"No," I said, as Grace sat back down beside me. "All of my wishes have already been granted."

"What were you wishing for?" Grace interrupted.

"To kiss you," I said to her. She leaned toward me, offering her neck, and I kissed her just behind her ear, pretending I couldn't still smell the almond scent of the wolf on her skin.

Isabel's eyes narrowed, though her lips stayed curved up, and I knew that, somehow, she had seen my reaction.

I looked away as the waitress came and took our order. Grace ordered coffee and a BLT. I got the soup of the day and tea. Isabel just ordered coffee, taking a bag of granola out of her small leather purse after the waitress had gone.

"Food allergy?" I asked.

"Hick allergy," Isabel said. "Grease allergy. Where I used to live, we had real coffeehouses. When I say *panini* here, everyone says *Bless you.*"

Grace laughed and took my napkin crane; she made it flap its wings. "We'll make a panini run to Duluth some day, Isabel. Until then, bacon will do you good."

Isabel made a face like she didn't much agree with Grace. "If by *good*, you mean *cellulite and zits*, sure. So, Sam, what's the deal on this corpse, anyway? Grace said that you said something about wolves getting fifteen years after they stop shifting."

"Nice, Isabel," Grace muttered, casting a sideways glance at me to see what my expression was at the word *corpse*. But she'd already told me over the phone that the wolf wasn't Beck, Paul, or Ulrik, so I didn't react.

Isabel shrugged, unapologetic, and flipped open her phone. She pushed it across the table to me. "Visual aid number one."

The phone scraped across invisible crumbs on the table as I spun it right side up. My stomach gripped in a fist when I saw the wolf on the screen, clearly dead, but my grief lacked force. I had never known this wolf as a human.

"I think you're right," I said. "Because I've only ever known this wolf as a wolf. It must've been from old age."

"I don't think this was a natural death," said Grace. "Plus, there were no white hairs on the muzzle."

I lifted my shoulders. "I just know what Beck told me. That we get . . . got" — I struggled with tense, since I wasn't one of them anymore — "ten or fifteen years after we stopped shifting. A wolf's natural life span."

"There was blood coming out of the wolf's nose," Grace said almost angrily, like it annoyed her to say it.

I slanted the screen back and forth, squinting at the muzzle. I didn't see anything on the blurry screen to suggest a violent death.

"It wasn't a lot," Grace said, in response to my frown. "Did any of the other wolves that died ever have blood on their faces?"

I struggled to remember the various wolves that had died while I was living in Beck's house. It was a blur of memories — Beck and Paul with tarps and shovels, Ulrik singing "For He's a Jolly Good Fellow" at the top of his lungs. "I don't really remember any of them clearly. Maybe this wolf got knocked in the head." I deliberately didn't allow myself to think about the person behind the wolf's pelt.

Grace didn't say anything else as the waitress set down our drinks and food. For a long moment there was silence as I doctored my tea and Isabel did the same to her coffee. Grace studied her BLT pensively.

Isabel said, "For a hick diner, they have really good coffee." Part of me appreciated the fact that she didn't even *look* to see if the waitress was within earshot before she said it — the sheer insensitivity was somehow rewarding to watch. But most of me was glad that I was sitting next to Grace instead, who shot

Isabel a look that said *Sometimes I don't know why I hang out with you.*

"Uh-oh," I said, glimpsing the opening door. "Incoming."

It was John Marx, Olivia's older brother.

I wasn't really looking forward to talking to him, and at first it appeared that I wouldn't have to, because John didn't seem to see us. He went straight to the counter and pulled out a stool, hunching his tall frame as he leaned on his elbows. Before he even ordered, the waitress brought him a coffee.

"John's hot," Isabel observed, with a voice that indicated that it was possibly a drawback.

"Isabel," hissed Grace. "Maybe turn down the insensitivity meter slightly?"

Isabel pursed her lips. "What? Olivia's not dead."

"I'm going to go ask him to come over and sit with us," Grace said.

"Oh, no, please don't," I said. "It's going to involve lying, and I'm not good at that."

"But I am," Grace said. "He looks pitiful. I'll be right back."

And so she returned a minute later with John and slid back in next to me. John stood at the end of the table, looking slightly uncomfortable as Isabel waited just a moment too long to make room for him on her side of the booth.

"So how are you?" Grace asked sympathetically, leaning her elbows on the table. I might have been imagining the leading tone to her voice, but I didn't think so. I'd heard that sound before, when she asked a question she already knew the answer to, and liked what she knew.

John glanced at Isabel, who was leaning away from him, in a fairly tactless way, arm against the windowsill. Then he leaned toward me and Grace. "I got an e-mail from Olivia."

"An e-mail?" Grace echoed. Her voice conveyed just the right combination of hope, disbelief, and frailty. Just what you'd expect from a grieving girl who was hoping her best friend was still alive. Only Grace knew Olivia *was* still alive.

I shot her a look.

Grace ignored me, still looking, all innocent and intense, at John. "What did it say?"

"That she was in Duluth. That she was coming home soon!" John threw his hands up. "I didn't know whether I should crap myself or scream at the computer. How could she do this to Mom and Dad? And then she's just like, 'So I'm coming back soon'? Like she just went off to visit friends and now she's done. I mean, I'm really happy, but, Grace, I'm *so* angry at her."

He sat back in his seat, looking a little surprised that he'd confessed so much. I crossed my arms and leaned on the table, trying to override the prickle of jealousy that had unexpectedly surfaced when John had said Grace's name with such a feeling of connection. Strange what love taught you about your faults.

"But when?" Grace pressed. "When did she say she would get back?"

John shrugged. "Of course she didn't say anything other than 'soon.' "

Grace's eyes shone. "But she's *alive*."

"Yeah," John said, and now I saw that his eyes were rather shiny as well. "The cops told us that — you know, that we shouldn't keep our hopes up — anyway. That was the worst, not knowing if she was alive."

"Speaking of the cops," Isabel said. "Did you show them the e-mail?"

Grace briefly turned a less-than-pleasant face to Isabel, but it had melted back into gentle interest by the time John turned back to her.

He looked guilty. "I didn't want them to tell me about how it might not be real. I guess — I guess I will. Because they can track it, right?"

"Yes," Isabel said, looking at Grace instead of at John. "I've heard cops can track IP addresses or whatever they're called. So they could find out the general area it was coming from. Like maybe even *right here in Mercy Falls.*"

In a hard voice, Grace replied, "But if it was from an Internet café from a pretty big city, like Duluth or Minneapolis, it wouldn't really be useful."

John interrupted, "I don't know if I really want to have Olivia dragged back here, kicking and screaming. I mean, she's almost eighteen, and she's not stupid. I miss her, but there had to be some reason for her to go."

We all stared at him — for different reasons, I think. I was just thinking that it was an awfully perceptive and selfless thing to say, if slightly uninformed. Isabel's stare looked more like an *are-you-a-total-idiot?* stare. Grace's was admiring.

"You're a pretty good brother," Grace said.

John looked down into his coffee cup. "Yeah, well, I don't know about that. Anyway, I'd better get going. I'm just on my way to class."

"Class on Saturday?"

"Workshop stuff," John said. "Extra credit. Gets me out of the house." He slid out of the booth, pulling a few bucks out of his pocket for the coffee. "Would you give this to the waitress?"

"Yup," Grace said. "See you around?"

John nodded and retreated. He had only been out of the diner for a moment when Isabel slid back into the center to face Grace.

"Wow, Grace, you never told me you were born without a brain," Isabel said. "Because that's the only way I can figure you would do something that incredibly stupid."

I wouldn't have put it in those terms, but I was thinking the same thing.

Grace waved it off. "*Psh.* I sent it the last time I was in Duluth. I wanted to give them some hope. And I actually thought it might keep the cops from looking so hard for her if they thought it was an annoying almost-legal runaway instead of a possible homicide-kidnapping thing. See, I *was* using my brain."

Isabel shook some granola into her palm. "Well, I think you should stay out of it. Sam, tell her to stay out of it."

The whole idea of it did make me uneasy, but I said, "Grace is very wise."

"Grace is very wise," Grace repeated to Isabel.

"Generally," I added.

"Maybe we should tell him," Grace said.

Isabel and I both stared at her.

"What? He's her brother. He loves her and wants her to be happy. Plus, I don't understand all the secrecy if it's scientific. Yeah, the greater world would definitely take it the wrong way.

But family members? You'd think they'd be better about it, if it's just logical instead of monstrous."

I didn't really have words for the horror that the idea inspired in me. I wasn't even sure *why* it elicited such a strong reaction.

"Sam," Isabel said, and I realized I was just sitting there, running a finger over one of my scarred wrists. Isabel looked at Grace. "Grace, that is the dumbest idea I have ever heard, unless your goal is to get Olivia rushed to the nearest microscope for poking and prodding. Also, John is clearly too highly strung to handle the concept."

This, at least, made sense to me. I nodded. "I don't think he's a good one to tell, Grace."

"You told Isabel!"

"We had to," I said, before Isabel could finish looking superior. "She had already guessed a lot of it. I think we should operate on a need-to-know basis." Grace was starting to get her blank face, which meant that she was annoyed, so I said, "But I still think you're very wise. Generally."

"Generally," repeated Isabel. "Now I'm getting out of here. I'm, like, sticking fast to the booth."

"Isabel," I said, as she got up, and she stopped at the end of the table, giving me this weird look, as if I hadn't called her by her name before. "I'm going to bury him. The wolf. Maybe today, if the ground's not frozen."

"No hurry," Isabel said. "It's not going anywhere."

As Grace leaned in toward me, I caught another whiff of the rotten smell. I wished I'd looked more closely at the photo on Isabel's phone. I wished the nature of the wolf's death had been more straightforward. I'd had enough mysteries for a lifetime.

Chapter Eight

· SAM ·

I was human.

The day after I buried the wolf was frigid, Minnesota March in all its volatile splendor: One day the temperatures would soar into the thirties, and the next it would be barely twelve or thirteen degrees. It was amazing how warm thirty-two felt after two solid months of single digits. I'd never had to endure such cold in my human skin. Today was one of the bitterly cold days, as far away from spring as you could get. Except for the brilliant red winterberries that clustered at the edges of the trees, there was no color left anywhere in the world. My breath frosted in front of me, and my eyes dried with the cold. The air smelled like being a wolf, and yet I wasn't.

The knowledge both thrilled and hurt me.

There'd only been two customers in the bookstore all day. I considered what I'd do after my shift. Most times, if my shift ended before Grace was done with school, I would linger in the loft of the store with a book rather than go home to the Brisbanes' empty house. Without Grace there, it was just a place to wait for her, a dull ache inside me.

Today, the ache had followed me to work. I had already written a song — just a piece of a song — *Is it still a secret if nobody cares / if having the knowledge in no way impairs / your living — and feeling — the way that you breathe / knowing the things that you know about me* — the hope of a song more than anything else. Now, I perched behind the counter reading a copy of Roethke, my shift about to end and Grace tutoring until late, my eyes drawn to the tiny flakes of snow drifting outside instead of Roethke's words: *"Dark, dark my light, and darker my desire. My soul, like some heat-maddened summer fly, keeps buzzing at the sill. Which I is I?"* I looked down at my fingers on the pages of my book, such wonderful, precious things, and felt guilty for the nameless wanting that plagued me.

The clock ticked to five. This was when I usually locked the front door, turned the sign to CLOSED — COME BACK SOON, and went out the back door to my Volkswagen.

But this time I didn't. This time I locked the back door, picked up my guitar case, and went out the front, sliding a little on the ice coating the threshold. I pulled on the skullcap that Grace had bought me in a failed attempt to make me look sexy while keeping my head warm. Stepping out into the middle of the sidewalk, I watched tiny flakes float down onto the abandoned street. As far as I could see, there were banks of old snow pressed into stained sculptures. Icicles made jagged smiles of the storefronts.

My eyes smarted with the cold. I held my free hand out, palm up, and watched as snow dissolved on my skin.

This was not real life. This was life as watched through a

window. Life watched on television. I couldn't remember when I hadn't hidden from this.

I was cold, I had a handful of snow, and I was human.

The future stretched before me, infinite and growing and mine, in a way that nothing had ever been before.

Sudden euphoria rushed through me, a grin stretching my face at this cosmic lottery I had won. I had risked everything and gained everything, and here I was, of the world and in it. I laughed out loud, no one to hear me but the audience of snowflakes. I leaped off the sidewalk, into the bank of graying snow. I was drunk with the reality of my human body. A lifetime of winters, of skullcaps, of collars turned against cold, of noses turning red, of staying up late on New Year's Eve. Skidding in the slick tire tracks in the road, I waltzed across the street, swinging my guitar case in a circle, snow falling all around me, until a car honked at me.

I waved at the driver and jumped up onto the opposite sidewalk, knocking the crisp snow off each parking meter as I came to it. My pants were frozen with snow stuffed into my shoes, my fingers numb and red, and still I was me. Always me.

I circled the block until the cold had lost its novelty, and then I doubled back to my car and checked my watch. Grace would still be tutoring, and I didn't feel like running the risk of getting to her house and finding one of her parents instead. Awkward didn't begin to describe those conversations. The more obvious Grace and I became with our relationship, the less her parents found to say to me. And vice versa. So instead I headed toward Beck's house. Even though I couldn't hope for any of the other wolves to have shifted, I could pick up some of my books. I wasn't a fan of the mysteries that filled Grace's bookshelves.

So I followed the highway in the dying gray light of day, Boundary Wood pressing up against the shoulder of the road, until I was on the deserted street that led to Beck's.

Pulling into the empty driveway, I climbed out of the car and took a deep breath. The woods here smelled different than the woods behind Grace's did — here, the air was filled with the sharp, wintergreen scent of the birches and the complex smell of wet earth near the lake. I could pick out the scent of the pack, too, musky and pungent.

Habit led me to the back door, the fresh snow squeaking beneath my boots, clumping at the cuff of my jeans. I dragged my fingertips through the snow on top of the bushes that grew against the house, as I walked around back and waited again for the surge of nausea that meant I was about to change. But it didn't come.

Beside the back door, I hesitated, looking out over the snowy backyard and into the woods. I had a thousand memories that lived in the span of ground stretching from the door to the woods.

Turning back to the door, I realized that it was not quite ajar, but not quite shut, either, pressed in just far enough to keep it from coming open with the intermittent wind. I looked down to the doorknob and saw a smear of red on it. One of the other wolves, shifting very, very early — it had to be. Only one of the new wolves could possibly become human this early, and even they couldn't realistically hope to keep that form while ice-slicked snow crusted the ground.

Pushing open the door, I called, "Hello?" There was rustling from the kitchen. Something about the way it sounded, scraping and scuffling across the tile, made me uneasy. I tried to think of something to say that would sound reassuring to a wolf but not sound insane to a human. "Whoever it is, I belong here."

I rounded the corner into the dim kitchen, then stopped short by the edge of the center island when I smelled the earthy reek of lake water. Reaching across the counter to flick on the light, I asked, "Who's there?"

I saw a foot — human, bare, dirty — jutting from behind the island, and when it jerked, I did, too, startled. Coming around the island, I saw a guy curled on his side, shaking hard. His dark brown hair was spiked with dried mud, and on his outstretched arms, I saw a dozen little wounds, evidence of an unprotected trip through the woods. He stank of wolf.

Logically, I knew he had to be one of Beck's new wolves from the year before. But I felt a weird prickle go through me when I thought about Beck handpicking him, when I realized that this was a brand-new member of the pack, the first one in a long time.

He turned his face to me, and though he had to have been in pain — I remembered that pain — his expression was quite composed. And familiar. Something about the brutal line of his cheekbones down to his jaw and the narrow shape of his brilliant green eyes was irritatingly familiar, attached to a name just on the edge of my consciousness. In more ordinary circumstances, I would've known it, I thought, but right then, it just tickled somewhere in the back of my head.

"I'm going to change back now, aren't I?" he said, and I was a bit taken aback by his voice — not just by the timbre, which was rather gravelly, and older than I had expected — but also by the tone. Completely level, despite the shudder of his shoulders and the darkening of his nails.

I knelt beside his head, trying out the words in my mouth, feeling like a kid wearing his father's clothing. Any other year, and it would've been Beck explaining this to a new wolf, not me. "Yeah, you are. It's too cold still. Look — next time you shift, find the shed in the woods —"

"I saw it," he said, his voice slipping more to a growl.

"It's got a space heater in there and some food and clothing. Try the box that says SAM or the one that says ULRIK — something in there ought to fit." In truth, though, I didn't know if they would or not. The guy had broad shoulders and muscles like a gladiator. "It's not as good as being in here, but it'll spare you the brambles."

He cast his brilliant eyes up at me and the sardonic look in them made me realize he'd never given me any reason to believe the wounds bothered him. "Thanks for the tip," he said, and my remaining words felt sour in my mouth.

Beck had told me that the three new wolves he'd created had been recruited — that they knew what they were getting into. I hadn't considered, before now, what sort of person would choose this life. Someone who would willingly lose themselves for more and more of the year until eventually it was good-bye to all of it. It was a sort of suicide, really, and as soon as I thought the word, it made me look at the guy in an entirely different way. As the newcomer's body twisted on the floor, his expression still controlled — expectant, if anything — I just had time to see the old track marks on his arms before his skin twisted into a wolf's.

I hurried to get the back door open so that the wolf, brownish and dark in the dim light, could escape into the snow and away from the too-human environment of the kitchen. This wolf didn't dart for the door, however, like other wolves would have. Like *I* would have, as a wolf. Instead, he stalked slowly by me, head low, pausing to look directly into my eyes with his green ones. I didn't look away, and finally he slid out the door, stopping once again in the backyard to look at me appraisingly.

Long after the new wolf had gone, the image of him haunted me: the puncture wounds in the bends of his elbows, the arrogance in his eyes, the familiarity of his face.

Retreating back to the kitchen to clean up the blood and dirt from the tile, I saw the spare key lying on the floor. I returned it to its hiding place, by the back door.

As I did, I felt watched, and I turned, expecting to see the new wolf at the edge of the forest. But instead it was a big, gray wolf, eyes steady on me, familiar in an entirely different way.

"Beck," I whispered. He didn't move, but his nostrils worked, smelling the same thing I did: the new wolf. "Beck, what did you bring us?"

Chapter Nine

• ISABEL •

I stayed after class for a student government meeting. The meeting was boring as hell and I didn't give a crap about how Mercy Falls High chose to organize itself, but it served the dual purpose of keeping me away from home and letting me sit in the back of the assembly with my silent smirk on, my eyes painted dark, being unattainable. I had my usual group of girls who sat around me, eyes painted like mine, looking unattainable — which was not the same as *being* unattainable.

Being popular in a town the size of Mercy Falls was ridiculously easy. You only had to believe you were a hot commodity, and you were. It wasn't like San Diego, where being popular was like a full-time career. The effects of attending the assembly — an hour-long ad for the Isabel Culpeper brand — would last for a week.

But finally I had to make my way home. Delightfully, both of my parents' cars were in the driveway. I was beside myself with joy. I sat in my SUV in the driveway, opened the Shakespeare I was supposed to be reading, and turned up my music loud enough that I could see the bass vibrating the rearview mirror.

After about ten minutes, my mother's silhouette appeared in one of the windows, with an exaggerated motion for me to come in.

And so the evening was under way.

Inside our vast stainless-steel kitchen, it was the Culpeper Show at its finest.

Mom: "I'm sure the neighbors love your white trash music. Thanks for playing it loud enough for them to hear it."

Dad: "Where were you, anyway?"

Mom: "Student assembly."

Dad: "I didn't ask you. I asked our daughter."

Mom: "Honestly, Thomas, does it matter who answered?"

Dad: "I feel like I have to hold a gun to her head to get her to speak to me."

Me: "Is that an option?"

Now they were both glaring at me. I didn't really need to add lines to the Culpeper Show; it was self-sustaining without me and played reruns all night.

"I told you she shouldn't go to public school," my father told my mother. I knew where this was going. Mom's next line was "I told you we shouldn't come to Mercy Falls," and then Dad would start throwing stuff, and eventually they would end up in separate rooms, enjoying different brands of alcoholic beverages.

"I have homework," I interrupted. "I'm going upstairs. See you next week."

As I turned to go, Dad said, "Isabel, wait."

I waited.

"Jerry told me you were hanging out with Lewis Brisbane's daughter. Is that true?"

Now I turned, to see what his expression was. His arms crossed, he leaned against the colorless counter, his shirt and tie still perfectly unwrinkled, one eyebrow raised in his narrow face. I raised mine to match. "What about it?"

"Don't take that tone with me," Dad said. "I just asked a question."

"Then fine. Yes. I hang out with Grace."

I could see a vein stand out on one of his arms as he closed his hands into fists and opened them again, over and over. "I hear that she has a lot to do with the wolves."

I made a little gesture in the air like, *What are you talking about?*

"Rumor is she feeds them. I've been seeing them around here a lot," he said. "Looking suspiciously well cared for. I'm thinking it's time to do some more thinning."

For a moment we just looked at each other. Me trying to decide if he knew I'd been feeding them and was doing his passive-aggressive thing to get me to say something, and him trying to stare me down.

"Yeah, Dad," I said, finally. "You should go shoot some animals. That'll bring Jack back. Good idea. Should I tell Grace to lure them closer to the house?"

My mother stared at me, a frozen piece of art: *Portrait of a Woman With Chardonnay.* My father looked like he wanted to hit me.

"Are we done?" I asked.

"Oh, I'm getting very close to done," my father said. He turned and gave my mother a meaningful look, which she didn't see because she was too busy filling her eyes with tears that had yet to fall.

I thought my part in this particular episode was definitely over, so I left them behind in the kitchen. I heard my dad say, "I'm going to kill all of them." And my mother said, voice full of tears, "Whatever, Tom."

The end. I probably needed to stop feeding the wolves.

The closer they got, the more dangerous it was for all of us.

Chapter Ten

· GRACE ·

By the time Sam got home, Rachel and I had been attempting to make chicken parmesan for a half hour. Rachel lacked the concentration to bread the chicken pieces, so I had her stirring the tomato sauce while I dredged an endless number of chicken parts through egg and then through breadcrumbs. I pretended to be annoyed, but really the repetitive action had a kind of relaxing effect, and there was a subtle pleasure in the tactile elements: the viscous swirling of the brilliantly yellow egg over the chicken, then the soft *shush* of the breadcrumbs rubbing against one another as they moved out of the chicken's way.

If only I didn't have this persistent headache. Still, the process of making dinner and having Rachel over was doing a pretty good job of making me forget about both my headache and the fact that it had gotten winter dark outside, the chill pressing in against the window above the sink, and Sam was still not here. I kept repeating the same mantra over and over in my head. *He won't change. He's cured. It's over.*

Rachel bumped her hip against my hip, and I realized, all at once, that she had turned up the music insanely loud. She bumped my hip again, in time with the song, and then spun into the center of the kitchen, wiggling her arms over her head in some sort of demented Snoopy dance. Her outfit, a black dress over striped leggings, paired with her dual ponytails, only added to the ludicrous effect.

"Rachel," I said, and she looked at me but kept dancing. "This is why you are single."

"No man can handle this," Rachel assured me, gesturing to herself with her chin. She spun and came face-to-face with Sam, standing in the doorway from the hall. The thumping bass must've drowned out the sound of the front door. At the sight of him, my stomach slid down to my feet, a weird combination of relief, nerves, and anticipation all in one, a feeling that never seemed to go away.

Still facing Sam, Rachel did a strange dance move with her index fingers extended; it looked like it had possibly been invented in the fifties, when people weren't allowed to touch each other. "Hi, The Boy!" she shouted over the music. "We're making Italian food!"

Still holding a piece of chicken, I turned and made a loud noise in protest. Rachel said, "My colleague informs me that I spoke too strongly. I am watching Grace make Italian food!"

Sam smiled at me, his always sad-looking smile maybe a little tighter than usual, and said, ". . ."

I struggled to turn down the radio with my hand that wasn't covered with breading. "What?"

"I said, 'What are you making?' " Sam repeated. "And then, 'Hi, Rachel.' And 'May I come into the kitchen, Rachel?' "

Rachel swept grandly out of his way, and Sam came to lean

on the counter next to me. His yellow wolf's eyes were narrowed, and he seemed to have forgotten that he was still wearing his coat.

"Chicken parmesan," I said.

He blinked. "What?"

"It's what I'm making. What were you up to?"

Sam said, stumbling, "I — was — at the store. Reading." With a quick glance toward Rachel, he sucked in his lips and said, "Can't talk. My lips are still cold from being outside. When will it be spring?"

"Forget spring," said Rachel, "when will it be *dinner*?"

I waved unbreaded chicken at her, and Sam looked around at the counter behind him. "Can I help?" he asked.

"Mostly I need to finish breading these eight million chicken breasts," I said. My head was starting to pound, and I really was beginning to hate the mere sight of uncooked chicken. "I never realized what happened to two pounds of chicken when you pounded it flat."

Sam gently shouldered past me to the sink to wash his hands, his cheek leaning against mine as he reached behind me for the dish towel to dry his hands. "I'll bread the rest while you fry them. Does that work?"

"I'll cook the water for the pasta," Rachel volunteered. "I'm excellent at boiling things."

"The big pot's in the pantry," I said.

As Rachel disappeared into the small pantry and began crashing through the pots and lids, Sam leaned over to me so that his lips pressed against my ear. He whispered, "I saw one of Beck's new wolves today. Shifted."

It took a moment for my brain to shuffle through the meaning of his words: *new wolves*. Was Olivia human? Did Sam have to try to find the other wolves? What happened now?

I turned sharply toward him. He was still close enough to me that it put us nose to nose; his was still cold from being outside. I saw the worry in his eyes.

"Hey, none of that while I'm here," Rachel said. "I like The Boy, but I don't want to watch you kiss him. Kissing in front of the loveless is an act of cruelty. Aren't you supposed to be frying something?"

So we finished making dinner. It seemed to take an agonizingly long time, knowing that Sam had something to say and knowing that he couldn't say it in front of Rachel. And there was guilt mixed in as well, making the time drag. Olivia was Rachel's friend, too. If she had known that Olivia might be coming back soon, she'd be over the moon and full of questions. I tried to avoid glancing at the clock; Rachel's mom was picking her up at eight.

"Oh, hi, Rachel. Mmm, food." My mother flowed through the kitchen, dropping her coat on one of the chairs by the wall as she did.

"Mom!" I said, not bothering to hide the surprise in my voice. "What are you doing home so early?"

"Is there enough for me? I ate at the studio, but it wasn't very filling," Mom said. I had no doubt. Mom was an excellent food burner; ceaseless movement did a lot in the calorie-destruction department. She turned, saw Sam. Her voice changed to something knowing and not entirely pleasant. "Oh. Hi, Sam. Here again?"

Sam's cheeks reddened.

"You practically live here," Mom went on. She turned and looked at me. Clearly it was supposed to convey some meaning, but it was lost on me. Sam, however, turned his face away from both of us as if it was clear enough to him.

Once upon a time, Mom had really liked Sam. She'd even flirted with him in her mom way and asked him to sing and pose for a portrait. But that was back when he was just a boy that I was seeing. Now that it was clear that Sam was here to stay, Mom's friendliness had evaporated and she and I communicated in the language of silence. The length of the pauses between sentences conveyed more information than the words within them.

My jaw tightened. "Have some pasta, Mom. Are you working more tonight?"

"Do you want me to get out of your way?" she asked. "I can go upstairs." She tapped my head with her fork. "No need to shoot me dagger eyes, Grace. I get it. See you later, Rachel."

"I didn't have dagger eyes," I said after she left, going over to hang up her coat. Something about the entire exchange had left a sour taste in my mouth.

"You didn't," Sam agreed, his voice a bit mournful. "She has a guilty conscience." His face was pensive, shoulders sagged, like he was carrying a weight he hadn't been carrying that morning. All of a sudden I wondered if he ever doubted that he'd made the right decision — if it had been worth the risk. I wanted him to know that I thought it was. I wanted him to know I'd shout it from the rooftops. That was when I decided to confide in Rachel.

"You better go move your car," I told Sam. He cast an anxious look toward the ceiling, as if Mom could read his thoughts through the floor of her home studio. Then toward Rachel. And then toward me, his unasked question clear in his expression: *Are you really telling her?* I shrugged.

Rachel looked at me quizzically. I made a gesture like, *Wait and I'll explain*, and Sam went to call up the stairs, "See you later, Mrs. Brisbane!"

There was a long pause. Then Mom said, not in a nice way, "Bye."

Sam came back into the kitchen. He didn't say that he felt guilty, but he didn't have to. It was written all over his face. He said, a little hesitant, "If I'm not back by the time you go, Rach, see you later."

"Back!" Rachel said in surprise as Sam went out the front door, car keys jingling. "What does he mean 'back'? What's he doing with his car? Wait — has The Boy been sleeping *here*?"

"Shhh!" I said hurriedly, with a glance toward the hallway. Taking Rachel by the elbow, I propelled her over toward the corner of the kitchen and released her quickly, looking at my fingers. "Whoa, Rachel, your skin is cold."

"No, you're hot," she corrected. "So what's going on here? Are you guys like — *sleeping* together?"

I felt my cheeks flush despite myself. "Not like that. Just like . . ."

Rachel didn't wait for me to figure out how to finish my thought. "Holy freakin' holy freakin' holy . . . I can't even think of what to say to that, Grace! Just like *what*? What do you guys *do*? No, wait, don't tell me!"

"Shhh," I said again, even though she wasn't being that loud. "Just sleep. That's it. Yeah, I know it sounds weird, but, I just . . ." I struggled for words to explain it. It wasn't all about almost losing Sam and wanting to keep him near. It wasn't all about lust. It was about falling asleep with Sam's chest pressed against my back so I could feel his heart slow to match mine. It was about growing up and realizing that the feeling of his arms around me, the smell of him when he was sleeping, the sound of his breathing — that was home and everything I wanted at the end of the day. It wasn't the same as being with him when we were awake. But I didn't know how to say that to Rachel. I wondered why I'd wanted to tell her. "I don't know if I can explain it. Sleeping *feels* different when he's there."

"I'll sure bet it does," Rachel said, her eyes wide.

"Rachel," I said.

"Sorry, sorry. I'm trying to be reasonable here, but my best friend just told me that she's been spending every night with her boyfriend without her parents knowing it. So he's sneaking back in here? You've corrupted The Boy!"

"Do you think I'm doing the wrong thing?" I asked, wincing a little, because I thought maybe I *had* corrupted Sam.

Rachel considered. "I think it's awfully romantic."

I laughed, a little shakily, with something like giddiness and relief. "Rachel, I'm so in love with him." But it didn't sound *real* when I said it. It sounded corny, like a commercial, because I couldn't quite invest my voice with the truth and depth of how I felt. "Swear not to tell?"

"Your secret is safe with me. Far be it from me to break up the young lovers. God! I can't believe you really are young lovers."

My heart was thumping with the confession, but it felt good, too — one less secret I was keeping from Rachel. By the time her mom arrived a few minutes later, we were both fairly giddy. Maybe it was time to tell her some of the other secrets, too.

· SAM ·

It was eighteen degrees outside. In the bright light of the moon, a flat, pale disc behind a tangle of leafless branches, I folded my bare arms tightly across my chest and stared at my socks, waiting for Grace's mother to vacate the kitchen. I softly cursed icy Minnesota springtimes, but the words swirled away in puffs of white in the darkness. It was strange to be standing in this cold, shaking with it, unable to feel my fingers or toes, my eyes burning with it, and to be no closer to being a wolf than I had been before.

Through the cracked sliding-glass door on the deck, Grace's voice was just audible; she was talking with her mother about me. Her mother wondered gently if I would be coming over tomorrow night as well. Grace mused vaguely back that I probably would be, as that's what boyfriends did. Her mother commented to no one in particular that some people might think that we were moving too fast. Grace asked her mother if she wanted any more chicken parmesan before she put it away in the fridge. I could hear the impatience in her voice, but her mother seemed oblivious, effectively holding me prisoner outside by her presence in the kitchen. Standing on the frigid wood of the deck in my jeans and thin Beatles T-shirt, I contemplated the possible wisdom of marrying Grace and living a young hippie life in the backseat of my Volkswagen, without parental constraints. It had never seemed like such a good idea as now, my teeth starting to chatter and my toes and ears going numb.

I heard Grace say, "Will you show me what you were working on upstairs?"

Her mom sounded vaguely suspicious as she said, "Okay."

"Let me just get my sweater," Grace said. She came over to the glass door of the deck, silently unlocking it as she got her sweater off the back of the kitchen table with her other hand. I saw her mouth *Sorry* to me. A little louder, she said, "It's cold in here."

I counted to twenty after they'd left the kitchen, and let myself in. I was shuddering uncontrollably with the cold, but I was still Sam.

I had all the evidence I needed that my cure was real, but I was still waiting for the punch line.

· GRACE ·

Sam was still shaking so badly by the time I met him in my room that I completely forgot about my lingering headache. I shoved my bedroom door shut without turning on the light and followed the sound of his voice to the bed.

"M-m-maybe we need to rethink our lifestyle choices," he whispered to me, teeth chattering, as I climbed into bed and wrapped my arms around him. My fingers brushed against the goose bumps that covered his arms; I could feel them even through the fabric of his shirt.

I tugged the blanket up to cover both of our heads and pressed my face against the frigid skin of his neck. It felt selfish to say it out loud. "I don't want to sleep without you."

He curled into a tiny ball — his feet, even through his socks, were freezing against my bare legs — and mumbled, "Me neither. B-but we have our whole —" His words piled up on top of one another; he had to stop and rub his hand over his lips to warm them before he went on. "Our whole lives ahead of us. To be together."

"Our whole lives, starting now," I said. Outside my bedroom door, I heard my dad's voice — he must've gotten home just as I came into the room — and listened to my parents' voices as they climbed up the stairs to their room, noisy and jostling against each other. For a brief moment, I envied their freedom to come and go as they pleased, no school, no parents, no rules. "I mean, you don't have to stay here, if it makes you uncomfortable. If you don't want to." I paused. "I didn't mean for that to sound so clingy."

Sam rolled over to face me. I couldn't see anything but the glint of his eyes in the darkness. "I'll never get tired of this. I just didn't want to get you in trouble. I just didn't want you to feel like you had to ask me to go. If it gets too difficult."

I touched his cold cheek with my hand; it felt good against my skin. "You can be pretty stupid sometimes for such a smart guy." I felt his smile curve against my palm as he pushed his body closer to mine.

"Either you're really hot," Sam said, "or I'm really cold."

"Duh, I'm hot," I whispered. "Soooo hot."

Sam laughed soundlessly — a little, shaky, exhaling sound.

I reached down to clutch his fingers in mine; we held them like that, smashed between our bodies in a knot, until his fingers stopped feeling so frigid.

"Tell me about the new wolf," I said.

Sam went still beside me. "There's something wrong with him. He wasn't afraid of me."

"That's weird."

"It made me wonder what kind of person would choose to be a wolf. They must all be crazy, Grace, every one of Beck's new wolves. Who would choose that?"

Now it was my turn to go still. I wondered if Sam remembered lying beside me last year, just like this, and me confessing that I wished I changed, too, to go with him. No, not just to go with him. To feel what it was like, to be one of the wolves, so simple and magical and elemental. I thought about Olivia again, now a white wolf, darting between trees with the rest of the pack, and something inside me felt a little raw. "Maybe they just love wolves," I said finally. "And their lives weren't so great."

Sam's body was right beside me, but his hand in mine was slack and I saw that his eyes were closed. His thoughts were far, far away from me, untouchable. Finally, he said, "I don't trust him, Grace. I just feel like no good will come from these new wolves. I just . . . I wish Beck hadn't done it. I wish he'd known to wait."

"Go to sleep," I told him, though I knew he wouldn't. "Don't worry about what might happen."

But I knew he wouldn't do that, either.

Chapter Eleven

• GRACE •

"Back again, Grace?"

The nurse looked up as I walked into her office. The three chairs that sat opposite her desk were full — one student's head lolled back in a sleep posture too embarrassing to not be real, and the other two kids were reading. Mrs. Sanders was pretty famous for letting kids who were overwhelmed with life hang out in her office, which was fine until someone who had a pounding headache and just wanted to sit down walked in and found all the waiting chairs full.

I came around to the front of her desk and crossed my arms across my chest. I felt like humming along to the throb of the ache in my head. Rubbing my hand over my face — a gesture that suddenly and fiercely reminded me of Sam — I said, "I'm sorry to bother you for something so dumb again, but my head is just killing me."

"Well, you do look pretty miserable," Mrs. Sanders agreed. She got up and gestured to the wheeled chair behind her desk. "Why don't you sit down while I track down a thermometer? You're a little flushed, too."

"Thanks," I said gratefully, and took her place as she headed into the other room. It felt odd being here. Not just in her chair, with her solitaire game still up on the computer and the pictures of her kids looking back at me from the desk, but in the nurse's office at all. This was only the second time I'd been here, and it was only a few days since my last visit. I'd waited outside the door for Olivia a few times, but never actually been inside as a patient, blinking under the fluorescent lights and wondering if I was getting sick.

Without Mrs. Sanders there, I didn't feel like I needed to appear stoic, and I pinched the top of my nose, trying to put pressure on the center of the headache. It was the same as the other headaches I'd been getting recently, a dull, radiating pain that burned along my cheekbones. They were headaches that seemed to threaten more: I kept waiting to get a runny nose or a cough or *something*.

Mrs. Sanders reappeared with a thermometer, and I hurriedly dropped my hand from my face. "Open, dear," she instructed me, which I would've found funny any other time, because Mrs. Sanders did not strike me as a "dear" sort. "I have a feeling you're coming down with something."

I accepted the thermometer and put it under my tongue; the plastic sleeve on it felt sharp edged and slimy in my mouth. I was going to observe that I rarely got sick, but I couldn't open my mouth. Mrs. Sanders chatted about classes with the two awake students on the chairs while three minutes dragged by, and then she returned and slid the thermometer out.

"I thought they made high-speed thermometers now," I said.

"For pediatrics. They figure you high school hellions have

enough patience to use the cheap ones." She read the thermometer. "You have a bit of a temperature. Teeny. You probably have a virus. There's a lot of it going around with the temperature going up and down. You want me to call someone to pick you up?"

I momentarily thought about the joy of escaping school and snuggling in Sam's arms for the rest of the afternoon. But he was working and I had a test in Chemistry, so I sighed and admitted the truth: I was not really sick enough to justify leaving. "There's not that much of the school day left. And I have a test."

She made a face. "A stoic. I approve. Well, here. I'm really not supposed to do this without getting ahold of your parents, but —" She stood beside me and opened one of her desk drawers. There was a bunch of loose change, her car keys, and a bottle of acetaminophen in there. Shaking two of the pills into my palm, she said, "That'll kick that temperature in the butt and probably take care of your headache, too."

"Thanks," I said, relinquishing her chair to her. "No offense, but hopefully I won't be back in here this week."

"This office is a cultural and social hot spot!" Mrs. Sanders said, feigning shock. "Take care."

I swallowed the acetaminophen and chased it with some water from the cooler by the door, then headed back to class. I could barely feel my headache. By the end of last period, the acetaminophen had done the trick. Mrs. Sanders was probably right. This nagging sensation of something *more* was just a virus.

I tried to tell myself that was all it was.

Chapter Twelve

· COLE ·

I didn't think I was supposed to be human right now.

Sleet cut into my bare skin, so cold that it felt hot. My fingertips were like clubs; I couldn't feel anything in them. I didn't know how long I'd been lying on the frozen ground, but it was long enough for sleet to have melted in the small of my back.

I was shaking almost too badly to stand, unsteady on my legs as I tried to figure out why I had changed back from a wolf. Before now, my stints as a human had been during warmer days and had been mercifully brief. This was a frigid evening — maybe six or seven o'clock, judging from the sun glowing orange through the leafless tree line.

I didn't have time to wonder at the instability of my condition. I was trembling from the cold, but I didn't feel even a hint of nausea in my stomach, or the twist of my skin that meant I was about to change into a wolf. I knew, with sinking certainty, that I was stuck in this body, at least for the moment. Which meant I needed to find shelter — I was stark naked, and I wasn't about to wait for frostbite to set in. Too many extremities that I preferred not to lose.

Wrapping my arms around myself, I took stock of my surroundings. Behind me, the lake reflected brilliant specks of light. I squinted into the dim forest ahead of me and could see the statue that overlooked the lake, and beyond the statue, the concrete benches. That meant I was within walking distance of the huge house I'd seen earlier.

So now I had a destination. Hopefully nobody was home.

I didn't see any cars in the driveway, so luck was with me so far.

"Damn, damn, damn," I muttered under my breath as I winced my way across the gravel to the back door. There were just enough nerves working in my bare feet for me to feel the stones cutting into the cold flesh. I healed quicker now than I had before, back when I was still just Cole, but it didn't make the initial bite of the stone any less painful.

I tried the back door — unlocked. Truly the Man Upstairs was smiling down on me. I made a note to send a card. Pushing open the door, I stepped into a cluttered mudroom that smelled like barbecue sauce. For a moment, I just stood there, shivering, briefly paralyzed by the memory of barbecue. My stomach — a lot flatter and harder than it had been the last time I'd been human — growled at me, and for a brief, brief moment, I thought about finding the kitchen and stealing food.

The idea of wanting something that bad made my lips curve into a smile. And then my painfully cold feet reminded me why I was here. Clothing first. Then food. I headed out of the mudroom and into a dim hallway.

The house was every bit as gargantuan as it had seemed from the outside and looked like some kind of spread in *Better*

Homes and Gardens. Everything was hung on the walls just so, in perfect threes and fives, perfectly aligned or charmingly asymmetrical. A spotlessly clean rug in a color that was probably called "mauve" led me silently down the wood-floored hallway. Glancing behind me to make sure the coast was still clear, I narrowly avoided tripping over a pricey-looking vase that held a bunch of artfully arranged dead branches. I wondered if real people actually lived here.

More pressingly, I wondered if anyone who wore my size lived here.

I hesitated as the hall opened up. To my left, more dim hallway. To my right, a massive, dark staircase that looked like a murder scene out of a gothic horror movie. I wrestled briefly with logic and decided to go upstairs. If I were a rich guy in Minnesota, I'd have my bedroom upstairs. Because heat rises.

The stairs led me to a hallway that was open on one side to the stairs below. My toes burned against the plush green carpet as feeling slowly returned to them. The pain was a good thing. It meant they still had blood flow.

"Don't move."

A female voice halted me. It didn't sound afraid, despite the fact that a naked guy was standing in the middle of her house, so I figured I would probably turn to find a rifle pointed at me. I was acutely aware of my heart beating normally in my chest; God, I missed adrenaline.

I turned around.

It was a girl. She was pretty much drop-dead gorgeous in an eat-your-heart kind of way, all huge blue eyes partially hidden behind a jagged fringe of blond hair. And a tilt to her shoulders like she knew it. When she swept her eyes up and down my body, I felt as if I'd been judged and found wanting.

I tried a smile. "Hi. Sorry. I'm naked."

"Nice to meet you. I'm Isabel," she said. "What are you doing in my house?"

There wasn't really a right answer to that question.

Below us, there was the sound of a door shutting, and Isabel and I both jerked to look down toward the noise. For a brief moment, my heart yammered in my chest and I was surprised to feel terror — to feel *something* after such a long stretch of nothing.

I couldn't move.

"Oh my *God*!" A woman appeared at the bottom of the stairs, staring straight up at me through the railing of the balcony. Her eyes swiveled to Isabel. "Oh my God. What in —"

I was going to be killed by two generations of beautiful women. While naked.

"Mom," Isabel snapped, interrupting. "Do you mind not staring? It's totally perv."

Both her mother and I blinked at her.

Isabel moved closer to me and leaned across the railing at her mother. "A little privacy, maybe?" she shouted down.

This brought her mother back to life. She shouted back, with a voice growing ever higher, "Isabel Rosemary Culpeper, are you even going to tell me what a *naked* boy is doing in this house?"

"What do you *think*?" Isabel replied. "What do you think I'm doing with a naked boy in this house? Didn't Dr. Carrotnose warn you that I might act out if you kept ignoring me? Well, here it is, Mom! Here's me acting out! That's right, keep staring! I hope you're liking it! I don't know why you make us go to therapy if you aren't even going to listen to what he has to say. Go on, punish me for your mistakes!"

"Baby," her mother said, in a much quieter voice. "But *this* —"

"At least I'm not standing on some street corner selling myself!" Isabel screamed. She turned to me, and her face instantly softened. In a voice a million times lighter, she said, "Kitten, I don't want you to see me like this. Why don't you go back to the room?"

I was an actor in my own life.

Down below, her mother rubbed a hand over her forehead and tried not to look in my direction. "Please, please just tell him to get some clothing on before your father gets home. In the meantime, I'm going to go have a drink. I don't want to see him again."

As her mother turned around, Isabel grabbed my arm — somehow it shocked me to feel her hands on my skin — and tugged me down the hall and through one of the doors. It turned out to be a bathroom, all tiled in black and white, with a giant claw-footed bathtub taking up most of the space.

Isabel shoved me into the room so hard that I nearly fell into the bathtub, and then she shut the door behind us.

"What the hell are you doing human so early?" she demanded.

"You know what I am?" I asked. Stupid question.

"Please," she said, and her voice oozed contempt in a way that threatened to turn me on. No one — *no one* — talked to me like that. "Either you're one of Sam's, or you're a random naked pervert who smells like dog."

"Sam? Beck," I said.

"Not Beck. Sam, now," Isabel corrected. "It doesn't matter. What matters is that you're naked, in my house, and you really ought to be a wolf right now. Why the crap aren't you a wolf right now? What's your name?"

For a single, crazy moment, I almost told her.

• ISABEL •

For a moment, his face flickered to someplace else, someplace uncertain, the first real expression he'd had on his face since I found him pretty much posing next to the balcony. And then the almost-smirk was back on his face, and he said, "Cole."

Like it was a gift.

I tossed it back at him. "Well, why aren't you a wolf right now, *Cole*?"

"Because I wouldn't have met you otherwise?" he suggested.

"Nice try," I said, but I felt a hard smile twist my face. I knew enough about flirting, out of habit, to recognize it in action. And he was a cocky bastard, too; rather than getting more self-conscious as we spoke, he reached up and held the shower rod behind him with both hands, stretching himself out rather beautifully as he studied me.

"Why did you lie to your mom?" Cole asked. "Would you have done that if I'd been a paunchy real estate broker turned werewolf?"

"I doubt it. Kindness isn't generally my thing." What was my thing was the way that stretching his arms above his head bunched his shoulder muscles and tightened his chest. I tried to keep my eyes on the arrogant curl of his lips. "That said, we ought to get you some clothing."

His lips curved more. "Eventually?"

I smiled nastily at him. "Yeah, let's get that freak show covered up."

He made a little *whoo* shape with his lips. "Harsh."

I shrugged. "Stay here and don't hurt yourself. I'll be right back."

Shutting the bathroom door, I headed down the hallway to my brother's old bedroom. I hesitated outside the door for just a moment, and then pushed it open.

It had been long enough since he'd died that being in his room no longer felt intrusive. Plus, it didn't really look like his room anymore. My mother had packed up a lot of his stuff in boxes on the advice of her last therapist, then had left the boxes in his room on the advice of her current one. All of his sports crap had been packed, as well as his big, homemade speaker system. Once you took those two things away, there wasn't anything left to say *Jack*.

Moving into the dark room, I knocked my shin on the corner of one of the therapy boxes on my way to the floor lamp. I swore softly, clicked on the light, and for the first time contemplated what I was doing: digging through my dead brother's stuff to find clothing for a totally swoonworthy but jerkish werewolf standing in my bathroom, after telling my mom that I'd been sleeping with him.

Maybe she was right and I did need therapy.

I twisted my way through the boxes and threw open the closet. A rush of Jack-smell came out — pretty gross, really. Partially washed jerseys and man-shampoo and old shoes. But for a second, just for a second, it made me stand still, staring at the dark shapes of the hanging clothing. Then I heard my mother, far away downstairs, drop something, and remembered that I needed to get Cole out of here before my father came home. Mom wouldn't tell him. She was good like that. She didn't like to see crap get broken any more than I did.

I found a ratty sweatshirt, a T-shirt, and a decent pair of jeans. Satisfied, I turned around — right into Cole.

I bit off another swearword, my heart thumping. I had to crane my head back a bit to see his face this close; he was pretty tall. The dim floor lamp cast his face in sharp relief, like a Rembrandt portrait.

"You were taking a long time," Cole said, taking a step back for politeness' sake. "I came to see if you'd gone to get a gun."

I shoved the clothing at him. "You'll have to go commando."

"Is there any other way?" He tossed the shirt and sweater onto the bed and half turned to pull on the jeans. They hung a little loosely on him; I could see the lines of his hip bones casting shadows as they disappeared into the waist.

I looked away quickly as he turned back around, but I knew he had seen me watching. I wanted to scratch the cocky lift of his eyebrows from his face. He reached for the T-shirt, and as it unfolded in his hands, I saw that it was Jack's favorite Vikings T-shirt, the bottom right edge of it smeared with a bit of white from when he'd painted the garage last year. He used to wear the shirt for days at a time, until eventually even he admitted it smelled. I'd hated it.

Cole stretched his arm above his head to put it on, and suddenly all I could think was that I couldn't stand to see anyone but my brother wear that T-shirt. Unthinking, I grabbed a handful of the fabric and Cole froze, looking down at me, expression blank. Maybe a little puzzled.

I tugged, indicating what I wanted, and still with a vaguely curious expression, he released his fist, letting me pull the shirt from his hands. Once I had the shirt, I didn't want to explain why I had taken it back, so I kissed him instead. It was easier kissing him, pressing him back up against the wall, trying out the shape of his smirk on my lips, than it was to sort out why Jack's shirt in someone else's hands made me feel so sharp and exposed inside.

And he was a good kisser. I felt his flat stomach and ribs slide up against mine, even though his hands didn't lift to touch me. This close, he smelled like Sam had on the first night that I met him, all musky wolf and pine. There was a certain earnest hungriness to the way Cole pressed his mouth against mine that made me think there was more truth in him here, kissing me, than there was when he spoke.

When I pulled back, Cole stayed where he was, leaned back against the wall, fingers hooked in the pockets of his still-unzipped jeans, his head cocked to one side, just studying me. My heart was thumping in my chest, and my hands were trembling with the effort of not kissing him again, but he didn't seem fazed. I could see how slow and soft his pulse was beating through the skin of his abdomen.

The fact that he wasn't as revved up as I was instantly infuriated me, and I took a step back, throwing Jack's sweatshirt at him. He reached up to catch it a second after it bounced off his chest.

"That bad?" he said.

"Yeah," I said, crossing my arms to keep them still. "It was like you were trying to eat an apple."

His eyebrows spiked as if he could tell I was lying. "Rematch?"

"I don't think so," I said. I pressed a finger into one of my eyebrows. "I think it's time for you to go."

I was afraid he was going to ask where he was supposed to go, but he just tugged on the sweatshirt and zipped up the jeans with an air of finality. "You're probably right."

Even though I saw that the soles of his feet were cut up pretty bad, he didn't ask for shoes and I didn't offer them. The weight of not explaining myself to him was choking the words out of me, so I just led him downstairs and back toward the door he'd come in.

I saw him hesitate, just a moment, as we passed by the door to the kitchen, and I remembered the feel of his ribs against mine. Part of me knew I should offer him something to eat, but most of me just wanted him gone as quickly as possible. Why was it so much easier to leave a dish out for the wolves?

Probably because wolves didn't have arrogant smirks.

In the mudroom, I stopped by the door and crossed my arms again. "My dad shoots wolves," I told him. "Just for the record. So you might want to keep out of the woods behind the house."

"I'll keep that in mind when I'm in the body of an animal with no higher thought," Cole said. "Thanks for that."

"I live to please," I said, throwing open the door. Sleet, coming in sideways from the dark night, dotted my arm.

I expected a hangdog expression, or something else meant to elicit sympathy, but Cole just looked at me, a weird, firm smile on his face. Then he walked right out into the sleet, pulling the door out of my hands to shut it behind him.

After the door had closed, I stood there for a long moment, softly cursing under my breath, not knowing why I was letting it bother me. Then I went to the kitchen and got the first thing I could see — a bagged loaf of bread — and returned to the back door.

I planned in my head what I would say — something like, *Don't expect anything else* — but when I opened the door, he was already gone.

I flicked on the back light. Dim yellow light splashed across the frozen yard, odd reflections thrown by the thin layer of crusted sleet. About ten feet from the door, I saw the jeans and tattered sweatshirt lying in a haphazard pile.

My ears and nose burning in the cold, I crunched slowly out to the clothing, stopping to study the shape of it. One of the sleeves of the sweatshirt was flung out, as if pointing to the distant pine woods. I lifted my eyes and, sure enough, there he was. A gray-brown wolf standing just a few yards beyond me, staring at me with Cole's green eyes.

"My brother died," I told him.

The wolf didn't flick an ear; sleet and snow drifted down and clung to his fur.

"I'm not a nice person," I said.

Still motionless. My mind bent, just a little, trying to reconcile Cole's eyes and that wolf's face.

I unwrapped the bread and held the bag so that the slices tumbled onto the ground next to my feet. He didn't flinch — just stared, unblinking, human eyes in an animal's face. "But I shouldn't have told you your kiss sucked," I added, trembling a little with the cold. Then I wasn't sure what else to say about the kiss, so I shut up.

I turned back to the door. Before I went in, I folded the clothing and flipped the empty planter by the door over it to protect it from the weather. Then I left him out in the night.

I could still remember his human eyes in that wolf face; they'd looked as empty as I felt.

Chapter Thirteen

· SAM ·

I missed my mother.

I couldn't explain this to Grace, because I knew all she could see when she thought of my mother were the savage scars that my parents had left on my wrists. And it was true, the memories of them trying to kill the tiny monster I had become were stuffed into my head so tightly that sometimes they seemed like they would split my skull; the old wounds dug so deep that I felt the razor blades again whenever I was near a bathtub.

But I had other memories of my mother, too, that snuck in between the cracks when I least expected them. Like now, when I was curled over the counter in The Crooked Shelf, my books lying inches from my empty hands, my eyes looking out the windows at the creeping brown evening. The last words I had read rested on my lips — Mandelstam, who wrote about me without having any way to know me:

But by blood no wolf am I

Outside, the last bit of sun glazed the corners of the parked cars with blinding amber and filled the puddles in the street with liquid gold. Inside, the store was already out of the reach of the dying day, dim and empty and half-asleep.

It was twenty minutes to closing.

It was my birthday.

I remembered my mother making me cupcakes on my birthdays. Never a cake, since it was just my parents and me, and I had the appetite of a bird, picking and choosing my culinary battles carefully. A cake would've gone stale before it was eaten.

So my mother made cupcakes. I remembered the vanilla scent of the frosting, hastily swirled onto the cake with a butter knife. By itself, it would've been ordinary, but this particular cupcake had a candle poked through the frosting. A tiny flame stretched from the wick, a bead of melted wax trembling just beneath it, and the cupcake was transformed to something bright and beautiful and special.

I could still smell the church scent of the blown-out match, see the reflection of the flame in my mother's eyes, feel the soft cushion of the kitchen chairs under my skinny, folded-up legs. I heard my mother tell me to put my hands in my lap and saw her set the cupcake in front of me — she wouldn't let me hold the plate, in case I knocked the candle onto my lap.

My parents had always been so careful with me, until the day they decided I needed to die.

In the store, I put my forehead in my hands and stared down at the curled corner of the book cover lying between my elbows. I could see how the cover was not really a single piece of paper, how it was really a printed piece of stock with a protective layer over the top, and how the topmost layer had peeled back to let a corner of the true cover get stained and yellow and tattered.

I wondered if I was really remembering my mother making me cupcakes, or if it was something my brain had stolen from one of the thousands of books I had read. Someone else's mother, pasted onto my own, slinking in to fill the void.

Without raising my head, I lifted my gaze, putting the matching scars on my wrists directly at eye level. In the dull evening light, my veins were visible below the translucent skin of my arms, but the light blue forks disappeared beneath the uneven scar tissue. In my head, I reached to take the cupcake from the plate with arms smooth and unmarked, still pristine with my parents' love. My mother smiled at me.

Happy birthday.

I closed my eyes.

I didn't know how long they'd been closed when the *ding* of the shop door made me jerk up. I was about to tell the newcomer that we were no longer open, but then Grace turned around, shoving the door shut behind her with her shoulder. She clutched a drink tray in one hand and a Subway bag in the other. It was like another light had been turned on in the store; the entire place seemed brighter.

I was too stunned to jump up to help her, and by the time it occurred to me, she'd already deposited her loot on the counter. Coming around the back of the counter, Grace threw her arms around my shoulders and whispered in my ear, "Happy birthday."

I wriggled my arms free of her embrace to wrap them around her waist. I held her tightly to me and pressed my face to her neck, hiding my surprise. "How did you know?"

"Beck told me before he changed," Grace said. "*You* should've mentioned it." She pulled back to look at my face. "What were you thinking about? When I came in?"

"Being Sam," I said.

"What a nice thing to be," Grace said. And then she smiled, bigger and bigger, until I felt my expression mirror hers, our noses touching. Grace finally stepped away to gesture to her offering on the counter, wrapped around my stack of books in a rather intimate way. "I'm sorry this is not more swank. There's not really a place to do romantic in Mercy Falls, and even if there were, I'm somewhat poor at this moment, anyway. Can you eat now?"

I slid around her and went to the front door, locking it and turning the OPEN sign around. "Well, it's closing time. Do you want to go home with it? Or upstairs?"

Grace glanced toward the burgundy-carpeted stairs that led to the loft, and I knew she'd made up her mind. "You carry the drinks with your big muscles," she said, with considerable irony. "And I'll take the sandwiches, since they're not breakable."

Switching off the lights for the first floor, I followed her up the stairs, cardboard drink tray in hand. Our feet went *swoof swoof* in the thick carpet as we climbed to the dim loft with its slanted ceilings. With every step we took, I felt like I was ascending further and further above that remembered birthday to something infinitely more real.

"What did you get me?" I asked.

"Birthday sandwich," Grace replied. "Duh."

I flicked on the lily lamp that sat on the low bookshelves; eight small bulbs cast an erratic pattern of rose-colored light over us both as I joined Grace on the battered love seat.

My birthday sandwich turned out to be roast beef with mayonnaise, the same as Grace's. We spread out the papers between us so that the edges overlapped and Grace hummed "Happy Birthday" in a terribly off-key way.

"And many more," she added in an entirely new key.

"Why, thanks," I said. I touched her chin, and she smiled at me.

After we'd finished our sandwiches — well, I had nearly finished mine, Grace had eaten the bread off hers — she gestured to the sandwich wrappers and said, "You should crumple up those papers. And I'll get your present out."

I looked at her, eyebrows raised, as she pulled her backpack from the floor onto her lap. "You shouldn't have gotten me anything," I said. "I feel silly getting a present."

"I wanted to," Grace said. "Don't ruin it by going all bashful. I said get rid of those papers!"

I bent my head and started to fold.

"You and those cranes!" She laughed as she saw that I was folding the tidier of the two sandwich papers into a big, floppy bird printed with the Subway logo. "What is it with you and them?"

"I used to make them for good times. To remember the

moment." I waved the Subway crane at her; it flapped its loose, wrinkled wings. "You know you'll never forget where this crane came from."

Grace studied it. "I think that's a pretty safe assumption."

"Mission accomplished," I said softly, and rested the crane on the floor beside the love seat. I knew I was stalling the moment before she presented her gift. It gave me a weird knot in my stomach to think she'd gotten me something. But Grace wouldn't be put off.

"Now, close your eyes," she said. Her voice had a little catch in it — anticipation. Hope. I silently said a prayer: *Please let me like whatever it is she got.* In my head, I tried to imagine the face that went with perfect delight, so that I could have it ready to pull out no matter what she had given me.

I heard her rezipping her backpack and felt the cushions rocking as she rearranged herself on the couch.

"Do you remember the first time we came up here?" she asked as I sat there, half-alone in the darkness of my closed eyes.

It wasn't a question meant to be answered, so I just smiled.

"Do you remember how you made me close my eyes, and you read me that poem from Rilke?" Grace's voice was closer; I felt her knee touch mine. "I loved you so much right then, Sam Roth."

My skin tightened in a shiver, and I swallowed. I knew she loved me, but she almost never said it. That alone could've been her birthday gift for me. My hands lay open in my lap; I felt her press something into them. She closed one of my hands over the top of the other. Paper.

"I didn't think I could ever be as romantic as you," she said. "You know I'm not good at that. But — well." And she did a funny little laugh at herself, so endearing that I nearly forgot myself and opened my eyes to see her face when she did it. "Well, I can't wait anymore. Open your eyes."

I opened them. There was a folded piece of computer paper in my hands. I could see the ghost of the printing that was on the inside, but not what it was.

Grace could barely sit still. Her expectation was hard to bear, because I didn't know if I could live up to it. "Open it."

I tried to remember the happy face. The upward tilt of my eyebrows, the open grin, the squinty eyes.

I opened the paper.

And I completely forgot about what my face was supposed to look like. I just sat there, staring at the words on the paper, not really believing them. It wasn't the hugest of presents, though for Grace, it must've been difficult to manage. What was amazing was that it was me, a resolution I hadn't been brave enough to write down. It was something that said she knew me. Something that made the *I love you*s real.

It was an invoice. For five hours of studio time.

I looked up at Grace and saw that her anticipation had melted away into something entirely different. Smugness. Complete and total smugness, so whatever my face had done on its own accord must've given me away.

"Grace," I said, and my voice was lower than I'd planned.

Her smug little smile threatened to break into a bigger one. She asked, unnecessarily, "You like it?"

"I . . ."

She saved me from having to compose the rest of a sentence. "It's in Duluth. I scheduled it for one of our mutual days off. I figured you could play some of your songs and . . . I don't know. Do whatever you hope you'll do with them."

"A demo," I said softly. The gift was more than she knew — or maybe she realized everything that it meant. It was more than just a nod to me doing more with my music. It was an acknowledgment that I could move forward. That there was going to be a next week and a next month and a next year for me. Studio time was about making plans for a brand-new future. Studio time said that if I gave someone my demo and they said, "I'll get back to you in a month," I'd still be human by the time they did.

"God, I love you, Grace," I said. Still holding the invoice, I hugged her, tight, around her neck. I pressed my lips against the side of her head and hugged her hard again. I put down the paper beside the Subway crane.

"Are you going to make it into a crane, too?" she asked, then closed her eyes so I could kiss her again.

But I didn't. I just stroked the hair away from her face so I could look at her with her eyes closed. She made me think of those angels that were on top of graves, eyes closed, faces lifted up, hands folded.

"You're hot again," I said. "Do you feel all right?"

Grace didn't open her eyes, just let me continue tracing around the edge of her face as if I were still pushing her hair away from her skin. My fingers felt cold against her warm skin. She said, "Mmm hmm."

So I kept teasing her skin with my fingers. I thought about

telling her what I was thinking, like *You're beautiful* and *You're my angel*, but the thing about Grace was that words like that meant more to me than to her. They were throwaway phrases to her, things that made her smile for a second but were just . . . gone after that, too corny to be real. To Grace, these were the things that mattered: my hands on her cheeks, my lips on her mouth. The fleeting touches that meant I loved her.

When I leaned in to kiss her, I caught just the tiniest trace of that sweet, nutty smell from the wolf she'd found, so faint that I could have been imagining it. But just the thought of it was enough to throw me from the moment.

"Let's go home," I said.

"This is your home," Grace said, with a playful smile. "You can't fool me."

But I stood up, tugging both her hands to pull her after me.

"I want to get home before your parents do," I said. "They've been getting home really early."

"Let's elope," Grace said lightly, bending to collect our leftover sandwiches and drinks. I held out the bag so that she could toss everything inside, and watched as she retrieved the sandwich-paper crane before we headed down the stairs.

Hand in hand, we retreated through the now-dark store and out back, where Grace's white Mazda was parked. When she got into the driver's seat, I lifted my palm to my nose, trying to catch a whiff of the scent from before. I couldn't smell it, but the wolf in me couldn't ignore the memory of it in that kiss.

It was like a low voice whispering in a foreign language, breathing a secret that I couldn't understand.

Chapter Fourteen

· SAM ·

Something woke me.

Surrounded by the dull, familiar darkness of Grace's bedroom, I wasn't sure what it was. There was no sound outside, and the rest of the house lay in the half-aware silence of night. Grace, too, was quiet, rolled away from me. I wrapped my arms around her, pressing my nose against the back of her soap-scented neck. The tiny blond hairs at her nape tickled my nostrils. I jerked my face away from them and Grace sighed in her sleep, curling her back tighter against the shape of my body as she did. I should've slept, too — I had inventory work at the store early the next day — but something in my subconscious hummed with an uneasy watchfulness. So I lay against her, close as two spoons in a drawer, until her skin was too hot to be comfortable.

I slid a few inches away, keeping a hand on her side. Normally, the soft up-and-down of her ribs under my palm lulled me to sleep when nothing else would. But not tonight.

Tonight, I couldn't stop remembering what it had felt like when I'd been just about to shift. The way the cold had crawled along my skin, trailing goose bumps behind it. The turn, turn, turn of my stomach, aching nausea unfurling. The slow sunburst of pain up my spine as it stretched according to memories of another shape. My thoughts slipping away from me, crushed and reformed to fit my winter skull.

Sleep evaded me, just out of my grasp. My instincts prickled relentlessly, urging me to alertness. The darkness pressed against my eyes while the wolf inside me sang *something is not right.*

Outside, the wolves began to howl.

• GRACE •

I was too hot. The sheets stuck to my damp calves; I tasted sweat at the corner of my lips. As the wolves howled, my skin tingled with the heat, a hundred tiny needle pricks all over my face and hands. Everything felt painful: the blanket's uncomfortable weight on me, Sam's cold hand on my hip, the wailing, high cries of the wolves outside, the memory of Sam's fingers pressed into his temples, the shape of my skin on my body.

I was asleep; I was dreaming. Or I was awake, coming out of a dream. I couldn't decide.

In my mind, I saw all the people I'd ever seen shift into wolves: Sam, mournful and agonized, Beck, strong and controlled, Jack, savage and painful, Olivia, swift and easy. They all observed me from the woods, dozens of eyes watching me: the outsider, the one who didn't change.

My tongue stuck to the roof of my sandpaper mouth. I wanted to lift my face from my damp pillow, but it felt like too much trouble. I waited restlessly for sleep, but my eyes hurt too much to close.

If I hadn't been cured, I wondered, what would my shift have been like? What sort of wolf would I have been? Looking at my hands, I imagined them dark gray, banded with white and black. I felt the weight of a ruff hanging on my shoulders, felt the nausea kick in my gut.

For a single, brilliant moment, I felt nothing but the cold air of my room on my skin and heard nothing but Sam breathing beside me. But then the wolves began to howl again, and my body shuddered with a sensation that was both new and somehow familiar.

I was going to shift.

I choked on the wolf rising up inside me, pressing against the lining of my stomach, clawing inside my skin, trying to peel me inside out.

I wanted it, and my muscles burned and groaned.

Pain split me

I had no voice

I was on fire.

I sprang from the bed, shaking off my skin.

· SAM ·

I jerked awake, stung by Grace's scream. She was one hundred million degrees, close enough to burn me but too far away for me to reach.

"Grace!" I whispered. "Are you awake?"

The sheets swept off my body as she rolled away from me,

crying out again. In the dim light, I could only see her shoulder, and I reached out for it, cupping her arm with my hand. She was drenched with sweat, and her skin trembled beneath my palm, an unstable, unfamiliar flutter.

"Grace, wake up! Are you okay?" My heart was pounding so loud that it felt like I wouldn't hear her even if she did answer.

She thrashed beneath my touch and then bolted upright, eyes wild, body volatile and quivering. I didn't know her.

"Grace, talk to me," I whispered, though whispering seemed pointless in light of her earlier scream.

Grace stared at her hands with a kind of wonder. I laid the back of my hand on her forehead; she was appallingly hot, hotter than I thought anyone could be. I laid my palms on both sides of her neck, and she shuddered as if they were ice.

"I think you're sick," I said, my own stomach turning over. "You have a fever."

She spread her fingers wide and studied her shaking hands. "I dreamed — I dreamed I shifted. I thought I —"

She suddenly let out a terrible wail and curled away from me, clutching her arms around her stomach.

I didn't know what to do.

"What's wrong?" I asked, not expecting an answer and not getting one. "I'm getting you some Tylenol or something. In the bathroom?"

She just whimpered. It was terrifying.

I leaned forward to see her face, and that's when I smelled it.

She stank of wolf.

Wolf, wolf, wolf.

From Grace.

The scent of wolf.

It wasn't possible. It had to be me. I prayed it was me.

I turned my face into my own shoulder, inhaled. Lifted my hand to my nose, the one that had just touched her forehead.

Wolf.

My heart stopped.

And then the door came open and light flooded in from the hall.

"Grace?" Her father's voice. The bedroom light came on, and his eyes found me sitting next to her. *"Sam?"*

Chapter Fifteen

· GRACE ·

I didn't even see Dad come into the room. The first moment I realized he was there was when I heard his voice, far away, like sound through water.

"What's going on here?"

Sam's voice was a murmured soundtrack to the pain that burned through me. I hugged my pillow and stared at the wall. I could see the diffuse shadow that Sam made and the sharper one of my father, closer to the hall lights. I watched them move back and forth, making one big shape and then two again.

"Grace. *Grace Brisbane.*" My father's voice became louder again. "Don't pretend I'm not here."

"Mr. Brisbane —" Sam started.

"Do not — *do not* — 'Mr. Brisbane' me," Dad snapped. "I can't believe you can look me in the face, when behind our backs —"

I didn't want to move because every movement made the fire inside me burn faster, but I couldn't let him say that. I rolled toward them, wincing at the thorns of pain that prickled through my stomach as I did. "Dad. No. Don't say that to Sam. You don't know."

"Don't think I'm not furious with you, too!" Dad said. "You have completely, utterly betrayed our trust in you."

"Please," Sam said, and now I saw that he was standing by the side of the bed in his sweatpants and T-shirt, fingers making white marks in his own arms. "I know you're angry with me, and you can keep being angry with me and I don't blame you, but there's something wrong with Grace."

"What's going on here?" Now Mom's voice. Then, in a strange, disappointed tone that I knew would kill Sam, "Sam? I can't believe it."

"Please, Mrs. Brisbane," Sam said, although Mom had told him before to call her Amy, and he normally did, "Grace is really, really warm. She —"

"Just get away from the bed. Where's your car?" Dad's voice fell into the background again, and I stared at the shape of the ceiling fan above me, imagining it coming on and drying the sweat on my forehead.

Mom's face appeared in front of me, and I felt her lay her hand on my forehead. "Sweetie, you do seem feverish. We heard you cry out."

"My stomach," I murmured, careful not to open my mouth too wide, in case what was inside me crawled out.

"I'm going to try to find the thermometer." She vanished from my sight. I heard Dad's and Sam's voices going on and on and on. I didn't know what they could possibly have to talk about. Mom reappeared. "Try to sit up, Grace."

I cried out as I did, claws scraping the inside of my skin. Mom handed me a glass of water while she peered at the thermometer.

Sam, standing by the bedroom door, jerked around when the glass slid from my unprotesting hand and landed on the floor with a dull and distant sound. Mom stared at the glass, and then at me.

My fingers still in a circle, cupping an invisible glass, I whispered, "Mom, I think I'm really sick."

"That's it," Dad said. "Sam, get your coat. I'm taking you to your car. Amy, take her temperature. I'll be back in a few minutes. I'll have my phone."

I turned my eyes toward Sam, and his expression pierced me. He said, "Please don't ask me to leave her like this." My breath came a little faster.

"I'm not asking," my father said. "I'm telling. If you *ever* want to be allowed to see my daughter again, you will get out of my house right now, because I am telling you to."

Sam scrubbed his hands through his hair and then linked them behind his head, eyes closed. For a moment, it was like we all held our breaths, waiting to see what he would do. The tension in his body was written so clearly that an explosion seemed imminent.

He opened his eyes, and when he spoke, I almost didn't recognize his voice. "Don't — don't even *say* that. Don't threaten me with that. I'll go. But don't —" And he couldn't even say anything else. I saw him swallow, and I think I said his name, but he was already down the hall with my father following him.

A moment later, I thought I heard the engine of Dad's car rev to life outside, but it was Mom's car, and I was in it, and I felt like my fever was eating me alive. Outside the car window, the stars swam in the cold night sky above me as we drove, and I felt small and alone and in pain. *Sam Sam Sam Sam where are you?*

"Sweetie," Mom said from the driver's seat. "Sam's not here."

I swallowed tears and watched the stars wheel out of sight.

Chapter Sixteen

· SAM ·

The night that Grace went to the hospital without me was the night I finally turned my eyes back to the wolves.

It was a night full of tiny coincidences that collided into something bigger. If Grace hadn't gotten sick that night, if her parents had been out late as they usually were, if they hadn't discovered us, if I hadn't gone back to Beck's house, if Isabel hadn't heard Cole outside her back door, if she hadn't delivered Cole to me, if Cole hadn't been equal parts junkie and asshole and genius — how would life have unfolded?

Rilke says: *"Verweilung, auch am Verstrautesten nicht, ist uns gegeben"* — *"We are not allowed to linger, even with what is most intimate."*

My hand already missed the weight of Grace's.

Nothing was the same after that night. Nothing.

After I got into the car with Grace's father, he drove me to the cluttered alley behind the bookstore where my Volkswagen was parked, navigating carefully so that he didn't rub his mirrors on the trash bins on either side. He pulled to a stop just behind my car, his silent face illuminated by the flickering streetlight that hung from the second story of the store. I was silent, too, my mouth sealed shut with a toxic paste of guilt and anger. We sat there together, and the windshield wiper scraped suddenly across the windshield, making us both flinch. He had accidentally turned it to intermittent when he signaled to enter the alley. He let it swipe the already-clear windshield once more before he seemed to remember to turn it off.

Finally, without looking at me, he said, "Grace has always been perfect. In seventeen years, she has never gotten into trouble at school. She's never done drugs or alcohol. She's a straight-A student. She has always been absolutely perfect."

I didn't say anything.

He went on. "Until now. We don't need someone to come along and corrupt her. I don't know you, Samuel, but I do know my daughter. And I know that this is all you. I am not trying to be threatening here, but I won't have you ruining my daughter. I think you seriously need to reconsider your priorities before you see her again."

For a brief moment, I tried out words in my head, but everything I thought of was too vitriolic or honest for me to imagine saying. So I just got out into the frigid night with everything still shut up inside me.

After he had gone, waiting just long enough to make sure that my car started before he backed out onto the empty street, I sat in the Volkswagen with my hands folded in my lap and stared at the back door of the bookstore. It seemed like days ago that Grace and I had walked through it, me still high with the memory of the studio invoice and her still high with my reaction and the pleasure of knowing just what to get me. I couldn't picture her smug face now, though. The only image my mind could pull up was the one of her twisting in pain on top of the sheets, face flushed, reeking of wolf.

It's only a fever.

That's what I told myself as I drove toward Beck's, my headlights the only illumination in the pitch-black night, bending and flickering against the black tree trunks on either side of the road. Again and again I said it, even as my gut whispered that it wasn't and my hands ached to jerk the wheel and drive right back to the Brisbane house.

Halfway to Beck's, I took out my cell phone and dialed Grace's number. I knew it was a bad idea even as I did it, but I couldn't help it.

There was a pause, and then I heard her father's voice instead of hers.

"I'm only picking this up to tell you not to call," he said. "Seriously, Samuel, if you know what's good for you, you will just leave it for tonight. I do not want to talk to you tonight. I do not want Grace talking to you. Just —"

"I want to know how she is." I thought about adding *please*, but couldn't bring myself to.

There was a pause, like he was listening to someone else. Then he said, "It's just a fever. Don't call again. I'm trying really hard to not say something I'll regret later." This time I did hear someone's voice in the background — Grace's or her mother's — and then the phone went dead.

I was a paper boat drifting in a massive night ocean.

I didn't want to go to Beck's, but I had nowhere else to go. I had no one else to go to. I was human, and without Grace, I had nothing but this car and a bookstore and a house full of countless empty rooms.

So I drove to Beck's — I needed to stop thinking of it as Beck's — and parked my car in the empty driveway. Once upon a time, I'd worked at the bookstore during the summers, when Beck was still human and I still lost my winters to being a wolf. I'd pull up in the summer evenings when it was still light, because during the summers, it was never night, and I would get out of Beck's car to the sounds of people laughing and the smell of the grill from the backyard. It felt strange to be stepping out into the still night now, the cold prickling my skin, and knowing that all those voices from my past were trapped in the woods. Everyone but me.

Grace.

Inside the house, I turned on the kitchen light, revealing the photographs stuck every which way all over the cabinets, and then switched on the hall light. In my head, I heard Beck say to my small nine-year-old self, "Why do we need every light in the house on? Are you signaling to aliens?"

And so I went through the house tonight and turned on every light, revealing a memory in every single room. The bathroom where I'd nearly turned into a wolf right after meeting Grace. The living room, where Paul and I had jammed with our guitars — his beat-up old Fender was still propped against the mantle. The downstairs guest room, where Derek had stayed with a girlfriend from town before Beck had chewed him out for it. I turned on the lights to the basement stairs and the lights in the library down there, and then came back up to get the lights in Beck's office that I'd missed. In the living room, I stopped just long enough to crank up the expensive stereo system that Ulrik had bought when I was ten so that I could "hear Jethro Tull the way it was meant to be heard."

Upstairs, I turned the knob on the floor lamp in Beck's room, where he had almost never slept, preferring to store books and papers on his bed and instead fall asleep in a chair in the basement, some book facedown on his chest. Shelby's room came to life under the dim yellow ceiling light, pristine and unlived in, no personal possessions except for her old computer. I was tempted for a brief moment to smash in the monitor, just because I wanted to hit something, and if anyone deserved it, Shelby did, but it didn't seem like there'd be any satisfaction in breaking it without her here to see me finally do it. Ulrik's room looked like it had been frozen in time. One of his jackets was still thrown across the bed next to a folded pair of jeans and an empty mug on the nightstand. Paul's room was next, where he had a mason jar on the dresser with two teeth in it — one belonging to him, and one belonging to a dead white dog.

I saved my own bedroom for last. Memories floated on strings from the ceiling. Books lined the walls, stacked and sloped against the desk. The room smelled stale and unused; the boy who had grown up in it hadn't stayed here for a long time.

I'd be staying in it now. One person rattling around in this house, waiting and hoping for the reappearance of the rest of his family.

But just before I reached inside the dark room for the light switch on the wall, I heard the sound of an engine outside.

I was no longer alone.

"Are you trying to land airplanes?" Isabel asked me. She didn't look real, standing in the middle of the living room in silky pajama bottoms and a padded white coat with a fur collar. I had never seen her without makeup, and she looked a lot younger. "I could see the house from a mile away. You must have every light turned on."

I didn't reply. I was still trying to work out how Isabel had ended up here at four o'clock in the morning with the boy I'd last seen changing into a wolf in the middle of the kitchen floor. He stood there in a battered sweatshirt and jeans that hung on him like they belonged to someone else, his bare feet an alarming mottled shade, and his fingers hooked in his pockets as if their terrible swelling and discoloration didn't bother him. The way that he was looking at Isabel and the way she going out of her way *not* to look at him made it seem, impossibly, like they had some kind of history.

"You're frostbitten," I said to the guy, because it was something to say that didn't require much thought. "You need to warm up those fingers or you're going to be very unhappy later. Isabel, you had to know that."

"I'm not an idiot," Isabel said. "But if my parents caught him in my house, he'd be dead, and that would make him even more unhappy. I decided the outside chance of them noticing my car missing in the middle of the night was a happier option."

If Isabel noticed me swallowing, she didn't pause. "By the way, this is Sam. *The* Sam." It took me a moment to realize that she was now talking to the cocky frostbitten guy.

The Sam. I wondered what she'd told him about me. I looked at him. Again, the familiarity of his face pricked at me. It was not a *real* familiarity, like someone I had met in person, but more like the familiarity of meeting a person who looks like an actor whose name you can't recall.

"So you're the one in charge now?" he said, with a smile that struck me as sardonic. "I'm Cole."

The one in charge now. That's the way it was, wasn't it?

"Have you seen any of the other wolves change yet?" I asked.

He shrugged. "I thought it was too cold for *me* to be changing."

His grotesquely colored fingers were bothering me enough that I moved away from him and Isabel, toward the kitchen, where I found a bottle of ibuprofen. I tossed it toward Isabel, who surprised me by catching it. "It's because you were just bitten. I mean, last year. Temperature doesn't have so much to do with you shifting yet. It's just going to be . . . unpredictable."

"Unpredictable," echoed Cole.

Sam, no, please, not again, stop — I blinked, and my mother's voice was gone, back into the past where it belonged.

"What are these for? Him?" Isabel held up the bottle of pills and jerked her chin toward Cole. Again, I got that flash of *history* between them.

"Yeah. It's going to hurt like hell when he warms up his fingers," I said. "That'll keep it bearable. Bathroom's that way."

Cole took the ibuprofen from me, but I could tell he wasn't going to use it. Whether because he thought he was some macho tough guy or for religious reasons or what, I didn't know. But when he went into the downstairs bathroom, I heard him hit the light switch and set down the pill bottle without opening it. Then I heard the water begin to run into the bath. Sam turned away with this strange, disgusted look on his face, and I knew that he didn't like Cole.

"So, Romulus," I said, and Sam turned around, his yellow eyes open wide. "Why are you here, all alone? I thought Grace would have to be surgically removed from your side." After spending the last hour with Cole, whose face revealed only the emotions he wanted me to see, it was strange to see undisguised pain on Sam's face. His thick dark eyebrows showed misery all by themselves. It occurred to me that he and Grace might have had a fight.

"Her parents kicked me out," Sam said, and he smiled for just a second, like people do when something's really not funny and they don't want to be telling you but they don't know what else to do. "Grace, uh, got sick and they, uh, found us together, and they kicked me out."

"Tonight?"

He nodded, very broken and honest, and I couldn't quite look at him. "Yeah. I got here a little before you did."

The fierce glow of every light in the house suddenly seemed more significant. I wasn't sure if I admired him for feeling everything so hard and fiercely, or if I was contemptuous of him for having so much emotion that he had to spill it out every window of the house. I didn't know how I felt.

"But, um . . ." Sam said, and in just those two words, I heard him getting himself back together, like a horse assembling its legs beneath itself before standing up. "Anyway. Tell me about Cole. How did you end up with him?"

I looked at him sharply until I realized he meant *How did you end up* here *with him?* "Long story, wolf-boy," I said, and crashed down on the sofa. "I couldn't sleep, and I heard him outside the house. It was pretty obvious what he was, and pretty obvious that he wasn't going to change back. I didn't want my parents to find out and freak, so, the end."

Sam's mouth did something unreadable. "That's awfully nice of you."

I smiled thinly. "It happens."

"Does it?" Sam asked. "I think most people would've left a naked stranger outside."

"I didn't want to step in a pile of his fingers tomorrow on my way to the car," I said. I felt like Sam was probing me to say something else, like he'd somehow guessed that this was the second time that we'd met and that the first time had involved my tongue introducing itself to Cole's, and vice versa. I used the topic of Cole's fingers to redirect the conversation. "Speaking of which, I wonder how he's getting along in there." I looked down the hallway toward the bathroom.

Sam hesitated. For some reason, I remembered that the light in the bathroom had been the only light not turned on. Finally, Sam said, "Why don't you go knock on the door and find out?

I'm going to go upstairs to get a room ready for him. I just — I need a minute to think."

"Okay, whatever," I said.

He nodded, and just as he turned to go upstairs, I caught a glimpse of some private emotion on his face that made me think he wasn't as much of an open book as I'd thought. It made me want to stop him and ask him to fill in the blanks of our conversation — how Grace was sick, why the bathroom light wasn't on, what he was going to do now — but it was way too late, and, anyway, I wasn't that girl yet.

· COLE ·

The worst of the pain was already over, and I was just lying in the water, floating my hands on top of the bathwater and imagining falling asleep in it, when I heard a knock on the bathroom door.

Isabel's voice followed the knock, the force of which opened the unlatched door an inch. "Have you drowned?"

"Yes," I said.

"Mind if I come in?" But she didn't wait for my answer; she just let herself in, sitting on the toilet beside the tub. The fluffy, fur-lined hood of her jacket made her look like she had a hunchback. Her hair was jagged on her cheek. She looked like an ad for something. For toilets. For jackets. For antidepressants. Whatever it was for, I'd buy it. She looked down at me.

"I'm naked," I said.

"So am I," Isabel replied. "Under my clothing."

I cracked a grin. Had to give credit where credit was due.

"Are your feet going to fall off?" she asked.

Because of the size of the bathtub, I had to lift and straighten my leg to look at my toes. They were a little red, but I could wiggle them and feel all of them except for my pinkie toe, which was still mostly numb. "Not today, I don't think."

"Are you going to stay in there forever?"

"Probably." I sank my shoulders farther into the water to show my commitment to the plan. I glanced up at her. "Care to join me?"

She raised a knowing eyebrow. "Looks a little small in there."

I closed my eyes with another smile. *"Zing."* With my eyes shut, I felt warm and floaty and invisible. They should invent a drug that made you feel like this. "I miss my Mustang," I said, mostly because it was the sort of statement that would make her react.

"Lying naked in a bathtub made you think of your car?"

"It had a rockin' heater. You could really cook the hell out of yourself in there," I said. It was a lot easier to talk to her with my eyes closed, too. Not so much of a pissing contest. "I wish I'd had it earlier tonight."

"Where is it?"

"Home."

I heard her take her coat off; it *shushed* on the bathroom counter. The toilet creaked as she sat back down. "Where's home?"

"New York."

"City?"

"State." I thought about the Mustang. Black, shiny, souped-up, sitting in my parents' garage because I was never home to drive it. It had been the first thing that I'd bought when my first big check came in, and, in the irony of the century, I'd been on tour too much to ever drive it.

"I thought you came from Canada."

"I was on" — I stopped just short of saying *tour*. I was liking my anonymity too much — "vacation." I opened my eyes and saw in her hard expression that she'd heard the lie. I was beginning to realize that she didn't miss much.

"Some vacation," she replied. "Must've sucked for you to choose this." She was looking now at the track-mark scars on my arms, but not in the way that I expected her to. Not like judging. More like hungry. Between that and the fact that she was wearing only a camisole beneath her coat, I was having a hard time focusing.

"Yeah," I agreed. "How about you? How do you know about the wolves?"

Isabel's eyes betrayed something for just a second, so fast that I couldn't tell what it was. In between that and her make-upless face, young and soft-looking, I felt bad for asking.

Then I wondered why I bothered to feel bad for this girl I hardly knew.

"I'm friends with Sam's girlfriend," Isabel said. I'd done enough lying, or at least telling of partial truths, to know what it sounded like. But since she hadn't called me out on my own partial truth, I returned the favor.

"Right. Sam," I echoed. "Tell me more about him."

"I already told you that he's like Beck's son and he's basically taking over for him. What more do you want to know? It's not like I'm his girlfriend." But her voice was admiring; she liked him. I didn't know what I thought of him yet.

I said the thing that had been bugging me since I'd met him. "It's cold. He's human."

"Yeah, so?"

"Well, Beck led me to believe that was a pretty hard thing to accomplish, if not impossible."

Isabel seemed to be contemplating something — I saw a tiny, silent battle waging in her eyes — and finally she shrugged and said, "He's cured. He gave himself a high fever and it cured him." This was a clue of some kind. To Isabel. Something in her voice wasn't quite right when she said it, but I wasn't sure how it fit into the overall picture.

"I thought Beck wanted us — the new ones — to take care of the pack because there aren't many left who turn human for long enough," I said. Truthfully, I was relieved. I didn't want responsibility; I wanted to slide into the darkness of a wolf's skin for as much time as possible. "Why didn't he just cure everybody?

"He didn't know Sam was cured. If he'd known, he would've never made more wolves. And the cure doesn't work for everybody." Now Isabel's voice was out-and-out hard, and I felt like I was somehow no longer a part of the conversation I'd started.

"Good thing I don't want to be cured, then," I said lightly.

She looked at me, and her voice was contemptuous. "Good thing."

Suddenly I felt sort of done. Like in the end, she was going to see the truth about me no matter what I said, because that was what she did. She was going to see that when you took away NARKOTIKA, I was just Cole St. Clair, and inside me was absolutely nothing.

I felt the familiar hollow hunger inside, like my soul was rotting.

I wanted a fix. I needed to find a needle to slide under my skin or a pill to dissolve under my tongue.

No. What I needed was to be a wolf again.

"Aren't you afraid?" Isabel asked, suddenly, and I opened my eyes. I hadn't realized I'd shut them. Her gaze was intense.

"Of what?"

"Of losing yourself?"

I told her the truth: "That's what I'm hoping for."

· ISABEL ·

I didn't have anything to say to that. I didn't expect him to be honest with me. I wasn't sure where we could go from here, because I wasn't prepared to return the favor.

He lifted a dripping hand from the water, his fingertips a little wrinkled.

"You want to see if my fingers are done?" he asked.

Something in my stomach turned over as I took his wet hand and ran my fingers from his palm to his fingertips. His eyes were half-closed, and when I was through, he took his hand back and sat up, making the water slosh and crest around him. He leaned his hands on the edge of the bathtub, putting his face at my eye level. I knew we were going to kiss again and I knew that we shouldn't, because he was already at rock bottom and I was getting there, too, but I couldn't help myself. I was starving for him.

His mouth tasted like wolf and salt, and when he put his hand at the base of my neck to pull me closer, lukewarm water trailed down my collarbone into my shirt and between my breasts.

"Ow," he said into my mouth, and I pulled back. But he didn't appear particularly concerned as he looked down at his shoulder, where my nails had broken the skin. I was still aching from kissing him, and this time, at least, he seemed to feel it, too, because when he dragged his still slightly damp hand flat down my neck to my breastbone, stopping just short of broaching the line of my camisole, I felt the *wanting* in the pressure of his fingertips.

"What do we do now?" I asked.

"Find a bed," he said.

"I'm not sleeping with you." The high of the kiss was starting to wear off, and it was like the first time I'd met him all over again. Why did I let him get to me? What was wrong with me? I stood up, got my coat off the counter, and put it back on. Suddenly, I was horribly afraid that Sam would know that we'd kissed.

"And again I'm left feeling like I must be a bad kisser," Cole said.

"I need to go home," I told him. "I have school tomorrow — today. I have to be home before my dad leaves for work."

"A really bad kisser."

"Just say thanks for your fingers and toes." I had my hand on the doorknob. "And let's leave it at that."

Cole should've been looking at me like I was crazy, but he was just looking at me. Like he didn't seem to get that this was a rejection.

"Thanks for my fingers and toes," he said.

I shut the bathroom door behind me and left the house without finding Sam. It wasn't until I was halfway home that I remembered how Cole had told me that he was hoping to lose himself. It made me feel better to think that he was broken.

Chapter Seventeen

· COLE ·

I woke up human, though the sheets were twisted and smelled of wolf.

After Isabel left the night before, Sam had led me past a pile of linens that had clearly just been torn from a bed, and set me up in a downstairs bedroom. The entire room was so yellow that it looked like the sun had thrown up on the walls and wiped its mouth afterward on the dresser and curtains. But it had a freshly made bed in the middle of the room, and that was all that mattered.

"Good night," Sam said, voice cool but not hostile.

I didn't reply. I was already under the covers, dead to the world, dreaming of nothing.

Now, blinking in the late morning sunshine, I left the bed unmade and padded into the living room, which looked entirely different in the daylight. All reds and tartans made brilliant by the sun pouring in the wall of windows behind me. It looked comfortable. Not at all like the stiff gothic perfection of Isabel's house.

In the kitchen, photos were stuck every which way on the cabinets, a mess of tape and pushpins and smiling faces. I immediately found Beck in dozens of them, and Sam, too, looking like a stop-motion video as he aged in each one. No Isabel.

The faces, for the most part, were all happy and grinning and comfortable, like they were making the best of a strange life. There were photos of grilling and canoeing and playing guitars together, but it was pretty obvious that they all took place either in this house or in the immediate vicinity of Mercy Falls. It was like there were two messages being given out by the cabinets of photos: *We are a family*, and *You are a prisoner.*

You chose this, I reminded myself. The truth was, I hadn't given much thought to the times in between being a wolf. I hadn't really given much thought to anything.

"How are your fingers?"

My muscles tensed for a second before I recognized the voice as Sam's. I turned toward it and found him standing in the wide doorway to the kitchen, a cup of tea in his hand, the light from behind haloing his shoulders. His eyes had a shadowed look that was equal parts sleep deprivation and uncertainty about me.

It was a weird and surprisingly freeing feeling, to have someone not take you at face value.

To answer his question, I lifted my hands beside my head and wiggled my fingers, a gesture with cavalier overtones that I hadn't initially intended.

Sam's unnervingly yellow eyes — I never got used to them — kept looking, looking at me, waging a battle with himself. Finally he said in a flat voice, "There's cereal and eggs and milk."

I raised an eyebrow.

Sam's shoulders had already ducked as he started to retreat back into the hall, but my raised eyebrow stopped him. He closed his eyes for a moment, then reopened them. "Okay, this." He set his mug on the island between us and crossed his arms. "This: Why are you here?"

The pugilistic tone made me like him slightly better. It offset his stupid floppy hair and sad, fake-looking eyes. Evidence of a spine was a good thing.

"To be a wolf," I said, flippant. "Which, coincidentally, *isn't* the reason you're here, if rumors are true."

Sam's eyes flicked to the photos behind me, so many of them containing him, and then back to my face. "It doesn't matter why I'm here. This is my home."

"I see that," I replied. I could've helped him out, but I didn't see the point.

Sam considered for a moment. I could actually see him mentally reviewing how much effort he wanted to put into the conversation. "Look. I'm not normally a jerk. But I'm having a really hard time understanding why someone would choose this life. If you could explain that to me, we'd be a lot closer to getting along."

I held out my hands as if I were presenting something. When I did that at shows, the audience went wild, because it meant I was about to sing something new. Victor would've gotten the reference and laughed. Sam didn't have the context, so he just looked at my hands until I said, "To make a fresh start, Ringo. The same reason your man Beck did it."

Sam's expression went totally flat. "But you *chose* this. On purpose."

Clearly Beck had given Sam a different story of his genesis than the one he'd given me; I wondered which one was real. I wasn't about to get into a lengthy discussion with Sam, however, who was looking at me like he expected me to debunk Santa Claus next. "Yeah, I did. Make of that what you will. Now can I get some breakfast, or what?"

Sam shook his head — not like he was angry, but like he was shaking gnats away from his thoughts. He glanced at his watch. "Yeah. Whatever. I've got to get to work." He stepped past me, not meeting my eyes, and then checked himself. He went back into the kitchen and jotted something on a Post-it note, which he then smacked onto the door of the fridge. "That's my cell and my work. Call me if you need me."

It was clearly killing him to be nice to me, but still, he was. An ingrained sense of politeness? Duty? What was it? I wasn't really a fan of nice people.

Sam started again to head out, but he stopped again, in the doorway, his car keys jingling. "You'll probably change back soon. When the sun goes down, anyway, or if you're outside too long. So try to stick around here, okay? So no one will see you shift?"

I smiled thinly at him. "Sure thing."

Sam looked like he was going to say something else, but then he just pressed two fingers to his temple and grimaced.

The gesture said all the things that Sam hadn't: He had plenty of problems, and I was just another one of them.

I was enjoying being not-famous more than I'd expected.

· ISABEL ·

When Grace wasn't in school on Monday, I ducked into the girls' bathroom and called her during lunch. And got her mom. At least, I was pretty sure it was her mother.

"Hello?" The voice that answered was obviously not Grace's.

"Uh, hello?" I tried not to sound too snarky, in case it really was her mom. "I *was* calling for Grace." Okay, so I couldn't keep all the attitude out of my voice. But seriously.

The other voice was friendly. "Who is this?"

"Who is *this*?"

I heard Grace's voice, finally. "Mom! Give me that!" There was a shuffling sound and then Grace said, "Sorry about that. I'm grounded, and apparently that means that people can screen my calls without asking me."

Color me impressed. Saint Grace got grounded? "What did you do?"

I heard a door shut on her side of the phone. Not quite a slam, but more defiant than I would've expected from Grace. She said, "Got caught sleeping with Sam."

My face in the bathroom mirror opposite me looked surprised, eyebrows hiked up toward my hairline, the black liner around my eyes making them look even bigger and rounder than they really were. "This is the good stuff! You guys were having *sex*?"

"No, no. He was just sleeping in my bed. They're completely overreacting."

"Oh, of course they are," I said. "Everyone's parents are cool with their daughters sharing bed space with their boyfriends. I know my parents would love it. So, what, they kept you from going to school? That seems . . ."

"No, that's because I was in the hospital," Grace said. "I got a fever, and again they overreacted and took me to the hospital instead of giving me Tylenol. I think they just wanted a good reason to take me in the opposite direction from Sam. Anyway, it took forever, of course, like it always does in a hospital, and I didn't get home until late. So I just woke up, basically."

For some reason my thoughts immediately ran to Grace looking up at Mr. Grant and asking to be excused for her headache. "What's wrong with you? What did the doctors say?"

"Virus, or something. It was just a fever," Grace said, so fast that I barely had time to get out my questions. It didn't sound like she believed herself.

The bathroom door came open slightly behind me and I heard, "Isabel, I know you're in there." Ms. McKay, my English teacher. "If you keep skipping lunch, I'm going to have to tell your parents. Just saying. Class is in ten minutes."

The door swung shut once more.

Grace said, "Are you not eating again?"

I said, "Shouldn't you be more worried about your problems at the moment?"

· COLE ·

After Sam had disappeared to "work," whatever that was, I poured myself a glass of milk and wandered back into the living room to look through some drawers. In my experience, drawers and backpacks were great ways to get to know a person. The end tables in the living room only offered up remote controls and PlayStation controls, so I headed into the office I'd passed on the way from my bedroom.

It was a way better jackpot. The desk was stuffed with papers, and the computer wasn't password protected. The room was practically made for ransacking, situated on the corner of the house with windows on two walls, one pair of them facing the street, so I would have plenty of warning if Sam returned. I set my glass of milk down next to the mouse pad (someone had drawn doodles all over the pad with a Sharpie, including a sketch of a very large-breasted girl in a schoolgirl outfit) and made myself comfortable in the chair. The office was like the rest of the house — homey and masculine and comfortable.

On top of the desk, there were some bills, all addressed to Beck and all marked PAID BY AUTOMATIC WITHDRAWAL. Bills were not interesting. A brown leather day planner sat next to the keyboard. Day planners were not interesting, either. I opened a drawer instead. A bunch of software programs, mostly utilitarian stuff, but a handful of games as well. Also not interesting. I went for the bottom drawer and was rewarded by a swirl of dust, which is what people use to cover their best secrets. Then, a brown envelope labeled SAM. Now we were getting somewhere. I pulled out the first sheet. Adoption paperwork.

Here we go.

I shook the contents of the envelope on the desk, reaching in to pull out some of the smaller sheets that stayed inside. Birth certificate: Samuel Kerr Roth, showing that he was about a year younger than me. A photograph of Sam, knobby and small but still bearing the same flop of dark hair and heavy-lidded eyes I'd noticed the night before. His expression was complicated. Last night, the freakish wolf-yellow of his eyes had caught my attention; when I pulled the photo closer, I saw that baby Sam had the same yellow irises. So they weren't colored contacts. Somehow that made me feel slightly friendlier toward him. I put down the photo. Beneath it was a sheaf of browning newspaper clippings. My eyes scanned the stories.

> Gregory and Annette Roth, a Duluth couple, were charged last Monday with the attempted murder of their seven-year-old son. Authorities have placed their child (not named here to protect identity) into state custody. His fate will be decided after the Roths' trial. The Roths allegedly held their son in a bathtub and cut his wrists with a razor. Shortly after the act, Annette Roth confessed to the next-door neighbor, saying that her son was taking too long to die. Both she and Gregory Roth told the police that their son was possessed by the devil.

I felt a thick, disgusted glob in the back of my throat that wouldn't go away when I swallowed. I was having a hard time not thinking of Victor's little brother, who was eight now. I flipped back to the photo of Sam holding Beck's hand and looked once more at Sam, his half-closed eyes staring at some point past the camera, vacant. The position of his small hand in Beck's turned his wrist toward the camera, clearly showing the recent red-brown slash across it.

A little voice in my head said *And you feel sorry for yourself.*

I shoved the newspaper clippings and the photograph back into the envelope so that I didn't have to look at them, and looked at the sheaf of paperwork underneath instead. It was trust paperwork, naming Sam as the beneficiary of the trust — which included the house — and the contents of a checking account and a savings account, both bearing Beck's and Sam's names.

Pretty heavy stuff. I wondered if Sam knew that he basically owned the place. Underneath the paperwork was another black day planner. Flipping through it, I saw journal entries with the efficient, backward-slanting writing of a left-hander. I turned to the first page: *"If you're reading this, I'm either a wolf for good, or you're Ulrik and you should get the hell out of my stuff."*

I jerked when the phone rang.

I watched it ring twice, and then I picked it up. I answered, "Da."

"Is this Cole?"

My spirits inexplicably rose. "Depends. Is this my mother?"

Isabel's voice was sharp over the phone. "I wasn't aware you had one. Does Sam know that you're picking up the phone now?"

"Were you calling for him?"

A pause.

"And is that your number on the caller ID?"

"Yeah," said Isabel. "Don't call it, though. What are you doing? You're still you?"

"For the moment. I'm looking through Beck's stuff," I said, shoving the SAM envelope and its contents back in the drawer.

"Are you kidding me?" Isabel asked. She answered her own question. "No, you're not." Another pause. "What did you find?"

"Come and look."

"I'm at school."

"Talking on the phone?"

Isabel considered. "I'm in the bathroom trying to work up enthusiasm for my next class. Tell me what you found. Some ill-gotten knowledge will cheer me up."

"Sam's adoption papers. And some newspaper clippings about how his parents tried to kill him. Also, I found a really bad sketch of a woman wearing a schoolgirl outfit. It's definitely worth seeing."

"Why are you talking to me?"

I thought I knew what she meant, but I said, "Because you called me."

"Is it because you just want to sleep with me? Because I'm not sleeping with you. Nothing personal. But I'm just not. I'm saving myself and all that. So if that's why you want to talk to me, you can hang up now."

I didn't hang up. I wasn't sure if that answered her question.

"Are you still there?"

"I'm here."

"Well, are you going to actually answer my question?"

I pushed my empty milk glass back and forth.

"I just want someone to talk to," I said. "I like talking to you. I don't have a better answer than that."

"Talking isn't really what we were doing either time we saw each other," she said.

"We talked," I insisted. "I told you about my Mustang. That was a very deep, personal conversation about something very close to my heart."

"Your car." Isabel sounded unconvinced. She paused, then finally said, "You want to talk? Fine. Talk. Tell me something you've never told anybody else."

I thought for a moment. "Turtles have the second-largest brains of any animal on the planet."

It took Isabel only a second to process this. "No, they don't."

"I know. That's why I've never told anybody that before."

There was a sound on the other side like she was either trying not to laugh or having an asthma attack. "Tell me something about you that you've never told anybody else."

"If I do, will you do the same?"

She sounded skeptical. "Yeah."

I traced the outline of the Sharpie schoolgirl on the mouse pad, thinking. Talking on a telephone was like talking with your eyes closed. It made you braver and more honest, because it was like talking to yourself. It was why I'd always sung my new songs with my eyes closed. I didn't want to see what the audience thought of them until I was done. Finally, I said, "I've been trying not to be my father my entire life. Not because he's so horrible, but because he's so impressive. Anything — *anything* I do can't possibly compare."

Isabel was silent. Maybe waiting to see if I was going to say more. "What does your father do?"

"I want to hear what you've never told anyone."

"No, you have to talk first. You wanted to talk. It means you say something, and I respond, and you talk back again. It's one of the human race's most shining achievements. It's called a *conversation*."

I was beginning to regret this particular one. "He's a scientist."

"A rocket scientist?"

"A mad scientist," I said. "A very good one. But really, I don't want to have any more of this conversation until a much later date. Like possibly after my death. Now can I hear yours?"

Isabel took a breath, loud enough for me to hear it over the phone. "My brother died."

The words had a ring of familiarity to them. Like I'd heard them before, in her voice, though I couldn't imagine when. After I finished thinking that, I said, "You've told someone that before."

"I never told anyone before that it was my fault, because everybody already thought he was dead by the time he actually died," Isabel said.

"That doesn't make any sense."

"Nothing makes any sense anymore. Like, why am I talking to you? Why am I telling you this when you don't care?"

This question, at least, I knew the answer to. "But that's *why* you're telling me." I knew it was true. If we'd had the opportunity to deliver our confessions to anyone who actually cared about their contents, there was no way either of us would've opened our mouths. Sharing revelations is easier when it doesn't matter.

She was quiet. I heard other girls' voices in the background, high, wordless streams of conversation, followed by the hiss of running water, and then silence again. "Okay," she said.

"Okay, what?" I asked.

"Okay, maybe you can call me. Sometime. Now you have my number."

I didn't even have time to say bye before she hung up.

Chapter Eighteen

· SAM ·

I didn't know where my girlfriend was, my phone battery had died, I was living in a house with a possibly insane new werewolf who I sort of suspected was suicidal or homicidal, and I was miles away from all of it, counting the spines of books. Somewhere out there, my world was slowly spinning out of orbit, and here I was in a beautifully ordinary splash of sunlight, writing *The Secret Life of Bees (3/PB)* on a yellow legal pad labeled INVENTORY.

"We should be getting goodies in today." Karyn, the shop owner, came in from the back room, her voice preceding her. "When the UPS man comes. Here."

I turned and found that she was holding a styrofoam cup at me.

"What's this for?" I asked.

"Good behavior. It's green tea. Is that right?"

I nodded appreciatively. I had always liked Karyn, from the moment I met her. She was in her fifties, with short, choppy hair that had gone entirely white, but her face — her eyes, especially — was youthful underneath still-dark eyebrows. She hid an iron core behind a pleasant, efficient smile, and I could see how the best parts of what was inside her were written on her outside. I liked to think that she'd hired me because I was the same way.

"Thanks," I said, taking a sip. The way I could feel the hot liquid's journey all the way down my throat and into my stomach reminded me that I hadn't eaten yet. I'd gotten too used to my morning cereal with Grace. I tilted the legal pad toward Karyn so she could see what progress I'd made.

"Nice. Find anything good?"

I pointed to the stack of misplaced books that sat on the floor behind me.

"That's wonderful." Peeling the lid off her own coffee cup, she made a face and then blew steam across the top of the liquid. She regarded me. "Are you excited about Sunday?"

I was clueless, and I was sure my face reflected it. I waited for my brain to present an answer, but when it didn't, I echoed, "Sunday?"

"Studio?" she said. "With Grace?"

"You know about that?"

Without putting her coffee down first, Karyn awkwardly picked up half the stack of misplaced books and said, "Grace called me to make sure it wasn't a day you were working."

Of course she had. Grace wouldn't have scheduled an appointment for me without making sure that everything was sorted out beforehand. I felt a pang somewhere in my stomach, the miserable twist of missing her. "I don't know if we're still on for that." I hesitated as Karyn's eyebrow raised, waiting for me to say more. And then I told her the details I hadn't told Isabel the night before — because Karyn would care, and Isabel wouldn't have. "Her parents found me in her room after curfew." I felt my cheeks warm. "She was sick and cried out, which was why they came in to check on her, and they made me leave. I don't know how she is. I don't even know if they'll let me see her again."

Karyn didn't answer straightaway, which was one of the things I liked about her. She didn't automatically spit out *It'll be okay* until she was sure that was the right answer. "Sam, why didn't you tell me you couldn't come in to work today? I would've given you the day off."

I said, helplessly, "Inventory."

"Inventory could have waited. We're doing inventory because it's March and it's freezing and no one is coming in," Karyn said. She considered for a few more minutes, sipping her coffee and wrinkling her nose as she did. "First of all, they're not going to keep you from seeing her again. You're practically adults, and, anyway, they have to know that Grace couldn't do better than you. Second of all, she probably just has the flu. What was wrong with her?"

"Fever," I said, and I was surprised at how quiet my voice came out.

Karyn watched me closely. "I know you're worried, but lots of people get fevers, Sam."

I said softly, "I had meningitis. Bacterial meningitis."

I hadn't said it out loud before now, and now that I had, it was almost cathartic, as if acknowledging my fears that Grace's fever might be something more dangerous than a common cold made them more manageable.

"How long ago?"

I rounded to the nearest holiday. "Christmastime."

"Oh, it wouldn't be contagious from then," she said. "I don't think meningitis is one of those diseases that you can catch months later. How is she feeling today?"

"Her phone went to voicemail this morning," I said, trying not to sound too sorry for myself. "They were really angry last night. I think they've probably taken her phone."

Karyn made a face. "They'll get over it. Try to see it from their point of view."

She was still shifting back and forth with the books to keep them from falling, so I set down my green tea and took them from her. "I can see it from their point of view. That's the problem." I walked over to the biography section to shelve a misplaced biography of Princess Diana. "If I were them, I'd be furious. They think I'm some bastard boy who has successfully worked his way into their daughter's pants and will shortly be on his way out of her life."

She laughed. "I'm sorry. I know it's not funny to you."

I said, sounding rather grimmer than I meant to, "It will be hilarious to me one day, when we're married and only have to see them at Christmas."

"You do know that most boys don't talk like that," Karyn said. Taking the inventory list, she headed behind the counter, setting her coffee next to the cash register. "You know how I got Drew to propose to me? A stun gun, some alcohol, and the Home Shopping Network." She looked at me until I smiled at her line. "What does Geoffrey think of all this?"

It took me too long to realize that she was talking about Beck; I couldn't remember the last time I'd heard his first name said out loud. And the realization that I was going to have to lie hit me right afterward. "He doesn't know yet. He's out of town." My words tumbled out too fast, with me too much in a hurry to get the lie over with. I turned toward the shelf so that she wouldn't see the way my face looked.

"Oh, that's right. I forgot about his Florida clients," Karyn said, and I blinked at the shelf in front of me, surprised at Beck's guile. "Sam, I'm going to open a Florida bookstore for the winter. I think Geoffrey has the right idea. Minnesota in March is just not a good idea."

I had no idea what story Beck had ever told Karyn to convince her that he was in Florida for the winter, but I was fairly impressed, as Karyn didn't strike me as gullible. But of course he must've told her something — he had spent enough time in here as both a customer and, later, when I got my first job here and before I got my license, as my chauffeur. Karyn had to have noticed his absence in the winter. I was even more impressed by the easy way that she said his first name. She'd known him well enough for *Geoffrey* to fall naturally from her lips, but not well enough to know that everyone who loved him called him by his last name.

I realized that there had been a long pause, and that Karyn was still watching me.

"Did he come here a lot?" I asked. "Without me?"

Behind the counter, she nodded. "Often enough. He bought a lot of biographies." She paused, contemplating this. She'd told me once that you could completely psychoanalyze someone based on the sort of books they read. I wondered what Beck's love of biographies — I had seen the shelves and shelves of them at home — told her about him. Karyn went on, "I do remember the last thing he bought, because it wasn't a biography, and I was surprised. It was a day planner."

I frowned. I didn't remember seeing it.

"One of those with spaces to write comments and journal entries on each day." Karyn stopped. "He said it was to write down his thoughts for when he couldn't remember to think them."

I had to turn to the bookshelves then because of the sudden tears burning in my eyes. I tried to focus on the titles in front of me to pull my emotions back from the edge. I touched a spine with one of my fingers, while the words blurred and cleared, blurred and cleared.

"Is there something wrong with him, Sam?" Karyn asked.

I looked down at the floor, at the way the old wooden floorboards buckled a bit where they met the base of the shelves. I felt dangerously out of control, like my words were welling, ready to spill. So I didn't say anything at all. I didn't think about the empty, echoing rooms of Beck's house. I didn't think about how it was now me who bought the milk and the canned food to restock the shed. I didn't think about Beck, trapped in a wolf's body, watching me from the trees, no longer remembering, no longer thinking human thoughts. I didn't think about how this summer, there was nothing — no one — to wait for.

I stared at a tiny, black knot in the floorboards at my feet. It was a lonely, dark shape in the middle of the golden wood.

I wanted Grace.

"I'm sorry," Karyn said. "I didn't mean to — I don't mean to pry."

I felt bad for making her feel awkward. "I know you don't. And you're not. It's just —" I pressed my fingers to my forehead, on the epicenter of the ghostly headache. "He's sick. It's — terminal." The words came out slowly, a painful combination of truth and lie.

"Oh, Sam, I'm sorry. Is he at the house?"

Not turning around, I shook my head.

"This is why Grace's fever bothers you so much," Karyn guessed.

I closed my eyes; in the darkness, I felt dizzy, like I didn't know where the ground was. I was torn between wanting to speak and wanting to guard my fears, keeping control of them by keeping them private. The words came out before I could think them through. "I can't lose both of them. I know . . . I know how strong I am, and I'm . . . not that strong."

Karyn sighed. "Turn around, Sam."

Reluctantly, I turned, and saw her holding up the legal pad with the inventory on it. She pointed with a pen to the letters *SR*, written in her handwriting at the bottom of my additions. "Do you see your initials on here? This is because I'm telling you to go home. Or somewhere. Go clear your head."

My voice came out small. "Thank you."

She ruffled my hair when I came over to collect my guitar and my book from the counter. "Sam," she said, just as I was heading past her, "I think you're made of stronger stuff than you think."

I made my face into a smile that didn't last to the back door.

Opening the door, I stepped right into Rachel. Through a tremendous stroke of luck or personal dexterity, I kept from dumping my green tea all over her striped scarf. She snatched it out of my way well after the danger of hot liquids had passed, and gave me a warning look.

"The Boy should watch where he's going," she said.

"Rachel should not manifest in doorways," I replied.

"Grace told me to come in this way!" Rachel protested. At my puzzled look, she explained, "My natural talents don't extend to parallel parking, so Grace said if I parked behind the store, I could just pull in and that nobody would mind if I walked in the back door. Apparently she was wrong because you tried to repel me with vats of burning oil and —"

"Rachel," I interrupted. "When did you talk to Grace?"

"Like, last? Two seconds ago." Rachel stepped backward to allow me enough room to step outside and close the door behind me.

Relief fell through me so fast that I almost laughed. Suddenly, I could breathe the cold air tinged with exhaust and see the tired green paint of the trash bins and feel the icy wind reaching an experimental finger into my shirt collar.

I hadn't expected to see her again.

It sounded melodramatic now that I knew Grace was well enough to talk to Rachel, and I didn't know why I would've jumped to that conclusion, but it didn't make it any less true.

"It is freezing cold out here," I said, and gestured to the Volkswagen. "Do you mind?"

"Oh, let's," Rachel said, and waited until I unlocked the doors to get in. I started the engine and put the heat up and pressed my hands over the air vents until I felt less anxious about the cold that couldn't harm me. Rachel was managing to fill the entire car with some very sweet, highly artificial scent that was probably meant to be strawberry. She had to fold her stocking-covered legs on the seat in order to make room for her overflowing bag.

"Okay. Now talk," I said. "Tell me about Grace. Is she okay?"

"Yeah. She went to the hospital last night, but she's back again. She didn't even stay overnight. She was fevered, so they doped her up with Tylenol out the wazoo and she got unfevered. She said she feels fine." Rachel shrugged. "I'm supposed to get her homework. Which is why" — she kicked her stuffed backpack — "I'm also supposed to give you this." She held out a pink phone with a cyclops smiley-face sticker on the back.

"Is this your phone?" I asked.

"It is. She said yours goes straight to voicemail."

This time I did laugh, a relieved, soundless one. "What about *hers*?"

"Her dad took it from her. I can't believe you two got caught. What were you guys thinking! You could've died from humiliation!"

I just gave her a look that was invested with as much dolor as physically possible. Now that I'd heard that Grace was alive and well, I could afford some melancholy humor at my own expense.

"Poor Boy," Rachel said, patting my shoulder. "Don't worry. They won't stay mad at you forever. Give them a few days and they'll be back to forgetting they have a daughter. Here. The phone. She's allowed to take calls again now."

I gratefully accepted it, punched in her number — "Number

two on speed dial," Rachel said — and a moment later I heard, "Hey, Rach."

"It's me," I said.

· GRACE ·

I didn't know what emotion it was that flooded me when I heard Sam's voice instead of Rachel's. I just knew that it was strong enough that it made two of my breaths stick together into one long, shuddering exhalation. I steamrollered over the unidentified feeling. "Sam."

I heard him sigh, which desperately made me want to see his face. I said, "Did Rachel tell you? I'm okay. It was just a fever. I'm at home now."

"Can I come over?" Sam's voice was odd.

I tugged my comforter up farther on my lap, jerking it when it didn't straighten the way I wanted it to, trying not to reinvoke the anger I'd felt earlier when talking to Dad. "I'm grounded. I'm not allowed to go to the studio on Sunday." There was a dead silence on the other end of the line; I thought I could imagine Sam's face, and it kind of hurt me, in a numb way that came from being upset for so long that you couldn't sustain it. "Are you still there?"

Sam's voice sounded brave, which hurt more than his silence. "I can reschedule."

"Oh, no," I said emphatically. And suddenly the anger broke through. I tried to speak through it. "I am making it to the studio on Sunday, I don't care if I have to beg them. I don't care if I have to sneak out. Sam, I'm so mad, I don't know what to do. I want to run away right now. I don't want to be in the house with them. Seriously, talk me down. Tell me I can't come and live with you. Tell me you don't want me over there."

"You know I wouldn't tell you that," Sam said softly. "You know I wouldn't stop you."

I glared at my closed bedroom door. My mother — my jailer — was somewhere on the other side of it. Inside me, my stomach still felt fever sick; I didn't want to be here. "Then why don't I?" My voice sounded aggressive.

Sam was silent for a long moment. Finally, he said, his voice low, "Because you know that's not how you want it to end. You know I'd love to have you with me, and it will be that way, one day. But this isn't the way it ought to happen."

For some reason, that made my eyes prick with tears. Surprised, I scrubbed them away with a fist. I didn't know what to say. I was used to me being the practical one and Sam being the emotional one. I felt alone in my fury.

"I was worried about you," Sam said.

I was worried about me, too, I thought, but instead I said, "I'm okay. I really want to get out of town with you. I wish it were Sunday already."

· SAM ·

It was weird to hear Grace this way. It was weird to be here, sitting in my car with her best friend when Grace was home, needing me for once. It was weird to want to tell her that we didn't need to go to the studio until things calmed down. But I couldn't tell her no. I physically couldn't say it to her. Hearing her like this . . . she was a different thing than I'd ever seen her be, and I felt some dangerous and lovely future whispering secrets in my ear. I said, "I wish it were Sunday, too."

"I don't want to be alone tonight," Grace said.

Something in my heart twinged. I closed my eyes for a moment and opened them again. I thought about sneaking over myself; I thought about telling her to sneak out. I imagined lying in my bedroom beneath my paper cranes, with the warm shape of her tucked against me, not having to worry about hiding in the morning, just having her with me on our terms, and I ached and ached some more with the force of wanting it. I echoed, "I miss you, too."

"I have your phone charger here," Grace whispered. "Call me from Beck's tonight, okay?"

"Okay," I said.

After she'd hung up, I handed the phone back to Rachel. I wasn't sure what was wrong with me. It was only forty-eight hours until I saw her again. That wasn't long. A drop in the bucket in the ocean of time that was our lives together.

We had forever now. I had to start believing that.

"Sam?" Rachel asked. "Do you know you have the saddest sad face ever?"

Chapter Nineteen

· SAM ·

After I parted ways with Rachel, I headed back to Beck's house. The day had become sunny; not so much warm as the promise of warm — summer in the making. I couldn't remember weather like this. It had been so many years since this nearly-spring hadn't kept me locked inside my wolf form. It was hard to convince myself that I didn't need to cling to the shelter of the warm car.

I would not be afraid. *Believe in your cure.*

I shut the car door, but I didn't go into the house; if Cole was still in there, I wasn't ready to face him. Instead, I headed around the back of the house, across the slimy dead grass from last year and into the woods. I had the thought that I ought to check the shed to see if there were any wolves inside. The building, buried a few hundred yards in the woods behind Beck's house, was a haven for new wolves as they shifted back and forth. It was stocked with clothing and tinned food and flashlights. Even a little combo TV/VCR and a space heater that could run off the boat battery. Everything a volatile new wolf would need to be comfortable while waiting to see if its human form would stick.

Sometimes, however, a new pack member would shift back to a wolf while inside the shed too fast to open the door, and then there was a wild animal, slave to instinct, trapped in walls that stank of humans and shifting and uncertainty.

I remembered one spring, when I was nine and still relatively uncertain in my wolf skin, the warm day had stripped my pelt from me and left me naked and embarrassed, curled on the forest like a pale new shoot. Once I was certain I was alone, I'd made my way to the shed as Beck had told me to. My stomach was still aching, like it did between the shifts back then. It was enough to double me over, my sharp ribs pressing against the tops of my legs as I crouched, biting my finger until the spasm passed and let me straighten up and open the door to the shed.

I spooked like a colt at the sound of a voice as I came through the door. After a minute, my heart quieted enough for me to realize that the voice was singing; whoever had been inside last had left the boom box on. Elvis asked whether I was lonely tonight while I dug through the bin marked SAM. I pulled on my jeans but didn't bother to find a shirt before I went for the food bin. I tore open a bag of chips, my stomach growling only when it was sure that it was about to be filled. Sitting there on the bin, scrawny knees pulled up to my chin, I listened to Elvis croon and thought about how song lyrics were just another sort of poetry. The summer before, Ulrik had been making me memorize famous poems — I could still remember the first half of "Stopping by Woods on a Snowy Evening." I tried to remember the second half as I crunched through the entire bag of corn chips, hoping to get rid of my stomach pains.

In the time it took me to notice that the hand holding the

bag of chips was shaking, the ache in my abdomen had turned into the inside-out squeeze of the change. I had no time to get to the door before my fingers were useless and stubby, my nails ineffective against the wood. My last human thought was a memory: my parents slamming my bedroom door, the lock snicking shut as the wolf bubbled out of me.

My wolf memories were hard to remember, but I did remember this: It took me hours to give up trying to get out that day.

It was Ulrik who found me.

"Ah, *Junge*," he said in a sad voice, running a hand over his shaved head as he looked around. I blinked at him blankly, somehow surprised that he was not my mother or father. "How long have you been in here?"

I was curled in the corner of the shed, staring at my bloody fingers, my brain slowly drifting out of my wolf thoughts and into fragmented human ones. Bins and their lids were scattered across the shed, and the boom box lay in the middle of the floor, the cord jerked from the wall. There was dried blood smeared on the floor, with prints both wolf and human through it. Chips and peelings from the door made a violent confetti, surrounded by torn bags of chips and pretzels, their ruined contents abandoned, uneaten.

Ulrik crossed the floor, his boots crunching softly across the fine sand of potato chips, and he stopped halfway to me as I shrank back. My vision danced, showing me by turns the trashed shed and my old bedroom, strewn with bed linens and shredded books.

He reached a hand toward me. "Come on, get up. Let's get you inside."

But I didn't move. I looked again at my blunted nails, bloody splinters shoved beneath them. I was lost in the small world of my fingertips, the shallow ridges of whorls outlined delicately with red, a single banded wolf hair caught in my blood. My gaze slid to the lumpy new scars on my wrists, spotted with crimson.

"Sam," Ulrik said.

I didn't lift my eyes to him. I had used all my words and all my strength trying to get out, and now I couldn't bring myself to want to stand.

"I'm not Beck," he said, voice helpless. "I don't know what he does to make you snap out of this, okay? I don't know how to speak your language, *Junge*. What are you thinking? Just look at me."

He was right. Beck had a way of pulling me back to reality, but Beck was not there. Ulrik finally picked me up, my body limp as a corpse in his arms, and carried me all the way back to the house. I didn't speak or eat or move until Beck shifted and came into the house — even now, I still didn't know if it had been hours or days.

Beck didn't come straight to me. Instead he went into the kitchen and clanged some pots. When he came back out to the living room, where I hid in the corner of the sofa, he had a plate of eggs.

"I made you food," he said.

The eggs were exactly the way I liked them. I looked at them instead of Beck's face and whispered, "I'm sorry."

"There's nothing to be sorry for," Beck said. "You didn't know any better. And Ulrik was the only one who liked those damn Doritos. You did us all a favor."

He set the plate down on the sofa beside me and went down the hall into his study. After a minute, I took the eggs and slid silently down the hall after him. Sitting down outside the open study door, I listened to the erratic patter of Beck's fingers on his keyboard as I ate.

That was back when I was still broken. It was back when I thought I'd have Beck forever.

"Hi, Ringo."

Cole's voice brought me back to the here and now, years later, no longer a nine-year-old guided by benevolent guardians. He stood at my elbow as I faced the shed door.

"I see you're still human," I said, more surprised than my voice let on. "What are you doing out here?"

"Trying to become a wolf."

A nasty chill ran down my skin at that, remembering fighting the wolf inside. Remembering the turn in my stomach before the shift. The sick feeling just when I lost myself. I didn't reply. Instead, I pushed open the door to the shed, fumbling for the light. The space smelled musty, unused; memories and dust motes suspended in the stale air. Behind me, a cardinal made its squeaking-sneaker noise again and again, but otherwise, there was no sound.

"Now's a good a time as any to get familiar with this place, then," I told him. I stepped into the shed, my shoes making dusty shuffling noises on the worn wood floor. Everything was in place as far as I could see — blankets folded neatly beside the dormant television, watercooler filled to the top, and jugs lined up obediently behind it, waiting their turn. Everything was waiting for wolves to fall into humans.

Cole stepped in after me, looking around at the bins and supplies with vague interest. Everything about him radiated disdain and restless energy. I wanted to ask him *What did Beck see in you?* Instead, I asked, "Is it what you expected?"

Cole had one of the bins opened a few inches and was looking inside; he didn't look away as he replied, "What?"

"Being a wolf."

"I expected it to be worse," he said, and now he looked at me, a sly smile on his face like he knew what I'd gone through to not be one. "Beck told me the pain was unbearable."

I picked up a dried leaf that we'd tracked into the shed. "Yeah, well, the pain's not the difficult part."

"Oh yeah?" Cole's voice was knowing. It was like he wanted me to hate him. "What's the difficult part, then?"

I turned away from him. I really didn't want to answer. Because I didn't think he'd care about the difficult part.

Beck had picked him. I would not hate him. I would *not.* There had to have been something in there that Beck saw. Finally, I said, "One year, one of the wolves — Ulrik — he decided it would be a great idea to start growing Italian herbs from seeds in pots. Ulrik was always doing crazy crap like that." I remembered him poking holes in the potting soil and dropping seeds in, tiny, dead-looking things disappearing into the deep black earth. "This had better work, dammit," he had said amiably to me. I'd been standing by his elbow the entire time, getting in his way while I watched, moving only when his elbow accidentally prodded my chest. "Think you can stand any closer, Sam?" he'd asked. Now, to Cole, I added, "Beck thought Ulrik was crazy. He told him that basil was only two bucks a bunch at the store."

Cole raised one of his eyebrows at me, his expression clearly indicating that he was indulging me.

I ignored his expression and said, "I watched Ulrik's seeds every day for weeks, waiting for any little bit of green in the dirt, anything to tell me that there was life waiting to happen. And that's it. That's the difficult part," I told Cole. "I am standing here in the shed, and I'm waiting to see if my seeds are going to poke out of the dirt. I don't know if it's too early to look for signs of life or if, this time, winter has claimed my family for good."

Cole stared at me. The contempt was gone from his expression, but he didn't say anything. His face held something empty, something I didn't know how to react to, so I didn't say anything, either.

There was no point in staying any longer. I did the last step while Cole hung back, checking the food bins to make sure no insects had gotten into them. I left my fingers hooked on the edge of the plastic bin for a moment as I listened. I didn't know what I was listening for; there was only silence and more silence and more silence again. Even the cardinal outside the still-open door had fallen quiet.

Pretending Cole wasn't there, I strained my ears like I had when I was a wolf, attempting to create a map of all the creatures in the nearby woods and the sounds that they made. But I heard nothing.

Somewhere, there were wolves in these woods, but they were invisible to me.

Chapter Twenty

· COLE ·

I was losing my grip on my human body, and I was glad.

Sam made me uncomfortable. I had a couple of different personas that pretty much worked across the board for everyone I had ever met, but none of them seemed right for him. He was painfully, annoyingly earnest, and how was I supposed to respond to that?

So I was relieved when we got back from the shed and he announced that he was going on a drive.

"I'd ask if you wanted to come," Sam said, "but you're going to change soon."

He didn't say how he came to this conclusion, but his nostrils pinched a bit, like he could smell me. A few moments later, the diesel engine of his Volkswagen thrummed noisily as it pulled out of the driveway, leaving me alone in a house that changed moods with the time of day. The afternoon got cloudy and cold, and suddenly, the house was no longer a comforting den but a foreboding maze of graying rooms, something out of a fever dream. Likewise, my body wasn't firmly human — but it wasn't wolf, either. Instead it was a strange, middle territory — human body, wolf brain. Human memories seen through wolf eyes. At first I paced the halls, the walls pressing in, not really believing Sam's diagnosis. When I finally felt a hint of the shift in the creep of my nerves, I stood at the open back door and waited for the cold to take me. But I wasn't there yet. So I shut the door and lay on my borrowed bed, feeling the gnaw of nausea and the crawl of my skin.

Through the discomfort, I was intensely relieved.

I had begun to think that I wasn't going to change back into a wolf.

But this miserable in-between — I got up, went to the back door again, stood in the frigid wind. I gave up after about ten minutes and retreated back to the couch, curling around the turmoil of my stomach. My mind darted through the gray halls, though my body stayed still. In my head, I walked down the hall, through unfamiliar rooms in shades of black and white. I felt Isabel's collarbone under my hand, saw my skin losing its color as I became a wolf, felt the microphone in my fist, heard my father's voice, saw him facing me across the dining room table.

No. Anywhere but home. I would let my memories take me anywhere but there.

Now I was at the photo studio with the rest of NARKOTIKA. It was our first big magazine spread. Well, really it was mine. The theme was "Under-18 Success Stories," and I was the poster child. The rest of NARKOTIKA was just there as supporting cast.

They weren't shooting us in the studio proper; instead the photographer and his assistant had taken us into the stairwell of the old building and were trying to capture the mood of the band's music by draping us over the railings and standing us on different stairs. The stairwell smelled like someone else's lunch — fake bacon bits and salad dressing you'd never order and some mysterious spice that might have been old foot.

I was coming off a high. It wasn't my first one, but it was pretty damn close. These brand-new highs pushed me into a humming flight of euphoria that still left me feeling a little guilty afterward. I had just written one of my best songs ever — "Break My Face (and Sell the Pieces)," destined to be my best-selling single — and I was in a great mood. I would've been in an even better mood if I hadn't been there, because I wanted to be smelling the outside air, thick with exhaust fumes and restaurant smells and every thrilling city scent that told me I was somebody.

"Cole. Cole. Hey, slick. Could you stand still for me? Stand next to Jeremy for a second and look down over here. Jeremy, you look at him," the photographer said. He was a paunchy, middle-aged guy, with an unevenly cut goatee that was going to bother me all day. His assistant was a twenty-something redheaded girl who had already confessed her love for me and thus became uninteresting. At seventeen, I hadn't yet discovered that a sardonic smile could make girls take their shirts off.

"I haven't stopped," Jeremy said. He sounded half-asleep. He always sounded half-asleep. Victor, on the other side of Jeremy, was smiling down at the ground just like the photographer had told him to.

I wasn't feeling the shot. How was shooting us looking over a balcony like some freaking Beatles album cover going to fit

NARKOTIKA's sound? So I shook my head and spit off the balcony and the photographer's flash went off and he and his assistant stared at the viewfinder and looked annoyed. Another flash. Another annoyed look. The photographer came to the landing and stood six stairs down from us. His voice was cajoling. "Okay, Cole, how about something with some life in it? You know, give me a smile. Imagine your best memory. Give me a smile you'd give your mom."

I raised an eyebrow and wondered if he was for real.

The photographer seemed to have a flash of insight, because his voice raised as he said, "Imagine you're onstage —"

"You want life?" I asked. "'Cause this isn't it. Life is unexpected. Life is about risk. That's what NARKOTIKA is, not some damn Boy Scout family picture. It's —"

And I leaped at him. I flew off the stairs, my arms spread out on either side, and I saw panic cross his face just as his assistant jerked her camera up and the flash blinded me.

I crashed down on one foot and rolled up against the brick wall of the stairwell, laughing my ass off. Nobody asked if I was okay. Jeremy was yawning, Victor was giving me the finger, and the photographer and the assistant were exclaiming over their viewfinder.

"Have some inspiration," I told them, and stood up. "You're welcome." I wasn't even feeling any pain.

After that, they let me do what I wanted for the shoot. Humming and singing my new song, I led them up and down the stairs, pressing my fingers against the wall like I was about to push it over; down to the lobby, where I stood in a potted plant; and finally into the alley behind the studio, where I jumped on top of the car that had brought us from the hotel, leaving dents in the roof so the car would remember me.

When the photographer called it a day, his assistant came over to me and asked for my hand. I offered my palm, and she pulled it around so that it faced the sky. Then she wrote her name and number on it while Victor watched from just behind her.

Victor grabbed my shoulder as soon as she'd gone back inside. "What about Angie?" he demanded, with a half smile on his face like he knew I was going to give him an answer he liked.

"What about her?" I asked.

The smile disappeared, and he gripped the hand with the number on it. "I don't think she'd be really happy about this."

"Vic. Dude. None of your business."

"She's my sister. It's my business."

The conversation was definitely ruining my good mood. "Well, then, here it is: Angie and I are over. We've been over so long, they're teaching it in history classes. And it's still none of your business."

"You bastard," Victor said. "You're going to leave her like that? You ruin her life and just walk away?"

It was *really* ruining my good mood. It was starting to feel like time for a needle or a beer or a razor. "Hey, I asked her. She said she'd rather go it alone."

"And you believed her? You know, you think you're so good. You and your goddamn *genius*. You think you're going to live forever like this? No one's going to remember your face when you're twenty. No one's going to remember you."

He was deflating, though. He was almost done. If I said sorry or even just stayed quiet, he'd probably turn away and go back to the hotel.

I waited a beat, and then I said, "At least the girls call me by my name, dude." I watched his face, a smirk on mine. "At least I'm not always 'NARKOTIKA's drummer.' "

Victor punched me. It was a good punch, but not everything he had. In any case, I was still standing, though I thought he'd probably split my lip. I could still feel my face and I could still remember what we were talking about. I looked at him.

Jeremy appeared by Victor's elbow, probably clued in by the sound of Victor's fist smacking my face that this wasn't one of our usual arguments.

"Don't just stand there!" Victor shouted, and he hit me again, right in the jaw, and this time I had to stagger to stay up. "Hit me, you piece of crap. Hit me."

"Boys," Jeremy said, but didn't move.

Victor slammed his shoulder into my chest, one hundred and eighty pounds of repressed anger, and this time I crashed to the ground, a piece of asphalt grinding into my back. "You're such a waste of space. Life is one big ego trip for you, you privileged son of a bitch." He was kicking me now, and Jeremy was watching, arms crossed.

"That's enough," Jeremy said.

"I — want — to — smash — that — smile — off — your — face," Victor said between kicks. He was out of breath now, and finally, one of his kicks threw him off balance and he fell heavily to the ground next to me.

I stared up at the rectangle of gray-white sky above us, framed in by the dark buildings, and felt blood trickle from my nose. I thought about Angie back at home and the way she'd looked when she told me she'd rather go it alone, and I wished she could've watched Victor kick the crap out of me.

Above me, Jeremy held out his camera phone and took a picture of the two of us lying on the asphalt in some city I couldn't even remember the name of.

Three weeks later, that photo of me flying off the stairs, Jeremy and Victor watching me, hit magazine stands and made the front page of the mag. My face was everywhere. No one was forgetting me anytime soon. I was everywhere.

Later in the afternoon, lying on the floor of Beck's house, the shift became urgent inside me, so insistent that I realized that my nausea earlier had only been pretend, nothing like the real thing, which bit and tore and ripped at my guts. I made my way again to the back door and opened it, standing and looking out at the grass. It was surprisingly warm outside, the overcast sky gone, but an occasional stiff breeze reminded me it was still March. This time, when a cold gust of wind blew, it cut right through my human body to the wolf inside. Goose bumps raced across my skin. I stepped onto the concrete stoop and hesitated, wondering if I should go to the shed and leave my clothing there to make it easier to retrieve later. But the next gust sent me double with shudders. I wasn't going to make it to the shed.

My stomach groaned and pinched; I crouched and waited.

But the shift didn't come right away, like it had before. Having been human for almost a day now, my body was more sure of its form, and it didn't seem like it wanted to give it up easily.

C'mon, shift, I thought, as the wind pulled another rack of shuddering from me. My stomach churned. I tried to remember that it was just a reaction to the shifting process; I didn't really need to throw up. If I just resisted the impulse, I'd be fine.

I braced my fingers against the cold concrete, willing the wind to push me into a wolf. Out of the blue, I remembered Angie's number, and I felt an irrational desire to go back inside and dial it, just to hear her say hello before I hung up. I wondered what Victor was thinking right now, after all this.

My chest ached.

Get me out of this body. Get me out of Cole, I thought.

But that was just one more thing out of my control.

Chapter Twenty-One

· GRACE ·

That night, there was nothing different about my bed without Sam there. There was nothing unfamiliar about the shape of the mattress. The sheets were no larger without him. I was no less tired without the steady sound of his breathing, and in the dark, I could not see the absence of his square shoulder beside me. The pillow still smelled like him, like he'd gotten up to get his book and had forgotten to come back.

But it made all the difference in the world.

My stomach aching, an echo of the pain of last night, I pressed my face into his pillow and tried not to remember those nights when I had thought he was gone for good. Imagining him over in Beck's house now, I rolled over and got my cell phone. But I didn't dial his number, because, stupidly, all I could think of was when we were lying together and Sam was shivering and he said, *Maybe we should rethink our lifestyle.* Then I thought of him telling me to stay over here, not to come over and stay with him.

Maybe he was glad to be over there, to have the excuse to be alone. Maybe he wasn't. I didn't know. I felt sick, sick, sick, in some new and terrible way that I couldn't describe. I wanted to cry and felt foolish for it.

I put my phone back on the nightstand and rolled back into his pillow and finally went to sleep.

· SAM ·

I was an open wound.

Restless, I roamed the halls of the house, wanting to call her again, afraid to get her in trouble, afraid of something nameless and huge. I paced until I was too tired to stand, and then I headed upstairs to my room. Without turning on the light, I went to my bed and lay down, my arm thrown across the mattress, my hand aching because Grace wasn't underneath it.

My thoughts festered inside me. I could not sleep. My mind slid away from the reality of the empty bed beside me and curved my thoughts into lyrics, my fingers imagining the frets they would press to find the tune.

I'm an equation that only she solves / these Xs and Ys by other names called / My way of dividing is desperately flawed / as I multiply days without her.

As the endless night crawled slowly by, innumerable minutes piling one upon another without getting anywhere, the wolves began to howl and my head began to pound. One of the dull, slow aches that the meningitis had left as its legacy. I lay in the empty house and listened to the pack's slow cries rise and fall with the pressure inside my skull.

I had risked everything, and I had nothing to show for it but my open hand, lying empty and palm up toward the ceiling.

Chapter Twenty-Two

· GRACE ·

"I'm going for a walk," I told Mom.

No day had ever passed as slowly as this Saturday. Once upon a time, when I was younger, I would've been thrilled to have an entire day with my mother in the house; now, I felt restless, like I had a houseguest. She wasn't really keeping me from doing anything, but I didn't feel like starting anything while she was around, either.

Currently, Mom was delicately folded on the end of the couch, reading one of the books that Sam had left behind. When she heard my voice, her head whipped around and her entire body stiffened. "You're *what*?"

"I'm going for a walk," I said, tempted to take Sam's book out of her hands. "I'm bored out of my mind and I want to talk with Sam, but you guys won't let me and I have to do something or I will start throwing stuff around my room like an angry chimp."

The truth was that without school or Sam, I needed to be outside. That's what I had always done in the summers before Sam — fled to the tire swing in the backyard, book in hand, needing the sound of the woods to fill the empty, restless space inside me.

"If you go chimp, I'm not cleaning your room," Mom warned. "And you can't go outside. You were just in the hospital two nights ago."

"For a fever that is now gone," I pointed out. Just beyond her, I could see the sky, deep blue and warm-looking, and, beneath it, the somehow pregnant-looking branches of the trees reaching into the blue. Everything in me itched to be outside, smelling the oncoming spring. The living room felt gray and muted in comparison. "Plus, vitamin D is great for sick people like myself. I won't stay out long."

When she didn't say anything, I found my clogs where I'd left them in the hall and slid them on. As I did, silence hung between us, speaking more strongly to what had happened that night than our few exchanged words had.

Mom looked profoundly uncomfortable. "Grace, I think we should talk. About" — she paused — "you and Sam."

"Oh, let's not." My voice conveyed exactly how much enthusiasm I had for the suggestion.

"I don't want to do it, either," she said, closing the book without checking the page number, which reminded me again of Sam, who always checked his page number, or folded the book temporarily closed around one of his fingers, before looking up to speak. Mom continued, "But I have to talk to you about it, and if you talk to me, then I'll tell your father you did, and you won't have to talk to *him*."

I didn't see why I had to talk to either of them. Until now, they hadn't cared what I did with myself or where I was when they were gone, and in a year, I'd be in college or at the very least out from under their roof. I thought about bolting but instead crossed my arms and faced her, waiting.

Mom got right to it. She asked, "Are you using protection?"

My cheeks burned. "Mom."

But she didn't back down. "Are you?"

"Yes. But that's not how it is."

Mom raised an eyebrow. "Oh, it isn't? How is it, then?"

"I mean that's not just how it is. It's —" I struggled to find words to explain, to convey just why her questions and her tone made me instantly bristle. "I mean, he's not just a boy, Mom. We're —"

But I didn't know how to finish the thought with her looking at me, her eyebrow already lifted in disbelief. I didn't know how I was supposed to tell her things like *love* and *forever*, and it struck me just then that I didn't want to. That sort of truth was something that you had to earn.

"You're what? In love?" The way Mom said it cheapened it. "You're seventeen, Grace. How old is he? Eighteen? How long have you known him? Months. Look — you've never had a boyfriend before. You're in lust as much as anything else. Sleeping together doesn't mean you're in love. It means you're in lust."

"You sleep with Dad. Aren't you two in love?"

Mom rolled her eyes toward the ceiling. "We're *married*."

Why was I even bothering? "This entire conversation will sound pretty stupid when Sam and I are visiting you at the old folks' home," I said, coldly.

"Well, I sincerely hope it does," Mom replied. And then she smiled, lightly, like the conversation was just casual chatter. Like we'd just made arrangements to go to a mother-daughter dance. "But I doubt we'll even remember it. Sam will probably be nothing more than a prom picture. I remember what I was like at seventeen and, believe me, it was not love that was in the air. Luckily for me, I had some common sense. Otherwise you might've had more siblings. I remember, when I was your age —"

"Mom!" I snapped, my entire face hot. "I am not you. I am *nothing like you*. You have *no idea* what goes on in my head, or how my brain works, or whether or not I'm in love with Sam or vice versa. So don't even try to have this conversation with me. Don't even — ugh. You know what? I'm done."

I snatched my forbidden phone from where it sat on the kitchen counter, got my coat, and stomped out. I slid the back door shut behind me and walked off the deck without looking back. Snapping at Mom should have made me feel guilty, but I couldn't feel one ounce of contrition.

I missed Sam so badly that it hurt.

Chapter Twenty-Three

· SAM ·

By the time I got done at the store, the day was freakishly warm, even warmer than the day before. The sun was warm on my cheeks when I got back to Beck's house and opened the car door. I stepped out and stretched my hands as far as they could go, closing my eyes until I felt like I was falling. In between gusts of wind, the air around me felt like the same temperature as my body, and it made it seem like I had no skin at all, like I was suspended, a spirit.

Birds, convinced that this afternoon meant that fickle spring had finally returned for good, shrilled excited love songs to one another from the bushes around the house. A song welled in me, too, the lyrics silent as I mouthed them, trying them out.

I walk through the seasons and always the birds
are singing and screaming and keening for love
When you're with me it seems so absurd
that I should be jealous of the jay and the dove.

It reminded me of the warm spring days that used to unfold me from my wolf form, days when I was so happy to get my fingers back.

It seemed so wrong to be alone right now.

I would check the shed again. I hadn't seen Cole yet today, but I knew he had to be human somewhere, with this kind of weather. And it was warm enough that at least one of the other new wolves might have changed as well. And it was something practical to do instead of listlessly wandering inside the house, waiting for tomorrow and wondering if I really was going to the studio, and if Grace was really coming with me.

Plus, Grace would've wanted me to watch for Olivia.

I knew someone was inside the shed as soon as I got within a few feet of it; the door was ajar, and I heard the sound of movement from inside. My sense of smell was nowhere near what it had been when I was a wolf, but my nose still conveyed to me that whoever was inside was one of us; the musky scent of the pack was only partially obscured by the scent of human sweat. As a wolf, I would've been able to tell exactly which pack member it was. Now, as a human, I was blind.

So I walked to the door and knocked the back of my knuckles on it three times. "Cole? All decent in there?" I asked.

"Sam?" Cole's voice sounded — relieved? It seemed odd for him. I heard the scrabbling of claws, then a groan. I felt the fine hairs on the back of my neck prickle to attention.

"Is everything okay?" I asked, cautiously pushing the door open. Inside the shed, it absolutely reeked of wolf, as if the walls bled with the smell. First I saw Cole, clothed, standing by the bins, one of his knuckles pressed against his lip in an uncertain gesture. And then I followed his eyes to the corner of the shed and saw a guy crumpled there, half covered by a bright blue polar fleece blanket.

"Who is *that*?" I whispered.

Cole removed his knuckle and looked away from both me and the figure in the corner.

"Victor," he said flatly.

At the name, the guy turned his face to look at us. Light brown hair, knotted and curled around his cheekbones. Maybe a few years older than me. My mind instantly went to the last time I'd seen him. Sitting in the back of Beck's Tahoe, wrists zip tied, looking at me. His lips silently forming the word *help*.

"Do you know each other?" I asked.

Victor shut his eyes, his shoulders shuddering, and then he said, "I — hold on —"

While I blinked, he shook out of his skin and into a pale gray wolf with dark facial markings, faster than I'd ever seen any of us shift. It was not quite effortless, but it worked naturally, like a snake rubbing out of its skin or a cicada stepping out of the brittle shell of its former self. No gagging. No pain. None of the agony of every other shift I'd ever witnessed or experienced.

The wolf shook itself, fluffing its coat, staring balefully up at me with Victor's brown eyes. I started to move away from the door, to give him an easy exit, but Cole said, voice strange, "Don't bother."

And then, as if on cue, the wolf sat down on its haunches

hard, ears trembling. He yawned, whining as he did, and then his whole body shook violently.

Cole and I turned our faces away at the same time, just as Victor gasped audibly, shifting back into his human form. Just like that. In and out. My mind couldn't quite grasp it. Out of the corner of my eye, I saw him tug up the blanket. More for the warmth than for the privacy, I was guessing.

Victor said, softly, "God*dammit*."

I looked at Cole, who had an utterly blank expression on his face, one that I was learning accompanied anything that mattered.

"Victor?" I said. "I'm Sam. Do you remember me?"

He was crouched on the floor now, rocking back and forth on his heels like he wasn't sure if he should sit or kneel. That and the shape of his mouth told me that he was in pain. He said, "I don't know. I don't think so. Maybe." He shot a glance at Cole, and Cole winced slightly.

"Well, I'm Beck's son," I said. Close enough to the truth and faster to spit out. "I'll help you, if I can."

· COLE ·

Sam was handling Victor a lot better than I had. I'd only stood and stared by the door, waiting to let him out if he managed to stay a wolf.

"That was . . . How do you shift that quickly?" Sam asked him.

Victor grimaced, glancing from Sam to me and back to Sam again. I could tell it was taking a big effort on his part to keep his voice steady. "It's worse from wolf to me. From me to wolf is easy. Too easy, man. I keep shifting back even though it's warm. That's what does it, right?"

"This is the hottest day we've had so far," Sam answered. "It's not supposed to be this warm the rest of the week."

"God," Victor said, "I didn't think it would be like this."

Sam looked at me, as if I had anything to do with anything. He stepped around me to get a folding chair, then sat down across from Victor. Suddenly, he reminded me of Beck. Everything about him was saying *interest* and *concern* and *sincerity*, from the curve of his shoulders to the lowering of his eyebrows over his heavy-lidded eyes. I couldn't remember if that was how Sam had first looked at me. I couldn't remember the first thing I'd said to him.

"Is this the first time you've shifted back?" he asked Victor.

Victor nodded. "That I can remember, anyway." He stared at me then, and I was very aware of my human body. At how I was just standing there, not in pain, not a wolf, just standing there.

Sam went on, like the whole thing was just a walk in the park, perfectly normal, "Are you hungry?"

"I —" Victor started. "Wait. I'm s—"

And he slid back to a wolf.

I could tell from the shock on Sam's face and the way he pressed a finger to one of his eyebrows that this wasn't normal, which made me feel a little better about finding the entire situation completely messed up. Victor the wolf stood there, eyeing the doorway and me and Sam, ears pricked and posture stiff.

I stared at Victor, remembering sitting in the hotel room after I'd met Beck, remembered saying, *You ready for the next big thing, Vic?*

"Cole," Sam said, not looking away from him. "How many times? How long have you been here?"

I shrugged, trying to look casual about it. "A half hour. He's been going back and forth the entire time. Is this normal?"

"No," Sam said emphatically, still looking at the wolf, who had crouched down close to the floor, staring back at him. "No, this isn't normal. If it's warm enough for him to stay human, he should be able to stay human for longer. Not this — I mean . . ." He trailed off as the wolf stood back up again.

Sam moved his knees away from Victor, in case he wanted to bolt, but suddenly Victor's ears flagged, and he began to tremble again. We both turned our faces away until he had changed into a human and had time to pull a blanket back over himself.

Victor groaned, lightly, and pressed his forehead into his hand.

Sam turned back around. "Does it hurt?"

"Ugh. Not a lot." He paused, shrugged his shoulders up by his ears, and kept them there. "God, I've been doing this all day. I just want to know when it will stop." He wouldn't look at me; his truthfulness was for Sam.

Sam said, "I wish I had an answer for you, Victor. Something is keeping you from staying in one form, and I don't know what it is."

Victor asked, "Is this the best it gets? I mean, I'm caught, right? This is what I get for listening to you, Cole. I should've figured out a long time ago that this is always how it goes."

But he still wasn't looking at me.

I remembered that day back in the hotel. Victor was crashing badly from one of his highs. These new lows of his were so low that even I, in my studied disinterest, could see that one day he wouldn't be able to climb back out of them. I'd been trying to help him when I convinced him to become a wolf with me. It wasn't entirely selfish. It wasn't just because I didn't want to try it alone.

If Sam hadn't been around, I would've told Victor that.

Sam knocked Victor's shoulder with a fist. "Hey. It's different when you're new. Everybody starts out unstable, and then we even out. Yeah, it's crap now, and you're taking crap to a whole new level, but when it gets really warm, this'll be behind you."

Victor looked bleakly at Sam, a face I'd seen a million times before because I had created it. Finally, he looked at me. "This should be you, you bastard," he said, and then he uncurled into a wolf again.

Sam threw up his hands, his palms open like an entreaty, and said, utterly frustrated, *"How — how — how . . ."* I realized how carefully he had been controlling his features and voice. It made my mind twist, almost as much as seeing Victor shift, to hear Sam go from oozing calm to being a hot mess. It meant that Sam had been perfectly capable of presenting a benevolent mask to me all along, but that he had *chosen* not to. Somehow it changed the entire way I thought of him.

Maybe that's what made me speak up. "Something is overriding the temperature," I said. "That's what I think. The heat is making him become human, but something else is telling his body to shift to wolf."

Sam looked at me. Not disbelieving, but not believing, either. "What else could do that?" he asked.

I looked at Victor, despising him for making this complicated. How hard would it have been to follow me into the wolf and back out, like he was supposed to? I wished I'd never come to the damned shed.

"Something in his brain chemistry?" I said. "Victor has a pituitary problem. Maybe the way it imbalances his levels is interfering with how he shifts."

Sam gave me a weird look then, but before he could say anything, the pale wolf's legs began to quiver. I looked away and then Victor was human again. Just like that.

• SAM •

I felt like I was watching the transformation of two people: Victor to wolf, and Cole to someone else. I was the only one standing here, staying the same.

I couldn't bring myself to leave Victor by himself like this, and so I stayed, and Cole stayed, too, minutes turning into hours while we waited for him to stabilize.

"There's no way to reverse it," Victor said flatly as the day began to ebb, not really a question.

I tried not to stiffen as my mind flashed back through the winter before I had rejoined Grace. Lying on the forest floor, fingers dug into the ground, head splitting open. Standing ankle deep in the snow, throwing up until I couldn't stand. Convulsed with fever, eyes shut against the agony of the light, praying for death.

"No," I said.

Cole's eyes were sharp on me, hearing my lie. I wanted to ask him, *If this is your friend, why am I the one sitting here next to him instead of you?*

As we sat there, waiting for Victor's next transformation, cooler air and dimming light stole in through the open door, evidence of the temperature dropping as the sun went down.

"Victor, I don't know how to make you stay human right now," I said. "But I think it's probably cold enough that if I got you outside, you'd probably stay a wolf. Do you want that? Do you want a break from shifting, even if it's not as you?"

Victor said, "Oh my God, yes," with such feeling that it stung.

"And who knows," I added. "Maybe once you get more stable, you'll —"

But there was no point finishing the sentence because Victor was already a wolf again, scrambling back from his proximity to me. "Cole!" I said hurriedly, jumping up. Cole jerked to life, pulling open the door. I was rewarded with a gush of cold air that made me wince, and the wolf shot out into the woods, tail low and ears flattened against his head.

I joined Cole in the doorway, watching Victor dart through the trees before stopping a safe distance away to gaze at us. Bare branches above his head trembled in the fitful breeze, touching the tips of his ears, but he didn't look away from us. We watched each other for several long minutes.

He stayed a wolf. I thought this feeling inside me was relief for him, but it pinched. I was already thinking about the next warm day and what would happen then.

I realized that Cole still stood beside me, his head cocked to one side, eyes on Victor.

Without thinking, I said, "If that's how you treat your friends when they need you, I'd hate to see how you treat other people."

Cole didn't exactly smile, but the edges of his mouth tightened into a vague expression that lived somewhere between contempt and disinterest. He didn't look away from Victor, but there was no compassion in his eyes.

I fought the desire to say something else, *any*thing else to get him to reply. I wanted him to hurt for Victor.

"He was right," Cole said from beside me, his eyes still on Victor. "That should be me."

I couldn't quite believe I'd heard him right. I'd underestimated him.

But then Cole added, "I'm the one who wants to get the hell out of this body."

Somehow, Cole never stopped amazing me.

I regarded him and said coldly, "And to think I thought for two seconds there that you gave a damn about Victor. It's all about your problems, *you* becoming a wolf. You just can't wait to get out of your own head, can you?"

"If you were in here, you might want that, too," Cole said, and now he did smile, a cruel, lopsided thing that crawled farther up one side of his face than the other. "I can't be the only one who wants the wolf."

He wasn't.

Shelby had preferred it, too. Broken Shelby, barely human, even when she wore the face of a girl.

"You are," I said.

Cole's smile broke into a silent laugh. "You're so naive, Ringo. How well did you know Beck?"

I looked at him, at his condescending expression, and I just wanted him gone. I wished Beck had never brought him back. He should've left Cole and Victor in Canada or wherever they'd come from.

"Well enough to know that he made a way better human than you ever will," I said. Cole's expression didn't change; it was like unkind words didn't make it to his ears. I clenched and unclenched my teeth, angry that I'd let him get to me.

"Wanting to be a wolf doesn't automatically make you a bad person," Cole said, voice mild. "And wanting to be human doesn't make you a good one."

I was fifteen again, sitting in my room in Beck's house, arms wrapped around my legs, hiding from the wolf inside me. Winter had already stolen Beck the week before, and Ulrik would be gone soon as well. Then me and my books and guitar would lay untouched until spring, just as Beck's books already lay abandoned. Forgotten in the self-oblivion that was the wolf.

I didn't want to have this conversation with Cole. I said, "Are you going to shift soon?"

"Not a chance."

"Then please go back to the house. I'm cleaning this place up." I paused. And then, as much to convince me as him, "And it's what you did to Victor that makes you a bad person. Not wanting to be a wolf."

Cole looked at me, the same blank expression on his face, and then he headed back toward the house. I turned away from him and went back into the shed.

Like Beck had done before me, I folded up the blanket Victor had left behind and swept out the dust and hair from the floor, and then I checked the watercooler and went through the food bins and made a note of what needed to be added to them. I went to the notepad that we kept by the boat battery — a list of scrawled names, sometimes with a date beside them, sometimes with a description of the trees, because they told time when we couldn't. Beck's way of keeping track of who was human and when.

The open page was still of last year's names, ending with Beck's, a far shorter list than that of the year before, which was in turn a shorter list than that of the year before it. I swallowed and flipped to the next page. I wrote the year on top and added Victor's name and the date beside it. Cole's name really ought to have been on there, too, but I doubted Beck had explained how we logged ourselves in. I didn't want to add Cole's name. It would mean officially admitting him to the pack, to my family, and I didn't want to.

For a long time I stood looking at that blank page with just Victor's name on it, and then I added my own.

I knew it didn't belong there anymore, not really, but it was a list of who was human, right?

And who was more human than me?

Chapter Twenty-Four

· GRACE ·

I headed into the trees.

The woods were still dormant and leafless, but the warmer air woke up a cacophony of damp spring smells that had been masked by the cold. Birds trilled at one another overhead, flicking from underbrush to higher branches, leaving shaking boughs in their wake.

I felt it in my bones: I was home.

Only a few yards into the wood, I heard the underbrush crackling behind me. My heart raced as I paused, interrupting the squish and crackle of the forest floor beneath my feet. Again, I heard the rustle again, no closer but no farther, either. I didn't turn, but I knew it had to be a wolf. I felt no fear — only companionship.

I heard the occasional stir of leaves as the wolf moved to follow me. Still not very close — just observing me from a careful distance. Part of me wanted to see which wolf it was, but the other part was too thrilled by the presence of a wolf to risk scaring it off. So we just walked together, me with steady progress and the wolf with intermittent bursts of movement to keep up with me.

The sun that shot through the still-naked branches above was warm on my shoulders, and I stretched out my hands on either side of me as I walked, soaking in as much of it as I could, trying to erase the feel of last night's fever. It felt like the further I got from my anger, the more I could feel that something wasn't right inside me.

Stepping through the underbrush, I remembered Sam taking me to the golden clearing in the woods and wished he was here with me now, listening to the unfamiliar racing of my heart. It wasn't like we spent all of our time together or like I didn't know how to occupy myself without him — he had his bookstore work and I had school and tutoring — but right now, I felt uneasy. Yes, the fever was gone, but I didn't feel like it was gone for good. I felt as if I could still sense it singing restlessly in my blood, waiting to reappear the next time the wolves called.

I kept walking. Here the trees were sparser, new saplings discouraged by the presence of the massive pine trees. The smell of the lake was stronger, and I saw a wolf paw print in the soft dirt of the forest floor. Underneath the dull green of the pines, I wrapped my arms around myself, cold without the sun on me.

To my left side, I saw a flash of movement: a brown-gray coat, the same color as the trunks of the pine trees. Finally, I saw the wolf who'd been accompanying me as he paused long enough for me to get a good look at him. He didn't flinch when

I took in his bright green, human eyes and the curious tilt to his ears. Beyond him, I saw the sparkle of the lake through the trees.

Are you one of the new wolves? I wondered in my head, but I didn't say it aloud, in case my voice startled him. He tilted his face upward, and I saw his nose working in my direction. I felt I knew what he wanted: I slowly lifted a hand in his direction, proffering my palm. He recoiled, as if from the scent, not from the movement, because after he had jerked back, his nose continued working.

I didn't have to bring my palm to my own nose to know what he was smelling, because I could still smell it myself. The sweet, rotten scent of almonds, trapped between my fingers and under my nails. It seemed more ominous than the fever itself had. It seemed to say, *This is more than just a fever.*

My heart thumped in my chest, although I still wasn't afraid of the brown-coated wolf. I crouched on the forest floor and clutched my arms around my knees, my limbs suddenly shaky with either knowledge or fever.

I heard an explosion of sound as several birds burst from the underbrush; both the brown wolf and I flinched. A gray wolf, the cause of the birds' surprise, slunk closer. He was larger than the brown wolf but not as brave; his eyes held interest but the set of both his ears and his tail were wary as he crept closer. His nose, too, twitched, scenting the air as he approached.

Motionless, I watched as a black wolf — I recognized him as Paul — appeared behind the gray one, followed by another wolf I didn't know. They moved like a school of fish, constantly touching, jostling, communicating without words. Soon there were six wolves, all keeping their distance, all watching me, all scenting the air.

Inside me, the wordless *something* that had given me my fever and slicked my skin with this scent hummed. Not painful, not at the moment, but not *right*, either. I knew why I wanted Sam so badly now.

I was afraid.

The wolves circled me, wary of my human form but curious of the smell. Maybe they were waiting for me to shift.

But I couldn't shift. This was my body, for better or for worse, no matter how hard the *something* inside me groaned and burned and begged to be released.

The last time I had been in these woods, surrounded by wolves, I had been prey. I had been helpless, pinned to the ground by the weight of my own blood, staring at the winter sky. They had been animals and I had been human. Now the line wasn't so distinct. There was no threat of attack from them. Just worried curiosity.

I moved, gingerly, to stretch out my stiff arms, and one of the wolves whined, high and anxious, like a mother dog to her pup.

I felt as if the fever was waking inside of me.

Isabel had told me that her mother, a doctor, once said that terminal patients often seemed to have an eerie sense of their condition, even before it was diagnosed. At the time, I'd scoffed, but now I knew what she meant — because I *felt* it.

There was something really wrong with me, something I didn't think doctors would know how to fix, and these wolves knew it.

I huddled under the trees, my arms wrapped around my legs again, and watched the wolves watching me. After several long moments, the large gray wolf, never taking his eyes from mine, sank to his haunches, slowly, as if he might change his mind at any moment. It was utterly unnatural. Utterly unwolflike.

I held my breath.

Then the black wolf glanced to the gray wolf and back at me before lying down as well, resting his head on his paws. He rolled his eyes toward me, ears still tilted watchfully. One by one, the wolves all lay down, forming a loose circle around me. The forest was still as the wolves remained, protective and patient. Waiting with me for something none of us had words for.

Far away, a loon called, eerie and slow. They always sounded plaintive to me. Like they were calling for someone they didn't expect to answer.

The black wolf — Paul — stretched his nose to me, nostrils moving slightly, and he whined. The sound was a soft, breathy echo of the loon, anxious and uncertain.

Just under my skin, something stretched and strained. My body felt like a battleground for an invisible war.

Surrounded by wolves, I sat on the forest floor as the sun sank in the sky and the shadows of the pines grew, and I wondered how much time I had.

Chapter Twenty-Five

· GRACE ·

Eventually, the wolves left me.

I sat there, alone, trying to feel every cell of my body, trying to understand what was happening inside. The phone rang — Isabel.

I answered. I had to return to the real world, even if it wasn't as real as I wanted it to be.

"Rachel was very happy to point out that you'd asked her, not me, to pick up your homework and copy notes for you," Isabel said after I said hello.

"She's in more of my cla —"

"Save it. I don't care; I didn't want the extra work of picking stuff up, anyway. I was more amused by the idea that she'd think that it was a status symbol." Isabel did sound amused; I felt a little bad for Rachel. "Anyway, I was calling to find out how infectious you are."

How could I explain how I felt? And to Isabel?

I couldn't.

I answered her truthfully by making it a narrow truth.

"I don't think I am infectious," I said. "Why?"

"I want to go someplace with you, but I don't want to get the bubonic plague if I do."

"Come to the backyard," I told her. "I'm in the woods."

Isabel's voice managed to convey equal parts disgust and disbelief. "The. Woods. Of course, I should've known; that's where sick people always go. Personally, I would rather go someplace and let off some steam with some good nonproductive retail therapy, but I guess the woods would be a rewarding and socially acceptable alternative. All the kids are doing it now. Should I bring skis? A tent?"

"Just you," I said.

"Do I want to know what you were doing in the woods?" she asked.

"I was walking," I told her. The truth, but not all of it.

I didn't know how to tell her the rest.

Later, Isabel had to shout for me beside the trees a few times and wait a few minutes for me to come out of the darkening forest, but I didn't feel guilty about it — I was still too lost in the revelation I'd had while surrounded by the wolves.

"Aren't you supposed to be dying or something?" Isabel demanded as soon as she saw me picking my way back in the direction of my house. I'd made my point with my mother; now it was time to go back, and I figured she wouldn't try to initiate a serious conversation if I had someone else in tow.

Isabel stood by the bird feeder, hands shoved in her pockets, the fur-lined hood on her shoulders hunched up around her ears. As I approached, her eyes flicked between me and a faded white stain of bird poop on the edge of the feeder. It was clearly bothering her. She was done up in full Isabel style — slashed haircut brutally and beautifully styled around her face and her eyes ink stained and dramatic. She really had been planning on going someplace with me; I did feel a little guilty, then, as if I'd refused her for frivolous reasons. Her voice was a few degrees colder than the air. "What part of your treatment involves trooping out through the woods when it's thirty-seven degrees outside?"

It *was* getting pretty cold; the ends of my fingers were bright pink. "Is it thirty-seven? It wasn't when I went out."

"Well, it is now," Isabel said. "I saw your mom when I was walking back here, and tried to convince her to let you go for a panini in Duluth tonight, but she said no. I'm trying not to take it personally." She wrinkled her nose when I came up alongside her, and together we headed back toward the house.

"Yeah, I'm trying to ignore how mad I am at her right now," I confessed. Isabel waited for me to slide the back door open for her. She didn't comment on my anger, and I didn't expect her to; Isabel was always angry at her parents, so I doubted it even registered on her radar as unusual. "I can fake paninis here, sort of. I don't really have good bread for it." I didn't really want to, though.

"I'd rather wait for the real thing," Isabel said. "Let's order pizza."

"Ordering pizza" in Mercy Falls meant calling up the local pizza joint, Mario's, and paying a six-dollar delivery charge. A price too dear after Sam's studio visit.

"I'm broke," I said regretfully.

"I'm not," Isabel replied.

She said this just as we came inside, and Mom, who was still parked on the couch with Sam's book, looked up sharply. Good. I hoped she thought we were talking about her.

I looked at Isabel. "Why don't we go to my room? Are we getting —?"

Isabel waved a hand at me to be quiet; she was already on the phone with Mario's, ordering a large cheese and mushroom pizza. She kicked off her fat-heeled boots on the back-door mat and followed me into my room, flirting effortlessly with whoever was on the other end of the phone as she did.

In my room, it seemed hideously warm in comparison to outside. I started to peel off my sweater as Isabel clicked her phone off and crashed sideways on the bed. She said, "We're getting free toppings. Bet me we're getting free toppings."

"I don't have to bet," I said. "That was practically phone sex on an extra-thin crust."

"It's what I do," Isabel said. "So look. I didn't bring my homework. I basically did it in my free period in school."

I gave her a look. "If you crap out of school now, you won't get into a good college, and then you'll be stuck here in Mercy Falls forever." Unlike Rachel and Isabel, I wasn't filled with horror at that idea. But I knew that neither of them could imagine worse fates.

Isabel made a face. "Thanks, Mom. I'll keep that in mind."

I shrugged and tugged out the book that Rachel had brought over earlier. "Well, I *do* have homework, and I want to get into college. At the very least, I have to do my reading for history tonight. Is that okay?"

Isabel laid her cheek on my comforter and closed her eyes. "You don't have to entertain me. It's enough to get out of the house."

I sat down at the head of the bed; the movement jostled Isabel but she kept her eyes shut. If Sam were here, and if he were me, he would have asked Isabel how bad things were and if she was doing okay. It wouldn't have occurred to me to ask the question before I'd met him, but I'd heard him ask things like that often enough now to know how it was done.

"How are things?" I asked. It felt weird in my mouth, like it must not sound as sincere as when Sam asked it.

Isabel made a loud, bored noise and opened her eyes. "That's what my mom's therapist asks." She stretched in a way that defined the word *languorous* and said, "I'm getting something to drink. Do you guys have soda?"

I was sort of relieved to be let off the hook so easily and wondered if I was supposed to ask again. Sam might have. I couldn't think like him for that long, though, so I just said, "There are some in the door of the fridge, and some in the drawer on the right."

"You want any?" Isabel asked, sliding off the bed. One of my bookmarks had fallen to the floor and stuck to her bare foot, and she made a triangle of one of her legs while she pulled it off.

I considered. My stomach felt a little twisty. "Ginger ale, if there's any left."

Isabel stalked out of the room and returned with a can of regular soda and a can of ginger ale, which she handed to me.

She clicked on the clock radio by the bed stand; it began humming out Sam's favorite alt station, a little fuzzy because it was from somewhere south of Duluth. I sighed; it wasn't my favorite music, but it reminded me of him, even more than his book sitting on the bed stand or his forgotten backpack on the floor beside my shelves. Missing him seemed bigger now that the sun was almost down.

"I feel like I'm at an open-mic night," Isabel said, and switched to a stronger Duluth pop station. She stretched on her stomach next to me where Sam would normally lie and popped the top of her soda. "What are you looking at? Read. I'm just chilling."

She seemed to mean it, so there was no reason for me to not open my history text. I didn't want to read, though. I just wanted to curl my arms around myself and lie on my bed and miss Sam.

· ISABEL ·

It was nice at first, just lying in bed doing nothing, with no parents or memories intruding. The radio played quietly next to me, and Grace frowned at her book, turning her pages forward and occasionally backward to frown harder at something. Her mother clunked around in the rest of the house, and the smell of burnt toast wafted under the door. It was comfortingly someone else's life. And it was nice to be with a friend but not have to talk. I could almost ignore the fact of Grace's illness.

After a while, I reached across to the nightstand, where a book with tattered edges lay by the clock radio. I couldn't imagine anyone ever reading a book enough to make it look like that. It looked like it had been driven over by a school bus after someone had taken a bath with it. The cover said it was poetry by Rainer Maria Rilke, with facing translations from the German. It didn't sound riveting, and I generally relegated poetry to one of the lower circles of hell, but I didn't have anything else to do, so I picked it up and opened it.

It fell open to a dog-eared page marked up with blue handwriting in the margins, and a few lines underlined: "*Ah, to whom can we fall apart? Not to angels, nor men, and even the most clever of animals see that we are not surely at home in our interpreted world*," and next to them was written, in ropey handwriting I didn't recognize, *findigen = knowing, gedeuteten = interpreted?* and other notes and random bits of German. I lifted the page closer to me to look at a tiny notation in the corner and realized that the book must've been Sam's, because it smelled like Beck's house. That scent brought back a rush of memories: Jack lying in a bed, seeing him turn into a wolf in front of my eyes, watching him die.

My eyes dropped again to the page. "*Oh and night, the night, when a wind full of infinite space gnaws at our faces.*"

I didn't think I liked poetry any better than before I'd picked up the book. I set the volume back down on the nightstand and laid my cheek on the bedspread stretched over the pillow. This must have been the side that Sam slept on when he snuck in here, because I recognized his scent. How ballsy he had been to come here night after night, just to be with Grace. I imagined him lying right here, Grace next to him. I had seen them kiss before — the way that Sam's hands pressed on Grace's back when he thought no one would see and the way that the hardness of Grace's face disappeared entirely when he did. It was easy to picture them lying together here, kissing, tangled. Sharing breath, lips pressed urgently against necks and shoulders and fingertips. I felt hungry suddenly, for something that I didn't have and couldn't name. It made me think of Cole's hand on my collarbone and how his breath had been so hot in my mouth, and suddenly I was sure that I was going to call him or find him tomorrow if such a thing was possible.

I pushed myself back up onto my elbows, trying to pull my brain from thoughts clouded with hands on hips and the smell of Sam on the pillow, and said, "I wonder what Sam's doing right now."

Grace had a page pinched between two fingers; she wasn't quite frowning — my words had wiped the frown off her face and replaced it with something more uncertain. I kicked myself for saying what I was actually thinking.

Grace gently laid down the page and smoothed it. Then she pressed her fingers to one of her flushed cheeks and smoothed the skin down to her chin with the same gesture. Finally, she said, "He said he'd try to call me tonight."

She was still looking at me in that blank, unsure way, so I added, "I was just wondering if any of the wolves are human right now, besides him. I met one of them." It was a line close enough to the truth that no bishops would blush while delivering it.

Grace's face cleared. "I know. He told me about one. You really met him?"

What the hell. I told her. "I brought him to Beck's the night you went to the hospital."

Her eyes widened, but before she had time to ask me more, the doorbell sounded — a loud, obnoxious bell that went on and on in multiple tones.

"Pizza!" her mom shouted, her voice too bright, and anything else Grace and I might have said to each other was lost.

· GRACE ·

The pizza arrived and Isabel gave a piece to Mom, which I wouldn't have done, and Mom retreated to her studio so we could have the living room. By now, the sky was black outside the glass door to the deck, and it was impossible to tell if it was seven P.M. or midnight. I sat on one end of the couch with a plate in my lap and a single piece of pizza staring back at me, and Isabel sat on the other end with two pieces on her plate. She blotted her pieces delicately with a paper towel, careful not to disturb the mushrooms. In the background, *Pretty Woman* was on and Julia Roberts's character was shopping at stores that Isabel would look at home in. The pizza lay in its box on the coffee table in between us and the television. There was a mountain of toppings.

"Eat, Grace," Isabel said. She offered me the roll of paper towels.

I looked at the pizza and tried to imagine it as food. It was amazing how just a single slice of cheese and mushroom pizza lying on a plate, with oozing, greasy strings of mozzarella trailing from it, could do what a walk in the woods hadn't: make me feel utterly sick. Looking at the food, my stomach was rolling inside me, but it was more than nausea. It was whatever had consumed me before: the fever that wasn't a fever. The sickness that was more than just a headache, more than just a stomachache. The illness that was me, somehow.

Isabel was looking at me, and I knew a question was coming. But I didn't really want to open my mouth. The vague something I'd felt in the woods was chewing at my belly now, and I was afraid of what I would say if I spoke.

The pizza sat in front of me, looking like nothing I could imagine swallowing.

I felt so much more vulnerable than I'd felt in the woods with the wolves around me. I didn't want Isabel with me now. Not Mom. I wanted Sam.

· ISABEL ·

Grace looked gray. She was staring at her pizza as if she was waiting for it to bite her, and finally she said, her hand on her stomach, "I'll be right back."

She pushed up off the couch, a little lethargic, and headed into the kitchen. When she returned, holding another ginger ale and a palm full of pills, I asked, "Are you feeling sick again?" I turned down the volume on the television a little, even though it was my favorite part of the movie.

Grace tipped all the pills into her mouth and swallowed them with a quick, efficient slug of ginger ale. "A little. People feel sicker in the evenings, right? That's what I read."

I looked at her. I thought that probably she knew. I thought probably she was already thinking what I was thinking, but I didn't want to say it. Instead, I asked, "What did they tell you at the hospital?"

"That it was just a fever. Just the flu," she said, and the way she said it, I knew she was remembering telling me about when she first got bitten. How she had thought she had the flu. How we both knew that it hadn't been the flu then.

So, finally, I said the thing that had been bothering me since I'd gotten to her house. "Grace, you smell. Like that wolf we found. You know this has to do with the wolves."

She rubbed a single finger back and forth on the rim of her plate where the decorative swirl was, as if she would rub it right off. "I know."

The phone rang, just then, and we both knew who it was. Grace looked at me and her fingers all went perfectly still.

"Don't tell Sam," she said.

Chapter Twenty-Six

· SAM ·

That night, because I couldn't sleep, I made bread.

Most of my sleeplessness was because of Grace; the idea of going up to bed and lying there alone, waiting for sleep again, was completely intolerable. But part of it was because Cole was still in the house. He was so full of restless energy — pacing the floor, trying out the sound system, sitting on the couch, watching television, then jumping up — that I was, too. It was like being in the presence of an exploding star.

So, bread making. It was something I had learned from Ulrik, who was a tremendous bread snob. He refused to eat most store-bought bread, and combined with the fact that when I was ten, I refused to eat anything but bread, a lot of baking got done that year. Beck thought we were both impossible, and wouldn't have anything to do with our neuroses. So that meant plenty of mornings were spent in each other's company, me on the floor leaning against the kitchen cabinets, curled around the guitar that Paul had gifted me, and Ulrik pounding some dough into submission and swearing pleasantly about me being in the way.

One day not long into the year, Ulrik pulled me to my feet to have me make the dough; it was also the same day that Beck had found out about Ulrik's doctor's appointment, a memory I'd been considering since I'd seen Victor struggling to stay human. Beck came storming into the kitchen, clearly furious, while Paul drifted in behind him, hovering in the door, looking less like he was concerned and more like he was hoping for an interesting collision.

"Tell me that Paul is a liar," Beck announced, while Ulrik handed me a can of yeast. "Tell me you did not go to a doctor."

Paul looked like he was about to bust out laughing, and Ulrik looked pretty close to that as well.

Beck raised his hands up like he wanted to strangle Ulrik. "You did. You really went. You crazy bastard. I told you it wouldn't do any good."

Paul finally started laughing as Ulrik grinned. Paul said, "Tell him what he gave you, Ulrik. Tell him what he wrote you."

But Ulrik seemed to realize that Beck wouldn't get the punch line, so, still smiling, he just pointed toward the fridge and said, "Milk, Sam."

"Haldol," said Paul. "He goes in for werewolfism, comes out with a script for antipsychotics."

"You think this is funny?" Beck demanded.

Ulrik finally looked at Beck and made a *so what* gesture with one hand. "Come on, Beck. He thought I was crazy. I told him everything that was going on — that I turned into a wolf in the winter, and the — the — what is it? — nauseous? nausea? — and the date I turned back into a human this year.

All the symptoms. I told him the honest-to-God truth, and he listened and nodded and wrote me a script for a crazy drug."

"Where did you go?" Beck asked. "Which hospital?"

"St. Paul." He and Paul hooted at Beck's expression. "What, you thought I marched into Mercy Falls General and told them I was a werewolf?"

Beck wasn't amused. "So — just like that? He didn't believe you? Draw blood? Anything?"

Ulrik snorted and, forgetting that I was supposed to be making the dough, started adding flour. "He couldn't get me out the door fast enough. Like crazy was catching."

Paul said, "I wish I could've been there."

Beck shook his head. "You two are idiots." But his voice was now fond as he pushed past Paul, out of the kitchen. "How many times do I have to tell you, you want a doctor to believe you, you're gonna have to bite them."

Paul and Ulrik exchanged looks. "Is he serious?" Paul asked Ulrik.

"I don't think so," Ulrik said.

The conversation drifted to something else as Ulrik finished the dough and put it in to rise, but I never forgot the lesson for the day: Doctors weren't likely to be any help in this particular battle of ours.

My mind returned to Victor. I couldn't shake the image of him sliding effortlessly from human to wolf and back again.

Apparently, Cole couldn't, either, because he walked into the kitchen and hiked himself up onto the center island with an annoyed expression. He wrinkled his nose at the heavy yeast scent in the kitchen and said, "I should be surprised that you're baking, but I'm not. So, I'm again struck with the unfairness that Victor can't stay human and I can't stay wolf. Should be the other way around."

I tried to keep the irritation out of my voice as I replied, "Yeah. I get it. You want to be a wolf. You do not want to be Cole. You want to be a wolf. You've made it really clear. Well, I have no magic formula to make you stay a wolf. Sorry." I noticed that he had a bottle of whiskey sitting on the countertop next to him. "Where did that come from?"

"Cabinet," Cole said. His voice was pleasant. "Why does it bother you so much?"

"I'm not really crazy about you getting drunk."

"I'm not really crazy about being sober," Cole replied. "I mean, you never really said what your big problem was with me wanting to be a wolf."

I turned away from him to the sink to scrub the flour off my hands; it became gluey between my fingers as the water hit it. I considered what I wanted to say, while I slowly scrubbed both hands clean. "I went through a lot of trouble to stay human. I know someone who died trying. I would give anything to have the rest of my family back right now, but they have to spend the winter in those woods, not even remembering who they are. Being human is a . . ." I was going to say *extraordinary privilege* but thought it sounded too grandiose. "There's no meaning to life as a wolf. If you don't have memories, it's like you never existed. You can't leave anything behind. I mean — how can I defend *humanity*? It's all that matters. Why would you throw that away?"

I didn't mention Shelby. Shelby, the only other person I'd ever known who wanted to be a wolf. I knew why she had abandoned her human life. Didn't mean that I agreed with it, though. I hoped she'd gotten her wish and was a wolf for good now.

Cole took a mouthful of whiskey and winced as he swallowed it. "You already answered the question right in there. The not remembering bit. Avoidance is a wonderful therapy."

I turned to face him. He seemed unreal in this kitchen. Most people had an acquired kind of beauty — they became better-looking the longer you knew them and the better you loved them. But Cole had unfairly skipped to the end of the game, all jaggedly handsome and Hollywood-looking, not needing any love to get there.

"I don't think so," I said. "I don't think that's a good reason."

"Don't you?" Cole asked curiously. I was surprised to see that there was no malice in his expression, just vague interest. "Then why do you piss in the upstairs bathroom?"

I looked at him.

"Oh, you didn't think I noticed it? Yeah. You always go upstairs to pee. I mean, I guess it could be because the downstairs bathroom is gross, but it seems fine to me." Cole jumped down from the counter, slightly unsteady when he landed. "So seems to me you're avoiding that tub. Am I right?"

I didn't see how he could know my backstory, but I guessed it wasn't a secret. Maybe Beck had even told him, though it made me feel a little weird to think that he had. "That's pretty minor," I said. "Avoiding a bathtub because your parents tried to kill you in one isn't the same as avoiding your entire life by becoming a wolf."

Cole smiled widely at me. The alcohol was making him an extremely jovial Cole. "I'll make you a deal, Ringo. You stop avoiding that bathtub and I'll stop avoiding my life."

"Yeah, right." The only time I'd been in a tub since my parents was when Grace had put me in one to get me warm last winter. But at that point, I'd been halfway to a wolf. I barely even knew where I was. And it was Grace, who I trusted. Not Cole.

"No, seriously. I'm a very goal-oriented person," Cole said. "Happiness, I think, comes from achieving goals, right? God, this stuff is good." He put the whiskey down on the counter. "I feel überwarm and fuzzy. So what do you say? You jump in that bathtub and I devote myself to keeping myself and Victor human? I mean, since the tub is such a minor thing?"

I smiled ruefully. He had known all along that there was no danger of me getting close to that bathroom. "Touché," I said, randomly remembering the last time I'd heard the expression: Isabel standing in the bookstore, drinking my green tea. It seemed like years ago.

· COLE ·

I smiled broadly at him. I was infused with the pleasant, slow warmth that could only be achieved through the consumption of hard liquor. I told him, "You see, we are both majorly messed up, Ringo. Issues up the wazoo."

Sam just looked at me. He didn't really look like Ringo; more like a sleepy, yellow-eyed John Lennon, if we were being specific, but "John" wasn't as catchy of a name to call him. I felt a sudden rush of compassion toward him. Poor kid couldn't even piss downstairs because his parents had tried to kill him. Seemed pretty harsh.

"Feel like an intervention?" I asked. "I think tonight feels like a good night for an intervention, man."

"Thanks, I'll deal with my issues on my own," Sam said.

"C'mon." I offered him the bottle of whiskey, but he shook his head. "It'll make you relax," I informed him. "Enough of this and you'll be paddling that tub to China."

Sam's voice was slightly less friendly. "Not tonight."

"Dude," I said, "I am trying to bond here. I am trying to help you. I am trying to help me." I took his arm in a comradely way. Sam pulled at my grip, but not like he meant it. I tugged him toward the kitchen door.

"Cole," Sam said, "you're completely smashed. Let go."

"And I'm telling *you* that this entire process would be easier if you were, too. Are you reconsidering the whiskey option?" We were in the hall now. Sam tugged again.

"I'm not. Cole. Come on. Are you serious?" He jerked at my grip. We were a few feet away from the bathroom door now. Sam bucked, and I had to use both my arms to keep him moving forward. He was surprisingly strong; I hadn't thought someone as weedy-looking as him could put up such a good fight.

"I help you, you help me. Just think of how much better you'll feel when you've faced your demons," I said. I wasn't sure if this was true, but it *sounded* good. I had to admit, too, that a big part of me was curious as hell to see what Sam would do when faced with the mighty bathtub.

I jostled us both into the doorway and used my elbow to hit the light switch.

"Cole," Sam said, his voice suddenly quieter.

It was just a bathtub. Just an empty tub of the most ordinary variety: ivory-colored tile surrounding it, white shower curtain pulled aside. A dead spider next to the drain. At the sight of it, Sam suddenly struggled in my arms, hard enough that it took all my strength to hold him. I felt his muscles knotted beneath my fingers, straining against me.

"Please," he said.

"It's just a bathtub," I said, bracing my arms around him. But I didn't need to. He'd gone completely limp in my arms.

· SAM ·

For one spare moment, I saw it for what it was, the way I must have seen it for the first seven years of my life: just an ordinary bathroom, faded and utilitarian. But then my eyes found the tub and I couldn't stand. I was

sitting at my dining room table. My father sat next to me; my mother hadn't sat next to me in weeks. My mother said

I don't think I can love him anymore. That's not Sam. That's a thing that looks like him, sometimes.

There were peas on my plate. I didn't eat peas. I was surprised to see them there because my mother knew this. I couldn't stop looking at them.

My father said

I know.

Now I was being shaken by Cole. "You aren't dying," he said. "It just feels like it."

And then my parents were holding my thin arms. I was being presented to a bathtub, though it wasn't evening and I hadn't been undressed. My parents were asking me to get in, and I wouldn't, and I think they were glad, because my refusal made it easier for them than trusting compliance. My father lifted me into the water.

"Sam," Cole said.

I was sitting in the bathtub in my clothing, the water turning my dark jeans black, feeling the water wick up through my favorite blue T-shirt with the white stripe, feeling the fabric stick to my ribs, and I thought, for a minute, for one, merciful moment, that it was a game.

"Sam," Cole repeated.

I didn't understand, and then, I did.

It wasn't when my mother wouldn't look at me, just gazing at the edge of the bathtub and swallowing, over and over. Or when my father reached behind him and said my mother's name to get her to look at him. Or even when she took one of the razor blades from his proffered hand, her fingers careful, as if she were selecting a fragile cracker from a plate of delicacies.

It was when she finally looked at me.

At my eyes. My wolf's eyes.

I saw the decision in her face. The letting go.

And that was when they had to hold me down.

Sam was somewhere else. That was the only way to put it. His eyes were just — empty. I hauled him out to the living room and shook him. "Snap out of it. We're out! Look around, Sam. We're out."

When I let go of his arms, Sam slumped to the floor, back against the wall, putting his head in his hands. He was suddenly all elbows and knees and joints folded up against one another, making him faceless.

I didn't know how I felt, seeing him there. Knowing I'd done it, whatever *it* was. It was making me hate him. "Sam?" I said.

After a long moment, he said, not lifting his head, his voice strange and low and thin, "Just leave me alone. Leave me alone. What did I ever do to you?" His breaths were uneven; I heard them catching in his chest. Not like sobs. More like suffocation.

I looked down at him, and suddenly anger bubbled up through me. It shouldn't have affected him this badly. It was just a damned bathroom. It was he who was making me this cruel — I hadn't done anything to him except shown him a damned tub. I wasn't that person he thought I was.

"Beck chose this, too," I told him, because he wouldn't say anything now to contradict me. "That's what he told me. He said that he got everything he wanted in life after law school, and he was miserable. He told me he was going to kill himself, but a guy named Paul convinced him there was another way out."

Sam was silent except for his ragged inhalations.

"That's the same thing he offered me," I said. "Only I can't stay a wolf. Don't tell me that you don't want to hear it. You're just as bad as I am. Look at you. Don't talk to me about damage."

He didn't move, so I did. I went to the back door and threw it open. The night had become savage and cold while I was drinking, and I was rewarded with a wrenching twist in my gut.

I escaped.

Chapter Twenty-Seven

· SAM ·

I went through the actions of punching down the dough and shaping the loaf and getting the bread in the oven. My head was humming with words that were too clipped and unrelated for me to form into lyrics. I was halfway here, halfway somewhere else, standing in Beck's same old kitchen on a night that could've been now or ten years ago.

The faces on the cabinet photos smiled back at me, dozens of different permutations of me and Beck, Beck and Ulrik, Paul and Derek, Ulrik and me. Faces waiting to be reinhabited. The photos looked faded and old in the dull nighttime of the kitchen. I remembered Beck taping them up, when they were brand-new, concrete proof of our ties.

I thought about how my parents so easily decided not to love me, just because I couldn't hold on to my skin. And about how I'd been so quick to shun Beck when I'd thought that he'd infected the three new wolves against their will. It was like I could feel my parents' imperfect love running through my veins. So quick to judge.

When I finally noticed that Cole was gone, I opened the back door and retrieved his clothing from the yard. I stood there, holding the cold bundle in my hands, and let the night air cut down inside me, past the layers of everything that made me Sam and human, to the creeping wolf that I imagined still lurking inside me. I played back Cole's dialogue in my head.

Was he really asking for my help?

I jumped when the phone rang. The phone was missing from the base in the kitchen, so I went into the living room and sat on the arm of the sofa while I picked up the receiver in there. *Grace,* I hoped fiercely. *Grace.*

"Hi?" It occurred to me, too late, that if Grace was calling this late, there was something wrong.

But it wasn't Grace's voice that answered, though it was female. "Who is this?"

"Excuse me?" I said.

"Someone called my cell from this number. Twice."

"Who is *this*?" I asked.

"Angie Baranova."

"When did they call?"

"Yesterday. Earlyish. No message."

Cole. Had to be. *Sloppy bastard.* "Must've been a wrong number," I said.

"Must've been," she echoed. "Because only, like, *four* people have this number."

I amended my opinion of Cole. *Stupid bastard.*

"Like I said," I insisted, "a wrong number."

"Or Cole," Angie said.

"Excuse me?"

She gave an unfunny, ugly little laugh. "Whoever you are, I know you wouldn't say anything even if he was standing right beside you. Because Cole's really good at that, isn't he? Getting you to do what he wants? Well, if he is there and it was him calling my number, tell him I've got a new cell. It's one 917-get-out-of-my-life. Thanks."

And she hung up.

I clicked TALK again to hang up the phone and leaned to return it to the cradle. I looked at Beck's stack of books on the end table. Beside them was a picture frame with a photo Ulrik had taken of Beck right after Paul had sprayed mustard on him while we barbecued burgers. Beck squinted at me, smears of unreal yellow caught in his eyebrows and globbed in his eyelashes.

"Sounds like you picked a real winner," I told Beck's photo.

· GRACE ·

That night, I lay in my bed, trying to forget the way the wolves had looked at me and trying to pretend that Sam was with me. Blinking in the blackness, I tugged Sam's pillow closer to me, but I'd used up all of his scent, and it was just a pillow again. I pushed it back to his side of the bed and lifted my hand to my nostrils instead, trying to tell if I still smelled like the wolves in the woods. I pictured Isabel's face when she said, *You know this has to do with the wolves*, and tried to interpret what her expression had meant. Disgust? Like I was contagious? Or was it pity?

If Sam were here, I would've whispered, *Do you think dying people know they're dying?*

I made a face at myself in the darkness. I knew I was being melodramatic.

I wanted to believe I was just being melodramatic.

Laying a hand flat on my belly, I thought about the gnawing ache that lived a few inches below my fingers. Right now, the pain seemed dull, slumbering.

I pressed my fingers into my skin.

I know you're there.

It seemed pitiful to be sitting awake in bed, contemplating my mortality alone, while Sam was within easy driving distance. I shot a futile glance up toward my parents' room, irritated that they'd deprived me of his company when I most needed it.

If I died now, I'd never go to college. I'd never live on my own. I'd never buy my own coffeepot (I wanted a red one). I'd never marry Sam. I'd never get to be Grace the way Grace was meant to be.

I had been so careful, my entire life.

I considered my own funeral. No way would Mom have enough common sense to plan it. Dad would do it between calls to investors and HOA board members. Or Grandma. She might step up to the plate once she knew what a crappy job her son was doing of raising her granddaughter. Rachel would come, and probably a few of my teachers. Definitely Mrs. Erskine, who wanted me to be an architect. Isabel, too, though she probably wouldn't cry. I remembered Isabel's brother's funeral — the whole town had turned out, because of his age. So maybe I would get a good crowd, even if I hadn't been a legend in Mercy

Falls, just by virtue of having died too young to have actually lived. Did people bring gifts to funerals like they did to weddings and baby showers?

I heard a creak outside my door. A sudden pop, a foot on a floorboard, and then the door creeping softly open.

For a single, tiny moment, I thought it might be Sam, somehow, miraculously sneaking in. But then from my nest in my blankets, I saw the shape of my father's shoulders and head as he leaned into my room. I did my best to look asleep while still keeping my eyes slitted open. My father came in a few, hesitant steps, and I thought, with surprise, *He's checking to see if I'm all right.*

But then he lifted his chin just a little bit, to look at a place just beyond me, and I realized that he wasn't here to make sure I was all right. He was just here to make sure Sam wasn't with me.

Chapter Twenty-Eight

· COLE ·

Crouched on the cold forest floor, pine needles pressing into my palms, blood smeared over my bare knees, I couldn't remember how long I'd been human.

I was suspended in a pale blue morning, fog tinting everything pastel as it moved slowly around me. The air reeked of blood, feces, and brackish water. It only took a glance at my hands to see where the smells came from. The lake was a few yards away from me, and between me and the water lay a dead deer, flat on her side. A flap of skin folded back from her ribs, presenting her innards like a gruesome gift. It was her blood that was smeared across my knees and, I saw now, my hands as well. In the overhead branches, invisible in the mist, crows called back and forth to one another, eager for me to lose interest in my kill.

I cast a glance around me, looking for the other wolves that must've helped me to take down the doe, but they had left me alone. Or, more truthfully, I'd left them, by shifting into a reluctant human.

Slight movement caught my eye; I darted a glance toward it. It took me a moment to realize what had moved — the doe.

Her eye. She blinked, and as she did, I saw that she was looking right at me. Not dead — dying. Funny how two things could be so similar and yet so far apart. Something about the expression in her liquid black eye made my chest hurt. It was like — patience. Or forgiveness. She had resigned herself to the fate of being eaten alive.

"Jesus," I whispered, getting slowly to my feet, trying not to alarm her further. She didn't even flinch. Just this: *blink*. I wanted to back away, give her space, let her escape, but the exposed bones and spilled guts told me flight was impossible for her. I'd already ruined her body.

I felt a bitter smile twist my lips. Here it was, my brilliant plan to stop being Cole and slip into oblivion. Here it was. Standing naked and painted with death, my empty stomach twisting with hunger while I faced a meal for something I wasn't anymore.

The doe blinked again, face extraordinarily gentle, and my stomach lurched.

I couldn't leave her like this. That was the thing. I knew I couldn't. I confirmed my location with a quick glance around — a twenty-minute walk to the shed, maybe. Another ten to the house, if there was nothing to kill her with in the shed. Forty minutes to an hour of lying here with her guts exposed.

I could just walk away. She was dying, after all. It was inevitable, and how much did the suffering of a deer count for?

Her eye blinked again, silent and tolerant. A lot — that was how much it counted for.

I cast around for anything that might serve as a weapon. None of the stones by the lake were large enough to be useful, and I couldn't imagine myself bludgeoning her to death, anyway. I ran through everything I knew of anatomy and instantly deadly car crashes and catastrophes. And then I looked back to her exposed ribs.

I swallowed.

It only took me a moment to find a branch with a sharp enough end.

Her eye rolled up toward me, black and bottomless, and one of her front legs twitched, a memory of running. There was something awful about terror trapped behind silence. About latent emotions that couldn't be acted out.

"I'm sorry," I told her. "I don't mean to be cruel."

I stabbed the stick through her ribs.

Once.

Twice.

She screamed, this high scream that was neither human nor animal but something terrible in between, the sort of sound that you never forget no matter how many beautiful things you hear afterward. Then she was silent, because her punctured lungs were empty.

She was dead, and I wanted to be. I was going to find out how to keep myself a wolf. Or I just couldn't do this anymore.

Chapter Twenty-Nine

· GRACE ·

I didn't think I'd slept, but a knock on my bedroom door woke me, so I must've. I opened my eyes; it was still dark in my room. The clock said it was morning, but only barely. The numbers glowed *5:30*.

"Grace," my mother's voice said, too loud for 5:30. "We need to talk to you before we go."

"Go where?" My voice was a croak, still half asleep.

"St. Paul," Mom said, and now she sounded impatient, like I should know. "Are you decent?"

"How can I be decent at five?" I muttered, but I waved a hand at her, since I was sleeping in a camisole and pj bottoms. Mom turned on the light switch, and I winced at the sudden brightness. I barely had time to see that Mom was in her billowy fair shirt before Dad appeared behind her. Both of them shuffled into my room. Mom's lips were pressed into a tight, businesslike smile, and Dad's face looked as if he had been sculpted from wax. I couldn't remember a time I'd seen them both looking so uncomfortable.

They both glanced at each other; I could practically see the invisible talk bubbles over their head. *You start. No, you start.*

So I started. I said, "How are you feeling today, Grace?"

Mom waved a hand at me as if it was obvious I was all right, especially if I was well enough to be sarcastic. "Today's the Artists Limited Series."

She paused to see if she had to clarify further. She didn't. Mom went every year — leaving before dawn with a vehicle packed full of art and not coming home until after midnight, exhausted and with a far emptier vehicle. Dad always went with her if he was off from work. I'd gone one year. It was a huge building full of moms and people buying paintings like Mom's. I didn't go again.

"Okay," I said. "So?"

Mom looked at Dad.

"So, you're still grounded," Dad said. "Even though we're not here."

I sat up a little taller, my head tingling in protest as I did.

"So we can trust you, right?" Mom added. "To not do anything stupid?"

My words came out slow and distinct with the effort of not shouting them. "Are you guys just . . . trying to be vindictive? Because I —" I was going to say *saved up forever to get this for Sam*, but for some reason, the idea of finishing the sentence closed my throat up. I shut my eyes and opened them again.

"No," Dad said. "You're being punished. We said you were grounded until Monday, and that's what's happening. It's unfortunate that Samuel's appointment happened to be during that time frame. Maybe another day." He didn't look like he found it unfortunate.

"They're booked for months in advance, Dad," I said.

I didn't think I'd ever seen the line of Dad's mouth look so ugly. He replied, "Well, maybe you should've considered your actions a little more, then."

I could feel a little pulsing headache just between my eyebrows. I pushed a fist into my skin and then looked up. "Dad, it was for his birthday. This was the only thing he got for his birthday. From anybody. It's a really big deal for him." My voice just — stopped. I had to swallow before I went on. "Please just let me go. Ground me Monday. Tell me to do community service. Make me scrub your toilets with my toothbrush. Just let me go."

Mom and Dad looked at each other, and for a single, stupid moment, I thought they were considering it.

Then Mom said, "We don't want you to be alone with him for that long. We don't trust him anymore."

Or me. Just say it.

But they didn't.

"The answer's no, Grace," Dad said. "You can see him tomorrow, and be glad that we're allowing even that."

"*Allowing* that?" I demanded. My hands fisted the covers on either side of me. Anger was rising up in me — I felt my cheeks, hot as summer, and suddenly, I just couldn't take it. "You've been ruling this particular part of the world via absentee ballot for most of my teenage years, and now you just ride in here and say, *Sorry, Grace, no, this little bit of life that you have managed to make for yourself, this person you've chosen, you should be happy we're not taking that, too.*"

Mom threw up her hands. "Oh, Grace, really. Stop overreacting. As if we needed any more proof that you were not mature enough to be with him that much. You're seventeen. You've got the rest of your life ahead of you. This is *not* the end of the world. In five years —"

"Don't —" I said.

To my surprise, she didn't.

"Don't tell me I'll have forgotten his name in five years or whatever you were about to say. Stop talking down to me." I stood up, throwing my covers to the end of the bed as I did. "You two have been gone too long to pretend that you know what's in my head. Why don't you go to some dinner party or a gallery opening or a late-night house showing or an all-day art show and hope that I'll be all right when you get back? Oh, that's *right*. You already are. Pick one, guys. Parents or roommates. You can't be one and then suddenly be the other."

There was a long pause. Mom was looking off into the corner of the room like there was a fantastic song playing in her head. Dad was frowning at me. Finally, he shook his head. "We're having a serious talk when we get home, Grace. I don't think it was fair of you to start this when you knew that we wouldn't be able to stay here to finish it."

I crossed my arms over my chest, my hands fisted. He wouldn't make me feel ashamed of what I'd said. He wouldn't. I'd waited too long to say it.

Mom looked at her watch, and the spell was broken.

Dad was already heading out the door as he said, "We'll talk about this later. We have to go."

Mom added, sounding like she was mimicking something Dad had told her, "We're trusting you to respect our authority."

But they weren't really trusting me with anything, because after they left, I walked into the kitchen and found that they'd taken my car keys.

I didn't care. I had another set they didn't know about in my backpack. There was something invisible and dangerous lurking inside me, and I was done being good.

I got to Beck's house just after daybreak.

"Sam?" I called, but got no answer. The downstairs was clearly unoccupied, so I headed to the second floor. In no time at all I had found Sam's bedroom. The sun was still below the trees and only anemic gray light came through the window in the room, but it was enough for me to see evidence of life: the sheets tossed aside on the bed and a pair of jeans crumpled on the floor next to a pair of inside-out dark socks and a discarded T-shirt.

For a long moment, I just stood by the bed, staring at the snarled sheets, and then I climbed in. The pillow smelled like Sam's hair, and after nights of bad sleep without him, the bed felt like heaven. I didn't know where he was, but I knew he'd be back. Already, it felt like I was with him again. My eyelids ached with sudden heaviness.

Behind my closed eyes I felt a tangled grip of emotions and feelings and sensations. The ever-present ache in my stomach.

The pang of envy when I thought of Olivia as a wolf. The rawness of anger at my parents. The crippling ferocity of missing Sam. The touch of lips to my forehead.

Before I knew it, I had fallen asleep — or rather, I had woken up. It didn't seem like any time at all had passed, but when I opened my eyes, I was facing the wall and the comforter was pulled up around my shoulders.

Usually when I woke up someplace other than my bed — at my grandmother's, or the few times I'd been in a hotel when I was younger — there was a moment of confusion as my body figured out why the light was different and the pillow wasn't mine. But opening my eyes in Sam's room, it was just . . . opening my eyes. It was like my body had been unable to forget where I was even while I was sleeping.

So when I rolled back over to look into the rest of the room and saw birds dancing between me and the ceiling, there was no surprise. Just wonder. Dozens of origami birds of every shape, size, and color danced slowly in the air from the heating vents, life in slow motion. The now-brilliant light through the tall window cast moving bird-shaped shadows all around the room: on the ceiling, on the walls, over the top of the stacks and shelves of books, across the comforter, across my face. It was beautiful.

I wondered how long I'd slept. Also, I wondered where Sam was. Stretching my arms above my head, I realized I could hear the dull roar of the shower through the open door. Dimly, I heard Sam's voice rise above the sound of the shower:

All these perfect days, made of glass
Put on the shelf where they can cast

perfect shadows that stretch and grow
on the imperfect days down below.

He sang the line over again, twice, changing *stretch and grow* to *shift and glow* and then *shift and grow*. His voice sounded wet and echoey.

I smiled, though there was no one to see it. The fight with my parents seemed like something that had happened to a long-ago Grace. Kicking back the blankets, I stood up, my head sending one of the birds into crazy orbit. I reached up to still it and then moved among the birds, looking at what they were made of. The one that had knocked against my head was folded out of newsprint. Here was one folded out of a glossy magazine cover. Another from a paper beautifully and intricately printed with flowers and leaves. One that looked like it had once been a tax worksheet. Another, misshapen and tiny, made out of two dollar bills taped together. A school report card from a correspondence school out of Maryland. So many stories and memories folded up for safekeeping; how like Sam to hang them all above him while he slept.

I fingered the one that hung directly over his pillow. A rumpled piece of notepaper covered with Sam's handwriting, echoing the voice I now heard in the background. One of the scribbled lines was *girl lying in the snow*.

I sighed. I had a weird, empty feeling inside me. Not a bad sort of empty. It was a sort of lack of sensation, like being in pain for a long time and then suddenly realizing that you're not anymore. It was the feeling of having risked everything to be here with a boy and then realizing that he was exactly what

I wanted. Being a picture and then finding I was really a puzzle piece, once I found the piece that was supposed to fit beside me.

I smiled again, and the delicate birds danced around me.

"Hi," Sam said from the doorway. His voice was cautious, unsure of where we stood this morning, after our days apart. His hair was all stuck out and crazy from his shower, and he was wearing a collared shirt that made him look weirdly formal, despite its rumpled, untucked appearance and his blue jeans. My mind was screaming: *Sam, Sam, finally Sam.*

"Hi," I said, and I couldn't keep from grinning. I bit my lip, but my smile was still there, and it only got bigger when Sam's face reflected it back at me. I stood there among his birds, with the shape of my body still impressed on the bed sheets beside me, the sun splashing over me and him, and my worries of last night seeming impossibly small in comparison to the vast glow of this morning.

I was suddenly overwhelmed by what an incredible person this boy was, standing in front of me, and by the fact that he was mine and I was his.

"Right now," Sam said — and I saw that he held the invoice for today's studio time in his hand, folded into a bird with sun-washed wings — "it's hard to imagine that it is raining anywhere in the world."

Chapter Thirty

· COLE ·

I couldn't get the smell of her blood out of my nostrils.

Sam was gone by the time I got to the house; the driveway was empty and the house felt echoey and hollow. I burst into the downstairs bathroom — the bath mat was still twisted from where Sam and I had struggled the night before — and turned the tap on as hot as I could get it. Then I stood in it and watched blood run down the drain. It looked black in the dull filtered light behind the shower curtain. Scrubbing my palms together and scratching my arms, I tried to get every last trace of the doe off me, but no matter how hard I worked my skin, I could still smell her. And every time I caught a whiff of her scent, I saw her. That dark, resigned eye looking up at me while I stared at her insides.

Then I remembered Victor looking up at me, lying on the floor of the shed, bitter, simultaneously Victor and wolf. My fault.

It occurred to me then that I was the opposite of my father. Because I was very, very good at destroying things.

I reached forward and turned the water temperature all the way to cold. There was a brief moment when there was enough hot water to make it the exact temperature of my body, turning me invisible. Then it became frigid. I swore and fought my instincts to jump out of the tub.

Goose bumps rose immediately on my skin, so fast that they hurt, and I let my head fall back. The water coursed over my neck.

Shift. Shift now.

But the water wasn't cold enough to force me to change; it was just cold enough to make my gut twist and nausea bubble through me. I used my foot to shut off the water.

Why was I still human?

It didn't make sense. If being a wolf was scientific, not magical, then it had to follow rules and logic. And the fact that the new wolves changed at different temperatures at different times . . . it didn't make sense. My head was full of Victor shifting back and forth, the white wolf watching me silently, sure in her wolf body, and me, pacing the halls of the house, waiting to shift. I grabbed the hand towel from the sink and used it to dry myself as I riffled through the downstairs closets for clothing. I found a dark blue sweatshirt that said NAVY on it and some jeans that were a bit loose but didn't fall off. The entire time that I was looking for clothing, my head hummed, turning over possibilities for new logic.

Maybe Beck had been wrong about hot and cold being the cause of the shifts. Maybe they weren't really causes; maybe they were just catalysts. In which case there might be other ways to trigger the shift.

I needed paper. I couldn't think without writing my thoughts down.

I got some paper from Beck's office, and Beck's day planner as well. I sat down at the dining room table, pen in hand, the heat rushing out softly through the vents making me feel warm and drowsy. My brain instantly traveled back to my parents' dining room table. I'd sat there every morning with my brainstorming notebook — my father's idea — and I would do my homework or write song lyrics or journal on something I'd seen on the news. That was back when I'd been sure I was going to change the world.

I thought about Victor, his eyes closed as he rode some new high. My mother's face when I told her she could go to hell with Dad. The countless girls waking up to find out they'd slept with a ghost, because I was already gone, if not in actuality, in some spiraling trip contained in a bottle or syringe. The way that Angie had one hand pressed flat against her breastbone when I told her I'd cheated on her.

Oh, yeah, I'd changed the world all right.

I opened the day planner and browsed through it, not even really reading, just skimming, looking for clues. There were little bits and pieces that might be useful but were meaningless on their own: *I found one of the wolves dead today; I looked at her eyes but she was no one to me. Paul said she'd stopped shifting fourteen years ago. There was blood on her face. Smelled like hell.* And *Derek changed into a wolf for two hours in the heat of summer; Ulrik and I have been trying to work that one out all afternoon.* And *Why does Sam get so many fewer years than the rest of us? He is the best of all of us. Why does life have to be so unfair?*

My gaze dropped to my hand. There was still a little bit of blood underneath the nail of my thumb. I didn't think that blood could stay on your skin when you shifted; it would've been on my fur, anyway, not on my skin. So that meant that blood underneath my fingernail had gotten there after I'd become a human. In those unmeasured minutes after I got my human body back but before I'd become Cole again.

I rested my head on the table; the wood seemed freezing cold on my skin. It seemed like far too much work to work out the werewolf logic. Even if I did — even if I figured out what really made us shift and where our minds went when they weren't following our bodies — what was the point? To become a wolf forever? All that work, just to preserve a life that I wouldn't remember. A life not worth preserving.

I knew from experience that there were easier ways to get rid of conscious thought. And I knew of one, one that until now I'd just been too cowardly to attempt, that worked permanently.

I'd told Angie once. It was back before she hated me, I think. I'd been playing the keyboard, home from my first tour, when the whole world lay out before me like I was both king and conqueror, full of possibilities. Angie didn't know yet that I'd cheated on her during the tour. Or maybe she did. When I'd stopped playing, my fingers still hovering over the keys, I said to her, "I've been thinking about killing myself."

Angie hadn't looked up from her position in the old La-Z-Boy we kept in the garage. "Yeah, I guessed that. How's that working out for you?"

"It's got its definite pros," I replied. "I can only think of one con."

She didn't say anything for a long moment, and then she said, "Why would you say something like that, anyway? You want me to talk you out of it? The only person who can talk you out of or into that is yourself. You're the genius. You know that. So that means you're just saying it for effect."

"Bull," I said. "I really wanted your advice. But whatever."

"What do you think I'm going to say? *'You're my boyfriend, go on, kill yourself. It's a nice easy way out.'* I'm sure that's what I would say."

In my head, I was in a hotel letting some girl named Rochelle who I'd never see again slide my pants off, just because I could. I closed my eyes and let self-loathing gently sing a siren song to me. "I don't know, Angie. I don't know. I didn't think. I just said what I was thinking, okay?"

She bit her knuckle and looked at the floor for a moment. "Okay, how about this. Redemption. That's the biggest con I can think of. You kill yourself, that's the end. That's the way you'll be remembered. That, and hell. You still believe in that?"

I'd lost my cross somewhere on the road. The chain had broken and now it was probably in some gas station bathroom or tangled in hotel sheets or kept as some shining souvenir by someone I hadn't meant to leave it with.

"Yeah," I said, because I still believed in hell. It was heaven I wasn't so sure about anymore.

I didn't mention it to her again. Because she was right: The only person who could talk me into it or out of it was me.

Chapter Thirty-One

· GRACE ·

Every minute took us farther away from Mercy Falls and everything in it.

We took Sam's car, because it was a diesel and got better mileage, but Sam let me drive, because he knew I liked to. The CD player still had one of my Mozart CDs in it when we got in, but I switched it to the fuzzy indie alt-rock station I knew he liked. Sam blinked over at me in surprise, and I tried not to look too smug that I was learning his language. Slower, maybe, than he was learning mine, but still, I was impressed with myself.

The day was beautiful and blue, the low areas of the road coated with a thin, pale mist that began to burn off as soon as the sun got above the trees. Some guy with a mellow voice and persuasive guitar hummed out of the speakers; he reminded me of Sam. Beside me, Sam leaned his arm across the back of my seat to softly pinch one of the vertebrae in my neck, and murmured along to the lyrics with a voice that conveyed both fondness and familiarity. Despite my slightly achy limbs, it was hard to shake the feeling of utter rightness with the world.

"Do you know what you're going to sing?" I asked.

Sam leaned his cheek on his outstretched arm and drew lazy circles on the back of my neck. "I don't know. You sprang it on me suddenly. And I was a bit preoccupied with being ostracized for the last few days. I guess I will sing — something. I may suck."

"I don't think you will suck. What were you singing in the shower?"

He was unself-conscious as he answered, both endearing and unusual for him. I was beginning to realize that music was the only skin he was truly comfortable in. "Something new. Maybe something new. Well . . . maybe something."

I got onto the interstate; this time of day, the road was lonely and we had the lanes to ourselves. "A baby song?"

"A baby song. More like a fetal song. I don't think it's even got legs yet. Wait, I think I'm getting babies confused with tadpoles."

I struggled to think of what it was that developed first on babies and failed utterly to manage it in a timely enough manner for a comeback. So I just said, "About me?"

"They're all about you," Sam said.

"No pressure."

"Not for you. You get to just float along through life being Grace and I'm the one who has to run to keep up creatively and lyrically with the ways you change. You're not a fixed target, you know."

I frowned. I thought of myself as frustratingly unchangeable.

"I know what you're thinking. But you're right here, aren't you?" Sam asked, using his free hand to point a finger into the fuzzy seat of the car. "You fought to be with me instead of letting yourself get grounded for a week. That's the stuff entire albums are based on."

He didn't even know the half of it. I was awash with some multicolored emotion that was guilt and self-pity and uncertainty and nerves all rolled into one. I didn't know what was worse: not telling him about still being grounded and the growing sickness inside me, or telling him. I did know this one thing: I wouldn't be able to untell either thing. And I didn't want to ruin this day for him. His one perfect birthday day. Maybe tonight. Maybe tomorrow.

I was more complex than I'd thought. I still didn't see how it would be album fodder, though I appreciated the idea that I had, in fact, done something that impressed Sam, who knew me better than I did. I changed the subject, a little. "What will you name your album?"

"Well, I'm not doing an album today. I'm doing a demo."

I waved off the clarification. "When you do an album, what will it be called?"

"Self-titled," Sam said.

"I hate those."

"Broken Toys."

I shook my head. "That sounds like a band name."

He pinched a tiny bit of my skin, just hard enough for me to squeal and say *ow*. *"Chasing Grace."*

"Nothing with my name in it," I said sternly.

"Well, you're just making this impossible. *Paper Memories*?"

I considered. "Why? Oh, the birds. It seems weird that I never knew about those birds in your room."

"I haven't made any since I met you for real," Sam reminded me. "The newest one is from the summer before last. All of my new cranes are at the store or in your room. That room is like a museum."

"Not anymore," I said, glancing over at him. He looked pale and wintery in this morning light. I changed lanes just to change lanes.

"True enough," he admitted. He sat back from me, pulling his hand from behind my head; he ran his fingers along the plastic divider in the air vent in front of him instead. I had missed his fingers. He said, not looking at me, "What sort of guy do you think your parents expect you to marry? Someone better than me?"

I scoffed. "Who cares what they think?" I realized, too late, what he had said, and by then, I didn't know what to say about it. I didn't know if he really meant it, or what. It wasn't like he'd actually asked me to marry him. It wasn't the same thing. I didn't know how it made me feel.

Sam swallowed and flicked the air vent open and shut, open and shut. "I wonder what would've happened if you hadn't met me. If you went on to finish high school and got that scholarship to be a math whiz at wherever it is that math geniuses go. And met some extremely charming, successful, and funny brain major."

Of all the things I found puzzling about Sam, this one was always the most puzzling: his sudden, self-deprecating mood swings. I'd heard Dad talk Mom out of her funks, though, and the content of them was similar enough to Sam's for me to recognize them as the same species. Was this what it meant to be creative?

"Don't be stupid," I told him. "I don't go around wondering what would've happened if you'd pulled some other girl out of the snow."

"You don't? That's sort of relieving." He turned up the heat and rested his wrists on the vents. The sun was already cooking both of us through the windshield, but Sam was like a cat — he was never too hot. "It's hard to get used to this idea of being a boy forever. I actually get to grow up. It makes me think I should get another job."

"Another one? You mean, other than the bookstore?"

"I don't know exactly how the finances of the house work. I know there is some money in the bank, and I see that it's making interest, and there are occasional payments into it from some fund or something, and the deductions come out for the bills, but I don't really know the details. I don't want to use up that money, so . . ."

"Why don't you talk to someone at the bank? I'm sure they'd be able to look at the statements and work it all out with you."

"I don't want to talk to anybody about it until I'm sure that B —" Sam stopped. Not just a pause. A full stop, the sort of stop that is better than a period. He looked out the window.

It took me a minute to work out what he'd been about to say. Beck. He didn't want to talk to anybody about it until he was sure that Beck was really not shifting back. Sam's fingertips were white on the dashboard where he had them pressed above the vents, and his shoulders were drawn up stiffly by his ears.

"Sam," I said, glancing at him as much as I dared while still keeping my eyes on the road. "Are you okay?"

Sam drew his hands into his lap, hard fists resting on top of each other. "Why did he have to make those new wolves, Grace?" he asked, finally. "It makes it that much harder. We were doing okay."

"He couldn't have known about you," I said, glancing at him. He was running a slow finger down his nose from his forehead and back again. I looked for an exit; somewhere to pull over. "He thought that" — and now I was the one who couldn't finish my sentence the way I'd meant to: *it was your last year.*

"But Cole — I don't know what to do about Cole," Sam confessed. "I just feel like there is something about him I should be getting, and I'm not. And if you saw his eyes, Grace. Oh, God, if you saw his eyes, you'd know there was something really wrong with him. There's something broken in there. And the other two, and Olivia, and I want you to go to college, and I need to — someone has to — I don't know what's expected of me, but it feels so huge. I don't know how much of it is what Beck would've wanted me to do and how much of it is what I expect myself to do. I'm just . . ." His voice faded off, and I didn't know how to comfort him.

We drove in silence for several long minutes, a bright guitar plucking rapid chords in the background while infinite white stripes flew by the car. Sam's fingers were pressed against his upper lip as if he had amazed himself by admitting his uncertainty.

"Still waking up," I said.

He looked at me.

"Your album. *Still Waking Up.*"

He looked at me, expression intense. Surprised, maybe, that I'd come close. "That's exactly how it feels. That's exactly it. One of these days, I'm going to get used to the idea that it's morning and I'm going to be a guy for the rest of the day. For all the rest of all the days. But until then, I'm stumbling around."

I darted a glance over at him, catching his eye. "Everybody does that, though. We all, one day, realize that we're not going to be kids forever and we're going to grow up. You just got to have that moment a little later than most people. You'll figure it out."

Sam's slow smile was rueful but genuine. "You and Beck were totally cut from the same cloth."

"Guess that's why you love both of us," I said.

Sam made the shape of a guitar chord on his seat belt and just nodded. A few moments later, he said, thoughtfully, "*Still Waking Up.* One day, Grace, I'm going to write a song for you and I'm going to call it that. And then I'll name my album after it."

"Because I am wise," I said.

"Yes," Sam said.

He looked out the window then, and I was glad, because it gave me time to dig in my pocket for a tissue without him seeing. My nose had started to bleed.

Chapter Thirty-Two

· ISABEL ·

Every third step I ran, my breath exploded out of me all in a rush. One step to suck in another cold lungful. One step to let it escape. One step of not breathing.

I hadn't been running in way too long, and I hadn't been running this far in even longer. I'd always liked jogging because it was a place to think, far away from the house and my parents. But after Jack died, I hadn't wanted to think.

Now, that was changing.

And so I was running again, though it was far too cold to be comfortable and I was out of shape. Even with my new, buoyant running shoes, my shins were killing me.

I was running to Cole.

It was too long of a run from my house to Beck's, even when I'd been running all the time, so I parked three miles away, warmed up in the transparent mist, and started.

Three miles gave me plenty of time to change my mind. But here I was, the house in sight, and I was still running. I probably looked like hell, but what did I care? If I was just there to talk, it didn't matter what I looked like, right?

The driveway was empty; Sam was already gone. I wasn't sure if I was relieved or disappointed. It meant, at least, that there was a good chance I'd find the house entirely empty, because Cole was probably a wolf.

Again, I couldn't tell if I was relieved or disappointed.

A few hundred feet from the house, I slowed to a walk, holding the stitch in my side. I'd almost gotten my breath back by the time I got to the back door. I tried the knob, experimentally; it turned and the door fell open.

I stepped into the house and hesitated by the back door. I was about to shout hello, when I realized that it might not be just Cole who was human. So I stood there in the dark little corner by the back door looking into the brighter area of the kitchen, remembering sitting in this house and watching Jack die.

It was easy for Grace to say that it wasn't my fault. Words like that didn't mean anything at all.

A sudden thunderous noise made me jump. There was a long pause, and then another burst of crashing and slamming and commotion from somewhere in the house. It was like a voiceless argument. For a long moment, I stood there, trying to decide whether or not I should just slip back outside and run back to my car.

You already sat back and did nothing once in this house, I thought grimly.

So I stepped deeper inside, making my way through the kitchen. I hesitated at the hall, looking into the living room, not quite understanding what was in front of me. I saw . . . *water.* Ragged trails of water shimmered in thin, uneven patterns across the wood floor, almost icy-looking in their perfection.

I lifted my eyes to the rest of the living room. It was completely trashed. A lamp was knocked onto the sofa, the shade askew, and picture frames littered the floor. The rug from the kitchen was thrown up against the side of one of the end tables, slicked with water on one side, and one of the chairs keeled on its back like a bystander too shocked to stand. I stepped slowly into the living room, listening for more sounds, but the house had gone quiet.

The destruction was so bizarre that it had to be intentional — books lying facedown in smears of water, pages ripped out; dented cans of food rolled against the walls; an empty wine bottle stuck upside down in a potted plant; paint shredded off the walls.

And then I heard the sounds again, scrabbling and smashing, and before I could react, a wolf came staggering down the hall to my left, ricocheting off the wall as it headed toward me. It was starting to become clear how the living room had gotten to its current state.

"Holy —" I said, and stepped backward into the kitchen. But it didn't seem like the wolf was interested in attack; water sheeted off its sides as it made its erratic way down the hall. It seemed oddly small in this context, its gray-brown fur soaked and slicked against its body, no scarier than a dog. The wolf got a few feet away and then looked up at me with insolent green eyes.

"Cole," I breathed, my heart doing a double thump. "You crazy bastard."

To my surprise, he flinched at the sound of my voice. It reminded me that he was, after all, only a wolf, and that his instincts must have been screaming about my presence between him and his exit.

I backed up, but before I could decide whether I should try to get the back door open for him, Cole began to twitch. By the time he was a few feet away from me, he was full-out convulsing and twisting and retching. I took a few steps back so he wouldn't puke on my nice running shoes and crossed my arms over my chest to watch him shift.

Cole scraped some new claw marks into the wall — Sam was going to love that *so much* — as he jerked on his side. Then, his body did magic. His skin bubbled and stretched, and I saw his long wolf mouth open wide in pain. He rolled onto his back, panting.

Newly human, he lay stretched on the floor, like a whale washed up on shore, arms marked up with faint pink memories of wounds. Then he opened his eyes and looked at me.

My stomach jerked. Cole had his face back again, but his eyes were still feral, lost in his wolf thoughts. Finally, he blinked, and his eyebrows ordered themselves in a way that told me he was really seeing me.

"Cool trick, right?" he said, his voice a little thick.

"I've seen better," I said coolly. "What are you doing?"

Cole didn't move, except to unfist his hands and stretch out his fingers. "Science experiments. On myself. Long, distinguished history of that."

"Are you drunk?"

"Possibly," Cole allowed, with a lazy smile. "I'm not sure if shifting metabolizes some of my blood alcohol. I don't feel too bad, though. Why are you here?"

I pressed my lips together. "I'm not. I mean, I was just going."

Cole stretched his arm in my direction. "Don't go."

"Because this looks like such a great time," I said.

"Help me figure it out," he said. "Help me figure out how to stay a wolf."

In my mind, I was sitting again at the foot of my brother's bed, my brother who had risked everything to stay human. I was watching him lose sensation in his fingers and his toes and whimper with the pain of his brain exploding. I didn't have words to describe my disgust for Cole at that moment.

"Figure it out yourself," I said.

"I can't," Cole told me, still lying on his back, looking at me upside down. "I can only get myself to shift, but it doesn't stick. The cold's a trigger, but so's adrenaline, I think. I tried an ice bath, but that didn't work until I cut myself, too, for the adrenaline. But it won't stick. I keep changing back."

"Boo hoo," I said. "Sam's going to be pissed when he sees what you've done to his house." I turned to go.

"Isabel, please." Cole's voice followed me, even if his body didn't. "If I can't make myself a wolf, I'm going to kill myself."

I stopped. Didn't turn around.

"I'm not trying to say it to manipulate you, okay? It's just the truth." He hesitated. "I've got to get out, somehow, and it's one or the other. I just can't — I need to figure this out, Isabel. You know more about the wolves. Please just help me with this."

I turned around. He was still lying on the floor, one hand over his chest, the other hand outstretched, reaching for me. I said, "All you're doing is asking me to help you kill yourself. Don't pretend it's anything else. What do you think it really is if you become a wolf forever?"

Cole closed his eyes. "Then help me do that."

I laughed. I heard how cruel my laugh sounded, but I didn't soften it. "Let me tell you something, Cole. I sat in this house, this very house" — I pointed to the floor as he opened his eyes — "in *that* room and I watched my brother die. I didn't do anything about it. You know how he died? He was bitten, and he was trying to keep from turning into a werewolf. I arranged for him to be injected with bacterial meningitis, which proceeded to give him a fever off the charts, basically set his brain on fire, destroyed his fingers and toes, and finally killed him. I didn't take him to the hospital because I knew that he would rather die than be a werewolf. And in the end, he got that wish."

Cole stared at me. That same dead look he'd given me before. I expected him to have a reaction, but there was nothing. His eyes were dull. Empty.

"I'm only telling you this so you know that I have wanted to escape about a hundred thousand times since then. I've thought about drinking — hey, it works for my mom — or drugs — hey, it works for my mom — and I've thought about taking one of my dad's eight million guns and putting it to my head and blowing my brains out. Sad part? Not even because I miss Jack. I mean, I do, but that's not why I want to do it. It's because I feel so damn guilty about how I killed him. *I* killed him. And some days I just can't live with that. But I do. Because that's life, Cole. Life's pain. You just have to get over as much of it as you can."

Cole said, simply, "I don't want to."

It seemed like he always sprang honesty on me when I least expected it. I knew it was making me empathize with him, even when I didn't want to, but I couldn't help it any more than I could help kissing him before. I crossed my arms again; I felt like he was trying to pull a confession out of me. And I didn't know if I had any more to confess.

· COLE ·

I was lying here, ruined, on the floor, and I had been so certain that today was the day I'd finally get up the nerve to end it.

And then it wasn't. Because somehow, watching her face when she talked about her brother, I just didn't feel the urgency anymore. I felt like I had been a balloon getting larger and larger, waiting to pop, and she had come in and burst herself first. And somehow that had let the air out of both of us.

It felt like everyone in this house had a reason to escape, and I was the only one trying to. I was so tired.

"I didn't realize you were actually human," I said. "As in, with actual emotions."

"Unfortunately."

I stared at the ceiling. I wasn't sure where I went from here.

She said, "You know what *I* don't want to do anymore? Watch you lying there naked." I rolled my eyes toward her and she added, "It's like you never wear clothes. You're always naked when I see you. Are you really stuck as a human?"

I nodded; the sound of my skull rubbing on the floor was loud inside my head.

"Good, then you won't do anything embarrassing while we're out. Get some clothes; let's go get some coffee."

I shot her a look that clearly said, *Oh, that will help.* She smiled her thin, cruel smile and said, "If you still feel like killing yourself after caffeine, there will be plenty of time left in the day."

"Ungh," I grunted as I got to my feet. I was taken aback by this perspective, standing, looking around at the hall and living room that I had trashed. I hadn't expected to be doing this again. My spine hurt like hell from shifting so many times in quick succession. "Better be some pretty amazing coffee."

"It's not great," Isabel admitted. She had a weird look on her face now that I was standing: relief? "But for the middle of nowhere, it's definitely better than what one would expect. Wear something comfortable. It's three miles back to my car."

Chapter Thirty-Three

· SAM ·

The studio was unimpressive from the outside. It was a squat, tired-looking rambler with a squat, tired-looking blue minivan parked in the driveway. An unmoving Labrador retriever lay in the unoccupied part of the driveway, so Grace parked on the street. She eyed the precipitous angle of the street and wrenched up the parking brake.

"Is that dog dead?" she asked. "Do you think this is *really* the place?"

I pointed to the bumper stickers on the minivan, all local Duluth indie bands currently in vogue: Finding the Monkey, The Wentz, Alien LifeForms. I hadn't heard any of them — they were too small to get radio play — but their names were tossed around enough in local advertisements for me to recognize them. "Yeah, I think so."

"If we get kidnapped by weird hippies, I'm blaming you," she said, opening her door. A rush of cold morning air got sucked into the car, smelling of city: exhaust, asphalt, the indefinable scent of a lot of people living in a lot of buildings.

"You picked the place."

Grace blew a raspberry at me and got out. For a moment she seemed a little unsteady on her feet, but she recovered quickly, clearly not wanting me to see it.

"Are you okay?" I asked.

"Couldn't be okayer," she said, popping the trunk.

When I reached down to get my guitar case, nerves punched me in the stomach, surprising me not by their presence but by the fact that they took so long to get there. I gripped the handle of my guitar case and hoped I wouldn't forget all of my chords.

We headed up to the front door. The dog didn't lift its head.

"I think it is dead," Grace said.

"I think it's one of those things to hide keys under," I told her.

Grace hooked her fingers in my jean pocket. I was about to knock on the front door when I saw a tiny wooden plaque with permanent-marker lettering: STUDIO ENTRANCE AROUND BACK.

So we went around the back of the rambler, where cracked concrete stairs too wide to easily fit our steps led us to an exposed basement and a hand-lettered sign that said ANARCHY RECORDING, INC. ENTRANCE HERE. Below it was a planter with some limp pansies that had been put out too early and battered by frost.

I turned to Grace. "'Anarchy, Incorporated.' That's ironic."

Grace gave me a withering look and rapped on the door. I wiped a suddenly clammy palm on my jeans.

The door opened, revealing another Labrador, this one very much alive, and a twenty-something girl with a red bandanna tied around her head. She was so interesting-looking and unpretty that she actually traveled through ugly to someplace on the other side that was almost as good as pretty: huge, beaked nose, sleepy-looking dark brown eyes, and sharp cheekbones. Her black hair was pulled up in a half a dozen interconnected braids coiled on top of her head, like a Mediterranean Princess Leia.

"Sam and Grace? Come on in." Her voice was gorgeous and complicated, a smoker's voice, though the smell pouring from inside was coffee, not cigarettes. Grace, suddenly motivated, stepped into the studio, following the scent of caffeine like a rat after the Pied Piper.

Once the door was shut behind us, it was no longer the basement of a shabby rambler but a high-tech escape pod in some other universe. We faced a wall of mixing boards and computer monitors; the entire room was dark and muted by soundproofing; recessed lighting illuminated the keypads and a chic low black sofa. One of the walls was glass and looked into a dark, soundproofed room with an upright piano and an assortment of microphones in it.

"I'm Dmitra," the girl with the braids said, reaching a hand out to shake. She looked unflinchingly at me at the same time that I lifted my gaze from her nose to her eyes, and just like that, we had made an unspoken pact: She would not stare at my yellow eyes because I would not stare at her nose. "Are you Sam or Grace?"

I smiled at her straight-faced delivery and shook her hand. "Sam Roth. Nice to meet you."

Dmitra shook hands with Grace, who was making friends with the Labrador, and said, "What are we doing today, kids?"

Grace looked at me. I said, "Demo, I guess."

"You guess? What sort of instrumentation are we looking at?"

I lifted the guitar case a few inches.

"Okay," she said. "You done this before?"

"Nope."

"A virgin. Sometimes just what you need," Dmitra said.

She reminded me a little of Beck. Even though she was smiling and joking, I could tell that she was watching and judging and making decisions about me and Grace as she did. Beck did that, too: gave the impression of intimacy while he was really deciding whether or not you were worth his time.

"You'll be in there, then," she continued. "Do you want to get some coffee before we get started?"

Grace made a beeline for the kitchenette that Dmitra indicated. While she did, Dmitra asked me, "What do you listen to?"

I set my guitar case on the sofa and extracted my guitar. I tried not to sound too pretentious. "A lot of indie rock. The Shins, Elliott Smith, José González. Damien Rice. Gutter Twins. Stuff like that."

"Elliott Smith," Dmitra repeated, as if I hadn't said anything else. "I see."

Grace reappeared with an ugly mug with a deer painted on it, as Dmitra did something with the computer that may or may not have been as useful as she was making it look. Finally, she directed me into the other room. She gave me an audience of microphones, one for my voice, one for my guitar, both leaning attentively toward me, and handed me a set of headphones.

"So we can talk to you," she said, disappearing back into the other room. Grace lingered, her hand on the Labrador's head beside her.

My fingers felt grimy and inadequate to the task ahead of them; the headphones smelled like they'd been worn by too many heads. From my perch on the chair, I looked plaintively up at Grace, who looked beautiful and peaked in the strange recessed lighting, like an edgy magazine model. I realized I hadn't asked her how she was feeling that morning. If she was still sick. I remembered her losing her footing outside the car and taking care to make sure I didn't see. I swallowed, my throat clinging to itself, and asked instead, "Can we get a dog?"

"We can," Grace said, magnanimously. "But I will not walk it in the morning. Because I will be sleeping."

"I never sleep," I said. "I'll do it."

I jumped as Dmitra's voice came through the headphones. "Would you just sing and play a little bit so that I can set up the levels?"

Grace leaned over and kissed the top of my head, careful not to spill her coffee into my lap. "Good luck."

I sort of wanted her to stay here while I sang, to remind me of why I was here, but at the same time, it wouldn't be the same to sing songs about missing her while looking at her, so I let her go.

· GRACE ·

I took my place on the sofa and tried to pretend that Dmitra didn't intimidate me. She didn't make small talk while she was rummaging on the mixing board, and I didn't know if talking would bother her, so I just sat there and watched her work.

Honestly, I was glad for the break in the conversation, the opportunity to be silent. My head was beginning its same slow thrumming, the strange heat spreading through my body again. Talking through the headache made my teeth ache; the warmth of the dull pain gathered in my throat and in my nostrils. I dabbed a tissue on my nose, but it was dry.

Just keep it together for today, I told myself. *Today isn't about you.*

I would not ruin the day for Sam. So I sat on the sofa and ignored my body the best I could and listened.

Sam had turned his back so that he faced away from us while he tuned his guitar, his shoulders hunched around the instrument.

"Sing for me for a moment," Dmitra said, and I saw him turn his head when he heard her voice in his headphones. He launched into some rapid fingerpicking piece that I'd never heard him play before, and began to sing. His very first note wavered, a hint of nerves, and then it was gone, disappearing into his voice, breathy and earnest. The song was this heart-breaking piece about loss and saying good-bye — I thought at first that it was about Beck, or even about me, and then I realized it was about Sam:

One thousand ways to say good-bye
One thousand ways to cry
One thousand ways to hang your hat before you
go outside

I say good-bye good-bye good-bye
I shout it out so loud
'Cause the next time that I find my voice I might
not remember how.

Hearing it coming out of speakers instead of Sam made it seem entirely different, like I had never heard him before. For some reason, my face just wanted to smile and smile. It felt wrong to be so proud of something that I had absolutely nothing to do with, but I couldn't help myself. In front of the mixing board, Dmitra had gone still, her fingers poised over the top of sliders. Her head was cocked, listening, and then she said, without turning around to face me, "We might end up with something good today."

I just kept smiling, because I'd known that all along.

Chapter Thirty-Four

· ISABEL ·

At three in the afternoon, we had Kenny's to ourselves. It still smelled like the morning's greasy breakfast offerings: cheap bacon, soggy hash browns, and a vague cigarette odor, despite the lack of a smoking section.

Across the booth from me, Cole slouched, his legs long enough that I kept accidentally hitting them with my feet. I didn't think he looked like he belonged in this hick diner any more than I did. He looked like he'd been put together by a swank designer who knew what he was doing — his distinctive features were brutal and purposeful, sharp enough to hurt yourself on. The booth seemed soft and faded around him, almost comically old-fashioned and country in comparison, like someone had dropped him here for a tongue-in-cheek photo shoot. I was sort of fascinated by his hands — hard-looking hands, all steep angles and prominent veins running across the back of them. I watched the deft way that his fingers moved while he did mundane things like putting sugar in his coffee.

"You a musician?" I asked.

Cole looked at me from under his eyebrows; something about the question bothered him, but he was too good to reveal much. "Yeah," he said.

"What kind?"

He made the kind of face real musicians make when they're asked about their music. His voice was self-deprecating when he said, "Just a bit of everything. Keyboards, I guess."

"We have a piano at my house," I said.

Cole looked at his hands. "Don't really do it anymore." And then he fell silent again, and it was that silence, heavy and growing and poisonous, that rested on the table between us.

I made a face that he didn't see because he didn't bother lifting his eyes. I wasn't big on making small talk. I considered calling Grace to ask her what I should say to a reticent suicidal werewolf, but I'd left my phone somewhere. Car, maybe.

"What are you looking at?" I demanded finally, not expecting an answer.

To my surprise, Cole stretched one hand out toward me, extending his fingers so that his thumb was closest, and he regarded it with an expression of wonder and revulsion. His voice echoed his expression. "This morning, when I became me again, there was a dead deer in front of me. Not really dead. She was looking at me" — and *now* he met my eye, to see my reaction — "but she couldn't get up, because before I'd shifted, I'd ripped her open. And I guess, well, I guess I was eating her alive. And I guess I kept doing it after, because my hands . . . they were covered with her guts."

He looked down at his thumb, and now I saw that there was a small ridge of brown beneath the nail. The end of his thumb trembled, so slightly that I almost didn't see it. He said, "I can't get it off."

I rested my hand on the table, palm up, and when he didn't understand what I wanted, I stretched my arm a few inches farther and took his fingers in mine. With my other hand, I got my nail clipper out of my purse. I flicked out the hook and slid it under his nail, scraping the bit of brown out.

I blew the grit off the table, put the clippers back in my purse, and let him have his hand back.

He left it where it was, between us, palm down, fingers spread out and pressed against the tabletop as if it were an animal poised for flight.

Cole said, "I don't think your brother was your fault."

I rolled my eyes. "Thanks, Grace."

"Huh?"

"Grace. Sam's girlfriend. She says that, too. But she wasn't there. Anyway, the guy she tried to save that way lived. She can afford to be generous. Why are we talking about this?"

"Because you made me walk three miles for a cup of old coffee. Tell me why meningitis."

"Because meningitis gives you a fever." His blank look told me that I was starting in the wrong place. "Grace was bitten as a kid. But she never shifted, because her idiot father locked her in the car on a hot day and nearly fried her. We decided that maybe you could replicate that effect with a high fever, and we couldn't think of anything better than meningitis."

"With a thirty-five percent survival rate," Cole said.

"Ten to thirty percent," I corrected. "And I already told you — it cured Sam. It killed Jack."

"Jack is your brother?"

"Was, yeah."

"And you injected him?"

"No, Grace did. But I got the infected blood to give to him."

Cole looked impatient. "I don't even have to bother to tell you why your guilt is self-indulgent, then."

One of my eyebrows shot up. "I don't —"

"Shhh," he said. He drew his outstretched hand back toward his coffee mug and stared at the salt and pepper shakers. "I'm thinking. So Sam never shifts at all?"

"No. The fever cooked the wolf out of him, or something."

Cole shook his head without looking up. "That doesn't make sense. That shouldn't have worked. That's like saying you shiver when you're cold and you sweat when you're hot, and so to stop you from shivering for the rest of your life, we're going to put you in a pizza oven for a couple minutes."

"Well, I don't know what to tell you. This was supposed to be Sam's last year, and he should've been a wolf right now. The fever worked."

He frowned up at me. "I wouldn't say the fever worked. I would say that something about meningitis made him stop shifting. And I'd say something about getting shut in a car made Grace stop shifting. Those are maybe true. But saying that the fever did it? You can't prove that."

"Listen to you, Mr. Science Guy."

"My father —"

"The mad scientist," I interjected.

"Yes, the mad scientist. He used to tell a joke in his classes. It's about a frog. I think it's a frog. It might be a grasshopper. Let's go with frog. A scientist has a frog and he says, 'Jump, frog.' The frog jumps ten feet. The scientist writes down *Frog jumps ten feet.* Then the scientist chops off one of the frog's legs and says, 'Jump, frog,' and the frog jumps five feet. The scientist writes *Cut off one leg, frog jumps five feet.* Then he chops off another leg, and says, 'Jump,' and the frog jumps two feet. The scientist writes down *Cut off two legs, frog jumps two feet.* Then he cuts off all the frog's legs and says, 'Jump,' and the frog just lies there. The scientist writes down the conclusions of the test: *Cutting off all a frog's legs makes the subject go deaf.*" Cole looked at me. "Do you get it?"

I was indignant. "I'm not a total idiot. You think we jumped to the wrong conclusion. But it worked. What does it matter?"

"Nothing, I guess, for Sam, if it's working," Cole said. "But I just don't think that Beck had it right. He told me that cold made us wolves and hot made us humans. But if that was true, the new wolves like me wouldn't be unstable. You can't make rules and then say that they don't really count just because your body doesn't know them yet. Science doesn't work that way."

I considered. "So you think that's more frog logic?"

Cole said, "I don't know. That's what I was thinking about when you came. I was trying to see if I could trigger the shift in a way other than cold."

"With adrenaline. And stupidity."

"Right. This is what I'm thinking, and I could be wrong. I think that it's not really cold that makes you shift. I think it's the way your brain reacts to cold that tells your body to shift.

Two entirely different things. One is the real temperature. The other one is the temperature your brain says it is." Cole's fingers headed toward his napkin and then stopped. "I feel like I could think better with paper."

"No paper, but —" I handed him a pen out of my purse.

His entire face changed from when I had first found him. He leaned over the napkin and drew a little flowchart. "See . . . cold drops your temperature and tells your hypothalamus to keep you warm. That's why you shiver. The hypothalamus does all kinds of other fun things, too, like . . . tells you whether or not you're a morning person, and tells your body to make adrenaline, and how fat you should be, and —"

"No, it does not," I said. "You're making this stuff up."

"I am not." Cole's expression was earnest. "This was polite dinner table conversation where I grew up." He added another box to his napkin flowchart. "So let's pretend there's another little box here of things that cold makes your hypothalamus do." He wrote *Become a wolf* in the new box he'd drawn; the napkin tore a bit as he did.

I turned the napkin around so that his handwriting — jagged, erratic letters piled on top of one another — was right side up for me. "So how does meningitis fit into this?"

Cole shook his head. "I don't know. But it might explain why I'm human right now." Without turning the napkin around again, he wrote, in big block letters across his hypothalamus box: METH.

I looked at him.

He didn't look away. His eyes looked very, very green with the afternoon light on them. "You know how they say drugs mess up your brain? Well, I'm thinking they were right."

I kept looking at him, and saw he was so obviously waiting for me to remark on his drug-life past.

Instead, I said, "Tell me about your father."

· COLE ·

I don't know why I told her about my father. She wasn't exactly the most sympathetic audience. But maybe that was why I told her.

I didn't tell her the first part, which was this: Once upon a time, before being a new wolf tied up in the back of a Tahoe, before Club Josephine, before NARKOTIKA, there was a boy named Cole St. Clair, and he could do anything. And the weight of that possibility was so unbearable that he crushed himself before it had a chance to.

Instead, I said, "Once upon a time, I was the son of a mad scientist. A legend. He was a child prodigy and then he was a teen genius and then he was a scientific demigod. He was a geneticist. He made people's babies prettier."

Isabel didn't say *That's not so bad.* She just frowned.

"And that was fine," I said. And it had been fine. I remembered photographs of me sitting on his shoulders while the ocean surf rushed around his calves. I remembered word games tossed back and forth in the car. I remembered chess pieces, pawns lying in piles by the side of the board. "He was gone a lot — but hey, I didn't care about that. Everything was great when he was home, and my brother and I had good childhoods. Yeah, everything was great, until we started to get older."

It was hard to remember the first time Mom said it, but I'm pretty sure that was the moment it all started to fall apart.

"Don't hold me in suspense," Isabel said sarcastically. "What did he do?"

"Not him," I said. "Me. What did *I* do."

What had I done? I must've commented cleverly on something in the newspaper, done well enough in school to get bumped forward a grade, solved some puzzle they hadn't thought I could solve. One day, Mom said for the first time, half a smile on her long, plain face that always looked tired — perhaps from being married to greatness for so long — "Guess who he's taking after."

The beginning of the end.

I shrugged. "I left my brother behind in school. My dad wanted me to come to the lab with him. He wanted me to take college classes. He wanted me to be him." I stopped, thinking of all the times I'd disappointed him. Silence was always, *always* worse than shouting. "I wasn't him. He was a genius. I'm not."

"Big deal."

"It wasn't, to me. But it was to him. He wanted to know why I didn't even try. Why it was I went running the other way."

"What was the other way?" Isabel asked.

I stared at her, silent.

"Don't give me that look. I'm not trying to find out who you are. I don't care who you are. I just want to know why it is you are the way you are."

Just then, the end of the table jostled, and I looked up into the bright, pimpled faces of three preteen girls. They had three matching pairs of half-moon eyes curved up in three matching expressions of excitement. The faces were unfamiliar but their postures were not; I immediately knew, with sinking certainty, what they were going to say.

Isabel looked at them. "Uh, hello, if this is about Girl Scout cookies, you can leave. Actually, if it's about anything, you can leave."

The ringleader preteen, who had hoop earrings — ankle holders, Victor had called them — thrust a pink notebook at me. "I *cannot* believe it. I *knew* you weren't dead. I knew it! Would you sign that? Please?"

The other two chorused "*omigod*" softly.

I guess what I should've been feeling was dread at being recognized. But all I could think while looking at them was that I'd agonized in a hotel room to write these brutal, nuanced songs, and my fan base was three squealing ten-year-old girls wearing *High School Musical* T-shirts. NARKOTIKA for kindergartners.

I looked at them and said, "Excuse me?"

Their faces fell, just a little, but the girl with the hoop earrings didn't withdraw the notepad. "Please," she said. "Would you autograph it? We won't bother you after that, I swear. I died when I heard 'Break My Face.' It's my ringtone. I love it so bad. It's, like, the best song, ever. I cried when you went missing. I didn't eat for days. And I added my signature to the petition for people who believed you were still alive. Oh my God, I can't even believe it. You're *alive*."

One of the girls behind her was actually crying, blinded by the sheer emotional good fortune of finding me with my heart still beating.

"Oh," I said, and proceeded to lie smoothly. "You think

I'm — yeah. I get that a lot. It's been a while. But no, I'm not." I felt Isabel's eyes on me.

"What?" Now the hoop-earring girl's face fell. "You look just like him. Really cute." She flushed a shade of red so deep it had to be painful.

"Thanks." *Please just go away.*

Hoop-earring girl said, "You're really not him?"

"I'm really not. You don't know how much I've heard that, since the news story." I shrugged apologetically.

"Can I at least take a picture with my phone?" she asked. "Just so I can tell my friends about it?"

"I don't think that's a good idea," I said, uneasy.

"That means *get out of here*," Isabel said. "Like, now."

The girls shot Isabel foul looks before turning and huddling around one another. We could still hear their voices clearly. "He looks just like him," one of the girls said wistfully.

"I think it *is* him," hoop-earring girl said. "He just doesn't want to be bothered. He ran away to escape the tabloids."

Isabel's eyes burned on me, waiting for an answer.

"Mistaken identity," I told her.

The girls had gotten back to their seats. Hoop-earring girl looked over the back of the booth and said, "I love you anyway, Cole!" before ducking back down.

The other two girls squealed.

Isabel said, "Cole?"

Cole. I was back where I started. Cole St. Clair.

As we left, the girls took my pic with their cell phones, anyway.

Beginning. of. the. end.

Chapter Thirty-Five

· SAM ·

I had never worked so hard on my music as I did the first two hours in the studio: Once Dmitra had decided that I wasn't an Elliott Smith wannabe, she shifted into high gear. We went over verses once, twice, three times, sometimes just trying a different arrangement, sometimes recording additional strumming guitar to go over my fingerpicking, sometimes adding percussive effects. On some tracks, I recorded over my voice with harmonies, sometimes more than once, until I was my very own pack of Sams crooning in polyphonic splendor.

It was brilliant, surreal, exhausting. I was beginning to feel how little sleep I'd gotten the night before.

"Why don't you take five?" Dmitra suggested after a few hours. "I'll work on mixing what we've done so far and you can get up, piss, get some coffee. You're starting to sound a little flat, and your girlfriend looks like she misses you."

Through the headphones, I heard Grace say indignantly, "I was just sitting here!"

I grinned and slid the headphones off. Leaving both them and my guitar behind, I came back into the main room. Grace, looking as exhausted as I felt, lounged on the sofa with the dog at her feet. I stood next to her while Dmitra showed me the shape of my voice on the computer screen. Grace hugged my hips and rested her cheek on my leg. "You sound amazing from out here."

Dmitra clicked a button, and my voice, compressed and harmonized and beautified, came through the speakers. I sounded — not like me. No . . . like me. But me, if I was on a radio. Me from outside myself. I stuffed my hands into my armpits, listening. If it was that easy to make a guy sound like a proper singer, you'd think everybody would be in the studio.

"It's brilliant," I told her. "Whatever you've done. It sounds brilliant."

Dmitra didn't turn around as she kept clicking and sliding. "That's all you, baby. I haven't really done much yet."

I didn't believe her. "Right. Yeah. Hey, where is the bathroom?"

Grace jerked her chin toward the hall. "Turn left at the kitchen."

I ran a hand over Grace's head and tweaked her ear with my fingers until she released me, and then I headed down the rat's maze of halls past the kitchenette. Now, in the hallway, lined with framed and signed album covers, I could smell the cigarette smoke. On the way back from the bathroom, I took my time going back to the studio, looking at the albums and signatures. Karyn might've believed that you could tell everything about someone by what sort of books they read, but I knew that you could tell even more by the music they listened to. If the wall was to be believed, Dmitra's tastes seemed to run toward electronica and dance. She had an impressive collection that I could admire even if the bands weren't really my thing. I made a note to joke with her about her impressive selection of Swedish album covers when I got back to the studio.

Sometimes, your eyes see something your brain doesn't. You pick up a newspaper and your head gives you a phrase that you didn't consciously read yet. You walk into a room and you realize something's out of place before you've bothered to properly look.

I felt that happening now. I saw Cole's face, or something that reminded me of it, though I didn't know where. I turned back to the wall and swept my eyes across the album covers again. Slower, this time. Scanning the artwork, the printed titles and artists, looking for what had triggered the image.

And there it was. Bigger than the others, because it was not an album cover but rather the glossy front of a magazine. On it, a guy leaped at the viewer, and behind it crouched his band members, staring at him. It was a famous cover. I remembered seeing it before. I remembered noticing the way the guy jumped toward the camera with his limbs completely outstretched, like the flight was all that mattered, like he didn't care what happened when he landed. I remembered, too, the main headline on the magazine, done in the same font that the band used on their album — BREAKING OUT: THE FRONT MAN OF NARKOTIKA TALKS ABOUT SUCCESS BEFORE 18.

But I had not remembered the guy having Cole's face.

I closed my eyes for a single moment, the cover still branded in my vision. *Please,* I thought. *Please let it just be an uncanny resemblance. Please don't let Beck have infected someone famous.*

I opened my eyes, and Cole was still there. And behind him, out of focus, because the camera only cared about Cole, was Victor.

I made my way slowly to the studio; they were listening to another one of my tracks, which sounded even better than the last. But it seemed suddenly disconnected from my life. My real life, the one that was dictated by the rise and fall of the temperature, even now that my skin was firmly human.

"Dmitra," I said, and she turned around. Grace looked up, too, frowning at something in my voice. "What's the name of the front man of NARKOTIKA?"

I'd already seen all the proof I needed, but I didn't think I would really believe it until I heard someone say it out loud.

Dmitra's face cracked into a grin, softer than she'd been the entire time we'd been in the studio. "Oh, man, that was a great concert. He is crazy as a fox, but that band was . . ." She shook her head and seemed to remember that I'd asked a question. "Cole St. Clair. He's been missing for months."

Cole.

Cole was Cole St. Clair.

And I had thought that my yellow eyes were hard to hide behind.

It meant there were thousands of eyes out there looking for him, waiting to recognize him.

And when they'd found him, they'd find all of us.

Chapter Thirty-Six

· ISABEL ·

"Where do you want me to drop you off? Back at Beck's house?"

We were sitting in my SUV, which was parked in the far corner of the Kenny's parking lot so no rednecks would open their car doors into it. I was trying not to look at Cole, who seemed huge in the front seat, his presence taking up far more room than his physical body.

"Don't do that," Cole said.

I slid my eyes toward him. "Do what?"

"Don't pretend like nothing happened," he said. "Ask me about it."

The afternoon light was dying quickly. A long, dark cloud slashed through the sky in the west. Not a rain cloud for us. Just bad weather on its way somewhere else.

I sighed. I didn't know if I wanted to know. It seemed to me that knowing would be more work than *not* knowing. But it wasn't like we could really put the genie back in the lamp now that it was out, could we? "Does it matter?"

Cole said, "I want you to know."

Now I looked at him, at his dangerously handsome face that even now called, in unsafe and dulcet tones, *Isabel, kiss me, lose yourself in me.* It was a sad face, once you knew to look for it. "Do you really?"

"I have to know if anybody other than ten-year-olds know who I am," Cole said. "Or I really will have to kill myself."

I gave him a withering look.

"Should I guess?" I asked. Without waiting for him to answer, I remembered his deft fingers and thought of his pretty face and said, "Keyboardist for a boy band."

"Lead singer of NARKOTIKA," Cole said.

I waited a long beat, waited for him to say *kidding.*

But he didn't.

· COLE ·

Her face didn't change. Maybe my target audience really was preteens. It was all very anticlimactic.

"Don't look at me like that," she said. "Just because I didn't recognize your face doesn't mean I haven't heard your music. Everyone and Jesus has heard your music."

I didn't say anything. What was there to say, really? The entire conversation felt very déjà vu or something; like I'd known all along I was going to have it with her, here in her car, the afternoon growing cold under the clouds.

"What?" Isabel asked, leaning over to look me straight in the face. "*What?* You think I give a crap about you being a rock star?"

"It's not about the music," I said.

Isabel pressed her finger into the crook of my elbow, on my track marks. "Let me guess. Drugs, girls, lots of swearing. What is there about you that you haven't already told me? This morning you were lying naked on the floor and telling me you wanted to kill yourself. So, what, you think that me knowing you're lead singer of omigod NARKOTIKA is going to change anything?"

"Yeah. No." I didn't know what I was. Relieved? Disappointed? Did I want it to change things?

"What do you want me to say?" Isabel asked me. "*'You're going to corrupt me, get out of my car'*? Too late. I'm already way beyond your influence."

At that, I laughed, though I felt bad for doing it because I knew she'd take it as an insult, though really it wasn't. "Oh, believe me, you are not. There are tiny, dirty rabbit holes that you have not been down that I have. I have taken people down into those tunnels with me, and they've never come out."

I was right. She was offended. She thought I found her naive.

"I'm not trying to piss you off. I'm just giving you fair warning. I'm far more famous for that than my music." Her face had gone utterly frosty, so I thought I was getting through to her. "I am, quite possibly, utterly incapable of making a decision that is not self-serving in absolutely every way."

Now Isabel started to laugh, a high, cruel laugh that was so sure of itself that it kind of turned me on. She put the car in reverse. "I keep waiting for you to tell me something that I don't already know."

I took Cole home, knowing full well it was a bad idea — and maybe doing it *because* it was a bad idea. By the time we got there, it was a dazzling evening, almost tacky in its beauty, the entire sky painted a color pink that I'd only ever seen here in northern Minnesota.

We were back where we'd first met, only now we knew each other's names. There was a car parked in the driveway: my dad's smoke blue BMW.

"Don't worry about it," I said as I pulled up on the other side of the circular driveway and put the SUV in park. "That's my dad. It's a weekend, so he'll be in the basement with some hard liquor to keep him company. He won't even know we're home."

Cole didn't comment, just slid out of the car, into the chilly, cloud-covered air. He rubbed his arms and looked at me, his eyes blank and dark in the shadows. "Hurry," he said.

I felt the bite of the wind and knew what he meant. I didn't want him to be a wolf right now, so I grabbed his arm and turned him toward the side door, the one that opened right at the base of the second staircase. "There."

He was shuddering by the time I shut the door behind him, trapping us both in a stairwell the size of a closet. He had to crouch, one hand braced against the wall, for about ten seconds while I stood over him with my hand on the doorknob, waiting to see if I'd have to open the door for him as a wolf.

Finally, he stood up, smelling wolfish but still wearing his own face. "That's the first time I've ever tried *not* to be a wolf," he told me. Then he turned and went up the stairs without waiting for me to tell him where to go.

I followed him up the narrow stairway, everything about him invisible except for the flash of his hands on the loose rail. I had this feeling that he and I, in this moment, were a car crash, and instead of putting on the brakes, I was hitting the accelerator.

At the top of the stairs, Cole hesitated, but I didn't. I took his hand and went past him, pulling him after me to another set of stairs, leading him all the way up to my room in the attic. Cole ducked to keep from hitting his head on the steeply slanted walls, and I turned and grabbed the back of his neck before he had time to straighten.

He smelled incredibly of wolf, which my head read as a weird combination of Sam and Jack and Grace, and Beck's house, but I didn't care, because his mouth was a drug. Kissing him, all I could think about was needing to feel his lower lip between my lips and his hands gripping my body to him. Everything in me was tingling, alive. I couldn't think about anything except the hungry way he kissed me back.

Far away downstairs, something *thumped* and *smashed.* Dad at work. It was a different planet, though, than this one with me and Cole. If Cole's mouth transported me so far from my life, how much further would the rest of him take me? I reached for Cole's jeans, my fingers fumbling over the waistband, and unbuttoned the button. Cole closed his eyes and sucked in a breath.

I broke away and backed onto my bed. My heart was

pounding a million miles an hour, watching him, imagining his weight pressing me down into the mattress.

He didn't follow me.

"Isabel," he said. His hands hovered by his sides.

"*What?*" I said. I was, again, out of breath, and he didn't even look like he was breathing. I thought about how I'd jogged that morning, hadn't been anywhere yet to reapply makeup, fix my hair. Was that it? I pushed myself up onto my elbows; my body was shaking. Something was rippling up inside of me that I couldn't identify. "What, Cole? Spit it out."

Cole just kept looking at me, standing there with his jeans unbuttoned and his hands half fisted by his sides. "I can't do this."

My voice came out derisive as I swept my eyes down him. "Doesn't look that way."

"I mean, I can't do this anymore." He buttoned his jeans and kept looking at me.

I wished he wouldn't. I turned my face away so that I didn't have to see the expression on his face. It felt condescending, whether or not he meant it that way. There wasn't anything he could say that wouldn't feel condescending.

"Isabel," he continued, "don't sulk. I *want* to. I really want to."

I didn't say anything. I stared at a feather from one of my pillows that had escaped onto my pale lavender bedspread.

"God, Isabel, don't make this harder, okay? I'm trying to remember how to be a decent person, okay? I'm trying to remember who I was before I couldn't stand myself."

"What, you didn't screw girls back then?" I snarled. A fat tear ran out of one of my eyes.

I heard him move; when I glanced up, he had turned to look out the dormer window, his arms crossed over his chest. "I thought you said you were saving yourself."

"What does that matter?"

"You don't want to sleep with me. You don't want to lose your virginity to some screwed-up singer. It'll make you hate yourself for the rest of your life. Sex does that. It's pretty awesome that way." His voice was bitter now. "You just don't want to feel anything, and it'll work great for about an hour. But then it'll be worse. Trust me."

"Well, you're the expert," I said. Another tear ran down my face. I hadn't cried since the week that Jack died. I just wanted Cole to go. Of all the people I might have wanted to see me finally cry, Cole St. Clair, king of the world, was not one of them.

Cole braced his arms on either side of the window; the last of the light coming through the clouds just barely illuminated his face. Not looking at me, he said, "I cheated on my first girlfriend. A lot. While I was on tour. When I got back, we fought about something else, so I told her I'd cheated on her with so many girls I couldn't remember their names. I told her that I'd seen enough now to know she wasn't anything special. We broke up. I guess I broke up with her. She was my best friend's sister, so I basically forced them to choose between me and each other." He laughed, a terrible, unfunny laugh. "And now Victor is out there in the woods somewhere, stuck as a wolf. Stuck as a guy becoming a wolf. I'm a great friend, aren't I?"

I didn't say anything. I didn't care about his ethical crisis.

"She was a virgin, too, Isabel," Cole said, finally looking at me again. "She hates me. She hates herself. I don't want to do that to you."

I stared at him. "I didn't ask for your help, did I? Did I invite you here for *therapy*? I don't *need* you to save me from myself. Or from you. How weak do you think I am?" For a brief moment, I didn't think I was going to say it. Then I did. "I should've just left you to kill yourself."

And again that face, always that face. Where he should have been looking at me like I'd hurt him, and there was . . . nothing.

Tears were burning down my cheeks, pricking when they met under my chin. I didn't even know what I was crying for.

"You're not that girl," Cole said, sounding tired. "Trust me, I've seen enough of them to know. Look. Don't cry. You're not *that* girl, either."

"Oh, yeah? What girl am I?"

"I'll let you know when I figure it out. Just don't cry."

The fact that he was pointing out my crying made it suddenly intolerable for him to see me doing it. I closed my eyes. "Just get out. Get out of my room."

When I opened them again, he was gone.

· COLE ·

Descending the stairs from her room, I was tempted to go outside and find out if the shivering gut-wrench I'd felt as I came in really meant what I thought it did. But I stayed in the warmth of the house. I felt like I knew something about myself that I hadn't before, a bit of knowledge so new that if I became a wolf now, I might lose it and not remember it whenever I became Cole again.

I wandered down the main stairs, mindful that her father was somewhere in the house's depths while Isabel stayed up in her tower alone.

What would it be like, growing up in a house that looked like this? If I breathed too hard it would knock some decorative bowl off the wall or cause the perfectly arranged dried flowers to weep petals. Sure, my family had been affluent growing up — successful mad scientists generally are — but it never looked like this. Our lives had looked . . . lived in.

I made a wrong turn on the way to the kitchen and found myself in the Museum of Natural Minnesota History instead: a massive, high-ceilinged room populated by an army of stuffed animals. There were so many that I would've doubted their realness, if not for the musty barnyard smell that filled the room. Weren't there animal extinction laws in Minnesota? Some of these animals looked pretty damned endangered; I'd never seen them in upstate New York, anyway. I peered at some sort of exotically patterned wildcat, which peered back at me. I remembered a snatch of earlier conversation with Isabel, back when I'd first met her — something about how her father had a penchant for shooting.

Sure enough, there was a wolf perpetually slinking by one of the walls, glass eyes glittering in the dim room. Sam must've been rubbing off on me, because suddenly, it seemed like a particularly horrible way to die, far away from your real body. Like an astronaut dying in space.

I glanced around at the animals — the line between them and me felt very thin — and pushed out a door on the other side of the room, one that I hoped would lead me back toward the kitchen.

I was wrong again. This was a plush round room, elegantly lit by the dying sunset coming through windows that made up half of the curving walls. At its center was a beautiful baby grand piano — and nothing else. Just the piano and the curving, burgundy walls. It was a room just for music.

I realized I couldn't remember the last time I'd sung.

I couldn't remember the last time I'd missed it.

I touched the edge of the piano; the smooth finish was cold beneath my fingertips. Somehow, right now, with the chill evening pressing in against the windows, waiting to change my skin, I was more human than I had been in a long time.

· ISABEL ·

I sulked for a while and then pushed myself off the bed and got cleaned up in my tiny bathroom. After I'd fixed my face, I got up and went to the window that Cole had been looking out from, wondering how many miles away he was by now. To my surprise, I could see a flashlight cutting an erratic path through the deep blue evening, heading down through the woods, toward the mosaic clearing. Was it Cole? He couldn't stay human in this weather, not when he'd been shuddering and close to the change before. My father?

I frowned at the enigmatic light, wondering if it meant trouble.

And then I heard the piano. I knew right off that it wasn't my father, who didn't even listen to music, and it had been months since my mother had played. Plus, it was not my mother's delicate, precise playing. It was an unsettling, creeping melody that repeated again and again on the upper keys, the spare tinkering of someone who expected other instruments to fill in the rest.

It was at such odds with how I imagined Cole that I *had* to see him playing. I silently made my way downstairs to the music room and hesitated outside the door, leaning in just enough to see without being seen.

And there he was. Not properly sitting on the bench, but leaning across it on one knee like he hadn't meant to stay that long. The musician's fingers that I'd spotted earlier weren't visible to me from this angle, but I didn't need to see them. All I had to see was his face. Unaware of an audience, lost in the repeated rhythm of the piano riff, lit by the evening, it was like all of Cole's armor had fallen off. This was not the aggressively handsome, cocky guy that I had met a few days ago. This was just a boy getting to know a tune. He looked young and uncertain and endearing, and I felt betrayed that he was somehow getting himself together when I couldn't.

Somehow, he was yet again being honest, sharing another secret, when I didn't have anything I was willing to give in return. For once, I saw *something* in his eyes. I saw that he was feeling again, and that whatever he was feeling was hurting him.

I wasn't ready to hurt.

Chapter Thirty-Seven

· SAM ·

The way home from Duluth was a collage of red taillights, highway signs suddenly looming out of the darkness only to disappear as quickly as they'd appeared, my voice coming out of the speakers and out of my mouth, Grace's face illuminated in little flashes and flickers by oncoming headlights.

Grace's eyes were half lidded with sleepiness, but I felt like I would never sleep again. I felt like this was the only day left in the world and I needed to be awake for it. I'd already told her about Cole, who he was, but I felt like there was more to say. I was probably annoying Grace, but she was being nice enough to not say anything about it. I said, again, "I *thought* he looked familiar. I just don't understand why Beck would do it."

Grace pulled her hands inside her sleeves and sealed the ends with her fingers. Her skin looked bluish by the light of the radio's display. "Maybe Beck didn't know who he was. I mean, I only kind of knew who NARKOTIKA was. I only know their one song. The one about breaking faces, or whatever."

"But he *had* to have an idea. Beck found him in Canada. While Cole was on tour. *On tour.* How long until someone in

Mercy Falls sees him and recognizes him? What if they come take him home and he turns into a wolf? Once he's human for the summer, will he just hide in the house and hope no one recognizes him?"

"Maybe," Grace said. She dabbed her nose with a tissue, then balled the tissue up and stuffed it in her coat pocket. "Maybe he wants to stay lost and it won't be a problem. I guess you should ask him. Or I could, since you don't like him."

"I just don't trust him." I ran my fingers back and forth across the steering wheel. Out of the corner of my eye, I saw Grace lean her head against the car door and sigh. She didn't look like herself.

Instantly, guilt flooded me. She'd worked so hard to make this the perfect day and I was ruining it. "Ah — I'm sorry. I'm being an ingrate. I won't worry about it anymore, okay? It can be tomorrow's problem."

"Liar."

"Don't be mad."

"I'm not mad. I'm just sleepy, and I want you to be happy."

I took one hand off the wheel to touch her hand where it lay on her lap. Her skin was very hot. "I am happy," I said, although now I felt worse than before. I was torn between wanting to lift up her hand to see if it smelled like wolf and wanting to leave it there and pretend that it didn't.

"This one is my favorite," she said softly. I didn't realize what she meant until she clicked back to the beginning of a track as soon as it ended. On the CD, the other Sam, the now-unchangeable one who stayed forever young, sang *I fell for her in summer, my lovely summer girl,* while another unchangeable Sam sang close harmonies over the first one.

My heart thumped in my chest as headlights striped across the interior of the car before leaving it dark again. I couldn't help but think about the last time I'd sung that song. Not in the studio, today, but the time before that. Sitting in a car as dark as pitch, like this one, my hand tangled in Grace's hair as she drove, right before the windshield exploded and turned the night into a good-bye.

It was supposed to be a happy song. It seemed wrong that it was forever poisoned by that memory, no matter how well things had turned out afterward.

Beside me, Grace turned her face to rest her cheek on the seat. She looked tired and faraway. "Will you fall asleep if I don't entertain you?" she asked, with a vague smile.

"I'm okay," I said.

Grace smiled at me, and tugged her jacket around her like a blanket. She kissed the air in my direction and closed her eyes. In the background, my voice sang *I'd be happy with this summer if it's all we ever had.*

Chapter Thirty-Eight

· SAM ·

The house was trashed. When I stepped into the living room, the first thing I saw was Cole with a broom and dustpan — a sight more ludicrous than him turning into a wolf — and then I saw shattered glass and tipped-over furniture behind him.

Grace said "Oh" behind me, in a sort of distressed way, and at the sound of her voice, Cole turned. He had the dignity to look surprised, though not enough to look apologetic.

I didn't know what to say to him. Every time I thought I might eventually work up some empathy and kindness toward him, he started some new fire. Did the rest of the house look like this? Or just every square inch of the living room?

Grace, however, looked at Cole, her hands stuck in her pockets, and said, "Problems?" in a light sort of way. With a smile in her voice.

And to my utter surprise, Cole smiled ruefully back at her, charming and *now* apologetic. "Herd of cats," he said. "I'm taking care of it." This last bit was with a glance in my direction, meant for me. Grace gave me a look that clearly said I was supposed to be nicer to him. I tried to remember if I'd ever been nice to him. I was sure I must've been, at the beginning.

I looked back at Grace. In the brighter light of the kitchen, she looked pale and tired, petal-thin skin showing darkness below. She probably ought to be in bed. She probably ought to be home. I wondered what her parents must be thinking and when they were supposed to return. I asked her, "I'll get the vacuum?" Meaning: *Is it okay if I leave you with him?*

Grace nodded firmly. "Good idea."

· GRACE ·

So this was Cole St. Clair. I'd never met a rock star before. I wasn't really disappointed, either. Even holding a broom and dustpan, he *looked* like a rock star, unreal and restless and *unsafe*. But I didn't agree with Sam about Cole's empty eyes. They looked full enough to me. Not that I was the greatest at reading people.

I looked straight at him and said, "So you're Cole."

"You're Grace," he said, though I didn't know how he would know.

"Yes," I said, and picked my way over to one of the living room chairs. I sank into it gratefully. I was beginning to feel like my body had been bludgeoned with rocks from the inside. I looked again at Cole. So this was the guy that Beck had hoped would take Sam's place. He'd obviously had good taste with Sam, so I was willing to give Cole the benefit of the doubt. I glanced at the stairs, to make sure Sam wasn't back yet from getting the vacuum, and said, "So. Is it what you expected?"

I liked Sam's girlfriend before she even opened her mouth, and then even more when she did speak. She wasn't what I'd expected, somehow, out of Sam's girlfriend. She was pretty in an undramatic way, and she had this great voice: very calm and matter-of-fact and distinctive.

I didn't understand her question at first. When I didn't answer right away, she clarified, "Being a wolf?"

I kind of loved that she just came out and said it.

"Better," I said, admitting the truth before I had time to censor it. She didn't look disgusted, like Isabel had. So I looked straight at her and told her the rest of the truth. "I became a wolf to lose myself, and that's just what I got. All I can think about when I'm a wolf is being with the other wolves. I don't think about the future or the past or who I was. It doesn't matter. All that matters is that moment, and being with the other wolves, and just being a ball of heightened senses. No deadlines. No expectations. It's amazing. It's the best drug ever."

Grace smiled at me as if I'd given her a present. It was such a nice smile, a knowing, genuine smile, that I thought in that moment that I would do anything to be her friend and to earn that smile again. I remembered what Isabel had said about Grace having been bitten but never shifting. I wondered if Grace was glad about that or if she felt cheated.

And so I asked her, "Do you feel cheated that you don't shift?"

She looked at her hand, which was resting gingerly on her stomach, and then back up at me. "I've always wondered what it would be like. I've always felt out of place. In between. I've always wanted — I don't know." She stopped. "Taking that vacuum on a walk, Sam?"

And then Sam was there, hauling an industrial vacuum cleaner into the room. He'd only been gone two seconds, but the room got brighter when they were together, as if they were two elements that became brilliant in proximity. At Sam's clumsy efforts to carry the vacuum, Grace smiled a new smile that I thought only he ever got, and he shot her a withering look full of the sort of subtext you could only get from a lot of conversations whispered after dark.

It made me think about Isabel, back at her house. We didn't have what Sam and Grace had. We weren't even close to having it. I didn't think what we had could get to this, even if you gave it a thousand years.

I was suddenly glad that I'd left Isabel on her bed and then alone at her house. It hurt to let myself remember I was poison to everyone I touched, but for once, it felt good to be self-aware. I couldn't stop myself from exploding, but I could at least learn to contain the fallout.

· GRACE ·

I felt bad sitting on the chair while Sam and Cole cleaned. Under normal circumstances, I would have jumped up to help. Cleaning a room that looked this bad was satisfying, because it really looked like you'd accomplished something by the end.

But tonight, I couldn't. It was all I could do to keep my eyes open. I felt like I'd been fighting something invisible all day and now it was catching up to me. My stomach felt warm and full under my hand; I imagined blood sloshing around inside it. And my skin was *hot hot hot*.

Across the room, I saw Sam and Cole working in silent concert, Cole crouched with the dustpan while Sam swept up the pieces too large to vacuum. For some reason, I was glad to see them working together. Again, I thought that Beck *must* have seen something in Cole. It couldn't have been a coincidence that he'd brought back another musician. He wouldn't have done something so risky as infecting a famous rocker if he hadn't thought there was a good reason behind it. Maybe he thought that if Sam managed to stay human, he and Cole would be friends.

It would be good for Sam to have a friend if I —

In my head, I saw Cole's face when he'd asked, *Do you feel cheated that you don't shift?*

When I was younger, I had imagined being a wolf. Running away with Sam the wolf into a golden wood, far away from my distant parents and the clutter of modern life. And again, when I'd thought I would lose Sam to the woods, I'd dreamed of going with him. Sam had been horrified. But now, finally, Cole had told me the other side of the coin. *All that matters is that moment, and being with the other wolves, and just being a ball of heightened senses.*

Yes.

It wouldn't be all bad. There was a payoff. To feel the forest floor under paws, to see and smell everything with brand-new senses. To know what it was like to be part of the pack, part of the wild. If I lost this battle, maybe it wouldn't be so terrible. To live in the woods that I loved, would that be such a great sacrifice?

Irrationally, I thought of the stack of unfinished mysteries on my bedroom shelf. I thought of lying on my bed with my jeans-covered legs tangled in Sam's, him reading his novel while I did my homework. Of riding in his car with the windows rolled down. Of us hand in hand on a college campus. Of an apartment full of our clutter, of a ring cupped in the palm of his hand, of life after school, of life as Grace.

I closed my eyes.

I hurt so much. Everything about me hurt, and there wasn't anything I could do. The promise of the woods was different when it wasn't a choice.

• SAM •

I thought she was tired. I figured it had been a long day. I didn't say anything until Cole noticed.

"She slept through the vacuum cleaner?" Cole asked, as if she were a small child or a dog and this was one of her more endearing habits.

I felt an irrational surge of anxiety, looking at her closed eyes, her slow breaths, her flushed cheeks. Then Grace lifted her head, and my heart started again.

I looked at the clock. Her parents would be getting back soon. We needed to get her home.

"Grace," I said, because she looked as if she might fall asleep again.

"Mmm?" She was still curled sideways on the armchair, her face resting on the arm.

"When did you say your parents wanted you back by?" I

asked. Grace's eyes darted to me, suddenly awake, and I saw in her expression that she hadn't been honest with me. My chest tightened. "Do they know you're gone?"

Grace looked away, cheeks colored. I'd never seen her look ashamed, and somehow it heightened how unwell she looked. "I should be home before they get back from the show. Midnight."

"So now," Cole said.

For a single, helpless, wordless moment, I thought Grace and I both had the same thought: that we didn't want this day to end. That we didn't want to part ways and climb into two cold beds far from each other. But there wasn't any use saying that out loud, so instead I said, "You do look really tired; you probably should get some sleep." Which was not at all what I wanted to say. I wanted to take her hand and lead her upstairs to my bedroom and whisper, *Stay. Just stay.*

But then I would be who her father thought I was, wouldn't I?

She sighed. "I don't want to."

I knelt in front of Grace so that I was eye to eye with her; her cheek was still pressed against the armchair. She looked so young and unguarded; I didn't realize how accustomed I was to her intense expression until it was gone.

"I don't want you to, either," I said, "But I also don't want you to get in trouble. Are you — okay to drive?"

"I have to be," Grace said, "I need my car for tomorrow. Oh, right. No school tomorrow; teacher work day. But for the next day."

She stood up, slowly, uncertainly. I was aware that both

Cole and I were just watching her as she found her keys and held them in her hand as if she wasn't sure what to do with them.

I didn't want her to go, but more than that, I didn't want her to drive.

"I'll drive her car," Cole said.

I blinked at him.

Cole shrugged. "I'll drive her car and she can ride with you. You can bring me back or . . ." He shrugged again.

Grace was giving me a look like she really wanted me to say yes, so I said yes. "Thanks," Grace told Cole.

"Don't mention it."

I was having a hard time believing Cole's transformation to a nice guy, but as long as he didn't wreck her car, I was happy to have the few extra moments with Grace and the peace of mind that she'd made it home.

So we went home, Cole a lonely figure in the driver's seat of Grace's car behind us, and me with Grace's hand held tightly in my lap. When we got to her parents' house, Cole deftly backed her car into the driveway while Grace leaned over and kissed me. It started off as a chaste kiss and then my mouth was parted and Grace's fingers held my shirt and I wanted to stay, oh God, I wanted to stay —

— and Cole tapped on the window. He was shuddering in the cold wind as I sheepishly rolled down the window.

"You might not want to put your tongue in her mouth; her dad's looking out the window. Also, *you*'d better hurry," he said, looking at Grace, "because in two seconds, I'm going to need *you*" — now he looked at me — "to pick up my clothes and I don't think you want a parental audience for that."

Grace's eyes got wide. "They're home?"

Cole jerked his chin toward the other car in the driveway. Grace stared at it, confirming my earlier suspicions about our visit being unapproved. "They said they'd be late. It's always after midnight for this show."

"I'll come in with you," I said, though I thought I'd rather hang myself. Cole was looking at me as if he was reading my thoughts.

She shook her head. "No. It'll be easier without you there. I don't want them yelling at you."

"Grace," I said.

"No," she said. "I'm not changing my mind. I can handle it. This needs to happen."

And that was my life, in a nutshell. Kissing Grace hurriedly good-bye, wishing her luck, letting her go, and then opening my car door to shield Cole's shift from prying neighborhood eyes.

Cole crouched on the asphalt, shaking, looking up at me. "Why's she grounded?"

I glanced at him and then returned my eyes to the house, making sure that no one was watching us. "Because her absentee parents decided they hated me. Probably because I was sleeping in her bed."

Cole spiked his eyebrows without commenting. He considered. He ducked his head while his shoulders shuddered. "Is it true they left her in a car to cook?"

"Yeah. That moment is a metaphor for their entire relationship."

"Nice," Cole said. After a moment, he said, "Why is this taking so long? Maybe I was wrong."

He already smelled of wolf. I shook my head. "It's because you're talking to me at the same time. Stop fighting it."

He was crouched like a runner now, his fingers spread on the asphalt, one knee bent, like he was ready to take off. He said, "Last night — I didn't think —"

I stopped him. And I said what I should've said before. "I was nobody when Beck brought me back, Cole. I was so damaged, I couldn't function. I barely ate and I used to scream when I heard running water. I don't remember that at all. I have giant holes in my memory. I'm still damaged, but not as bad as I was. Who am I to question Beck choosing you? Nobody."

Cole gave me a strange look, and then he threw up on the road. Jerking and shivering, he backed out of his human form, tearing his T-shirt as he thrashed against the side of my car. Cole as a wolf shuddered on the pavement for a long time before I was able to convince him to head toward the woods behind Grace's house.

After Cole had gone, I lingered by the open door of my car, looking at Grace's house, waiting for the light to come on in her bedroom and imagining myself there. I missed the sound of her shuffling her homework while I listened to music on her bed. I missed the cold of her feet against my legs when she climbed into bed. I missed the shape of her shadow where it fell across the page of my book. I missed the smell of her hair and the sound of her breath and my Rilke on her nightstand and her wet towel thrown over the back of her desk chair. It felt like I should be sated after having a whole day with her, but it just made me miss her more.

Chapter Thirty-Nine

· GRACE ·

It was oddly freeing, knowing that I was walking into trouble. I realized that all day I'd been wondering if I was going to get caught, what would happen, if they would find out later. And now I didn't have to wonder anymore.

I knew.

I shut the front door behind me and stepped into the hall. At the end of it, I could see my father standing with his arms crossed over his chest. My mother stood a few feet away from him, partially hidden by the door to the kitchen, her posture identical. They didn't say anything, and I didn't, either.

I wanted them to scream at me. I was ready for screaming. My whole body felt like it was shaking on the inside.

"Well?" my father asked when I got to the kitchen. That was it. No shouting. Just "Well?" as if he expected me to confess any number of sins.

"How was the show?" I asked.

My father gazed at me.

Mom broke first. "Don't pretend like nothing happened, Grace!"

"I'm not pretending," I said. "I'll say it: You told me not to go out, and I went out."

Mom's knuckles were white, pressed into fists at her sides. "You're acting like you didn't do anything wrong."

I felt deadly calm inside. It had been right to tell Sam not to come in; I wouldn't have been able to be this resolute with him here. "I didn't. I went to a studio in Duluth with my boyfriend, had dinner, and then came back home before midnight."

"We told you not to," Dad said. "That's what makes it wrong. You're grounded, and you went out anyway. I cannot believe how deeply you have betrayed our faith in you."

"You are completely blowing this out of proportion!" I snapped. I expected my voice to sound louder than his, but it sounded thin in comparison; the second wind I'd gotten driving back with Sam was gone. I could feel my pulse in my stomach and throat, hot and sick, but I pushed through it and kept my voice steady. "I'm not doing drugs or failing school or getting any hidden body parts pierced."

"How about —" He couldn't even say it.

"Having sex?" Mom finished for him. "In our house? How about being amazingly disrespectful. We've given you room to roam and you have —"

Now I found the fuel to be loud. "*Room to roam?* You've given me a planet to myself! I have sat in this house alone for hundreds and hundreds of nights, waiting for you two to come home. I've answered the phone a million times to hear 'Oh, we'll be late, honey.' I've arranged my own way home from school a thousand times. *Room to roam.* I finally have someone I've chosen for myself, and you guys can't handle it. You —"

"You're a teenager," Dad said dismissively. As if I hadn't just shouted. I would've doubted that I'd even raised my voice if my blood hadn't been pounding in my ears, punishingly painful. He continued, "What do you know about a responsible relationship? He's your first boyfriend. If you want us to believe you're responsible, prove it. And that doesn't involve underage sex and ignoring a direct order from your parents. Which is what you did."

"I did," I said. "I'm not sorry."

Dad's face turned red, the color rising from his collar to his hairline. In the light of the kitchen, it made him look very, very tanned. "How about this, then, Grace? You're never seeing him again. Does that make you sorry?"

"Oh, come on," I said. His words were starting to sound faraway and unimportant. I needed to sit down — lie down — sleep — something.

Dad's words were nails in my temples. "No, *you* come on. I'm not fooling around here. I don't like the person you are with him. He clearly doesn't respect us as your parents. I'm not letting you ruin your life for him."

I crossed my arms over my chest to hide that they were shaking. Part of me was in the kitchen having this conversation and part of me was thinking, *What is wrong with me?* My cheekbones pinched, warmed. I finally found my voice. "You can't do that. You can't keep me from seeing him."

"Oh, I can," Dad said. "You're seventeen and living under my roof, and as long as both those things are true, I absolutely can. When you're eighteen and out of high school, I can't tell you what to do, but right now, the entire state of Minnesota is on my side."

My stomach did something weird, a little twist, like nerves, at the same time that my forehead tingled. I put my finger to my nose, and it came away with a touch of red. I wouldn't let them see it; put me on the spot even more. Grabbing a tissue from the table and pressing it to my nostrils, I said, "He's not just a boy."

Mom turned away, waving her hand in the air like she was just tired of the whole thing. "Right."

At that moment, I hated her.

Dad said, "Well, for the next four months he is. You're not seeing him again, as long as I have anything to say about it. We're not doing more nights like this. And this conversation is over."

I couldn't stand to be in the same room as them a second longer. I couldn't stand to see the way Mom was looking back over her shoulder at me, eyebrow lifted like she was waiting for my next move. And I couldn't stand the pain.

I rushed to my room and slammed the door hard enough that I felt everything inside me shake.

Chapter Forty

· GRACE ·

"Dying is a wild night and a new road."

I had words stuck in my head instead of a song. I couldn't remember who wrote them, only that I had heard Sam read them out loud, looking up from the book and trying out the way they sounded. I remembered the moment, even: sitting in my dad's old office here in the house, riffling through notes for an oral presentation while Sam slouched over a book. In the comfort of that room, icy rain sliding down the windows, spoken in Sam's soft voice, the quote had seemed innocent. Clever, maybe.

Now, in the dark, empty silence of my room, the words running feverishly through my head again and again, they seemed terrifying.

The sickness inside me was impossible to ignore now. I waited a long time for my nose to stop bleeding, using toilet paper after I ran out of tissues. It seemed like it wouldn't ever stop. My guts were twisted inside me, my skin boiling.

All I wanted was to know what was really wrong with me. How long it would take. What it would do to me at the end. If

I knew all those things, if I had something concrete to hold on to instead of the pain, I could make my peace with it.

But I didn't have any answers.

So I could not sleep. I could not move.

I kept my eyes closed. The space beside me where Sam was supposed to be seemed huge. Before all this, when I had him with me, I would just roll over and press my face into his back when I woke up in the night. Let his breathing lull me back to sleep. But Sam wasn't here tonight, and sleep seemed far away and irrelevant with the crawling heat inside me.

In my head, I heard Dad forbidding me to see him again. My breathing caught a little at the memory. He'd change his mind. He couldn't mean that. I pushed my thoughts onto something else. My red coffeepot. I didn't know if such a thing actually existed, but if it did, I was buying one. Immediately. It seemed incredibly important to make it a goal. Get some money, buy a red coffeepot, move out. Find a new place to plug it in.

I flipped onto my back and laid my hand on my stomach, trying to see if I could actually feel the rolling of stomach under my fingers. I was so hot again, and my head felt weird and floaty, disconnected from the rest of me.

The back of my mouth tasted like copper. No matter how much I swallowed, I couldn't get the taste out of my mouth.

I felt *wrong.*

What's happening to me?

There was no one to ask, so I added up the clues for myself. The stomachache. The fever. Nosebleeds. Fatigue. The smell of wolf. The way the wolves had looked at me; the way Isabel had looked at me. Sam's fingers on my arm as I left, turning to me for one last hug. They all seemed like so many good-byes.

Finally, my denial fell away.

Even though it could be just a virus. Even though it could be something serious but treatable. Even though I really had no way of knowing . . .

I knew.

This pain I was feeling — it was my future. A change I couldn't control. I could dream about red coffeepots all I wanted. But my body would have the final say.

I sat up in the darkness, pushing back against the wolf inside me, tugging the blankets so they pooled in my lap. I wanted to be with Sam. The cool air bit at my cheeks and bare shoulders. I wished I were still at Beck's house, back in Sam's bed under his bedroom sky of birds. I swallowed down the pain, forced it deeper. If I were there now, he would wrap his arms around me and he'd tell me it would be all right, and it *would* be all right, at least for tonight.

I imagined myself driving back there tonight. The look on his face.

I rubbed the bare bottoms of my feet against each other. It was foolish, of course. There were a thousand reasons to stay, but . . .

I pushed back the barbed static in my head. Focused. Mentally made a list of what I needed. I'd get a pair of jeans from the middle drawer of my dresser and slide on a sweater and some socks. My parents wouldn't hear. The floor didn't creak much. It was possible. I hadn't heard any movement upstairs for a long time now. If I didn't turn on my car lights, they might not notice me pulling out of the driveway.

My heart was pounding now with the idea of escape.

I knew it wasn't worth getting in more trouble with my parents, not as angry as they were. I knew it wasn't going to be easy to drive with this roar of blood in my ears, the fever trailing across my skin.

But I couldn't really *get* into more trouble. They'd already forbidden me to see him. What could they do that was beyond that?

And I didn't know how many more nights I had.

My thoughts went to Mom, scoffing over the difference between love and lust. Me walking in the woods afterward, trying to dredge up guilt for yelling at her. I thought about my dad opening my door to look for Sam. How long it had been since they had asked me where I'd been, how I was doing, if I needed anything from them.

I'd seen my parents together; they were family. They still cared about the little details in each other's lives. I'd seen Beck, too, and the way that he *knew* Sam. The way he loved him. And Sam, the way he still orbited Beck's memory like a lost satellite. That was family. My parents and me . . . we lived together, sometimes.

Could you outgrow your parents?

I remembered the way the wolves had watched me. Remembered wondering how much time I had. How many nights I had to spend with Sam, how many nights I was wasting here alone.

I could still taste the copper. The sickness inside me wasn't getting any smaller. It raged, but I was still stronger than it. There were still things I had control over.

I got out of bed.

A sort of deadly calm filled me as I padded around my room, getting my jeans and underwear and shirts and two extra pairs of socks. The eye of the hurricane. I stuffed the clothes in my backpack with my homework and Sam's beloved copy of Rilke from the bed stand. I touched the edge of my dresser, held my pillow, stood by the window where I'd once stared down a wolf. My heart hummed in my chest, expecting at any moment for my mother or my father to open the door and find me in the midst of my preparations. Surely someone would have to just *feel* the seriousness of what I was doing.

But nothing happened. I got my toothbrush and hairbrush from the bathroom on my way down the hall, and the house stayed silent. I hesitated by the front door, my shoes in my hand, and listened.

Nothing.

Was I really doing this?

"Good-bye," I whispered. My hands were trembling.

The door *shushed* across the welcome mat as I pulled it shut behind me.

I didn't know when I'd come back.

Chapter Forty-One

· SAM ·

Without Grace, I was a nocturnal animal. I stalked ants in the kitchen, waiting by the insufficient light of the recessed bulbs with a glass and a piece of paper so that I could transport them outside. I took Paul's dusty guitar from its perch by the mantel and tuned it. First properly, then to drop D, then to DADGAD, then back to proper. In the basement, I browsed Beck's nonfiction until I found a book on taxes and another on winning friends and influencing people and another on meditation. I stacked them into a cairn of books I never intended to read. Upstairs, in my bathroom, I sat on the tile and experimented with the right way to trim my toenails. Cupping my fingers beneath my feet only caught the flying nails half the time, and if I left them to fly where they would, I could only find half the nails on the white tile. So it was a losing battle, with fifty percent casualties either way.

Partway through the process, I heard the wolves begin to howl, loud through Beck's bedroom window. Their songs sounded different from night to night, depending on how I felt.

They could be sonorous, beautiful, a heavenly choir in heavy, wood-scented pelts. Or an eerie, lonely symphony, notes falling against one another into the night. Joyful, voices lifted, calling down the moon.

Tonight, they were a cacophonous mob, howls vying for attention, barks interspersed. Restless. A pack discordant. A pack dispersed. They usually howled like that on nights when either Beck or Paul was human, but tonight they had both their leaders. I was the only one missing.

I stood up, cold floorboards pressing up against the soles of my human feet, and went to the window. I hesitated for a moment, then flicked the lock and threw open the window. Frigid night air rushed in, but it didn't do anything to me. I was just human. Just me.

The wolves' howls poured in as well, surrounding me.

Do you miss me?

The disorganized cries continued, more protest than song.

I miss you guys.

And, with dull surprise, I realized that was all there was to it. I missed them. I didn't miss *it.* This — this person leaning on the sash, full of human memories and fears and hopes, this person who would grow old — was who I was, and I didn't want to lose that. I didn't miss standing amongst them, howling. It would never compare to the feel of my fingers on the strings of my guitar. Their poignant song could never be as triumphant as the sound of me saying Grace's name.

"Some of us are trying to sleep!" I shouted out into the darkness, which swallowed the lie.

The night went quiet. The darkness was frozen into silence; no birdcalls or rustling of leaves in this still, still night. Just the distant hiss of tires on a far-off road.

"Roooooooooooo!" I called out the window, feeling clownish as I prompted my pack.

A pause. Long enough that I realized how badly I wanted for them to need me.

Then they began to howl again, just as loud as before, their voices spilling over one another with new purpose.

I grinned.

A familiar voice behind me made me jerk; I caught myself just before I put a hand through the screen.

"I thought you were supposed to have animal cunning and the ability to hear a pin drop a mile away."

Grace. Grace's voice.

When I turned, she was standing in the doorway, a backpack slung on her shoulder. Her smile was . . . shy.

"And here I am, sneaking up on you while you — what were you doing, anyway?"

I pushed down the window and turned back around, blinking. Grace was standing here in the doorway to Beck's bedroom. Grace, who was supposed to be home in her own bed. Grace, who haunted my thoughts when I couldn't dream. I felt like I couldn't be surprised. Hadn't I known all along that she'd appear here? Hadn't I just been waiting to find her in my doorway?

I finally regained control of my muscles and crossed the room to her. I was close enough to kiss her, but instead I reached for the dangling, loose strap of her backpack and ran my thumb along its ridged surface. The backpack's presence answered one of my unasked questions. Another question was answered by the still-lingering wolf scent on her breath. And the host of other questions I wanted to ask — *Do you know what will happen when they find out? Do you know this will change everything? Are you all right with how they will see you? How they will see me?* — had already been answered "yes" by Grace, or she wouldn't be here. She wouldn't have set a foot outside her bedroom door without thinking through everything.

Which meant I only had one question to ask: "Are you sure?"

Grace nodded.

And just like that, everything changed.

I tugged the backpack strap gently and sighed. "Oh, Grace."

"Are you mad?"

I took her hands and rocked them back and forth, dancing without lifting a foot. My head was a jumble of Rilke — *"You who never arrived in my arms, Beloved, who were lost from the start"* — her father's voice — *I'm trying really hard to not say something I'll regret later* — and longing personified, a physical being here, finally, in my wanting hands.

"I'm scared," I said.

But I felt a smile on my face. And when she saw my smile, an anxious cloud that I hadn't even noticed on her face sailed away, leaving only clear skies and finally, the sun.

"Hi," I said, and I hugged her. I missed her more now that I actually had her in my arms than when I hadn't.

· GRACE ·

I felt hazy and slow, moving in a dream.

This was someone else's life, where the girl ran away to her boyfriend's house. This wasn't reliable Grace, who never turned in homework late or stayed out partying or colored outside the lines. And yet, here I was, in this rebellious girl's body, carefully laying my toothbrush beside Sam's brand-new red one like I belonged here. Like I was going to be here a while. My eyes ached from fatigue, but my brain kept *whirring*, wide awake.

The pain was quieter now, calmed. I knew it was just hiding, pushed away by the knowledge that Sam was near, but I was glad of the respite.

On the bathroom floor, I saw a little half-moon of a toenail lying on the tile next to the base of the toilet. Its utter normalcy sort of drove home, with utter finality, that I was standing in Sam's bathroom in Sam's house and I was planning on spending the night in Sam's bedroom with Sam.

My parents would kill me. What would they do first, in the morning? Call my cell phone? Hear it ringing wherever they'd hidden it? They could call the police, if they wanted to. Like my dad said, I was still under eighteen. I closed my eyes, imagining Officer Koenig knocking on the door, my parents standing behind him, waiting to drag me back home. My stomach turned over.

Sam softly knocked on the open bathroom door. "You okay?"

I opened my eyes and looked at him standing in the doorway. He had changed into some sweats, and a T-shirt with an octopus printed on it. Maybe this was a good idea after all.

"I'm okay."

"You look cute in your pajamas," he told me, his voice hesitant as if he were admitting something he hadn't meant to.

I reached out and put a hand on his chest, feeling the rise and fall through the thin fabric. "You do, too."

Sam made a little rueful shape with his mouth and then peeled my hand from his chest. Using it to steer me, he switched off the bathroom light and led me down the hall, his bare feet padding on the floorboards.

His bedroom was illuminated only by the hall light and the ambient glow from the porch light through the window; I could just barely see the white shape of the blanket tidily turned down on the bed. Releasing my hand, Sam said, "I'll turn off the hall light once you're in, so you don't smack into anything."

He ducked his face away from me then, looking shy, and I sort of knew how he felt. It was like we were just meeting each other again for the first time, like we'd never kissed or spent the night together. Everything felt brand-new and shiny and terrifying.

I crept into the bed, the sheets cool under my hands as I edged toward the side of the mattress that met the wall. The hall went dark and I heard Sam sigh — a weighty, shaky sigh — before I heard the floorboards creak with his steps. The room was just light enough for me to see the edge of his shoulders as he climbed into the bed with me.

For a moment, we lay there, not touching, two strangers, and then Sam rolled toward me so that his head was on the same pillow as mine.

When he kissed me, his lips soft and careful, it was all the thrill of our first kiss and all the practiced familiarity of the accumulated memory of all our kisses. I could feel the beat of his heart through his T-shirt, a rapid *thud* that sped even more when I twined our legs together.

"I don't know what will happen," he said softly. His face was right next to my neck, his words spoken right into my skin.

"I don't, either," I said. Nerves and the thing inside me twisted my stomach.

Outside, the wolves still intermittently sang, their cries rising and falling, hard to hear now. Sam, beside me, was very still. "Do you miss it?" I asked him.

"No," he said, so fast that I couldn't believe he'd actually considered my question. After a moment, he gave me the rest of his answer, stumbling and hesitant. "This is what I want. I want to be me. I want to know what I'm doing. I want to remember. I want to matter."

He was wrong, though. He had always mattered, even when he was a wolf in the woods behind my house.

I turned my face quickly, to wipe my nose on a tissue I'd brought with me from the bathroom. I didn't have to look at it to know that it would be dotted with red.

Sam took a deep breath and wrapped his arms around me. He buried his head in my shoulder, and I felt him take handfuls of my pajama top in his fists as he breathed in my scent. "Stay with me, Grace," he whispered, and I balled my shaking fists up against his chest. "Please stay with me."

I could smell my own skin, the sick-sweet almond smell of me, and I knew he wasn't talking about just tonight.

Folded in my arms you're a butterfly in reverse
giving up your wings inheriting my curse
you're letting go of
me
you're letting go

Chapter Forty-Two

· SAM ·

The longest day of my life began and ended with Grace closing her eyes.

The next morning I awoke with Grace not quite in my arms, but rather sprawled indelicately across me and my pillow, pinning me to the bed. Sunlight framed both of us; the rectangle square of sun from the window bordered our bodies perfectly. The day had gotten late while we slept it away. It seemed like forever since I had slept like that, dead to the world, unmindful of the sunlight. Propping myself up on one elbow, I had a weird, falling sensation, the weight of thousands of unlived days stacked upon one another as I looked down at Grace. She mumbled as she awoke. When she turned her face toward me, I saw a flash of red before she ran her arm across her face.

"Ew," she said, opening her eyes to look at her wrist.

"Do you need a tissue?" I asked.

Grace groaned. "I'll get it."

"That's okay," I said. "I'm already up."

"You are not."

"I am. See, I'm leaning on my elbow. That is one thousand

times more up than you." Normally at this point I would've leaned in for a kiss or to tickle her or to run my hand down her thigh or to rest my head on her stomach, but today, I was afraid of breaking her.

Grace looked at me as if the lack of contact was conspicuous. "I could just wipe my nose on your shirt."

"Point taken!" I said, and slid out of bed to get a tissue. When I came back, her hair was mussed and hung down around her face, hiding her expression. Without comment, she wiped her arm, balling the tissue up quickly, but not quickly enough for me to miss the blood on it.

I felt wound tight.

Handing her a wad of tissues, I said, "I think we should take you to the doctor."

"Doctors are useless," Grace said. She dabbed at her nose, but there was nothing there anymore. She wiped off her arm instead.

"I want to go anyway," I said. Something had to put to rest this anxiety inside my chest.

"I hate doctors."

"I know," I said. This was true. Grace had waxed poetic about this before; personally, I thought it had more to do with her aversion to wasting time than it did to any fear or disdain of those in the medical profession. I thought what she really had was an aversion to waiting rooms. "We'll go to the health center. They're fast."

Grace made a face, then shrugged an agreement. "Okay."

"Thank you," I said, relieved as she *thumped* back down onto a pillow.

Grace closed her eyes. "I don't think they'll find anything."

I thought she was probably right. But what else could I do?

· GRACE ·

Part of me wanted to go to the doctor, in case they could help. But more of me was afraid to, in case they couldn't. What option was left if this failed?

Being in the health center added to the surreal aspect of the day. I'd never been, though Sam seemed familiar enough with it. The walls were a putrid shade of sea green and the exam room had a mural featuring four misshapen killer whales frolicking in sea green waves. All the while the nurse and the doctor were questioning me, Sam kept putting his hands in his pockets and taking them out. When I shot him a look, he quit doing it for a few minutes, then started cracking his knuckles with his thumb instead.

My head was swimmy, which I told the doctor, and my nose obligingly demonstrated its bleeding for the nurse. I could only describe my stomachache, however, and both of them looked mystified when I tried to get them to smell my skin (the doctor, however, did).

Ninety-five minutes after we'd entered, I left with a prescription for a seasonal allergy medication, a recommendation to get an over-the-counter iron supplement and saline nose spray, and the memory of a lecture on teens and sleep deprivation. Oh, and Sam was sixty dollars poorer.

"Do you feel better?" I asked Sam as he opened the door to the Volkswagen for me. He was a hunched bird in this spring weather, black and stark against the gray clouds. It was impossible to tell from the occluded sky if it was the beginning of the day or the end of one.

"Yes," he said. He was still a terrible liar.

"Good," I said. I was still a fantastic one.

And the thing inside my muscles groaned and stretched and ached.

Sam took me for a coffee, which I did not drink, and while we sat in Kenny's, Sam's cell phone rang. Sam tipped the phone toward me so I could see Rachel's number.

Leaning back, he handed me the phone. He had his arm curled around the back of my neck in a way that was very uncomfortable but very charming, so I couldn't move. I leaned my cheek against his arm and flipped the phone open.

"Hello?"

"Grace, oh my God, are you totally crazy?"

My stomach twisted. "You must've talked to my parents."

"They called my house. Probably the Tundra Queen's as well. They wanted to know if you were with me, because *apparently you did not spend last night in your bed*, and you were not near your phone today, and they were growing slightly concerned, in a way that is very disturbing for Rachel to be involved in!"

I pressed my hand into my forehead and leaned my elbow on the table. Sam politely pretended not to listen, though Rachel's voice was clearly audible. "I'm sorry, Rachel. What did you tell them?"

"You know I'm not a good liar, Grace! I couldn't tell them you were at my house!"

"I know," I said.

Rachel said, "So I told them you were at Isabel's."

I blinked. "You *did*?"

"What else was I supposed to do? Tell them you were at The Boy's, and have them kill both of you?"

My voice came out sounding a bit more pugnacious than I intended. "They're going to find out eventually."

"What do you mean? Grace Brisbane, you do not mean that you're not going back home again. Tell me that this was just because you were momentarily angry at them for grounding you. Or even tell me it's because you could not live without The Boy's stunning Boyfruits for another night. But don't tell me you think it's forever!"

Sam's face was twisted into a weird shape at the mention of his Boyfruits. I told Rachel, "I don't know. I hadn't thought that far ahead. But no, I don't really feel like going back anytime soon. Mom helpfully told me she thought that me and Sam were just a fling and that I needed to learn the difference between love and lust. And last night, Dad told me I wasn't allowed to see him until I was eighteen."

Sam looked stricken. I hadn't told him that part.

"Wow. Again, the limited understanding of parental types never fails to surprise me. Especially because The Boy is . . . well, The Boy is clearly incredible, so what is their problem? But, anyway, what should I do? Are you going to . . . um. Yeah, what's going to happen?"

"Eventually I'll get tired of wearing the same two shirts over and over, and I'll have to go home and confront them," I said. "But until then, I guess . . . I guess I'm not talking to them." It felt weird to say it. Yes, I was furious at them for what they'd said. But even I knew that those things weren't really worthy, on their own, of running away. It was more like they were the tip of the iceberg, and I wasn't so much running away as making their emotional distance from me official. They had seen no less of me today than they had most other days of my teen years.

"Wow," Rachel said. You knew she was nonplussed when that was all she could say.

"I'm just done," I said, and I was surprised to hear my voice waver, just a little. I hoped Sam hadn't caught it; I made sure my voice was firm when I said, "I'm not pretending we're a happy family anymore. I'm taking care of myself for once."

It seemed suddenly profound, this moment, sitting in a faded little booth in Kenny's, the napkin holder on the table reflecting an image of Sam leaning against me, and me feeling like an island floating farther and farther from shore. I could feel my brain taking a picture of this scene, the washed-out lighting, the chipped edge of the plates, the still-full coffee mug in front of me, the neutral colors of the layered T's Sam wore.

"Wow," Rachel said again. She paused, for a long moment. "Grace, if you're really serious about this . . . be careful, okay? I mean . . . don't hurt The Boy. It just seems like this is the kind of war that leaves lots of bodies behind and leaves the villages of the surrounding areas exhausted and war-weary from all the pillaging."

"Believe me," I said, "The Boy is the one thing in all this that I'm determined to keep."

Rachel breathed out a huge sigh. "Okay. You know I'll do whatever you need me to do. You probably ought to touch base with she-of-the-pointy-boots to make sure that she knows what's going on."

"Thanks," I said, and Sam leaned his head on my shoulder as if he were suddenly as exhausted as I was. "I'll see you tomorrow, okay?"

Rachel agreed and hung up. I slid the phone back into the pocket of Sam's cargo pants before resting my head against his head. I closed my eyes, and for a moment I just let myself inhale the scent of his hair and pretend that we were already back at Beck's house. I just wanted to be able to curl up with him and sleep without having to worry about confronting my parents or Cole or the odor of almonds and wolf that was starting to blossom on my skin again.

"Wake up," Sam said.

"I'm not sleeping," I replied.

Sam just looked at me. Then he looked at my coffee. "You didn't drink any of your liquid energy, Grace." He didn't wait for my answer; he simply took some bills out of his wallet and slid them underneath his own empty mug. He looked tired and older, dark circles beneath his eyes, and suddenly I was suffused with guilt. I was making things so hard on him.

My skin felt weird and tingly; I tasted copper again.

"Let's go home." I said.

Sam didn't ask me which home I meant. The word meant only one place now.

Chapter Forty-Three

• SAM •

I should've known it would come to this. And maybe, in some way, I did, because I wasn't surprised when I saw a blue SUV in Beck's driveway, one of the glossy, huge ones that were the size of a small convenience store. The license plate said CULPEPR, and Tom Culpeper stood in front of it. He was gesturing wildly to Cole, who looked profoundly unimpressed.

I had no hard feelings about Tom Culpeper, other than those generated by him staging a hunt on the wolves and shooting me in the neck. So my stomach clenched when I saw him standing in the driveway.

"Is that Tom Culpeper?" Grace said, voice conveying all the lack of enthusiasm I felt. "Do you think he's here about Isabel?"

As I parked on the street, an uneasy tingle shot down my limbs.

"No," I said. "I don't think he is."

· COLE ·

Tom Culpeper was a prick.

Being one myself, I was allowed to think such things. He'd been trying to get Beck's whereabouts out of me for about five minutes when Sam's little gray Volkswagen pulled up at the curb. Sam, in the driver's seat, looked tight mouthed as he got out of the car. Clearly he had some history with this tool.

Tom Culpeper stopped running his mouth as Sam walked across the brittle lawn, casting no shadow in the sunless afternoon.

"What can I do for you?" Sam asked.

Culpeper put his thumbs in the pockets of his khakis and eyed Sam. Suddenly he was jovial, confident. "You're Geoffrey Beck's kid. The adopted one."

Sam's smile was brittle. "I am."

"Do you know if he's around?"

" 'Fraid not," Sam replied. Grace joined us, standing between me and him. She had a vague frown on her face, like she was hearing music no one else did and she didn't like it. Culpeper's amiable expression sharpened when he saw her. Sam added, "I'll let him know you stopped by."

"He won't be back today?" Culpeper asked.

"No, sir," Sam said, managing to sound both polite and insolent. Perhaps unintentionally.

"That's too bad. Because I had something for him that I really wanted to give to him in person. But you know, I think you can probably handle it for him." He gestured with his chin toward the back of the SUV.

Sam's face was as gray as the sky above, as he and I followed; Grace lagged behind.

"Do you think this looks like something that might interest Mr. Beck?" Culpeper asked. He lifted the tailgate.

This moment. There are moments that change you forever, and this was one of mine.

In the back of the SUV, among plastic grocery bags and a fuel can, was a dead wolf. It lay on its side, shoved a bit to make it fit, its legs crossed over each other. Blood matted the fur at its neck and again at its stomach. Its jaw was slightly slack, the tongue lying limply across the canines.

Victor.

Sam put the back of his fist to his mouth, very softly, and then lowered it. I stared at the pale gray face with the dark markings, and at Victor's brown eyes staring blankly at the carpeted wall of the SUV.

Crossing my arms, I balled my hands to keep them from shaking. My heart was thumping in a frenzied, desperate way. I needed to turn away, but I couldn't.

"What is this?" Sam asked coldly.

Culpeper grabbed one of the wolf's back legs and, with a single jerk, tugged the body over the bumper. It made a sickening *thump* when it hit the driveway. Grace cried out, her voice full of the horror that was just starting to rise up inside me.

I had to turn around. My gut felt like it was unwinding inside me.

"You tell your father this," Culpeper snarled. "You tell him to stop feeding these things. I see another one on my property, I *will* shoot it. I will shoot every single wolf I can get in my sights. This is Mercy Falls, not *National Geographic*." He looked at Grace, who appeared as sick as I felt. To her, he said, "I would've thought you'd know to keep better company, considering who your father is."

"Better company than your daughter?" Grace managed to shoot back.

Culpeper gave her a thin smile.

Sam had gone very, very quiet, but Grace's voice seemed to bring him back to life. "Mr. Culpeper, I'm sure you're aware of my adopted father's profession."

"Very. One of the very few things we have in common."

Sam's voice was disturbingly even. "I'm pretty sure there are legal implications to tossing a dead wild animal on private property. It's out of hunting season for pretty much every animal, and most certainly for wolves. And I'm guessing if anyone knew about those implications, it would be him."

Tom shook his head and headed back around toward the driver-side door. "Right. Wish him luck on that. You have to spend better than half the year in Mercy Falls if you want the judge on your side."

I wanted to hit him so badly it hurt. I wanted to pound the waxy smug smile from his mouth.

I didn't think I could stop myself.

I felt a touch on my arm and looked down to see Grace's fingers circling my wrist above my fisted hand. She looked up at me, biting her lip. From the look in her eyes and the set of her shoulders, I could see that she wanted to pound the living crap out of him, too, and that was what stopped me.

"Better move that thing if you don't want me to back over

it," Culpeper called as he slapped the driver's door shut, and the three of us rushed forward to pull Victor's body off the driveway, right before the SUV's engine roared and he backed out.

It had been forever since I'd felt so damn young, so absolutely powerless against an adult.

As soon as the blue SUV was out of sight, Grace said, "He's gone. The bastard."

I dropped to the ground next to the wolf and lifted the muzzle. Victor's eyes looked back at me, dull and lifeless, losing meaning every second this side of death.

And I said what I should've said a long time ago — "I'm sorry, Victor. I'm so sorry" — to the last person I would ever destroy.

Chapter Forty-Four

· SAM ·

I felt like I had dug too many graves this year already.

Together, Cole and I got the shovel from the garage and took turns digging through the partially frozen ground. I didn't know what to say to him. My mouth felt stuffed full of words that I should've said to Tom Culpeper, and when I tried to find some left over for Cole, I came up short.

I wanted Grace to wait inside, but she insisted on coming along. She watched us from among the trees, arms folded tightly across her chest, eyes red.

I had chosen this site, sloped and sparse, because of its beauty in summer; when it rained, the leaves flipped up to reveal glowing white undersides that rippled in the wind. However, I had never been human here to appreciate its equally beautiful presence this time of year. While we dug, the evening transformed the woods, making ribbons of warm sunlight across the forest floor and painting stripes of blue shadows over our bodies. Everything was splashes of yellow and indigo, an impressionist painting of three teens at an evening funeral.

Cole had transformed yet again from the guy I'd seen last. When I handed off the shovel to him, we exchanged glances. And for the first time since I'd met him, his expression wasn't empty. When our eyes met, I saw pain and guilt . . . and Cole.

Finally, Cole.

Victor's body lay a few feet away from us, partially wrapped in a sheet. In my head, I came up with lyrics for him as I dug.

Sailing to an island unknown
Failing to find your way home
you walk under a sea
leagues beneath us

Grace caught my eye, as if she knew what I was doing. The lyrics could also be about her, so I shoved them out of my mind. Digging and waiting to dig. That was what I thought about as the sun crept down.

When the grave was deep enough, we both hesitated. From here, I could see Victor's belly and the blast that had killed him. In the end, he died as an animal.

It could have so easily been Beck's or Paul's body that Culpeper pulled out of the back of his truck. Last year, it could have been me. It was almost me.

· GRACE ·

Cole couldn't do it.

When the grave was finally dug and he was finally standing by Sam and looking down at the body next to the pit, I saw that

Cole couldn't do it. I recognized the veneer of control as he stood, his breaths ragged enough to make his body sway with each exhalation.

I'd been there.

"Cole," I said, and both Sam's head and Cole's jerked toward me. They had to look down, because I had long before gotten too tired to stand. From my place in the cold, dry leaves, I gestured toward Victor. "Why don't you say something? I mean, to Victor."

Sam blinked at me, surprised. I think maybe he'd forgotten that I'd already had to say good-bye to him once. I knew how it felt.

Cole didn't look at either of us. He pressed his knuckles to his forehead and swallowed. "I can't, um . . ." He stopped, because his voice was unsteady. I saw his throat move as he swallowed again.

We were making it harder for him. We were making him fight both grief and tears.

Sam picked up on this, and said, "We can go if you want some privacy."

"Please don't," Cole whispered.

His face was still dry, but a tear, cold against my hot cheek, streaked off my chin.

Sam waited a long moment for Cole to speak, and when he didn't, Sam recited a poem, his voice low and formal, "*Death arrives among all that sound, like a shoe with no foot in it, like a suit with no man in it . . .*" I watched Cole go completely still as Sam spoke. Still like not moving. Not breathing. A sort of still so deep you know it went all the way through him.

Sam took a step toward Cole and then, carefully, he put a hand on Cole's shoulder.

"This isn't Victor. This is something Victor wore, for a little while. Not anymore."

They both looked at the body of the wolf, stiff and small and defeated-looking in death.

Cole sank to the ground.

· COLE ·

I had to look at his eyes.

I uncovered the body so there was nothing between me and Victor's brown eyes. They were empty and faraway, ghosts of his real eyes.

The cold shook my shoulders, a soft threat of what was to come, but I pushed it away, out of my head. I looked into his eyes and tried to pretend that there was no wolf around them.

I remembered the day I'd asked Victor if he wanted to start a band with me. We were in his room, which was one part bed and three parts drum kit, and he was slamming out a solo. The echo was so loud in the small room that it sounded like there were three drummers. His poster frames jittered on the walls and his alarm clock was slowly jerking toward the edge of his bedside table. Victor's eyes were shining with manic fervor, and he made a crazy face at me every time he kicked the bass drum.

I could barely hear Angie's shout from the next room. "Vic, you're making my ears bleed! Cole, shut that stupid door!"

I shut Victor's bedroom door behind me.

"Sounds hot," I told him.

Victor tossed me one of his drumsticks. It arced past my head, and I had to jerk to catch it. I took a whack at his cymbals.

"Victor!" howled Angie.

He called, "These are magic hands!"

"One day, people will *pay* for the privilege of listening!" I shouted back.

Victor grinned at me and did a fast run with just one stick and the bass drum.

I smashed the cymbal again to piss Angie off and turned to Victor.

"What's up?" Victor asked. He pounded at the drums again, smacking his stick off the one I held in my hand in the middle of the run.

"So you ready to do this thing?" I asked him.

Victor lowered his drumstick. His eyes were steady on me. "What?"

"NARKOTIKA," I said.

Now, in this freezing cold wind, the sun disappearing, I reached out and touched the fur on Victor's shoulder. I said, my voice gravelly and uneven, "I came here to get away. I came here to forget everything. I thought . . . I thought I didn't have anything to lose."

The wolf lay there, small and gray and dark in the failing light. Dead. I had to keep looking at his eyes. I wouldn't let myself forget that this was not a wolf. This was Victor.

"And it really worked, Victor." I shook my head. "You know it, don't you? It's all gone when you're a wolf. It's just what I wanted. It is so, so good. It's absolute nothing. I could be a wolf right now, and I wouldn't remember this. It would be like it never happened. I wouldn't care if you were dead, because I wouldn't even remember who you were."

Out of the corner of my field of vision, I saw Sam turn his face away from me. I was profoundly aware of him not looking at me, not looking at Grace.

I closed my eyes.

"All . . . this . . . pain. This . . ." My voice was failing me again, suddenly dangerously unsteady. But I wouldn't let myself stop. I opened my eyes. "Guilt. Because of what I've done to you. Because of what I've always done to you. It would — it would be gone." I stopped, rubbed my hand across my face. My voice was nearly inaudible. "But that's what I always do, isn't it, Vic? Screw things up and then make myself disappear?"

I reached out and touched one of the wolf's front paws; the fur was coarse and cold beneath my fingertips. "Ah, Vic," I said, and my voice caught in my throat. "You were so good. *Magic hands.*" He'd never have hands again.

I didn't say the next part out loud. *Never again, Victor. I'm done running. I'm sorry this is what it took for me to see.*

Out of the corner of my eye, I saw something, the darkness shifting.

Wolves.

As a human, I had never seen so many of them, but now, the dark spaces between the trees seethed with them. Ten? A dozen? They were far enough away that I could almost believe I was imagining the dim shapes.

Grace's eyes were on them, too. "Sam," she whispered. "Beck."

"I know," he said.

We were all frozen, waiting to see how long the wolves would stay, and if they would come any closer. Crouched there beside Victor, I was aware that the glinting eyes meant something different to each of us. Sam's past. My present. Grace's future.

"Are they here for Victor?" Sam asked, voice soft.

Nobody answered him.

I realized: I was the only one mourning Victor for who he really was.

The wolves remained where they were, specters in the oncoming night. Finally, Sam turned to me and asked, "Are you ready?"

I didn't think it was something you could be ready for, but I covered Victor's face with the sheet. Together, Sam and I hefted his weight — it felt like nothing between us — and gently lowered him into the grave, with Grace and the pack as our audience.

The woods were utterly silent.

Then Grace stood up, finally, unsteady on her feet, one of her hands pressed to her stomach.

Sam startled as one of the wolves began to croon. It was a low, sad sound, far more like a human voice than I thought possible.

One by one, the other wolves added their voices; as the evening grew darker, the song swelled, filling every crevice and gully in the forest. It prickled some wolf memory, buried deep in my mind, of me tipping my head back to the sky, calling the spring.

The lonely song drove home the fact of Victor's cold body in the grave like nothing else, and I realized that my cheeks were wet as I lowered my face to my palms.

Lowering my hands, I saw Sam cross the few steps to Grace and hold her swaying form.

Holding tight, denying the fact that eventually we all had to let go.

Chapter Forty-Five

· SAM ·

When we got back inside, it was hard to tell who looked worse — Cole, so racked with grief, or Grace, her eyes looking huge in her pale, pale face. It hurt to look at both of them.

Cole sank down into one of the chairs at the dining room table. I led Grace to the couch and sat next to her, meaning to turn on the radio, to talk to her, to do something, but I was all used up. So we all sat in silence, lost in our thoughts.

An hour later, when we heard the back door come open, all of us jerked, relaxing only a little when we saw that it was Isabel, bundled in her white, fur-lined jacket and her usual boots. Her eyes slid from Cole sitting at the table, his head on his crossed arms, to me, and then finally to Grace, who lay against my chest.

"Your father was here," I said, stupidly, because I couldn't think of anything else.

"I know. I saw, after it was too late. I didn't know he was going to bring it here." Isabel's arms were held tightly to her sides. "You should've heard him crowing when he got back. I couldn't get away until after dinner; I told him I was going to the library, because if there's one thing that man doesn't know, it's the hours the library is open." She paused, half turning her head back toward Cole's still-motionless form and then back to me. "Who was it? The wolf, I mean."

I glanced toward the dining room table, just visible from where we were on the couch. I knew he could hear us. "It was Victor. Cole's friend."

Isabel jerked her attention back to Cole. "I didn't realize he had any . . ." She seemed to realize how awful that sounded, because she added, "Here."

"Yes," I said emphatically.

She looked uncertain, glancing back at Cole and then back at us. Finally, she said, "I came to see what the plan was."

"Plan?" I asked. "For what?"

Isabel looked at Cole again, and then at Grace a little longer, and then she pointed a finger at me. With a gritted smile, she said, "Can I have a moment with you? In the kitchen?"

Grace lifted her head dully and frowned at Isabel, but she moved off me so that I could follow Isabel to the kitchen.

I had barely crossed over the threshold when Isabel said, voice biting, "I *told* you that the wolves were around our house and that my father was not a fan. What were you waiting for?"

My eyebrows raised at the accusation. "What? What your father did today? I was supposed to prevent that?"

"*You're* in charge. They're your wolves now. You can't just sit there."

"I didn't really think your father was going to go out —"

Isabel interrupted me. "Everyone knows my dad will shoot at anything that can't shoot back. I expected you to do something!"

"I don't know what I would do to keep the wolves from the property. They go around the lake because the hunting's good there. I really didn't think your trigger-happy father would blatantly flout hunting and firearms laws to prove his point." My voice came out accusing, which I knew wasn't fair.

Isabel laughed; it sounded like a bark, short and humorless. "You, of all people, ought to know what he is capable of, for God's sake. In the meantime, how long are you going to pretend there's nothing wrong with Grace?"

I blinked at her.

"Don't give me those lamb eyes. You're sitting there with her, and she looks like a cancer patient or something. I mean, she looks awful. And she smells just like that dead wolf. So what's going on?"

I winced. "I don't know, Isabel," I said. My voice sounded tired, even to me. "We went to the clinic today. Nothing."

"Well, then, take her to the hospital!"

"What do you think they'll do at a hospital? Maybe, *maybe* they'll do blood work on her. What do you think they'll find? I'm guessing 'werewolf' won't show up on most panels, and there isn't a diagnosis for 'smells like a sick wolf.' " I didn't mean to sound so angry; I wasn't angry at Isabel — I was angry at me.

"So you're just going to — what? Wait for something bad to happen?"

"What am I supposed to do? Take her into the hospital and demand they fix a problem that hasn't really appeared yet? That isn't in their *Merck Manual*? You don't think that I've been worrying about this all day? All week? Don't you think it's killing me to not know what's happening? It's not like we can be sure. There's no — no precedent. There's never been anyone like Grace. I'm stabbing in the dark here, Isabel!"

Isabel glared at me; I noticed her eyes were a little red behind her dark eye makeup. "*Think.* Be proactive instead of reactive. You ought to be looking at what killed that first wolf instead of just staring at Grace with moon eyes. And what were you thinking, letting her stay over here? Her parents have left me voicemails that could cook bacon. What happens if they find out where you live and show up here while Cole's shifting? *That* would be a great conversation starter. And speaking of Cole — do you know who he is? What the hell are you doing, Sam? What the hell are you waiting for?"

I turned away from her, linking my hands behind my head. "God, Isabel. What do you want from me? What do you want?"

"I want you to grow up," she snapped. "What did you think, that you could just work in that bookstore forever and live in a dream world with Grace? Beck's gone. You're Beck now. Start acting like an adult, or you're going to lose everything. Do you think my dad is really going to stop with just one? 'Cause I can tell you right now, he's not done. And what do you think is going to happen when people come after Cole? When whatever happened to that wolf happens to Grace? Were you *really* at a *recording studio* yesterday? Unreal."

I turned back around to face her. Her hands were fists stuffed in her armpits, her jaw was set. I wanted to ask her if she was doing this because Jack died and she couldn't stand to see it happen to someone else. Or if she was doing it because I had lived and Jack hadn't. Or was it because she was a part of us now, inextricably tied to me and Grace and Cole and the rest?

Ultimately, it didn't really matter why she was here, or why she was saying what she was saying. Because I knew she was right.

· COLE ·

I looked up when I heard the raised voices in the kitchen; Grace and I exchanged looks. She got up and came to sit across from me at the table, holding a glass of water and a few pills in her hand. She swallowed the pills and set the glass down. The entire process seemed to take a lot of effort, but I didn't say anything, because she hadn't. She had dark smudges under her eyes and her cheeks were bright red with a rising temperature. She looked exhausted.

In the other room, Sam's and Isabel's voices were raised. I felt the tension in the air, stretched between all of us tight as wires.

"I can't believe this is happening," I said.

Grace asked, "Cole? Do you know what will happen when people find out you're here? Do you mind me asking?" The way she asked it was completely frank and simple. No judgment about my famous face.

I shook my head. "I don't know. My family won't care. They gave up on me a long time ago. But the media will care." I thought about those girls snapping photos of me on their cell phones. "The media will love it. It would be a lot of attention for Mercy Falls."

Grace exhaled and laid a hand on her stomach, carefully, like she was afraid of crushing her skin. Had she looked like that earlier?

Grace asked, "Do you want to be found?"

I raised an eyebrow at her.

"Ah," she said. She considered this. "I guess Beck thought you would be a wolf more."

"Beck thought I was going to kill myself," I said. "I don't think he thought about it any more than that. He was trying to save me."

In the other room, Sam said something inaudible. Isabel said, "I know you and Grace talk about everything else, so why not that?"

Just then, when she said that, the way she said it, like the knowledge was painful, made it seem like Isabel had a crush on Sam. The possibility of that gave me a weird, numb feeling.

Grace just looked at me. She had to have heard it. But she kept her reaction to herself.

Isabel and Sam came into the living room then, Sam looking hangdog, Isabel looking frustrated. Sam came over behind Grace's chair and slid a hand onto her neck. It was a simple gesture that didn't say *possession* so much as *connection*. Isabel's eyes were on that hand, the same way I guess mine were.

I closed my eyes and opened them again. In between, I saw Victor. And I just couldn't do it anymore — be conscious.

"I'm going to bed," I said.

Isabel and Sam stared at each other again, a silent argument still waging, and then Isabel said, "I'm leaving. Grace? Rachel said you were staying at my place. I told them you were, too, but I know they didn't believe me. Are you really staying here tonight?"

Grace just reached up and held Sam's wrist.

"So it comes down to me being the voice of reason," Isabel snapped. "How ironic. The unlistened-to voice of reason."

She stormed out. I waited a second, and then I followed her out into the black night, catching up with her by the door of her white SUV, the night air cold enough to burn the back of my throat.

"What?" she said. "Just, *what*, Cole?"

I guess I was still raw from hearing her voice when she talked to Sam. "Why are you doing that to him?"

"To Sam? He needs it. Nobody else is telling him." She stood there, furious, and now that I'd seen her crying on her bed, it was easy to see that the same emotions were chewing her up inside right now, only she never let them out.

"And who's telling you?" I asked.

Isabel just looked at me. "Believe me, I do it to myself all the time."

"I believe you," I said.

For a second, she looked like she was going to cry again, and then she got into the driver's seat and jerked the door shut behind her. She didn't look at me as she reversed out of the driveway. I stood in the driveway, gazing after where she'd gone, the cold wind tugging at me without enough force to change me.

Everything was ruined, and everything was wrong, and not being able to shift should've been the end of the world. But instead, for once, it was okay.

Chapter Forty-Six

• SAM •

Here we were again, always saying good-bye.

Grace lay on my bed, flat on her back, knees up. Her T-shirt had pulled up just a little, revealing a few inches of her pale belly. Her blond hair was spread out on one side of her head as if she were flying through the air or floating in the water. I stood by the light switch, looking at her and just . . . wanting.

"Don't turn it off yet," Grace said, her voice a little strange. "Just come sit with me for a little bit. I don't want to sleep yet."

I turned off the light, anyway — in the sudden darkness, Grace made an annoyed noise — and then I leaned down to hit a switch, turning on a string of Christmas lights stapled around the ceiling. They sparkled through the strange shapes made by the slowly spinning birds, and cast moving shadows, like firelight, across Grace's face. Her noise of annoyance changed to one of wonder.

"It's like . . ." she started, but didn't finish.

I joined her on the bed, sitting cross-legged next to her instead of lying down. "Like what?" I asked, running the back of my fingers across her stomach.

"Mmmm," said Grace, half closing her eyes.

"Like what?" I asked again.

"Like looking at the stars," she said. "With a giant flock of birds flying past."

I sighed.

"Sam, I really want to buy a red coffeepot, if they exist," Grace said.

"I'll find you one," I said, and laid my hand flat on her belly; her skin was shockingly hot against my hand. Isabel had told me to ask Grace how she felt. To not wait for her to tell me, because she wouldn't until it was too late. Because she didn't want to hurt me.

"Grace?" I said, removing my hand, scared.

Her eyes drifted from the birds spiraling slowly above us to my face. She caught my hand and moved it so that our hands cupped around each other, her fingertips on my lifeline and mine on hers. "What?" When she spoke, her breath smelled both copper and medicinal; blood and acetaminophen.

I knew I should ask her what was happening, but I wanted just one more minute of peace. One more moment before we faced the truth. So I asked a question that I knew, now, had no correct answer. A question that belonged to a different couple, with a different future. "When we're married, can we go to the ocean? I've never been."

"When we're married," she said, and it didn't sound like a lie, though her voice was soft and sad, "we can go to all the oceans. Just to say that we did."

I lay down beside her, our hands still in a knot on her stomach, shoulder to shoulder, and together we looked up through the flock of happy memories flying above us, caught in this room. The Christmas lights winked above us; when the swaying wings eclipsed the bulbs, it made me feel like we were moving, rocking on a giant boat, looking up at unfamiliar constellations.

It was time.

I closed my eyes. "What is happening with you?"

Grace was quiet for so long that I started to doubt that I'd said my question out loud. Then she said, "I don't want to go to sleep. I'm afraid to go to sleep."

My heart didn't so much skip a beat as slow to a crawl. "What does it feel like?"

"It hurts to talk," she whispered. "And my stomach — it really . . ." She laid my hand flat on her stomach and then put her hand on top of mine. "Sam, I'm afraid."

It almost hurt too much to speak after her confession. I said, softly, because it was all I could manage, "It's from the wolves. Do you think you caught it from that wolf, somehow?"

"I think it *is* a wolf," Grace said. "I think it's the wolf that I never was. That's what it feels like. It feels like I want to shift, but I never do."

My mind riffled rapidly through everything I'd ever heard about the wolves and our brilliantly destructive disease, but there was no precedent for this. Grace was the only one of her kind.

"Tell me," she said, "do you still feel it? The wolf inside you? Or is it gone now?"

I sighed and leaned to rest my forehead against her cheek. Of course it was still there. Of course it was. "Grace, I'm going to take you to the hospital. We'll make them find out what's wrong with you. I don't care what we have to tell them to make them believe."

Grace said, "I don't want to die in a hospital."

"You're not going to die," I told her, lifting my head to look at her. "I'm not done writing songs about you yet."

Her mouth smiled on one side, and then she tugged me down so she could rest her head on my chest as she closed her eyes.

I didn't close mine. I watched her and I watched the birds' shadows flit across her face, and I . . . wanted. I wanted more happy memories to hang up on the ceiling, so many happy memories with this girl that they would crowd the ceiling and flap out into the hall and burst out of the house.

An hour later, Grace started throwing up blood.

I couldn't call 911 and help her at the same time, so I left her curled up against the hallway wall, a thin trail of her own blood showing our path from the bedroom, while I stood in the doorway with the phone, never taking my eyes off her.

Cole — I didn't remember calling for him — appeared at the top of the stairs and silently brought towels.

"Sam," Grace said, voice miserable and thin, "my hair."

It was the smallest thing in the world, blood on the ends of her hair. It was the biggest thing in the world, her being out of control. While Cole helped Grace press a towel to her nose and mouth, I clumsily pulled her hair back into a ponytail, out of the way. Then, when we heard the ambulance pull into the drive, we helped her to her feet and tried to get her downstairs without her throwing up again. The birds fluttered and flapped around us as we hurried out, like they wanted to come with us, but their strings were too short.

Chapter Forty-Seven

· GRACE ·

Once upon a time, there was a girl named Grace Brisbane. There was nothing particularly special about her, except that she was good with numbers, and very good at lying, and she made her home in between the pages of books. She loved all the wolves behind her house, but she loved one of them most of all.

And this one loved her back. He loved her back so hard that even the things that weren't special about her became special: the way she tapped her pencil on her teeth, the off-key songs she sang in the shower, how when she kissed him he knew it meant forever.

Hers was a memory made up of snapshots: being dragged through the snow by a pack of wolves, first kiss tasting of oranges, saying good-bye behind a cracked windshield.

A life made up of promises of what could be: the possibilities contained in a stack of college applications, the thrill of sleeping under a strange roof, the future that lay in Sam's smile.

It was a life I didn't want to leave behind.

It was a life I didn't want to forget.

I wasn't done with it yet. There was so much more to say.

Chapter Forty-Eight

· SAM ·

Flickering lights
anonymous doors
my heart escaping in drips
i'm still waking up
but she's still sleeping
this ICU is
hotel for the dead

Chapter Forty-Nine

· COLE ·

I didn't know why I went with Sam to the hospital. I knew I could get recognized — though the odds seemed slim of anyone recognizing me with my stubbled face and the bags under my eyes. I also knew I could shift, if my body decided to succumb to the whims of the cold. But as Sam went to put his key into his car door to follow the ambulance, he'd looked at his bloody hand for a long second, and he'd had to try twice to get the key in the lock.

I had been hanging back, ready to disappear if it felt like the black morning cold would jerk me into a wolf, but when I saw Sam's hand, I stepped forward and took the key.

"Get in," I said, jerking my head toward the passenger seat.

And he did.

So here I was, standing in the hospital room of a girl I barely knew with a guy I knew only slightly better, and I still wasn't quite sure why I cared. The room was full of people — two doctors, a guy who I thought was a surgeon, and an absolute army of nurses. There was a lot of hushed talking back and forth, with enough technical jargon to gag a maggot, but I got the gist of it: They had no idea what was going on, and Grace was dying.

They wouldn't let Sam stand next to her, so he sat in a chair in the corner, his elbows on his knees and his face crumpled in one of his hands.

I didn't know what to do, either, so I stood beside him, wondering if, before I'd been bitten, I would've been able to smell all the death that hung in the air of the ICU.

A cell phone rang at my feet, a brisk, businesslike tone, and I realized it was coming from Sam's pocket. In slow motion, Sam took it out and then looked at the front of the phone.

"It's Isabel," he said, hoarse. "I can't talk to her."

I took it from his unresisting hands and answered it. "Isabel."

"Cole?" Isabel asked. "Is this Cole?"

"Yeah."

And then, the most sincere words I had ever heard out of Isabel's mouth: "Oh, no."

I didn't say anything. But the noise behind me must have said it all.

"Are you at the hospital?"

"Yeah."

"What are they saying?"

"What you said. They have no idea."

Isabel swore softly, over and over again. "How bad is it, Cole? Can you tell me?"

"Sam's right here."

"Great," Isabel said, harshly. "That's just great."

Suddenly, one of the nurses said, "Watch —!"

Grace half sat up, just enough to throw up more blood, all over the front of the nurse who had just spoken. The nurse matter-of-factly stepped back to scrub off her hands as another nurse took her place, with a towel for Grace.

Grace fell back onto the bed. She said something that the nurses couldn't catch.

"What, honey?"

"*Sam*," Grace wailed, a horrible sound both animal and human, hideously reminiscent of the doe's scream. Sam jerked to his feet just as a man and a woman pushed their way into the already-crowded room.

I saw one of the nurses open her mouth to protest the intrusion as the couple headed straight for us, but she didn't have time to say anything before the man said, "You son of a bitch," and punched Sam in the mouth.

Chapter Fifty

· SAM ·

Lewis Brisbane's punch took several moments to start hurting, like my body couldn't believe what had just happened to it. By the time the pain started to finally take hold, my hearing was buzzing and popping in my left ear, and I had to grab for the wall to keep from falling back over a chair. I was still sick from the sound of Grace's voice.

For a single fragment of a moment, I caught a perfectly clear image of Grace's mother watching, face blank as if waiting for an expression to land on it, doing nothing, and then Grace's dad swung at me again.

"I'll kill you," Grace's dad said.

I just stared at his fist, my ears still hissing from the first punch. Most of my mind was still with Grace, in the hospital bed, and what little I had left to devote to Lewis Brisbane couldn't quite believe he was going to punch me again. I didn't even flinch.

Before his fist connected again, her dad staggered back, struggling to keep his footing, and as my vision and hearing came back, all in a rush, I saw Cole dragging him backward. Like he was nothing but a bag of potatoes.

"Easy, big guy," Cole said. Then, to the nurses: "What are you staring at? Help the guy he just punched." I shook my head a little at the nurses' offer of ice but accepted a towel for my busted forehead. As I did, I heard Cole say to Mr. Brisbane, "I'm going to let you go. Don't make me get us both thrown out of this hospital."

I stood there, watching Grace's parents force their way to the side of the bed, and I didn't know what to do. Everything solid in my life was fracturing, and I didn't know where I belonged right now.

I saw Cole staring at me, and somehow his stare reminded me of the towel in my hand and the slow tickle of the blood as it welled from my skin. I lifted the towel to my head. Raising my arm made colorful dots spiral at the edge of my vision.

At my elbow, a nurse said, "I'm sorry — Sam? But since you're not an immediate relative, you can't stay in here. They've asked us to have you leave."

I just looked at her, feeling utterly empty. I didn't know what I was supposed to say to her. *My life is in that bed. Please let me stay.*

The nurse made a face. "I *really* am sorry." She glanced to Grace's parents and back to me. "You did good bringing her in here."

I closed my eyes; I could still see the swirling colors when I did. I had an idea that if I didn't sit down soon, my body was going to do it for me. "Can I tell her I'm going?"

"I don't think that's a good idea," said one of the other nurses, darting past with something in her arms. "Let her think he's still here. He can come back if—" she stopped herself before adding, "Tell him to stay close."

For a moment, I forgot how to breathe.

"Come on," Cole said. He looked back over his shoulder at Mr. Brisbane, who was looking at me with a complicated expression as I left. Cole pointed at him and said, "*You're* a son of a bitch. He belongs here more than you do."

But love isn't quantifiable on paper, so I had to leave Grace behind.

· COLE ·

By the time Isabel got to the hospital, dawn was just starting to seep through the warped glass of the cafeteria windows.

Grace was dying. I'd gotten that much out of the nurses before I left. She was throwing up all her blood and they were giving her vitamin K and transfusions to slow it down, but eventually, she was going to die.

I hadn't told Sam yet, but I thought he knew.

Isabel slapped a napkin down onto the table in front of me, next to Sam's stained towel. It took me a moment to recognize the napkin as my scribbled flow chart from the diner. It said METH in large letters, reminding me how much I'd told Isabel. She threw herself down into the plastic chair opposite me; everything about her screamed *angry angry angry*. She wasn't wearing any makeup except for a smudged heavy line of mascara around each eye that looked like it had been there a while.

"Where's Sam?"

I gestured to the cafeteria windows. Sam was a darker blot against the still-dark sky. His arms were linked behind his head as he stared out into nothing. Everything else had moved in this room as time passed: the light across the freakishly orange walls as the sun slowly rose, the chairs back and forth as hospital staff came and left with their breakfasts, the janitor with his mop and WET FLOOR sign. Sam was the pillar they all pivoted around.

Isabel fired another question. "Why are you here?"

I still didn't know. I shrugged. "To help."

"Then help," Isabel said, and pushed the napkin closer to me. Louder, she said, "Sam."

He lowered his hands but didn't turn around. Frankly, I was surprised he'd moved at all.

"Sam," she repeated, and this time, he did turn toward us. She pointed at the self-service bar and cashier at the other end of the room. "Get us some coffee."

I didn't know what was more amazing: that Isabel had just told him to get coffee, or that he did, albeit with no expression whatsoever. I turned my gaze back to Isabel. "Wow. Just when I think I've seen you at your coldest."

"That was me being nice," Isabel snapped. "What good is he doing, staring outside?"

"I don't know, remembering all the great days he and his girlfriend had, before she dies."

Isabel looked me right in the eye. "Do you think that will help you with Victor? Because it never really saves me when I think about Jack." She pressed a finger into the napkin. "Talk to me. About this."

"I don't understand what this has to do with Grace."

Sam set two coffee cups down, one in front of me and one in front of Isabel. Nothing for himself.

"What's wrong with Grace is the same thing that killed that wolf that you and Grace found," Sam said, his voice sounding gritty, like he hadn't used it in a while. "That smell is just too distinctive. It's the same thing."

He stood by the table, as if sitting down would mean that he was agreeing to something.

I looked at Isabel. "What makes you think that I can do something these doctors can't?"

"Because you're a genius," Isabel said.

"These people are geniuses," I replied.

Sam said, "Because you know."

Isabel pushed the napkin at me again. And once again, it was my father and me at the dining room table, and he was presenting me with a problem. Or I was sitting in one of his college classes when I was sixteen, and he was looking at my written work beside my solutions, searching for signs that I would follow in his footsteps. Or it was me at one of his award presentations with the ironed shirts and old school ties surrounding me, and my father telling them, in a voice that stood for no argument, that I was going to be great.

I thought of just that simple gesture from earlier, when Sam had laid his hand on Grace's collarbone.

I thought of Victor.

I took the napkin.

"I'm going to need more paper," I said.

Chapter Fifty-One

· SAM ·

There was no longer night than this: Cole and I in the cafeteria, going over every detail of the wolves until Cole's brain was full and he sent both Isabel and me away so that he could sit at a table with his head in his hands and a piece of paper in front of him. It seemed amazing to me that everything I wanted, everything I'd ever wanted, hung on the shoulders of Cole St. Clair, sitting at a plastic table with a scribbled-on napkin, but what else did I have?

I escaped from the cafeteria to sit outside her room, my back to the wall, my head in my hands. Against my will, I was memorizing everything about these walls, this place, this night.

I had no hope that they would let me in to see her.

So all I prayed for was that they would not come out to tell me that she was gone. I prayed for the door not to open. *Just stay alive.*

Chapter Fifty-Two

· SAM ·

Isabel came and got me and dragged me through the morning-busy halls to an empty stairwell where Cole waited for me. He was full of restless energy, his hands in two fists that he kept knocking lightly against each other, one on top of the other.

"Okay, I can't promise anything," Cole said. "I am just guessing here. But I have a — a theory. The thing is that, even if I'm right, I can't be proved right. Just wrong, really." When I didn't say anything, he said, "What is the big thing in common between Grace and that wolf?" He waited. I guessed I was supposed to answer.

"The smell."

Isabel said, "That's what I thought, too. Though it's pretty obvious, once Cole pointed it out."

"The shifting," Cole said. "Both the wolf and Grace haven't shifted for — what — a decade or more? That's the magic number for when wolves that don't shift anymore die, right? I know you said that that was the natural life span of a wolf, but I don't think that's it. I think that every wolf that's died without shifting has died like that wolf — *of* something. Not old age. And I think that's what's killing Grace."

"The wolf she never was," I said, suddenly remembering something she'd said the night before.

"Exactly," Cole said. "I think that they die because they aren't shifting anymore. I don't think shifting is the curse. I think whatever it is that is telling our bodies to shift is the bad guy here."

I blinked.

"It's not the same thing," Cole said. "If the shifting is the disease, it's one thing. If you're shifting because of the disease, it's something else entirely. So here's my theory, and this is such crap science, I don't have to tell you. It's science without microscopes, blood tests, or reality. Anyway. Grace was bitten. When she's bitten, wolf toxin, for lack of a better term, is introduced. Whatever it is in this wolf spit is really bad for you. Let's say that shifting is the good guy, and that something about this wolf spit initiates a defensive response in your body — shifting, to purge the toxin. Every time you shift, the toxin's put at bay. And for some reason, these shifts are timed with the weather. Unless, of course —"

"You stop yourself from shifting," Isabel said.

"Yeah." Cole glanced up toward the bottom of the stairwell, toward Grace's floor. "If you somehow destroy your body's ability to use hot and cold as a trigger, you look cured, but you're not. You're . . . festering."

I was tired, and I was not a science person. Cole could've told me that wolf toxin made you lay eggs and I would've thought it sounded reasonable at this point. "Okay. So it sounds fine, if vague. What's the upshot? What are you suggesting?"

"I think she needs to shift," Cole said.

It took me too long to realize what he was saying. "Become a wolf?"

Cole shrugged. "If I'm right."

"Are you right?"

"I don't know."

I closed my eyes. Without opening them, I asked, "And I'm guessing you have a theory on how to get her to shift."

Oh, God, Grace. I couldn't believe what I was saying.

Cole said, "Simplest is easiest."

I had a sudden image in my head of Grace's brown eyes looking out from a wolf's face. I wrapped my arms around myself.

"She needs to get bitten again."

My eyes flew open and I stared at Cole. "Bitten."

Cole made a face. "It's an educated guess. Something got messed up in the shifting chain of command, and if you reintroduced the original trigger, it might start her over from square one. Only this time don't cook her in the car."

Everything in me rebelled against the idea. Of losing Grace, losing what made her Grace. Of attacking her while she was dying. Of making decisions like this, on the fly, because there was no time. I said, "But it takes weeks or months to shift after you get bitten."

"I think that's how long it takes for the toxin to build up initially," Cole said. "But she's already there, obviously. If I'm right, she'd shift immediately."

I linked my arms behind my head and turned away from Cole and Isabel, staring at the pale blue concrete wall. "If you're wrong?"

"She has wolf spit in an open wound" — Cole paused, then added, "that she'll probably bleed to death from right now, because it sounds like the toxin is destroying her ability to clot."

They let me pace for several long moments, and then Isabel, a low voice out of the silence said, "If you're right, Sam's going to die, too."

"Yes," Cole said, in such an even way that I knew he'd already considered that. "If I'm right, when Sam gets ten or thirteen years down the road, his cure won't be a cure, either."

Could I believe the science concocted in a hospital cafeteria over lukewarm coffee and crumpled napkins?

It was all I had.

I turned, finally, and looked at Isabel. With her smudged makeup, her hair rumpled, her shoulders hunched up with uncertainty, she looked like an entirely different girl, trying to wear an Isabel disguise.

I asked, "How would we get into the room?"

Chapter Fifty-Three

· ISABEL ·

It fell to me to get Grace's parents out of the room. They hated Sam, so he was out, and Cole's brawn would be needed elsewhere, so he was out. It occurred to me, as I clicked down the hallway to Grace's room, that we were counting on Cole's solution not working. Because if it did, we were all going to be in big trouble.

I waited for a nurse to exit Grace's room, and then I opened the door a crack. I was in luck; only her mom was sitting by her bed, looking out the window instead of at Grace. I tried not to look at Grace, who lay silent and white, her head turned limply to the side.

"Mrs. Brisbane?" I asked in my best schoolgirl voice.

She looked up, and I noted, with some satisfaction for Grace's benefit, that her eyes were red. "Isabel?"

I said, "I came as soon as I heard. Could I — could I talk to you about something?"

She stared at me for a moment, and then she seemed to realize what I had asked. "Of course."

I hesitated at the door. *Sell it, Isabel.* "Um. Not near Grace. You know, where she could . . ." I pointed to my ear.

"Oh," her mother said. "Okay." She was probably curious about what I was going to say. Honestly, I was, too. My palms were sticky with nerves.

She patted Grace's leg and stood up. When she got out into the hall, I pointed behind my hand at Sam, who was, as we'd advised, standing a few feet on the other side of the door. He looked like he was going to throw up, which was about how I felt. "Not near him, either," I whispered. I remembered, suddenly, having told Sam that he wasn't cut out for deception. As my stomach churned and I planned what I was going to confess to Grace's mother, I thought that karma was a terrible thing.

· COLE ·

As soon as Isabel had gotten Mrs. Brisbane out — Was she the only person in there? Only one way to find out, I supposed — it was my turn. While Sam watched out to make sure no nurses came in, I slipped into the room. It stank of blood, rot, and fear, and my wolfish instincts crawled up inside me, whispering at me to get out.

I ignored them and went straight to Grace. She looked like she was made up of separate parts that had all been brought to the bed and assembled at awkward angles. I knew I didn't have much time.

I was surprised, when I knelt by her face, to find her eyes open, although the lids were heavy on them.

"Cole," she said. It was the long, low timbre of a sleepy little girl, someone who just couldn't stay awake much longer. "Where's Sam?"

"Here," I lied. "Don't try to look."

"I'm dying, aren't I?" whispered Grace.

"Don't be afraid," I said, but not for the reason she said. I pulled out drawers on the cart by the bed until I found what I was looking for: an assortment of shiny sharp things. I selected one that looked logical and took Grace's hand.

"What are you doing?" She was too far gone to care, though.

"Making you into a wolf," I said. She didn't flinch, or even look curious. I took a breath, held her skin taut, and made a tiny cut on her hand. Again, she didn't move. The wound was bleeding like hell. I whispered, "I'm sorry, this is going to be disgusting. But unfortunately, I'm the only guy who can do the job."

Grace's eyes opened just a little further as I worked up a big mouthful of saliva. I didn't even know how much she would need to be reinfected. I mean, Beck had had it down to a fine science, had thought everything out. He'd had a tiny syringe that he kept in a cooler.

"Believe me, less scarring this way," he'd said.

My mouth was getting dry as I thought about Isabel losing her hold on Grace's mother. The blood was pumping out of the tiny cut like I'd slashed a vein.

Grace's eyes were falling shut, though I could see her fighting to keep them open. Blood was pooling on the floor underneath her hand. If I was wrong, I'd killed her.

· SAM ·

Cole came to the door, touched my elbow, pulled me inside. He latched the door and pushed a surgery cart up against it, as if that would stop anything.

"Now's the moment of truth," he said, and his voice was uneven. "If it doesn't work, she's gone, but you get this moment with her. If it's going to work, we're . . . gonna have to get her out of here in a hurry. Now. I want you to brace yourself, because . . ."

I stepped around him and my vision shimmered. I had seen this much blood before, when the wolves made a kill, and there was so much blood that it stained the snow crimson around it for yards. And I had seen this much of Grace's blood before, years ago, back when I was just a wolf and she was just a girl, and she was dying. But I hadn't really been ready to see it again.

Grace, I said, but it wasn't even a whisper. It was just the shape of my mouth. I was at her side, but I was a thousand miles away.

Now she was shaking, and coughing, and her hands were gripping on the rails of the hospital bed.

Across the room, Cole stared at the door. The knob was jiggling.

"The window," he told me.

I stared at him.

"She's not dying," Cole said, and his own eyes were wide. "She's shifting."

I looked back down at the girl on the bed, and she looked back up at me.

"Sam," she said. She was jerking, her shoulders hunching. I couldn't watch her. Grace, going through the agony of the shift. Grace, becoming a wolf. Grace, like Beck and Ulrik and every other wolf before her, disappearing into the woods.

I was losing her.

Cole ran to the windows and jerked up on the latch. "Sorry, screens," he said, and busted them out with his foot. I was just standing there. "Sam. Do you want them to find her like this?" He rushed over, and together we picked Grace off the bed.

I heard the door crashing now; people calling on the other side.

There was a four-foot drop outside the hospital window. It was a brilliantly sunny, clear morning, perfectly ordinary, except that it wasn't. Cole jumped down first, swearing when he landed in the short shrubs, while I steadied Grace on the sill. She was becoming less Grace in my arms every moment, and when Cole lowered her onto the ground outside the window, she retched on the grass.

"Grace," I said, my vision swirling now because of her blood smeared across my wrists. "Can you hear me?"

She nodded and then stumbled to her knees. I knelt beside her; her eyes were huge and afraid and my heart was breaking. "I'll come find you," I said. "I promise I'll come find you. Don't forget me. Don't — don't lose yourself."

Grace grabbed for my hand and missed, catching herself from falling onto the ground instead.

And then she cried out, and the girl I knew was gone, and there was only a wolf with brown eyes.

I could not bring myself to stand. I knelt, bereft, and the dark gray wolf slowly cringed back from me and Cole. From our humanness. I didn't think I could breathe.

Grace.

"Sam," Cole said, "I can send you with her. I can start you over, too."

For a brief moment, I saw it. I saw myself again shuddering into the wolf, I saw my springs, hiding from drafts, I heard the sound I made when I lost myself. I remembered the moment I knew it was my last year and that for the rest of my life I'd be trapped in someone else's body.

I remembered standing in the middle of the street in front of The Crooked Bookshelf, filled with the certainty of a future. I had heard the wolves howling behind the house and remembered how glad I had been to be human.

I couldn't. Grace had to understand. I couldn't.

"Cole," I said, "get out of here. Don't give them any more reason to look at your face. Please —"

Cole finished my sentence. "I'll get her to the woods, Sam."

I slowly climbed back to my feet, walked back into the emergency department through the silently swishing glass doors, and, covered in my girlfriend's blood, lied perfectly for the first time in my life.

"I tried to stop her."

Chapter Fifty-Four

· SAM ·

So it comes to this: I would have lost her either way.

If Cole hadn't reinfected her, I would have lost her in the hospital bed. And now Cole's wolf toxin pumps through her veins, and I lose her to the woods, like I lose everything I love.

So here is me, and I am a boy watched — by her parents' suspicious eyes, since they cannot prove that I kidnapped Grace but believe it nonetheless — and I am a boy watchful — because Tom Culpeper's bitterness is growing palpable in this tiny town and I will *not* bury Grace's body — and I am a boy waiting — for the heat and fruitfulness of summer, waiting to see who will walk out of those woods for me. Waiting for my lovely summer girl.

Somewhere fate laughs in her far-off country, because now I am the human and it is Grace I will lose again and again, *immer wieder*, always the same, every winter, losing more of her each year, unless I find a cure. A real cure this time, not some parlor trick.

Of course, it's not just her cure. In fifteen years, it's my cure, and Cole's cure, and Olivia's cure. And Beck — does his mind still sleep inside his wolf's pelt?

I still watch her now, like I always did, and she watches me, her brown eyes looking out from a wolf's face.

This is the story of a boy who used to be a wolf, and a girl who became one.

I won't let this be my good-bye. I've folded one thousand paper crane memories of me and Grace, and I've made my wish.

I will find a cure. And then I will find Grace.

Acknowledgments

Once again, I feel unequal to the task of thanking everyone involved in the making of *Linger*. So many folks have been part of making *Shiver* and *Linger* that I'm afraid I'm bound to leave people out.

First of all, I have to thank my absolutely incredible editor, David Levithan, who helped me laugh hysterically as I transformed *Linger* from a house cat to a tiger. I have learned so much writing this book with you. And I have to thank the entire Scholastic team, for their tireless support of me and the series. Special mentions to Tracy van Straaten (we'll always have Chicago), Samantha Wolfert, Janelle DeLuise and Rachel Horowitz (Eastern Europe is putty in your hands), Stephanie Anderson (my intrepid production editor, for her tireless work on the books), and Rachel Coun (founding member of the *Shiver* fan club). I would list everyone at Scholastic who made me laugh or helped make the books a success, but it would take all day. Suffice to say: I love all of you.

I have to single out Chris Stengel, my jacket designer, for

special thanks. Chris, you are a graphic god, and you have chosen to use your powers for good. Thank you for that.

My agent, Laura Rennert, and her dog, Lola, have been tireless champions and listeners, and without them, I would be puddles of ooze. Ooze does not make for great fiction.

Thanks to random folks: Jennifer Laughran, for NARKOTIKA. Marian, for tea with almond extract. Beau Carr, for shouting from the rooftops. To all of the Gothic Girls, for returning my sanity. Vera, for accuracy in acetaminophen dispersal. To dead Germans, for writing excellent poetry.

I couldn't have written this without the help of my critique partners, Tessa Gratton and Brenna Yovanoff. I know you're in every acknowledgments page I write, but heck, it's true. You could cackle evilly when I beg for a lifeline, but instead you guys always throw it out to me.

My family: Kate, you know you're my first reader and best friend. Dad, you make werewolf logic possible. Mom, you always manage to know just when I'm at the end of my rope. Andrew, for helping me work out what made Cole tick. Jack, for countless wagon rides. Mom-in-law Karen, for wrangling Things 1 & 2 while I tore up NYC. Thank you.

And finally Ed, always Ed. It always comes back to you.

About the Author

Maggie Stiefvater is the #1 *New York Times* bestselling author of the novels *Shiver*, *Linger*, *Forever*, and *Sinner*. Her novel *The Scorpio Races* was named a Michael L. Printz Honor Book by the American Library Association. Her most recent acclaimed series, The Raven Cycle, includes *The Raven Boys* and *The Dream Thieves*. She lives in Virginia. You can visit her online at www.maggiestiefvater.com.

The story continues in
the *New York Times* bestseller,

forever

PROLOGUE

· SHELBY ·

I can be so, so quiet.

Haste ruins the silence. Impatience squanders the hunt.

I take my time.

I am silent as I move through the darkness. Dust hangs in the air of the nighttime wood; the moonlight makes constellations of the particles where it creeps through the branches overhead.

The only sound is my breath, inhaled slowly through my bared teeth. The pads of my feet are noiseless in the damp underbrush. My nostrils flare. I listen to the beat of my heart over the sound of the muttering gurgle of a nearby creek.

A dry stick begins to pop under my foot.

I pause.

I wait.

I go slowly. I take a long time to lift my paw from the stick. I am thinking, *Quiet*. My breath is cold over my incisors. I hear a live, rustling sound nearby; it catches my attention and holds it. My stomach is tight and empty.

I push farther into the darkness. My ears prick; the panicked animal is close by. A deer? A night insect fills a long moment with clicking sounds before I move again. My heart beats rapidly in between the clicks. How large is the animal? If it's injured, it won't matter that I'm hunting alone.

Something brushes my shoulder. Soft. Tender.

I want to flinch.

I want to turn and snap it between my teeth.

But I am too quiet. I freeze for a long, long moment, and then I turn my head to see what is still brushing my ear with a feather touch.

It is a something that I can't name, floating in the air, drifting in the breeze. It touches my ear again and again and again. My mind burns and bends, struggling to name it.

Paper?

I don't understand why it is there, hanging like a leaf in the branch when it is not a leaf. It makes me uneasy. Beyond it, scattered on the ground, there are items imbued with an unfamiliar, hostile smell. The skin of some dangerous animal, shed and left behind. I shy away from them, lip curled, and there, suddenly, is my prey.

Only it is not a deer.

It is a girl, twisting in the dirt, hands gripping soil, whimpering. Where the moonlight touches her, she's stark white against the black ground. Fear ripples off her. My nostrils are full of it. Already uneasy, I feel the fur at the back of my neck prickle and rise. She is not a wolf, but she smells like one.

I am so quiet.

The girl doesn't see me coming.

When she opens her eyes, I am right in front of her, my nose nearly touching her. She was panting soft, heated breaths onto my face, but when she sees me, they stop.

We look at each other.

Every second that her eyes stay on mine, more fur raises along my neck and spine.

Her fingers curl in the dirt. When she moves, she smells less wolf and more human. Danger hisses in my ears.

I show her my teeth; I ease backward. All I can think of is retreating, getting only trees around me, putting space between us. Suddenly I remember the paper hanging in the tree and the shed skin on the ground. I feel fenced in — this strange girl in front of me, that alien leaf behind me. My belly touches underbrush as I crouch, tail tucked between my legs.

My growl starts so slowly that I feel it on my tongue before I hear it.

I am trapped between her and the things that smell like her, moving in the branches and lying on the ground. The girl's eyes are on mine still, challenging me, holding me. I am her prisoner and I cannot escape.

When she screams, I kill her.

Chapter One

· GRACE ·

So now I was a werewolf and a thief.

I'd found myself human at the edge of Boundary Wood. Which edge, I didn't know; the woods were vast, stretching for miles. Easily traveled as a wolf. Not so easy as a girl. It was a warm, pleasant day — a great day, by spring-in-Minnesota standards. If you weren't lost and naked, that is.

I ached. My bones felt as if they'd been rolled into Play-Doh snakes and then back into bones and then back into snakes again. My skin was itchy, especially over my ankles and elbows and knees. One of my ears rang. My head felt fuzzy and unfocused. I had a weird sense of déjà vu.

Compounding my discomfort was the realization that I was not only lost and naked in the woods, but naked in the woods near civilization. As flies buzzed idly around me, I stood up straight to look at my surroundings. I could see the backs of several small houses, just on the other side of the trees. At my feet was a torn black trash bag, its contents littering the ground. It looked suspiciously like it may have been my breakfast. I didn't want to think about that too hard.

I didn't really want to think about *anything* too hard. My thoughts were coming back to me in fits and starts, swimming into focus like half-forgotten dreams. And as my thoughts came back, I was remembering being in this moment — this dazed moment of being newly human — over and over again. In a dozen different settings. Slowly, it was coming back to me that this wasn't the first time I'd shifted this year. And I'd forgotten everything in between. Well, almost everything.

I squeezed my eyes shut. I could see *his* face, his yellow eyes, his dark hair. I remembered the way my hand fit into his. I remembered sitting next to him in a vehicle I didn't think existed anymore.

But I couldn't remember his name. How could I forget his *name*?

Distantly, I heard a car's tires echo through the neighborhood. The sound slowly faded as it drove by, a reminder of just how close the real world was.

I opened my eyes again. I couldn't think about him. I just wouldn't. It would come back to me. It would all come back to me. I had to focus on the here and now.

I had a few options. One was to retreat back into these warm, spring woods and hope that I'd change back into a wolf soon. The biggest problem with that idea was that I felt so utterly and completely human at the moment. Which left my second idea, throwing myself on the mercy of the people who lived in the small blue house in front of me. After all, it appeared I'd already helped myself to their trash and, from the look of it, the neighbors' trash as well. There were a lot of problems with this idea, however. Even if I felt completely human right now, who knew how long that would last? And I was naked and coming from the woods. I didn't know how I could explain that without ending up at the hospital or the police station.

Sam.

His name returned suddenly, and with it a thousand other things: poems whispered uncertainly in my ear, his guitar in his hands, the shape of the shadow beneath his collarbone, the way his fingers smoothed the pages of a book as he read. The color of the bookstore walls, how his voice sounded whispered across my pillow, a list of resolutions written for each of us. And the rest, too: Rachel,

Isabel, Olivia. Tom Culpeper throwing a dead wolf in front of me and Sam and Cole.

My parents. Oh, God. My parents. I remembered standing in their kitchen, feeling the wolf climbing out of me, fighting with them about Sam. I remembered stuffing my backpack full of clothing and running away to Beck's house. I remembered choking on my own blood. . . .

Grace Brisbane.

I'd forgotten all of it as a wolf. And I was going to forget it all again.

I knelt, because standing seemed suddenly difficult, and clutched my arms around my bare legs. A brown spider crawled across my toes before I had a chance to react. Birds kept singing overhead. Dappled sunlight, hot where it came through full strength, played across the forest floor. A warm spring breeze hummed through the new green leaves of the branches. The forest sighed again and again around me. While I was gone, nature moved on, normal as always, but here I was, a small, impossible reality, and I didn't know where I belonged or what I was supposed to do anymore.

Then, a warm breeze, smelling almost unbearably of cheese biscuits, lifted my hair and presented me with an option. Someone had clearly been feeling optimistic about this fair weather and had hung out a line of clothing to dry at the brick rambler next door. My eye was caught by the garments as the wind fluffed them. A line of neatly pinned-up possibilities. Whoever lived in the rambler was clearly a few sizes larger than me, but one of the dresses looked like it had a tie around the waist. Which meant it could work. Except, of course, it meant stealing someone's clothing.

I had done a lot of things that a lot of people might not consider strictly right, but stealing wasn't one of them. Not like this. Someone's nice dress that they probably had to wash by hand and hang up to dry.

And they had underwear and socks and pillowcases up on the line, too, which meant they were probably too poor to have a dryer. Was I really willing to take someone's Sunday dress so I would have a chance at getting back to Mercy Falls? Was that really the person I was now?

I'd give it back. When I was done.

I crept along the woodline, feeling exposed and pale, trying to get a better look at my prey. The smell of cheese biscuits — probably what had drawn me as a wolf in the first place — suggested to me that someone must be home. No one could abandon that smell. Now that I'd caught the scent, it was hard for me to think of anything else. I forced myself to focus on the problem at hand. Were the makers of the cheese biscuits watching? Or the neighbors? I could stay mostly out of sight, if I was clever.

My unlucky victim's backyard was a typical one for the houses near Boundary Wood, littered with the usual suspects: tomato cages, a hand-dug barbecue pit, television antennae with wires leading to nowhere. Push mower half covered with a tarp. A cracked plastic kiddie pool filled with funky-looking sand, and a family of lawn furniture with plasticky sunflower-printed covers. A lot of stuff, but nothing really useful as cover.

Then again, they'd been oblivious enough for a wolf to steal trash off their back step. Hopefully they were oblivious enough for a naked high school girl to nick a dress from their clothesline.

I took a deep breath, wished for a single, powerful moment that I could be doing something easy like taking a pop quiz in Calculus or ripping a Band-Aid off an unshaved leg, and then darted into the yard. Somewhere, a small dog began to bark furiously. I grabbed a handful of dress.

It was over before I knew it. Somehow I was back in the woods, stolen garment balled in my hands, my breath coming fast, my body hidden in a patch of what may or may not have been poison sumac.

Back at the house, someone shouted at the dog to *Shut up before I put you out with the trash!*

I let my heart settle down. Then, guiltily and triumphantly, I slid the dress over my head. It was a pretty blue flowered thing, too light for the season, really, and still a little damp. I had to cinch the back up quite a bit to make it fit me. I was almost presentable.

Fifteen minutes later, I had taken a pair of clogs off another neighbor's back steps (one of the clogs had dog crap stuck to one heel, which was probably why they'd been put outside to begin with) and I was strolling along the road casually, like I lived there. Using my wolf senses, giving in like Sam had showed me so long ago, I could create a far more detailed picture of the surrounding area in my head than I could with my eyes. Even with all this information, I had no real idea where I was, but I knew this: I was nowhere near Mercy Falls.

But I had a plan, sort of. Get out of this neighborhood before someone recognized their dress and clogs walking away. Find a business or some kind of landmark to get my bearings, hopefully before the clogs gave me a blister. Then: somehow get back to Sam.

It wasn't the greatest of plans, but it was all I had.